Praise for *A Murder a*

"Susanna Calkins makes Restoration England come alive in her terrific debut. Murder, romance, and flawless social history combine into a beautifully crafted mystery that captivates until the very last page."
—Stefanie Pintoff

"Richly detailed . . . Calkins, who became fascinated with seventeenth-century England while pursuing her doctorate in British history, puts her knowledge to eloquent use in *A Murder at Rosamund's Gate*. Combined with an intricate plot and an amiable, intelligent and courageous heroine, Calkins's debut leaves the reader eagerly anticipating Lucy's next sleuthing adventure in what promises to be a first-rate historical series."
—*Richmond Times-Dispatch*

"Calkins's debut mystery places her unusual detective in a world rich in carefully researched historical detail. Even mystery mavens who winkle out the killer may well enjoy the story anyway."
—*Kirkus Reviews*

"Set in 1665, Calkins's debut brings London on the eve of the Great Plague to vivid life . . . the high-quality writing augurs well for future outings."
—*Publishers Weekly*

"Calkins brings London in 1665 to life in this upstairs-downstairs tale of mayhem and murder . . . A clever plot."
—*Mystery Scene Magazine*

"Calkins makes Lucy's efforts to find the [killer] entirely plausible, leading to a nail-biter climax with London in flames. This history-mystery delivers a strong heroine making her way through the social labyrinth of Restoration London."

—*Booklist*

"[An] excellently written, well-researched, and engaging debut."

—*Washington Independent Review of Books*

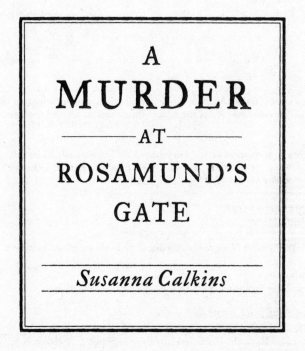

A
MURDER
AT
ROSAMUND'S
GATE

Susanna Calkins

MINOTAUR BOOKS ❧ NEW YORK

A MURDER AT ROSAMUND'S GATE. Copyright © 2013 by Susanna Calkins. All rights reserved. Printed in the United States of America. For information, address St. Martin's Press, 175 Fifth Avenue, New York, N.Y. 10010.

www.minotaurbooks.com
www.stmartins.com

The Library of Congress has cataloged the hardcover edition as follows:

Calkins, Susanna.
    A murder at Rosamund's Gate / Susanna Calkins. — First edition.
        p. cm.
    ISBN 978-1-250-00790-2 (hardcover)
    ISBN 978-1-250-00791-9 (e-book)
    1. Women—England—History—17th century—Fiction. 2. Murder—
Investigation—Fiction. 3. Great Britain—History—Restoration, 1660–1688—
Fiction. 4. London (England)—History—17th century—Fiction. 5. Mystery
fiction. 6. Historical fiction. I. Title.
    PS3603.A4394M87 2013
    813'.6—dc23

                                                                    2013002522

ISBN 978-1-250-03699-5 (trade paperback)

Minotaur books may be purchased for educational, business, or promotional use. For information on bulk purchases, please contact Macmillan Corporate and Premium Sales Department at 1-800-221-7945, extension 5442, or write specialmarkets@macmillan.com.

First Minotaur Books Paperback Edition: April 2014

10 9 8 7 6 5 4 3 2 1

To Matt

ACKNOWLEDGMENTS

Before I was a writer, I was a reader. To this end, I must thank my bibliophilic parents, James and Diane, for literally lining the walls of our house with books, and instilling in me a deep love of reading. I must also thank my siblings—Vince, Becky, and Monica Calkins—for sharing (or letting me steal) so many of their books growing up. For my love of writing, I owe great thanks to the dedicated teachers at J. R. Masterman Laboratory and Demonstration School in Philadelphia, especially Mitzi Brown. For my curiosity about English history, I thank my first history professor, George Stow, at La Salle University.

A Murder at Rosamund's Gate began with an image that came to me after Professor Melinda Zook first introduced me to seventeenth-century murder ballads and broadsides at Purdue University. For about ten years, I worked on the manuscript in bits and pieces, until I finally had a draft to share. With the encouragement of my husband, I offered it to my first readers—Franny Billingsly, Maggie Dalrymple, Denise Drane, Margaret Light, Steve Stofferahn, and Shyanmei Wang—who patiently read through odd passages and dangling clues, offered gentle feedback, raised hard questions, and most importantly, gave me the confidence to pursue my dream as a writer. To them I owe my deepest appreciation. I also wish to thank the many friends and family who celebrated my writing and helped me feel like an "author," especially Lisa and Nikhel Bagadia, Jeremy Beck and Chris Ehrick, Jolly and Chris Corley, Noyna Debburman, Marilyn Kelley, Robin Kelley, and Angie Betz, Andrea and Rob Lemke, Olivia Lemke, Greg Light, Sonal and Vas Maniatis, Elizabeth Marquardt, Jennie McNaughton, Marina Micari, Duane Swierczynski, and Steve Wagner. I am also grateful to my late mother-in-law, Terry Kelley, who always had faith in me.

The journey from manuscript to book continued with David Hale Smith, the best literary agent in the world and all-around good guy. I appreciate his belief in my book and in me—and for connecting me to Kelley Ragland. I am extremely grateful to Kelley for understanding my characters, and for her reflective and compassionate approach to editing my story. I also wish to thank all the wonderful people at Minotaur, especially Elizabeth Lacks and India Cooper, who made my dream tangible. A writer could not ask for a better team, and to everyone who worked on my book, I offer my deepest gratitude.

I could not have written this book without the love and understanding of my family. My children, Alex and Quentin Kelley, never seemed to mind little Rosamund dragging me away to coffee shops or tagging along on vacations, and for that I am very grateful.

Most importantly, I thank my husband, Matt Kelley, for giving me the confidence, space, and time to put the images in my mind to real words on paper. He took on many roles as I completed this book, most notably Alpha Reader (his favorite title), Senior Vice President for Continuity Management (double-checked all my dates, events, character descriptions, street names, etc. to make sure I hadn't goofed), Acting Head of Public Relations (bragged about me to all his friends), and Executive Administrative Assistant (made sure I always had time to write). To my partner and best friend, I dedicate *A Murder at Rosamund's Gate*.

LONDON

March 1665

· I ·

A great pounding at the door startled the chambermaid bending to light the morning hearth. Jerking upright, Lucy Campion swore softly as a bit of hot beeswax stung her wrist. Slapping the taper on the mantel, she sneaked a glance over her shoulder. She could hear Bessie and Cook rattling pots in the kitchen, but the rest of the magistrate's household was still. Her muttered oath had not carried. Though theirs was not a stringent Puritan family, the magistrate frowned on ill language, and Lucy always took care not to annoy him.

Lucy was feeling out of sorts, though, having been awakened an hour too early—not to the usual sound of roosters crowing but instead to their frantic squealing. Local boys had been casting stones at the witless birds, all mercilessly shackled to wooden stakes on the street outside her window. Although the Church officially did not condone such activities, the community accepted that boys would have their fun. Fortunately only the servants, light sleepers that they all were, had been awakened by the disturbance. The rest of the household, the magistrate's family, had slept blissfully on.

Now, tugging her skirts into place, Lucy moved across the long wooden floor into the great hall. Who could be calling? Deliveries from the haberdasher or the vintner usually were made at the kitchen entrance, and no decent visitor would call before the family had broken their morning fast.

As Lucy swung open the heavy oak door, her scolding words withered on her lips. Instead of a journeyman plying his trade, a straight-backed man in uniform regarded her sternly. Lucy recognized his red coat and insignia immediately. He was one of King Charles's own men. Although Redcoats were a common enough sight throughout London, a soldier at the stoop, even at the magistrate's household, disquieted her. Ever since she was a child, soldiers had filled her with unease.

He spoke without preamble. "I'm Duncan, the new constable. I must speak with the magistrate at once."

Youthful mischief, no doubt. The boys had probably caused some damage with their early-morning antics. Lucy took a deep breath. "Of course, sir. I'll fetch my master. Pray, warm yourself by the fire."

Inside, Lucy saw the constable's otherwise set face twitch in appreciation. The magistrate's home was fine enough, it was true. The place was not quite so decorated as some, for the master had a mean practical streak and would not let his wife furnish as lavishly as she would like. Still, it had a pleasing elegance that well suited the master and his family. The house had three floors, with the living quarters on the first floor, the sleeping chambers on the second, and the maids' cramped quarters on the very top floor. John, the master's servant, slept with Cook, his wife, in the tiny niche behind the kitchen hearth, among the potatoes and onions. How they fit, Lucy had often wondered, as John was a great burly man and Cook an ample woman herself.

Even as she turned to locate John, the master himself appeared. He could have been in full magisterial garb instead of a simple sleeping gown, so dignified was his bearing. This morning, the habitual twinkling of his eye and rueful grin were missing, replaced by the slightest of frowns. He summoned the constable to his private chamber, and they disappeared down the hallway.

Bessie came from the kitchen then, her blue eyes wide, having passed the constable in the corridor. Like Lucy, she had been awake for some time, tending to the early-morning duties of the household.

Two years older than Lucy, Bessie was a farm girl from Lambeth hired by the master at a Michaelmas hiring fair some five years back. Before coming to the Hargraves, Bessie had been a nursery maid in a "family of quality," tending to three small children. As she had confided to Lucy once, however, the master grabbed at her more than the tots did, and she was nearly thrown out when the mistress discovered her husband's sneaking ways. She was in that household two years before ending her contract with the family. Bessie had quickly found the Hargraves' household to her liking, just as Lucy did later. Master Hargrave paid well, son and father treated her courteously, and the mistress was not jealous of her pleasing ways.

Now Bessie giggled, revealing a large gap in her mouth where her tooth had cracked some years before. "So handsome, isn't he?" she whispered. "I just love the gold on the constable's red coat. I've never seen him before, though. Have you? I wonder where he came from."

"I don't know. Maybe Yorkshire?" Lucy guessed, for the soldier's voice reminded her a bit of a distant cousin she had met once. But who could know? After King Charles was restored to the throne, he had dispersed many of his men throughout England, Ireland, and Wales, to help restore order. Likely as not, the soldier was far from his childhood home.

Cook soon swatted Bessie. "You'd best be getting to your chores and forget that constable. It's not likely he brings good tidings at this hour," she said, her pockmarked face growing impish. She winked at Lucy. " 'Twould be best if you kept your mind on good honest boys like my Samuel."

Bessie flounced off to tend to the mistress, her curls bouncing beneath her cap. Lucy hid a smile. Bessie despised Samuel, a stocky lad of fourteen years who as a child used to pull her curls with sticky fingers, and who now would pinch her rear when out of his mother's sight. Thankfully, they saw him only rarely these days, for he had lately begun work as a fishmonger in Leadenhall.

Regarding the closed study door, Lucy wondered what business had brought the constable to the magistrate at such an hour. This was not altogether unusual, to be sure, since the magistrate often had constables and the like stopping by the household, but the grim set to this soldier's jaw made her especially curious.

After a half hour, the constable left, and Lucy brought out the master's breakfast to the dining room. There, the master downed his kippers and bread with a bit of wine, not lingering long, preferring to remain in his study until the noon meal. A member of the King's Bench before the war, and a magistrate since Charles II's return, he was beginning to write his memoirs when the assize courts were not in session. Lucy watched him closely. If he was bothered by the news Constable Duncan had brought, he hid it well.

Lucy's curiosity about the stranger faded as she spent the next hour emptying chamber pots into the cesspit and shaking out rush mats on the stones outside the stoop. These heavy tasks numbed her fingers and made the sweat run down the back of her woolen dress. She had received the dress when she first entered service with the Hargraves two years before, when her dear mother had come down with consumption. When she bent over now, she realized anew how the dress was pulling across her front, although not as tightly as it had on Bessie, who had worn the dress before her.

Lucy was just starting to rub the pewter with marestail, a plant that smelled and turned her fingers green, when Cook called her into the kitchen. "Where's your pocket?" she asked Lucy, taking down an old stone jar from an alcove above the cutting bench. "We've got guests for supper, and I need some ox tongue, coffee, and eggs from the market." She counted out a few coins and handed them to Lucy. "Don't pay more than six shillings, you hear me?"

"Oh, yes!" Lucy said, dropping the coins carefully in the pocket she kept hidden beneath her skirts. The promise of the unexpected jaunt made her fairly dance down the front path, despite the chill in the air.

As she opened the gate, someone called to her from the doorway. "Hold on a moment, Lucy." It was Adam, the magistrate's son. "I'll accompany you to market."

"Sir?" she asked. She did not know the magistrate's son very well. He'd been at Cambridge for the last few years and had only just returned to the household three weeks ago to finish up his studies in law at the Inns of Court. Unlike Sarah, the magistrate's daughter, and Lucas, the magistrate's ward, Adam always heeded the difference in their relative stations. He treated Lucy and the other servants courteously but never teased them in the playful way he did his sister and Lucas. Certainly he'd never volunteered to walk her into town.

"'Tis no day for a lass to be traveling alone." He started down the narrow cobblestone path. Seeing that she was still standing there, he tilted his head at her. "Coming?"

"Yes, sir," she said, scrambling to keep up with his lanky pace.

A moment later they passed the cocks Lucy had heard that morning. Now they were battered, plucked, and no longer squawking. Mercifully, the birds were all dead, and their youthful tormentors had long fled. Some of their neighbors were cutting them off the stakes to pop into their kettles. Adam frowned but didn't say anything.

"Yoo-hoo, Lucy!" one of the neighbors called, elbowing another servant in the ribs. It was Janey, the most miserable gossip on the street. "Where are you off to?"

"Market," Lucy responded through gritted teeth, trying not to flush at Janey's knowing smirk. She'd already been treated to Janey's vile opinions about what the gentry believed was their due. Seeing Lucy with the magistrate's son would certainly fuel the morning's gossip. Lucy shook her basket at her. "See?" With that, Lucy picked up her step, Adam matching her easily. Soon they were beyond sight of their neighbors' spying eyes.

As they walked along the dusty road to the market, Lucy found herself chattering far more than she usually did, trying to mask her discomfort at his presence. Why had Adam chosen to accompany her? she wondered. Did he think she wasn't safe?

Adam barely spoke at all during their half hour trek, and indeed, she was not even sure he was listening to her nervous chatter. He seemed distracted, ignoring all her comments about the weather, Lent, what Cook would be making for supper, and the new foal arriving in their neighbor Master Whitcomb's stable. Only when Lucy speculated aloud about whether the Whitcombs' groom would have to turn the foal in the womb did Adam give her a sidelong glance. She laughed a little to herself, feeling far less tense.

Even with that minor victory, Lucy was getting tired of the one-way conversation. She finally asked the question that had been on her mind all morning. "Why do you suppose, sir, that Constable Duncan came to see your father this morning?" She hopped over a muddy puddle, landing with a *squish* on the still-sodden ground.

Adam brushed off some drops of mud that had landed on his coat. "My father's business is his own, Lucy. It is not our concern."

"So early he came, don't you think?" she persisted. "It must have been a matter of great importance. The pounding he made, why, I thought he'd knock the door down!" She opened her eyes wide in pretended dismay.

Adam shrugged, refusing to take the bait. " 'Tis best if you put the constable's visit out of your head, I think, Lucy," he said.

"Do you think it had something to do with those boys mischief? That was some carousing!"

Seeing Lucy's hopeful look, Adam sighed. "The constable's visit did involve a crime, and a serious one at that. As you know it, is my father's right and duty as magistrate to be informed of ill happenings in his area of jurisprudence. Regardless, Father's business is—"

"I know," Lucy interrupted, "his own. You said so already." She almost winked at him, as she would have, had she been talking to Sarah or Bessie, but stopped herself just in time. "Don't worry. I'll pretend I never saw the constable." *Besides,* she thought to herself, *someone will know what happened. This crime won't stay secret for long.*

Nearing the market, the cobbled streets grew crowded and noisy. The ever-present din of London grew louder, and the foggy haze made everything a little darker. The second stories of the build-ings jutted into the narrow lanes, teetering on timbers some two or three centuries old.

As always, Lucy found herself ducking so that she would not be struck by the low-hanging wooden signs that swung into the streets. Since she could read better than most towns-people, she did not need to rely on the images painted on the signs to tell her the kinds of shops below. A picture of Adam and Eve hung above the apple sellers, a cradle hung above the basket makers, a cupid and torch above a glazier, an elephant above an ivory-comb maker, and so forth. She shuddered when she passed the bloodied bandages hanging from the windows of the barber surgeons. Brave souls, those who ventured inside.

A thin haze of smoke, arising from many ill-kept chimneys, lay dimly in the air. Steaming dung heaps littered the stones, and wild cats sniffed around doorways.

"Mind your step," said Adam.

Lucy grimaced. The corpse of a dog lay in one corner, where it would remain until the chief ditcher carted it off to Hounds-ditch.

No one gave Lucy and Adam any mind as they made their way through the streets, but Lucy looked about, always eager to connect with the life that teemed about her. Servants from large houses and the wives of merchants scurried about with baskets, bargaining for fresh vegetables, meats, breads, and other goods. All about, traders sang their wares.

"Candles and ribbons!"

"Spices from the East!"

"Woolens to keep you dry and warm!"

"Fresh fish!"

The market was full of children, some darting in and out of narrow shops, some playing, others clutching bundles and baskets or clinging to their mother's skirts. Almost all were dirty and pale, nothing like the red-cheeked children Lucy had known growing up outside London.

As she chose a bit of tongue from the fleshmarket, Lucy noticed two boys about her age, or maybe a little younger, sidling up to a woman bargaining with a butcher over a succulent cut of meat. Balancing three packages under one arm, the woman reached for her pocket to pay him.

Just then, one of the boys grabbed her purse, snapping the flimsy cord. The other boy scooped up two of her packages, and they took off, out of the market, in separate directions.

The woman, first stunned and mute, shook herself and began to wail, a shrieking, piteous sound. Nearby faces turned and conversations stopped, but after a moment, everyone returned to business. Pickpockets were a fair menace to the streets, but as the woman was a stranger, no one raised a hand to help her.

Shocked, Lucy turned to Adam. Had he witnessed it? It seemed he had.

"Come on. There's no constable about." His tone, like his face, was flat. "No bellman at hand, no soldiers. There is nothing to be done."

Her uncertain protest quelled, Lucy picked up her basket again. She could not stop looking back at the woman, who had begun to weep openly. With her purse and day's purchases gone, she might have little left. Her husband or master, unless he was a particularly forgiving man, might well beat her for her loss. Or worse. Lucy shuddered.

When they turned the corner, though, Lucy noticed that one of the young pickpockets had circled back, slinking among the crowded stalls. Without saying anything to Adam, she kept her head down, watching the lad as he helped himself to an apple here, a scrap of cloth there. He stood for a moment before an enormous leg of mutton. For a crazy moment, Lucy thought he was actually trying to figure out how to get the gamy leg inside his knapsack. The woman's purse, she imagined, was still inside his doublet.

"I'm to get some eggs and a bit of coffee," she told Adam, her eyes not leaving the boy.

Adam nodded, looking toward Fleet Street. Lucy had rarely been on the long, winding street where the printers and book-sellers lived and hawked their wares.

"See that shop there?" Adam asked, pointing halfway down the narrow road. "The fifth one in from the corner? 'Tis Master Aubrey's. Join me there in a quarter hour's time, and I shall see you home."

"Yes, sir," she said, distantly wondering at his grim tone. Right now, she was thinking about something else. Seeing that Adam was waiting for her to respond, she added, "Yes, sir. A quarter hour. I'll be there."

When Adam had walked away, Lucy looked again at the boy. She did not see his partner, but that was better for what she was about to do. Saying a soft prayer to her patron saint, she opened her pocket as if searching for a coin, walking straight toward the boy. An instant later, she collided with him, her hands right on his chest, then slipping easily into his shirt, where she seized the woman's purse and whisked it from view.

"Oh, my," Lucy said, so he could feel the full effect of her gaze. His frown was replaced by a look of confusion, under the onslaught of her smile. Lucy spent little time before a looking glass, but his somewhat dazed response gave her an unexpected sense of satisfaction. "I'm so sorry. I should have been paying more attention," Lucy said, tucking a loose strand of hair back under her muslin cap. For a moment, she wished she had Bessie's great blond curls, but no matter, she seemed to be doing fine.

The boy rubbed his hand against his shirt. "Oh, yes, miss, I mean, no, miss," he stammered. "A comely lass like yourself, you must watch for cutthroats. There's them that would take advantage of you, burying your nose down like that."

Lucy widened her eyes. "Oh, my. I hadn't thought of that. Cutthroats! In the market! To be sure, my dear aunt always says I must take more care, lest something dreadful happen."

"Indeed, you must, miss." He looked her up and down, taking in her servant's garb. He seemed to like what he saw, and he took a step closer. Lucy had to keep herself from stepping back, for his teeth suddenly looked a little sharper, a little more predatory, than they had a moment before. He went on, puffing up his chest. "Shall I walk with you a bit? Perhaps you'd like an ale? The Cheddar Cheese is just ahead."

Protect me from the likes of you, Lucy thought spitefully. Out loud, she said, "Oh, I don't think so. I don't even know your name, and my auntie—"

"My name's Sid, miss. Sid Petry, miss." He squeezed her upper arm.

His sudden liberty made her feel afraid and anxious to get away. What if Sid discovered what she had done? She looked about. "I have a friend meeting me, and he'll be wondering where I am. Sorry again, Sid, for being so careless."

It took all she had to get away from Sid's wheedling, and she was afraid he would follow her. Moving quickly through the stalls, Lucy stepped over piles of dung and refuse that lay scattered across the cobblestones. Looking about, she finally spied Sid's victim, now sitting dully at the edge of the cobblestone street, her arms wrapped around her skirts. No one was paying her any mind, and she looked quite forlorn indeed. Lucy strode up to her. "Pardon, ma'am."

"What do you want?" the woman growled. "Can't you see I'm not in a good way? Just got my pocket stolen and two good bones. What I shall tell my master, I don't know."

Lucy held out the woman's worn pocket. "Yes, I saw what that witless lad did. But wouldn't you know it? He dropped your pocket, the clumsy oaf."

The woman's mouth parted, but she said nothing.

Lucy turned away. Before she had taken two steps, however, she felt a hand claw at her elbow, forcing her to turn around. The woman twitched the left half of her lips in what might have been a smile. Lucy nodded. There didn't seem to be anything else to say.

Doubling back, Lucy entered the print shop where she was to meet Adam, a heavy acrid smell jolting her nose. Two men were working the presses, shouting back and forth. Adam was nowhere to be seen. As she waited, she read haltingly through some of the ballads and broadsides drying on the great racks. All told stories of monstrous births, unnatural events, and the like, or else offered quick recipes or advice. Having gone to petty school as a girl, Lucy had learned her letters and numbers but little else. Only in the last two years, when she'd found ways to listen to Sarah's tutors in secret, had she figured out how to pick through her letters and read at a reasonable pace.

The title of one of the woodcuts now caught her eye. " 'Murder, or a Vengeance Cast upon a Candlemaker,' " Lucy read out loud.

"Murder most foul," said a man stepping into the room, followed by Adam. Lucy guessed he was Master Aubrey. A fat and balding man, the printer had spilled ink all across his person, so that it had stained his beard, his forehead, and his smock, as well as his hands. "But fortunate, too," he added. Seeing Lucy's quizzical look, he explained, "The dismal act of murder—vile, disgusting, *monstrous*—will make this piece easy to sell. Watch."

Stepping out of his shop, Master Aubrey climbed onto a small bench. Adam and Lucy followed him outside. "Good people!" the printer called. "Let me tell you the true and most horrible story of Anne Johnson of Scarsbruck, a she-devil who poisoned her husband with an ill-begotten stew."

Hearing Master Aubrey's call, several passersby stopped to listen. A good story was always a treat, a murder even more enjoyable. Pushing up his sleeves on his heavy, sweaty arms, Master Aubrey launched into a sordid tale of greed, lust, and murder—the desperate plot of a woman weary of her husband's adulterous ways. "The moral of this candlemaker's sad end?"

The printer wagged his finger at the men in the crowd. "Do not dip your wick in the neighbor's tallow!"

The crowd let out a collective satisfied sigh. A few people cheered. The story complete, the people began to drift away, returning to their homes and stalls, with details of the murder carefully memorized. Master Aubrey and one of his printer's devils scurried about, collecting coins from people who purchased the penny broadside to share with their families and neighbors, or even to post on their walls at home.

As they took their leave, Master Aubrey murmured something to Adam that Lucy did not catch. Lucy wondered what his business with the printer had been, but she knew she could not be so forward. Instead, she asked Adam how he knew the man.

"What? Oh, I've known Aubrey for some time now," he said, sidestepping the question. "Say, Lucy, you have a brother? Will, is that right?" When Lucy nodded in surprise, he continued. "I know Aubrey's looking for an apprentice, a turner. He wants an eager lad who knows his letters and who could belt out a right good story. Father says you're quick enough, so I thought it might run in the family."

Lucy shook her head. "Will cannot read so well. 'Sides, he's fair settled with the smithy. I thank you for thinking of him, sir." Her lips twisted ruefully. "Although if I were a man, I could think of no finer trade in which to apprentice."

They fell silent as they walked along. Adam glanced at her. "So there was no coffee to be had at the market?" He looked pointedly at her basket.

Lucy flushed. Had he seen her talking to that rogue Sid?

No, he could not have, he'd have been with the printer. The lie came out quickly. "No, the price was too dear. I should not like to waste the magistrate's money."

"No eggs to be had either?"

Lucy glanced at him, but his tone was casual, disinterested. "No," she said. "I got to looking at a piece of Holland cloth for the mistress and forgot to get the eggs."

Her cheeks burned, but she kept her gaze straight ahead. She thought he did look at her then, but he just said, "That's too bad. I should have liked an egg at supper."

"I'm sorry, sir."

"Indeed. So am I."

They did not speak again, each lost in thought, for the rest of the walk home. Back at the magistrate's house, Adam disappeared. Lucy had barely had time to pass the shilling she had saved to Cook when Bessie pulled her aside. "Did you hear about the body?" she whispered, her whole face animated. "The woman who got herself murdered?"

·2·

Lucy leaned back against the larder, pushing aside several jars of dried fruits and spices, thinking about the true account she had just heard from Master Aubrey. "Well, I did hear tell of Anne Johnson, who did poison her husband, a candlemaker—"

"No, no, not a candlemaker. Not a monstrous tale!" Bessie interrupted. "I mean a real murder. Happened in these parts."

"Truly?" Lucy asked, studying Bessie's face. The girl was alight with excitement. "Who was it?"

"No one knows," Bessie said. "The watchman found her body last night in the north fields. That's why the constable was here. To bring the magistrate the news."

Instinctively, Lucy made the sign of the cross over her heart. The old faith stayed with them all when confronted by ungodly acts. Bessie nodded at the gesture and continued. "Edna—you know, the Thompsons' maid?—said she heard it was a woman, but no one could be sure if she was from around these parts."

"But why say murder?" Lucy pressed, seeking to find sense in Bessie's words. "Could it have been an accident?"

Certainly the field in that area was generally flat, but tall grasses often hid rocks and small hillocks that made any false step treacherous. She said as much to Bessie.

Bessie smirked, reveling in the best part of the story. "Unless she ran her own innards through with a knife, certainly 'twas no accident!"

"No!" Lucy's hands flew to her mouth. "How awful!"

Bessie continued, happy with the effect of her words. "Yes! Edna said Tom said there was blood everywhere and"—her voice lowered significantly—"she was near naked! Clad only in a few bits of cloth!"

That did not suggest a virtuous woman. Still, Lucy felt a pang of sorrow for this luckless person who had met such a fate. No one deserved such a death.

"And the north fields are not so very far away," Bessie whispered.

Lucy shivered. What if the murderer had come their way instead? Now that she knew what had happened, she was grateful that Adam had walked her to and from town earlier. There were many empty, desolate fields between here and there. Many fields where a stranger could wait. She shook her head, trying to clear the disturbing images from her mind.

The girls continued to speculate in hushed tones until they heard Cook's footsteps by the pantry. "Plenty of time for your tongues to wag later, girls," the older woman said, bustling about. "Supper is upon us, and we're hardly ready for the master's guests. The brawn is ready, but the cabbage is not done, and I've not even started the pancakes. And surely," Cook looked hard at Bessie, "I didn't see you press the mistress's new India silk. Would you have her wrinkled before the Mistresses Larimer and Chalmers?"

Bessie bobbed her head, mindful of her charge. Despite her flippant ways, she took her duties as the mistress's lady's maid as seriously as she took anything. Her good intentions did not keep her on the path to their mistress's chamber, however, when she encountered Lucas just returning home. Lucy could hear Bessie whispering fervently to him in the hallway, rather than collecting the mistress's gown. Lucy could not see them, but she could imagine Lucas nodding, a slight smile on his face as he took in Bessie's excitement.

Lucas was a friendly sort, a lively presence in the household. Although the red of his cheeks might have been more becoming on a lass, he was handsome enough, even if his slight plumpness kept him from cutting as fine a figure as Master Adam. Lucy knew the local gossips whispered about Lucas's history— "Was he from the wrong side of the blanket?"—yet the truth was far more sad than sordid. Bessie had told her, in confidence, that Lucas's mother, dying of pleurisy, had begged the magistrate to take her son as his ward. Apparently there was some distant relationship to the family. Having shown no inclination to be a soldier, Lucas had only one other option: to enter the clergy, a decision he accepted easily enough. "Treat me with respect," he would tease the girls, "or when I deliver my sermons, I'll have you cast from the Church."

Laying out the pewter in the dining room, Lucy fought a small pang of disappointment. When the family did not have guests, the servants were allowed to join them for the evening meal and sit together afterward, provided the day's chores were done. That was Lucy's favorite part of the evening. Or at least it had been, before Adam had returned to the household. Before, the magistrate would read passages from the Bible and, more interestingly, from other texts. She didn't always understand what he was reading, but she always attended to his words and on occasion ventured a question. She'd stunned everyone, including herself, the first time she'd spoken up during his reading. The magistrate had been talking about how a man freed from prison would be hard-pressed to regain his liberty. "Because no one would ever trust him again," she had murmured. No one else had been listening—Sarah, Bessie, and Lucas had been playing jackstraws, Cook was dozing in the corner, and the mistress had already retired—but when she whispered these words, everyone had stared at her, causing her to flush painfully. The magistrate had paused and peered at her, his expression in the candlelight inscrutable, although his eyes were kind. "That's right, Lucy." Before long, the magistrate would regularly query her. The rest of the household had taken notice, amused at his interest in his chambermaid's opinions. Still, as Sarah said, "At least Papa has someone to discuss those deadly dull texts with him."

This all had changed when Adam had returned and real debates between son and father ensued. Lucy would usually take her little stool from the kitchen and sit by the women, positioned so that she could sew in the light of the hearth while she listened to them debate politics, religion, and the law. Shy before Adam's superior words, Lucy stopped venturing her point of view. Only once did the magistrate ask her for her opinion straight out. "What say you, Lucy?" the master had asked. When father and son looked at her, she grew tongue-tied, staring at the mending in her lap. Adam and the magistrate were both surprised, Adam that his father was seeking the serving girl's opinion, and the magistrate at Lucy's silence. After that, Master Hargrave never pressed her again.

This evening, Lucy brought fruits and sweetmeats to the withdrawing room, lingering as much as she dared, hoping to hear some interesting conversation. Sarah and Lucas were playing draughts at a small table in the corner while Adam and the magistrate conversed quietly with their guests, Sir Herbert Larimer, an important physician from the Royal Academy, and Sir Walcott Chalmers, a barrister at the Inns of Court. Their wives sat with Mistress Hargrave in another corner, engaged in their own private conversation, which as far as Lucy could gather seemed to be something about a recent scandal involving one of the king's mistresses.

Accepting a mug of beer from Lucy's carefully polished tray, Sir Walcott turned to the bespectacled man sitting in an embroidered chair by the hearth. "Well, Larimer, what do you make of this recent business? Who was this lass found in the field?"

At the barrister's words, the women abruptly stopped their own conversation. "A horrible business," Mistress Hargrave sniffed. Lady Chalmers murmured agreement, but both women hung on the physician's response. He was often called to serve as coroner for suspicious or important deaths and could offer some fascinating detail that did not make it to the printed account.

Lucy lit another candle and brought it over next to Adam. He nodded at the gesture but was intent on hearing what Dr. Larimer had to say.

Larimer leaned back in his chair, touching his pipe stem to his lips. "'Tis an odd thing, that is certain. The body is being brought around to my office tomorrow morn; I will conduct my investigation then."

"A doxy, do you suppose?" Lucas asked from the corner, chewing on a date.

"Lucas!" both the master and mistress cried at once.

Master Hargrave jerked his head at his daughter. "We'll have no such talk here!"

Catching Lucy's eye, Sarah giggled behind her handkerchief. They'd certainly heard of women who sold their bodies for a bit of gold. Lord, didn't the Reverend Marcus speak of whores and lust and temptation every Sunday? He had done as much to inform them of the wages of sin as any boys joking about could have done.

"I don't mind telling you, Christopher, I don't like it. Not one bit," Larimer said, pulling at his beard. "Two young women in the last few months, taken nearly the same way. What monsters walk among us!" The physician frowned at Lucas. "And no, young man, not one of them a known lady of the evening."

"Similar deaths, you say?" Adam asked, glancing at his father. "Could they be connected in some way?"

"Young man, I think it highly unlikely that two monsters met together to plan out these young girls' deaths. Dashed near impossible, one might say." Larimer took a drink. "I say, is this your Cambridge education showing? We Oxford men would not make such wild speculations."

"But," Adam persisted, "you would agree, perhaps, that one man may have seen the popular accounts of the first murder and then—"

"Copied the other?" Larimer stared at Adam. "How strange. I cannot presume to know the mind of a murderous criminal. Would one copy the heinous acts of an irrational man?"

"Or it was the work of one man," Lucas suggested. "But I'm afraid I've neither Oxford nor Cambridge to blame for my irrational views."

"One deranged man? Stalking the lasses of London?" Mistress Larimer shivered. "How singular."

"And quite unlikely, my dear," the physician reassured his wife. He turned back to the magistrate. "Have you heard what Sam Pepys had to say today?"

With that, the conversation turned to lighter topics, though a slightly bilious feeling remained in the room.

The next day, after wiping her brow, Lucy poured hot water into a great tub set out in the courtyard. As the day was bright and fine, Mistress Hargrave had declared it perfect for the monthly washing. Even Sarah had to pitch in for the day's labors, although she would usually disappear once her mother had left.

It fell to Lucy to bring down pile after pile of shirts, shifts, and drawers from throughout the household. Thinking Adam was with his Cambridge mates, Lucy boldly pushed into his room to retrieve his linens, then drew back in dismay.

Adam was sitting at his small desk by the window, regarding a portrait that fit into the palm of his hand. Lucy could not see the image, but she supposed it was a young woman he fancied. Or even just her eye, as was sometimes the custom, if the woman was married or sought to conceal her identity.

His pen and ink jar were out, as if he had been writing. She could see a long sheet of notes in his careful, elegant script. Startled, Adam closed his hand over the miniature.

"Oh, I'm terribly sorry, sir. Pardon me! I didn't know you were in here, I thought . . ." She trailed off. It was one thing to talk to the magistrate's son in the drawing room, or even on a trip to the market, and quite another to be alone with him in his bedchamber.

"Yes?" he asked, trying to mask his annoyance. "Is there something you need?"

Unbidden, Lucy recalled how Miss Sarah's nurse used to say, *A maiden who does not protect her virtue will soon see it lost.* Maybe that was just for gentry, but she thought her mother would agree.

She ducked her head. " 'Tis washing day."

Barely sparing her a glance, Adam stood up and thrust a pile of linens into her arms. As she backed from the room, she saw him slip the miniature into a box on his desk.

———

Once outside, Lucy tossed the linens onto the sticks that lay across the buck tub, placing the cleaner clothes on top, still thinking about Adam's miniature. Together, Lucy and Bessie poured in the lye, their eyes stinging from the mixture of urine and ashes. Despite the chill in the air, the hard work and the fire kept them warm.

As they worked, Janey stopped by, holding a smudged penny piece out to Lucy. "Read it," she demanded.

Lucy rolled her eyes but took the paper. " 'Jane Hardewick, a servant from a good house in Lincoln Fields but a trollop by any measure,' " Lucy read, " 'was found stabbed in the glen by her master's household, that of the good family Elton.' "

"Jane Hardewick!" Bessie exclaimed, clutching her knotted skirts. She sat down on an overturned pail.

"Oh, no!" Lucy said. "Bessie, did you know this poor woman?"

Bessie frowned. "Yes, I did. She was no trollop, or at least, not as I've heard tell."

John brought buckets of cold water then, dumping them into the tub. Lucy and Bessie, sweat trickling unpleasantly under their clothes, took turns vigorously pulling the staff as they stirred the garments together. Cook helped pull and twist the heavy linen, squeezing away the water. Even Lucas came out to help.

Janey watched, tapping her foot. "Read the rest!" she urged, her eyes gleaming. "Tell 'em about what she was wearing."

Lucy wrinkled her nose but, seeing that everyone was waiting, continued. " 'Though last seen in a gray muslin dress and an embroidered red sash, the serving wench was *found only in her underskirts*—'" Lucy and Bessie looked at each other. The rumor they had heard seemed to be true. "'She had no coin upon her person,'" Lucy continued, her voice dropping at the dramatic bits, "'but upon closer inspection of the grounds, the constable did find a handkerchief embroidered with the letter *R* and a note—'"

"A note!" Bessie exclaimed. "How odd!"

"'—a note addressed to the unfortunate girl,'" Lucy read. "'This note implored her to meet the same-said R in that very field upon which she did encounter her most treacherous fate.'"

"R," Bessie breathed. "Who could that have been?"

Lucy read through the account carefully. "'The local constable who found her said that *R* may have referred to one Robert Preswell, who had of late pressed his suit upon her, despite being "of the married state himself." However, it was just as likely that she may have been set upon by ruffians or highwaymen.'

"Oh, look!" Lucy exclaimed. "Here's something about Sir Herbert." She read, "'The good Dr. Larimer, a royal physician, examined her and duly avowed, "She was not heavy with child, but no doubt was expecting a babe in arms in four or five months' time.'"

"Oh, that's a shame." Cook clucked. "What else does it say?"

Only that the Eltons' neighbor, one Goodwife Croft, had long warned that the trollop would come to no good end. Lucy thought about that for a moment. Every community seemed to have a Goodwife Croft or a Janey, women who carried tales, whispered stories, and always assigned the most sinister of motives to the most innocent of actions.

Lucy turned back to the account. The author, identified only as J.L., wrapped up by offering several opinions about the murderer's motives. He seemed certain that "R" had most likely murdered Jane to conceal their liaison from his wife. On the other hand, as J.L. jested, "'R's wife had threatened to take a rolling pin to his head, if he did not take care of his mistress.'"

Lucy raised her eyebrow. "His wife asked him to kill off his mistress in such a way? Does that even make sense?"

John chuckled. "A mistress and a wife? The man would do better to kill himself."

"Think that's funny, do you?" Cook asked, frowning at her husband. "I ought to take a rolling pin to you."

Ignoring Cook and John's playful squabbling, Lucy skimmed the last paragraph of the broadside. Here, J.L. delivered his judgment on the criminal and offered his readers a customary warning.

On a whim, Lucy climbed upon the bench, mimicking Master Aubrey's expression. "'R must be apprehended. He must be brought to justice.'" With a great flourish of her hands, she read the final words. "'He must be hanged—*ere he strike again*!'" Stepping down to mock applause, she caught sight of Bessie's expression.

Bessie's rosy cheeks had completely drained of color. "Make fun, will you?" Bessie asked. "Poor, poor Jane. She was one of us."

Lucy could tell that Jane's murder continued to weigh heavily on Bessie's thoughts. Throughout the next day, every time she saw Bessie pull the broadside out and look at it, she felt her friend's rebuke sting her heart. When she tried to express her sorrow, Bessie had just shaken her head. "Don't you understand, Lucy? Jane Hardewick had her whole life in front of her, and now it's gone. And no one cares, because they think she deserved it."

"I didn't think she deserved it—" Lucy began, but Bessie cut her off.

"There's Evensong," Bessie said, hearing St. Peter's bells chime. "Time to ready supper. The Embrys have been invited to dine."

Already out of sorts because of her tiff with Bessie, Lucy felt her mood sink even lower knowing the Embrys would be joining the family for supper. When Lord Embry and his friends had visited before, they'd spent most of the evening drinking the magistrate's finest madeira, with no care to depleting his stores. She'd also spent most of the evening fending off their roving eyes and hands in the corridors; when out of sight of the Hargraves, they'd try to catch her unaware.

Their noble status notwithstanding, Lucy wondered what the magistrate saw in the Embrys. Lord Embry did not seem clever or interesting, and indeed often said things that she could see made the magistrate flinch. To her surprise, Mistress Hargrave asked her to bring out the best pewter goblets and plates and the real silver emblazoned with the family's mark.

She understood later, though, when she overheard a whispered conversation between the mistress and Sarah. "Lord Embry is bringing his wife and daughter," the mistress said. "Your father is hoping that Adam will get on with Lady Judith." She pressed her hand to her forehead, sounding ever so slightly puzzled. "I suppose since her father is so important in the House of Lords."

Ah, that's it, Lucy thought. *They are hoping a match with the Embrys' daughter will help advance Adam's career.* Such arrangements were customary among the gentry, of course, but she could not help but curl her lip for a man who would make a match for such reasons.

Although nervous of grasping fingers, Lucy quickly realized that Lord Embry was all courtesy and good manners before his wife and daughter. As she filled goblets and plates, Lucy studied the Embrys under her lashes.

Lady Embry was crisp and polite, sitting straight-backed in her chair. Judith was lovely, her blond hair pulled on top of her head, revealing fine, if icy, features. Her teeth were even but overlarge, Lucy thought, somewhat crossly. She did not like how mother and daughter looked about in a calculating way. When they thought no one was watching, they seemed to be appraising the magistrate's furniture, the flagons on the table, the tiny silver spoons. Throughout supper, Sarah twisted the linen in her lap, obviously disconcerted by the elegance of the Embrys, and the mistress kept a distant smile on her face, inclining her head courteously to Lady Embry. Lucas chatted amiably enough with Judith while Adam spoke with his father and Lord Embry.

When the company moved to the drawing room, Sarah tried to engage Judith, but Judith seemed more interested in talking brightly to Adam. "This is lovely wine," Judith said, looking meaningfully at the jug in Lucy's hand.

"Oh, let me fill that for you," Lucy said, moving across the room. In her haste, a bit of wine sloshed onto Judith's silk dress.

"Stupid!" Judith exclaimed, jerking back in her chair. "Look what you've done!"

"Oh, miss, I'm so sorry!" Lucy stammered, her face red. She looked about for a bit of linen to dab at Judith's dress.

"I should say you are," Judith said, smoothing her skirts, conscious that the men had stopped talking. To Mistress Hargrave she said, "Your servant has spilled the wine. In our household, she'd be discharged for such sloppiness. So uncommon is it for us, I daresay it surprises us when we come upon it elsewhere."

"Yes, my dear," Lady Embry purred, with a quick glance at her daughter, "but we should not expect servants to be so well trained as ours. We get ours early on indeed, sometimes as young as nine or ten, and train them from the start. This way, they know how to handle themselves in the presence of their betters. A few were even from the palace, where such happenstance is unheard of."

Lucy looked down, her cheeks burning.

Master Hargrave coughed slightly. "Indeed," he said, smiling at Lucy. "Such accidents are rare here, too. In any case, we should not like to sack a lass like Lucy, for such loyal and trustworthy servants are worth far more than the trouble a few drops of wine can bring."

"Moreover," his wife put in, "I know how to take that stain out." Mistress Hargrave then dabbed a clean piece of linen into her goblet before carefully rubbing at the stain on Judith's dress. As if she had performed an act of sorcery, the stain disappeared. "See, the white Rhenish wine takes out the red straight away." She laid the linen on the table. "A little trick I learned at the palace."

Judith and her mother exchanged glances. "At the palace?" Lady Embry asked, her haughty tone catching a bit.

"Yes, when I was one of Her Majesty's own ladies-in-waiting. I was but a young girl, of course, not much over twelve when I first came." The mistress smiled blandly at her guests. Lucy could have hugged her. "And I can tell you, during the time of Charles and Henrietta, there was no small amount of wine spilled at the palace, by nobles and servants alike."

The mistress sat back, dabbing her mouth daintily. Lucy could have sworn she was hiding a smile but was far too well bred to show it. To have served the queen as a beautiful lady-in-waiting was no small honor. Few could say the same, and this was quite a triumph. Lady Embry nodded slightly, acknowledging the added status of her hostess, and seemed to lose her chill somewhat.

The rest of the night passed pleasantly enough with Master Hargrave pulling out the fiddle and passing it around for the household to play a merry tune. He had long insisted his children and ward learn to play. Sarah was quite good, Lucy noted with a little smile. Sarah's music teacher had been attractive enough to keep her interest. Lucas, too, though coming to the instrument a bit late, played a few quick jigs passably.

Dutifully, Adam took his turn, his eyes half shut, ignoring Judith's rapt attention. He seemed neither interested nor disinterested in the piece but played with little of the fervor she had seen in him on some evenings. Indeed, he seemed distracted.

Placing the violin back in the case, he caught Lucy's eye. She raised an eyebrow, and he gave a little shrug. *I do not perform for strangers,* he seemed to say.

Especially ones that insult a hardworking lass in his household, Lucy added mentally on his behalf. Whether that gallantry was true, she did not know.

The next morning, Bessie and Lucy stepped out of the magistrate's house, eager to have a day off. The mist today was tentative, a few wisps that the wind easily chased away. Since both were visiting their families south of London, the girls planned to walk together as far as Southwark. Although they didn't admit it, neither wanted to walk alone. There were several long, lonely fields ahead of them, and Jane Hardewick's death reminded them how vulnerable they were on their own.

Lucy was glad that their tiff had smoothed over, and Bessie seemed to feel the same way. By unspoken agreement, neither mentioned the murder again.

"Shall we pass through Aldgate?" Bessie asked.

"Aldgate?" Lucy asked, surprised. "That will add nearly three-quarters of an hour to our journey."

"Well, I thought perhaps your brother, Will, might have the day off, too," Bessie said, a trifle too carelessly. "We could all journey through Lambeth together."

Lucy narrowed her eyes. She knew Will had taken Bessie to the plays a few times, but she also knew that her brother had a roving eye. "He did not mention his next day off, so I do not know his plans," she said.

Seeing Bessie smirk out of the corner of her eye, Lucy added, "However, I'm sure if he *is* free today, he will be quite eager to see Cecily, his sweetheart from home. They are all but promised, you know." She wasn't trying to be unkind, but she did hope to dampen Bessie's hopes about Will.

"I don't think they are promised," Bessie said.

Lucy snorted, but pretended she had sneezed when she saw Bessie's hurt expression. "You may be right," she said, trying to make amends.

"I am right," Bessie said smugly. "You'll see."

When they arrived at the smithy, Lucy was irritated to see that Will, indeed, was waiting for them. Clearly, he and Bessie had arranged to meet, and neither of them had told her. For a little while Lucy pouted, but then gave up when neither seemed to notice. Finally, when Will stopped to buy them some apples, Bessie linked her arm in Lucy's. "Do you mind? About Will?" Her blue eyes seemed enormous in their worry as she waited for Lucy to respond.

"Why didn't you tell me?" Lucy whispered.

Bessie shrugged. "I should have. You are my own true sister." She paused. "There's something else, too," she began, but broke off when Will tossed them both an apple.

By and by, Lucy gave in to the pleasure of spending time with her brother. She could not help but eye him happily. Truly William, with twenty years behind him, was fast becoming the handsomest man she knew. His boots were of fine black leather, and his cloak was of soft spun linen.

When she remarked upon his finery, he laughed. "Yes, my master often allows us to trade our services to men in town. He let me work for Master Brumley, whose good wife made me this cloak. I brought something for Mother, too." This spoke well of Will, for most guildsmen were strict about allowing their apprentices to work for themselves.

The three continued on, chattering all the while. Several young men, making merry with a leather flask, passed by them, no doubt off to the playhouses for a bit of afternoon fun. Since the Puritan ban on theatergoing had been lifted four years ago, plays were even allowed on the Lord's Day and during Lent.

Lucy sighed, wishing she could spare the three shillings required to attend, but such coins came dear. Will went frequently, but she suspected that he might have been less drawn to the plays and more to the actresses who cavorted about. The only time he'd taken her to the Globe, he'd also pointed out a comely orange seller who might have been another of his lady loves. Perhaps, Lucy thought, in that regard Bessie would be good for her brother, although she could not imagine he'd be ready to settle down.

When they reached London Bridge, Lucy caught herself humming a few words of a popular song.

London Bridge is broken down,
Dance over my Lady Lee,
London Bridge is broken down,
With a gay lady.

Not for the first time, Lucy wondered what poor Anne Boleyn had been thinking as she was being carted to death across this very bridge. What had it been like, knowing that her husband, the king, had ordered that her head be chopped off once she reached the other side? Had she cried on the shoulder of her faithful attendant, Lady Margaret Lee? How despairing she must have felt, that God had not seen fit to give her a male heir. That pitiful queen would never know, of course, that her daughter, dear Queen Bess, would bring such an era of peace and prosperity to England.

As they neared the south end of the bridge, Lucy willed herself not to look up. She knew, from the few other times she had passed through the south gate, that the rotting heads of criminals were set on pikes, warning all who would commit crimes against the king and the people of the realm. It sickened her, hearing the crowd jest and make fun.

"Mind the fresh ones," they would poke each other, "lest you get a bit of gristle on your clothes."

Instinctively, Lucy gripped Will's arm and buried her face in his shoulder. She felt him pat her cheek and was comforted by his touch.

At the crossroads by St. Mary Overy dock, as Bessie was about to take her leave, William caught her hand. "Now, you will be careful, won't you, lass? We can't have our girls running about alone, can we?"

Lucy watched him then whisper in Bessie's ear and saw her nod before she walked away.

Suddenly, she felt quite irritated with her brother. "Don't you even remember Cecily at all? Weren't you promised to her?" She stamped her foot.

Will kicked a tuft of dirt. "We were never promised, and you know it."

"Are you courting Bessie now?"

"I like Bessie. She's very sweet." Will touched her shoulder. "Lucy, before Father died, long before the Troubles, he told me that he did not want me to be a farmer. He wanted me to learn a trade, make some money, and support Mother, you, and little Dorrie. That's what I'm trying to do. I'm just not ready to settle down with anyone. Bessie understands that."

"I'm not so sure."

"I am! Besides, Lucy, I want to master my own trade!" he said, throwing his head back, looking like a young lion. "I don't want you to be serving gentry your whole life. I want something better for you, too. You should have a dowry."

"Well, if I live with you, I won't need a dowry," Lucy said, catching his excitement, her earlier annoyance forgotten. "You can buy me books instead. I shall learn to write books myself. Then you can set me up as a lady pamphleteer, and I can bring in my own income."

Will stopped and stared at his sister, horrified. "Lucy!"

Lucy giggled, lest he think her mad. "Nay, Will. I was just teasing. I think it's quite unlikely I'll become a petticoat author; I can scarcely write. Of course, I shall wed in time. Perhaps you can provide me with a dowry that will convince an earl to come a-calling."

"Indeed, Lucy. Indeed."

The next morning, Lucy was walking back from the market, just a few bruised apples in her basket. Hopefully Cook could make a pie. Though it was cold, she decided to take the long way home, sticking to the main roads, not crossing through the fields as she usually did. Jane Hardewick's murder still sat uncomfortably on her thoughts. Why hadn't she asked if Bessie or John could accompany her to market? she wondered. The road, though bright and sunny, was fairly desolate, and trees were thick in this part. Plenty of places for highwaymen and cutthroats to hide.

Then, to her dismay, Lucy heard someone cry out. She stiffened, looking this way and that. Was someone—crying?

Hesitating, she cocked her head toward the sound. It did not sound like a baby, or even a child. Taking a deep breath, she pulled aside a branch and peered into the brush.

Lucy stared. A man, tattered and mud splattered, was huddled in the dusty grasses, swaying back and forth and moaning. Controlling her enormous desire to flee, Lucy heard herself speak to the man. "Sir?" she asked. "Is there something the matter?"

At her voice, the man's head popped up, his mouth slack

jawed. Drawing back, Lucy recognized him. She had seen him before, in town, where small laughing boys had taunted him with sticks and rotten apples, making sport of his drooling lips, his missing fingers, and the frightening patch he wore over one eye.

Sickened now by the memory of the children's cruel taunts, Lucy knelt beside him. "Why are you crying?" she whispered.

Not replying, he wrapped his arms around his knees and began to rock slowly back and forth. Lucy tried not to look at his maimed hand. "Avery has lost his kitten, and she but a wee little thing, too. She was here"—he patted his leather pouch, which lay open on the ground—"in Avery's pocket. She just done gone and run off." He blew his nose noisily into his sleeve.

Lucy sighed. His mind was no doubt touched, but she felt sorry for him. How could he take care of a kitten? He seemed hardly able to take care of himself. Lucy knew she shouldn't tarry, but surely, she reasoned, she could spare a minute to help the poor addled soul.

Within moments of crawling through the brush, Lucy regretted her impulsive decision. Though Avery might be harmless enough, how could she be sure? What if this were a trap? Her mind flashed again to Jane Hardewick, killed in a field not so far away. Her heart started to pound. "I must get out of here," she whispered to herself. "This is folly."

She began to edge away but then heard a little mewing sound. Pausing, she watched a leaf move, and then a little white kitten popped up its head. Lucy scooped up the kitten, its orange and white tail wrapped around its frail, shivering body. Under her cloak, she felt the kitten begin to purr. "Avery, look here!" she called. "This must be your kitten!"

The big man bounded over, his face wreathed in smiles. "Kitty!" he scolded, gently taking the kitten from her out-stretched hands. "Why did you run away? Avery missed you!"

Avery sat down with his back against the tree, stroking the kitten in his lap. "We take care of each other, me and Kitty. Avery had another cat once. During the war. But that one's all gone now." His face clouded over.

"You were a soldier?" Lucy asked, somewhat taken aback. Yet, as she admitted to herself, there were many men like Avery still about, scarred and missing limbs, at the edge of public places, not venturing much among the people, except to beg.

"Aye," Avery answered. "One of King Charles's own men. Avery dunna remember much. The cannon he was feeding did done blow up in his face." He cocked his head, listening to the kitten purr. " 'Twas lucky enough Avery lost only a few fingers. He's still got the other hand to do his bidding. Some poor devils, the surgeons had to keep sawing and sawing." Stroking the kitten, he added, "Avery still hears screams sometimes."

Lucy shuddered, imagining the gore of battlefield surgery. A wave of sympathy poured over her as she thought bitterly of the blood that had ruined her father's fields. Holding out her hand, she smiled gently. "I'm Lucy."

He took her hand tenderly in both of his own—one hand perfectly formed, if grimy, and the other a claw—and a funny expression crossed his face. For a moment, she saw a glimpse of the man he once was. "You're lovely." She smiled and was about to thank him when he added, "Near as lovely as the other one."

Lucy supposed he meant some long-ago sweetheart, and she felt sad. The war had robbed so many people of so much. She did not pretend to understand much about politics, but she did understand suffering. Idly, she wondered how the magistrate would explain the great conflict that had torn so many families and communities apart.

Avery's dribbling mask returned, and he dropped her hand. They sat in silence for a moment, watching the kitten nestle on his knee. "That lass was an angel," he said, stroking the kitten's fur. "A fair angel."

"Was she your beloved?" Lucy asked gently.

"Beloved?" He seemed confused by her words, and then his brow cleared. "No, Avery doesn't have a sweetheart. Me and Kitty just have each other. Avery meant the girl sleeping in the field."

"In the field?"

"She looked like a sleeping angel, she did. Her hair was spread out so fine. Me and Kitty were hid behind a tree, but we could see her, lying in the grasses. Peaceful, she looked. But Avery did not like that the witches stole her clothes while she was asleep."

"She didn't wake up? When people were taking her clothes?" asked Lucy, sitting straight up. Something seemed off.

Avery rubbed his nose in the kitten's soft fur. "Like the men in the war. They didn't wake up either," he muttered. "All kinds of things happened to them."

An unpleasant thought occurred to Lucy. Her heart tripped faster. "Asleep, like the men—you fought with?" Lucy asked casually. "Did those people—witches, did you say?—help her, the angel, er, fall asleep?"

Avery shook his shaggy head. "No, they just took her clothes. She looked cold and alone. Avery wanted to cover her up. Poor angel." Then his face changed. He looked unbearably sad and fully comprehending. "She was dead."

·3·

The next day, being Palm Sunday, the whole household rose early, good members of the king's Church that they were. They walked together to St. Peter's, Master Hargrave carefully guiding the mistress over mislaid stones and puddles in the street. A light mist drifted about them, softly billowing against the line of trees and the houses they passed. Adam and his parents were speaking in hushed tones. Lucy caught the word "plague." She shuddered, focusing instead on the sweet smell of lavender coming from her hair and skin. She had been the last to use the bathwater the night before, and Bessie had added a few drops of her special perfume to freshen the cold tub.

Lucas and Sarah walked nimbly along, chattering about a gypsy who'd been fortune-telling at Covent Garden and was known to have set up camp in nearby Linley Park.

"Did she tell you about the man you were going to marry?"

Lucas asked, guiding Sarah around a heap of still-steaming manure.

"Oh, yes," Sarah said, giggling. "She said he would not be so handsome." Then she remembered something else. "Oh, and Father! The fortune-teller told me that I am to travel a great deal, across many rivers, she said, but that you would not like it. I wonder why? I should always come back to visit."

"I should hope so," the magistrate said drily, turning to look at his daughter. "However, I do not think the goodly Reverend Marcus would like us talking about fortune-telling on the Sabbath. Especially now that Lucas has begun his studies with him."

Lucas looked abashed. "Oh, yes, sir. You're right, sir."

Once inside St. Peter's, a gray stone church built in the fourteenth century, the family took their seats in their accustomed row, with the Hargraves toward the front and the servants standing next to the pew, alongside the wall. When Lucy had first starting attending the parish church with the Hargraves, she had been glad to be able to hear the minister so clearly. Now she wished she could sit in the back of the church with the common folk, since the new minister had a way of staring at a body with a scorching gaze, verily reading one's soul. His stories of hell and damnation made her heart beat painfully.

Lucy leaned against the oak wall, the stone floor hard on her feet. She shifted her weight carefully, so as not to attract anyone's attention. Stifling a sigh, Lucy tried to focus on the minister's words. Master Hargrave would question them on the walk home. He saw it as his godly duty, as head of the household, to make sure they were properly instructed in the faith.

Today, the reverend was speaking on the weakness of woman, one of his favorite topics. In his great voice, he pronounced, "Woman is a weak creature, not endued with the like strength and constancy of mind as men. They are prone to all manner of weak affections and dispositions of mind, that—"

Lucy had heard this opinion before. She thought of Avery, and other men harmed by war and illness who, if they were lucky, were housed by family or a kind neighbor. Who were the truly afflicted among them?

Her woolgathering was interrupted when the door at the back of St. Peter's banged open, letting in a refreshing stream of chill air. Heads swung around, and murmurs arose from the pews.

Bessie nudged her, and Lucy's mouth fell open. A woman, naked but for a bit of sackcloth covering her female parts, was striding down the center aisle. Her skin was rubbed dark with ashes, and her eyes were intent on the reverend at the pulpit.

Lucas looked stunned and angry. "How dare she?" Lucy heard him say to Sarah.

The congregation grew silent, watchful. Old men, slumping in their pews, sat up. Mothers covered their children's eyes. A man's low whistle carried in the silence, only to be hushed, probably by his missus. The reverend scowled.

Standing before the pulpit, the woman raised her hands heavenward. She laughed, but Lucy shivered at the sound. "Who amongst thee is not a sinner?" the woman hissed.

Lucy was struck by the woman's unfamiliar form of ad-

dress. Thee. The sackcloth and ashes. A Quakeress! One of that
wretched sort who were always getting themselves dragged off
by the magistrate's men and hauled away in carts. Pitiful crea-
tures really, some not so much older than herself. The strange-
ness of their faith made them outsiders, outcasts from the
community that had raised them.

"I am the trumpet of the Lord! I am his handmaiden!" The
Quakeress cried, her sackcloth slipping precariously down one
shoulder. "Heed my words! His judgment is coming upon thee,
all thee who are sinners, thee who are false pretenders! A great
plague upon thee all!"

Aghast and captivated by the spectacle, no one moved. The
reverend, whose face had been growing a more mottled purple
with each passing moment, finally regained his senses. "Harlot!"
he shouted, shaking his finger at her. "How dare you interrupt
this holy service of the Church of England!"

The crowd began to mutter in the pews. "Abomination!"
Lucy heard someone hiss.

"Quackers!" someone else called.

The minister jerked his head at two men seated nearby.
Jumping up, they each grabbed the woman under an arm and
hauled her from the church, her feet dragging against the stone
floor. Lucy blushed to see the woman's sackcloth ride farther
up her legs. The woman's screams were cut off as the great oak
door slammed shut.

The buzz that filled the pews died down with a single glare
from the minister. Lucy wondered what would happen to the
woman. Hauled off to jail, she supposed, probably to Newgate.

Finally, the minister offered the closing prayer, and the congregation began to move out of the dim church. The mist had
cleared, and the day was bright but chilly. Blinking, Lucy was
pulled up short by the sounds of a woman wailing and bursts
of raucous laughter. She turned to see several boys casting rotten tomatoes at a hunched gray figure.

Shocked, Lucy saw that the Quakeress had been tied to
makeshift stocks, even in this freezing cold. As Lucy watched,
a rotten egg hit the woman square on her forehead, so that egg
and shell dripped into her mouth. Her face was flushed and
bleeding. Wrinkling their noses from the stench, some of the
crowd began to move away from the spectacle.

"What in the name of heaven?" Adam had pushed his way
through the crowd. His face creased. "Who strung this woman
up?"

Some of the boys shifted their feet. A tall, skinny man dressed
in tattered clothes stepped forward. He looked wiry and mean,
like someone accustomed to a fight. "What's it to you?" he
sneered, kicking a small rock toward where Adam stood. The
crowd that had begun to disperse began to sidle back, hoping
for a bit of fisticuffs, some unexpected revelry on the Lord's
Day.

Adam drew up his frame, squaring his shoulders. "You
have no right to treat this woman in such a fashion. It is a matter
for the courts, and the law of this realm, to determine justice for
this woman."

The man scowled. "This here bunter has made a mockery
of God's law, or have you forgotten that? Perhaps you have

some sympathies for her? We could make room for you here in the stocks!"

As the crowd snickered, the man smirked, pulling the scarf from the woman's head. Her dark hair, thick and matted, fell loose. Lucy could see that the woman's lower lip was trembling fiercely. Drops of blood trickled from her nose. Lucy willed her not to weep, fearing that her ridicule would be worsened. As if she heard Lucy's pleas, she steadied her chin and spoke. "Thee hast thyself made sport with God's law, and thee shalt suffer in the bowels for tormenting one of his own handmaidens, picked to deliver his truth!"

"Who dares make such sport on the Lord's own day?" The reverend's voice boomed from the steps of St. Peter's. For a moment he stood still, the stone magnificence of the church adding to his stature. Lucas stood behind him, taking in the scene uncertainly, looking more serious and pale than Lucy had ever seen him.

A great rumble of hooves and a cloud of dust moved before the church. Alerted to the disturbance, two king's men appeared on horses.

The magistrate, who had just emerged from the church, hailed the king's guardsmen. "You there! Bring a cart around! And you! Cut this woman loose!"

At the presence of the magistrate, the jeering men and women began to slink away. Master Hargrave turned back to the woman, who still crouched, trembling, in the mud. One of her eyelids was matted shut, and her nose was swelling purple. She began to mumble feverishly.

"Miss? Could you tell me your name?"

The woman stopped mumbling and looked directly at the magistrate with her one good eye. Without a curtsy or even a nod to his authority, she answered him. "Dorcas White."

The magistrate looked at her sternly. "I do not condone the violence that has been taken against you today, Mistress White. Only the courts should punish such wrongdoing. I am sorry that you have been treated so injuriously, on the Lord's Day at that. You say that your conscience guides your actions—"

Mistress White interrupted, protesting. "It is God's will! I am his voice and mouthpiece. He has told me to speak out against the wickedness of—"

Master Hargrave held up his hand. "Enough!"

The woman fell silent. The magistrate continued. "I do not wish to debate the merits of your beliefs, as misguided as they are. It is not for me to challenge the heresies that you speak. It is for the reverend here"—he nodded to the minister, who gravely nodded back—"to counter such lunacy.

"I am concerned only with keeping the peace," Master Hargrave continued, "and with punishing those who transgress it. As I am sure you are well aware, you are accused of violating the Peace Act, by disrupting this church service and propagating your heretical beliefs among the godly. For this transgression, you will be imprisoned and stand trial."

A few people nodded, approving. Lucy looked down for a moment so no one could see her face. She had never seen the magistrate issue a charge, and she felt confused. No doubt the woman had disrupted the king's own service—appearing in such shocking dress!—and yet, had she not been punished enough?

Who knew how long she had been tormented, how long she had been mistreated by those bullying men, before the service had ended. Now she was to be carted off to jail?

"So be it," the Quakeress said, biting her lip. "Thee cannot take a righteous woman from her path to God, even if thee do throw me in chains!"

"Get her to Newgate," the magistrate told the soldiers. "I'll tend to her on the morrow."

·4·

I don't know how you got me to do this," Lucy muttered to Bessie, drawing her cloak closer around her body. It was nearly midnight, and they were on their way to Linley Park to see the gypsies. Ever since yesterday at church, when she had heard that the gypsies had encamped nearby, Bessie had insisted she needed to speak with them.

Now they were making their way through gaping shadows and dark fields, against Lucy's better judgment. Visiting gypsies during Lent seemed a bad idea, let alone in the deep of night.

"I am deathly afraid to go alone," Bessie had pleaded with her, "but I will, I swear it, if you won't come with me."

Try as she might, Lucy could not get Bessie to tell her what question she was seeking to answer. Lucy had frowned, but she knew she could not let her friend go alone.

Thankfully, the moon was bright and full. Moving quickly, they began to warm up. Sporadic shouts and boisterous laughter from late-night revelers reached their ears, but as the girls moved away from the public thoroughfares, the world grew steadily darker and quieter. The sound of an occasional branch breaking behind them would make them whirl around, fearing a wolf or a wild dog at every turn.

Bessie stopped abruptly, gripping Lucy's arm. "There!" she said, pointing to a hill that loomed before them. Tiny flickers of campfires could be seen in the distance. For a moment, the two girls huddled together, uncertain whether to venture forward or to run home.

A moment later, the decision was out of their hands when a hoarse voice called to them out of the darkness. "Come you to hear your fortune, did you now?"

Lucy could not tell if the voice was of a man or a woman, so rasping and harsh it was. She waited for Bessie to speak, but she seemed struck dumb. A heavily shrouded figure stepped out of the shadows and appeared to be waiting.

Lucy found her tongue. "Yes, we wish to have our fortunes read." She hesitated. "If you please, ma'am."

The old woman barked, a rough mirthless sound. She jerked her thumb toward a campfire. "Over there. Maraid, she's waiting for you."

Gripping each other's arms, the girls sat down, warily watching the woman called Maraid. The fire made Maraid's hair and skin shine, as if the flames dwelled within her deepest being. Frankly, it unnerved Lucy.

Bessie passed her a bit of silver. The woman took Bessie's

hand and held it to the light of the fire. She looked up at Bessie and then at Lucy. She sighed, a long weary breath. "I remember you, child."

Lucy looked at Bessie in surprise. She wondered when Maraid had read her fortune before.

The gypsy continued. "I remember your hand. 'Tis no new fortune I can tell you, I'm afraid. There is a darkness upon you, but as I told you before, it does not have to be that way."

Seeing Bessie's face blanch, she added more gently, "But you have not come all this way to hear the same fortune. You have paid your silver. You may ask me one question."

Bessie whispered something in the gypsy's ear. The woman frowned, shadows dancing across her ageless face. She shook her head. "This I cannot see. There is a veil down across that time. From what you have told me, I do not believe it shall pass as you like."

Seeing Bessie's crestfallen face, Maraid added, "You have many who love you and will tend to you, including this loyal friend here."

The gypsy turned to Lucy. Something about Maraid drew Lucy in, almost against her will. The crackling fire added odd sparks, so it looked almost as if there were fire within her eyes.

Lucy looked at her tattered clothes, a hodgepodge of colors, including a brightly embroidered red sash wrapped around her waist. It caught her attention. She pointed at it. "That's lovely."

Maraid's eyes flickered to the beautiful young woman tending the fire. "Yes, it is," she agreed, "but it comes from a dark place."

The young woman scowled, and a new tension tightened

around them. A shadow passed, scratching a cold place upon Lucy's neck. Eager to be off, Lucy urged Bessie to stand. "We'd better go."

As the girls scurried out of the gypsy's camp, Lucy felt they were being watched, a feeling she could not shake for all the dark journey home. Adding to her unease, although Lucy pressed, Bessie refused to tell her what she had sought from the gypsies.

Lucy sighed a bit impatiently, pulling the cloak closer around her shoulders, watching the sun set. Since their visit to the gypsies the day before, Bessie had grown more jumpy and anxious. To make matters worse, Bessie had been gone for much of today, and Lucy had been covering all her duties. This could work during the day, when Sarah and the mistress did not need to be tended to, but tonight they were dining out and would soon require Bessie's expert hairdressing skills.

Lucy bit her lip, peering down the dimly lit road to see if she could make out Bessie or her red cape. "Where *is* she?" The sound of her own voice startled her. Soon someone would surely notice their absence from the house. She had a package holding Adam's shoes, and she thought they could pretend they'd been at the shoemaker, although there was no good reason that two of them would have been needed to tend to this task.

Even in her head, the story sounded false. She could hear their questions. "Why did you not say you would return when the shoemaker had finished Master Adam's shoes? Why did you both need to stay?" Most frightening of all, "Where were you?

What have you been doing?" If they were caught, surely the
mistress would punish them. Most likely, she would refuse to
let them attend Lady Embry's Easter masquerade coming up in
a few days' time.

Lucy sighed. Perhaps no one would ask them to explain
their absence. Cook would be easy enough to satisfy, to be sure.
But Master Hargrave! She gulped. It would almost be like lying
to God. She shivered. Bessie just had to make haste.

Hearing a quick step behind her, she jumped.

"Lucy!" Bessie whispered. "It's me!"

Lucy faced her. Two red spots stood high in Bessie's cheeks.
Her hair was falling from her cap, and her skirt was rumpled
as though she had run a long way. "Fix your skirts!" Lucy whispered fiercely. "We were at the shoemaker's this long while,
understand?"

Lucy's fears, however, were for naught. The master and mistress had decided to stay in for the evening and had taken a
small, quiet supper in their room. The mistress had not needed
Bessie to help her dress. Adam and Lucas were out, no doubt
at the tavern. Cook accepted their explanation without question and set them to work preparing for tomorrow's dinner.
John, sharpening knives by the fire, glanced at them but said
nothing.

Not until they were preparing for bed did Lucy press Bessie
about her whereabouts that afternoon. A sudden color rose in
Bessie's cheeks and she half smiled, revealing the little dimple
in her cheek and her slightly cracked tooth. With her golden
curls loosened about her face, she looked like an angel.

"Were you with Will again?" Lucy demanded.

Bessie looked away. "Lucy, actually, Will and I quarreled. I was—somewhere else." She stammered, "I, uh, went out, um, to see my sister. Her little boy was, um, sick. I wanted to see if she needed me."

As if she'd heard how feeble her reply was, Bessie's next words came out a little strongly, tumbling over one another. "He's so prone to the sickness, you see, ever since he had the ague."

"Did he have need of a bleeding?" Lucy asked slowly, climbing into the bed beside Bessie.

Bessie pulled the cover up. "Oh, no, he's looking to recover soon, the doctor said. And Lucy . . ."

"Hmmmm?"

"Thank you."

Lucy felt Bessie roll over to go to sleep. Listening to her friend's deep breaths, Lucy brooded silently. *How, Bessie. How did you know the baby was sick?* No messenger had come to the house. Poor Bessie, who could not make up a lie to save her life.

"You weren't at your sister's house," Lucy whispered. "Where were you?"

·5·

Easter arrived, and as soon as they returned from the church on Sunday, the women began to prepare for the Embrys' masquerade that evening. Lucy knew that the magistrate didn't really approve of the Embrys holding such an extravagant affair on a holy day, but he didn't wish to refuse his wife and daughter the delights of the ball, and of course no one wanted to be viewed as a Puritan these days. Even the servants would be allowed to share in a bit of the festivities, though naturally they wouldn't be mixing with the Embrys' guests. Only Lucas would not be attending the masquerade, having decided to help the reverend with the Easter evening service instead.

Lucy did not dare touch the shining silk brocades that Bessie had spent several hours ironing to perfection. Instead, she brushed shoes, smoothed petticoats, and found Sarah's tiny silver combs. Finally, Mistress Hargrave, her hair curled and dress pressed, waved Lucy and Bessie away with a smile. "Go," she said. "Make yourselves gorgeous."

Once in their own room, Bessie helped Lucy pull on her only dress suitable for such an affair, a heather blue taffeta that Miss Sarah had given Bessie the year before. Slight watermarks had stained the sleeves and the skirt but no longer showed after Bessie's expert alterations. Bessie's dress was a soft mossy green taffeta that emphasized her well-formed figure.

Lucy twirled in her dress, enjoying the feel of the soft fabric against her body. Bessie had also loaned Lucy her second-best petticoat, a black one that was full enough to let the skirt flare out softly.

Bessie sniffed her underarms. "Yuck," she scowled. With a bit of cloth, she lightly powdered each armpit with alum. "You want some?"

"No, thank you," Lucy said. Better to have a little sweat under the arms than to have that unpleasant tingling all night.

"How about this?" Bessie uncorked a small bottle of scent, dabbing a few drops of the liquid behind her ears. She handed the vial to Lucy. "For your complexion, my lady," she said, mimicking the gypsy's wheedling tone. "Tonight, when you meet the man of your dreams, he will be unable to withstand your charms."

Laughing, Lucy put a few drops behind her ears, careful not to spill on her beautiful dress. Why not? Indeed, Bessie's own skin glowed, and she was flushed and lovely in the twilit room. To be sure, she looked like a princess, or at least like one of the king's lady loves. For a moment, Lucy was filled with great admiration and love for this girl who had become like a sister.

"Oh!" Bessie recalled herself with a start, becoming a well-trained servant again. "I forgot! The vizard! The mistress wanted me to fix it. And I must still do my hair." She pulled out one long blond curl forlornly. "Perhaps it is good that Will shall not see me so."

The vizard was a harlequin mask that the women would use to court mystery and mischief at the ball. It would not do for the mistress to appear without hers, and several feathers still needed to be attached.

"Oh, I can take care of it," Lucy reassured her. "I know where it is. You finish getting ready."

Lucy ran lightly down the stairs, enjoying the unaccustomed luxury of taffeta against her skin. It was not silk, of course, but it was a great improvement over the wools and heavy cottons to which she was accustomed.

Retrieving the vizard, Lucy rushed out of the mistress's chamber, keeping her head down so as not to put her foot through her skirts. In her haste, she collided with Adam walking swiftly down the narrow corridor, smashing her nose on his book. The book and vizard flew in the air. Losing her balance, Lucy stumbled backward, hovering over the steps.

For a dizzying moment, Lucy felt she was going to plunge backward down the hard steps and break her neck. Frantically, blindly, she grasped for Adam. The next instant, he had grabbed her arms and swung her safely back to the landing. She leaned into him, breathing hard.

"Lucy!" Adam exclaimed, still gripping her tightly. "Are you all right?" Managing to nod, she stepped back, a little unsteady on her feet.

"Easy, there!" he said. "You're liable to plunge right back down the stairs. I'd like to avoid that." Then he looked at her closely. "Hey! Your nose is bleeding."

"Oh, no!" Lucy wailed, putting her hand to her face. It felt strange, swollen. She started to move past him.

He put his hand on her shoulder. "Wait a minute, Lucy." Removing a handkerchief from the pocket of his new plush-lined cloth suit, Adam raised her chin, holding the linen lightly to her nose. "Here, tilt your head back. That should stanch the blood."

Lucy could smell the slight, pleasant aroma of tobacco, soap, and something else. Suddenly, she was acutely aware that they were alone in the hallway, standing not even a pace apart. No man, not even her brother, had ever held her face.

Their eyes met. For the first time, she realized that his eyes were a deep blue-gray, not the brown that she always supposed. Now something flickered in them as he gazed down at her intently. He dropped his hand abruptly.

She flushed, taking a step back, smoothing her dress. Reaching for the cloth with a trembling hand, she stammered, "Thank you, sir. I'm fine. I'll wash out your kerchief."

Adam nodded, seeming to be searching for words. Seeing the vizard, which had fallen to the floor, he picked it up, smiling slightly. "Yours?"

"No, sir, it belongs to my mistress. Your mother, I mean." She looked down at her simple taffeta. The elaborate mask was not something servants would wear. He might have followed her thoughts.

"Indeed. Well." Adam's manner grew brisk. "Have a care

tonight. Mind you're not running down hallways at the Embrys'. I doubt they'd like it much." He turned abruptly on his heel, leaving Lucy alone with her flurried thoughts.

Moments later, her nose still aching, Lucy pushed open the door to her chambers to find Bessie rummaging through her wooden chest. Bessie started, hiding something under her spring muslin dress. Why did Bessie look guilty? Lucy wondered. She looked like she'd been caught eating the master's own mutton pie.

Then Bessie caught sight of Lucy's face, and nothing else was important. "Oh, dear, Lucy! What happened to you? Why's your nose all red and swollen?"

Adam's face flashed into Lucy's thoughts, and just as quickly she put the image away. She didn't want to share the odd moment with anyone, even Bessie. Besides, if Bessie could have secrets, then so could she. "I ran into something," she hedged, "but, oh! I must look awful!"

Wordlessly, Bessie pulled out the tarnished old looking glass that the mistress had allowed them to use for the evening. Horrified, Lucy looked at her nose, which looked misshapen and huge. She groaned, sure that her lovely night would be ruined.

Instantly, Bessie's arm came around her, comforting and sweet. "Oh, Lucy! Don't you worry. We'll have Cook prepare a poultice. You'll feel better right quick!"

In the kitchen, Cook took one look at her and began to bustle about. From one stone jar, she pulled a piece of dried fruit off a medlar. She crushed it into a fine powder, then mixed in the juice of red roses, adding a few cloves and nutmeg.

Lucas, quite comfortably eating a bit of cold turkey pie by the fire, gave a low whistle when he saw Lucy's face. "Been in a scrap?" he teased. "Your conk's out of sorts!"

Her nose now throbbing, Lucy responded tartly, raising her hand. "Yea, and you keep laughing at me, you'll be getting a right knock across your kisser!"

Lucas grinned at her country expression. "Is that so? Then come here. I could use a knock across my kisser, particularly if it came from you. You look lovely, even if your nose is fast looking like a goose's egg."

Startled, Lucy looked at him. Though he was joking, the compliment seemed real. Then he winked at her, continuing to chew. Cook tousled his hair and wagged her finger at him. "None of your nonsense, now," she said, and then to Lucy, "Don't ye worry, lass—I've just the thing." Adding a crust of old bread and some water to the fragrant concoction, Cook soon had a paste, which she then smoothed gently around Lucy's tender nose. "This will do the trick."

After washing her face in cold rainwater a little while later, Lucy surveyed herself critically in the cracked looking glass. She could not compare to Bessie's plump loveliness, with her dimpled cheeks and full lips that begged for a kiss. Even so, she thought her own dark lashes were wonderfully long and framed her brownish green eyes nicely, and when she moved her head just so, her brown hair glinted with golds and reds like the setting sun.

Then her mother's voice came dancing to her ears. *The devil loves a looking glass.* She put the mirror down abruptly.

Later that evening, Lucy and a few of the maids from the Embry household peered from behind the curtain into the great room at the feast and the dancing. The festivities of Lady Embry's Easter masquerade in the great room were being mimicked happily by the servants in the lower kitchens and the servants' dining hall. Barrels of beer and ale were flowing freely among the servants, while near fifty guests in fancy costumes and masques dipped their mugs into open barrels of Rhenish and French wine.

The musicians hired for the occasion played fashionable new pieces from France on beautiful stringed instruments. Lady Embry's newly imported spinet and harpsichord were widely admired at their prominent location by the great fire. Men and women danced gracefully together in sets of sixes and eights, the ladies holding their masks and fans coyly to their faces, the men leading confidently through the intricate steps. Jewels winked softly in candlelight, and a number of lovers, some acknowledged, others not, laughed and murmured together in the shadows.

From her vantage point of the hidden balcony, Lucy found herself looking for the Hargraves. The magistrate was deep in conversation with three dour-looking men, all of whom looked like they'd rather be in someone's home, sipping sherry, than caught in this gorgeous and flamboyant display. Lucy recognized them as frequent visitors to the house. Two were members of Parliament; the other was a justice of the peace.

Mistress Hargrave was sitting with several other matrons, watching her daughter whirl from one handsome partner to the next and allowing herself to be fanned by a young whelp. Adam was listening politely to a beautiful young heiress who, if the whispers in the alcove could be believed, had just been presented at court, her vizard held to one side so he could see her fine features. As Lucy watched, the young woman daringly laid her hand on Adam's sleeve and, with great pleasure evident in her face, allowed him to lead her into the next set.

Others had been watching Adam, too. "He's really the best dancer of the lot," one of the maids said with a sigh.

"I wonder what else he's good at?" asked another young woman, grinning wickedly. Lucy recognized her as one of Lady Harrington's lady's maids. "I may aim to find out, one of these days!"

"I expect he's already had his way with *you,* Lucy?" Janey asked, her smile bright but her features hard. Seeing Lucy flush, she continued, "Do tell, did he have you over the kitchen table? Or spread your skirts as you bent to pick up his linens?"

"Not when Bessie's around for the taking, I'd say!" chimed Mariah, Janey's companion.

"I'd trouble myself to have a brat with him!" a much younger girl added. Lucy did not know her. "He'd be one to take care of his own, I wager."

"Stupid git!" Janey said. "Them that think like nobles think themselves too fine for the likes of us. It's all sweet talk till they get the chit with child, and that's the end of it."

Janey's fierceness chilled Lucy a bit. The sorry fate of a serving lass done in by her master was all too well known a tale, usually ending with the mistress casting her out of the house, with nary a reference but with plenty of names for the girl and her babe—hoyden and bastard but two.

"He's not like that," Lucy said. "Neither is the magistrate."

Janey sneered. "You must not be pleasing enough for them, then."

"Oh, poo!" Bessie's voice sounded in her ear. Lucy had not heard her under the taunts of the other girls. "Who wants to watch *them* dancing! Come, Lucy, they've started dancing downstairs, and I mean for us to have some fun!"

They made their way downstairs, and there to the servants' dining hall, which connected to the Embry's large kitchen. Lucy found a quite different party. The servants had moved the tables and benches out of their dining hall, creating a cramped but lively dancing area. Several couples were already whirling about, the weariness of their dreary servant's days forgotten, while others clapped and stamped their feet in time with the old familiar country dances. When Bessie and Lucy walked through the door, each was seized about the waist by a young man eager for a partner to bounce about with in merry confusion.

Breathless with laughter and the quickness of the steps, both girls found themselves passed playfully among a number of different men. Some of the men she knew from houses along the Hargraves' street; others she did not know. These Lucy assumed were members of the Embrys' extensive livery and household.

After she grew tired of dancing, Lucy moved into the kitchen, where men and women, young and old, perched about the room, trading quips and jests. Some couples began stumbling out of the kitchen, flagons of ale in their hands. Young serving girls, freed from their normal routines, flirted outrageously.

Squeezing onto a bench, Lucy smiled at the woman next to her, holding a sleeping babe in her lap. Lucy marveled at the baby's ability to sleep through the good-natured revelry. Accepting a mug of ale, Lucy laughed along with the others as jokes and outrageous stories continued to fly. She saw Bessie in the corner, flirting a bit with some men from the Embrys' stable. Looking at Bessie, laughing and happy, it was hard to see the moody girl she'd been these last few weeks.

Richard, one of the Embrys' liverymen, heaved himself up onto the edge of the wooden table, his tongue clearly loosened by ale. "I heard tell of an old thief, Jack Grubb, who was to meet with the hangman one fine morning," Richard began. "When the hangman placed the noose around his neck, our good man Jack said, 'Nay, good sir! Do not bring the rope too near my throat. For I am,' says he, 'so ticklish about that place that I shall hurt myself, laughing so hard, that the rope will like to throttle me!'"

Everyone roared and clinked their pewter mugs. A strumpet snuggled beside Richard, slipping under his arm. When he put his arm around her waist, she smirked at the other girls, for Richard was easily one of the most handsome men there.

Yet a few minutes later, he came over to Lucy and poured more ale into her mug.

"Thank you." She smiled up at him.

Richard caught her look and seated himself beside her on the long low bench. "Oh, little minx," he said, taking a hearty swig of ale. "I did not catch your name. I'm Richard."

Lucy murmured her name, her head beginning to swim from her three cups of ale. Richard covered her free hand with his and spoke in a caressing tone. "Lucy. What a lovely name to match a lovely face. Are you enjoying yourself, my little sweet?"

Not sure what to say, Lucy nodded and managed a tremulous smile. As the man began to whisper things in her ear that made her blush, she felt confused and stood up. The room wavered around her. She put her hand on the wall to steady herself, saying, "I think I'm off, then."

Moving toward the door, Lucy paused as the room spun around her. Once she was outside, the fresh night air welcomed and soothed her, and she was glad to leave the noisy din behind. Shouts of laughter and music drifted from the house. She saw a man stride out of the main door, a woman following after him. Squinting, she sighed when she saw Adam and Judith Embry.

Lucy stepped quickly into the shadows of a gracious elm tree, so that she would not be seen. A chill breeze blew, reminding her she had left her wrap inside. Not wanting to return to the house just yet, she wrapped her hands around her bare arms.

Judith's voice carried in the still air, allowing Lucy to catch snatches of their conversation. "Father, you know, believes—"

Lucy heard Judith say, but her words were lost in the light wind that had arisen. Although unsure why, Lucy moved closer, keeping care to keep her figure hidden in the bushes.

Adam appeared to pull away slightly. "Yes, I'm well aware of what your father thinks."

"Oh, Adam," Judith continued. "You can do anything you want. Father doesn't think lawyers really are too important."

Hearing her brittle little laugh, Lucy shuddered.

"Indeed?" Adam asked idly, lazily.

This time, Judith seemed to sense that she had gone too far. "Oh, dear," Judith said soothingly, caressing his arm. "I've made you angry, Adam. Come, let's have a kiss and make up."

Lucy watched as Adam regarded Judith. She could not tell what he was thinking. She wondered if he liked what he saw. He paused. "Why not?" she heard him say.

Averting her gaze, Lucy crept away, a deep dismay rising up inside her. *Adam deserves better than her,* she thought. As if on cue, her nose began to throb, painfully reminding her of the odd encounter with Adam on the stairs.

Suddenly desperate to go home, she stumbled away, only to quickly become disoriented as the fog grew heavier. Without a lantern, she could not find the path. A hand on her arm made her jump.

It was Richard. "Are you lost, my sweet?" he asked, smiling. "I know that I lost you, and I came out here to see if I could find you."

"I was on my way home."

"Home? Nonsense! The evening is still young! No one goes home until the morning chores are to be done! 'Tis the night for servants to frolic and play as lords! Come, be my lady, and sit with me a bit."

Still smiling, Richard began to pull her toward the Embrys' stable. She did not object when he put his arm firmly around her waist. When she stumbled over a root and his grip around her tightened, she heard him laugh, a deep sound that rumbled from his chest. She laughed, too, suddenly giddy. Richard opened the stable door, kicking aside some straw as they entered. Lucy halted in confusion, but he deftly maneuvered them inside.

For the second time that day, a man held her face in his hands. This time, however, his eyes did not meet hers, and he planted his lips hungrily on her mouth. He pulled the door shut behind them, and she heard the latch click. At that, something inside her began to sound an alarm, like church bells proclaiming fire.

Fear making her stomach lurch, Lucy tried to pull away, but Richard pressed her tightly against the stable wall with his body, his hands fumbling at the strings on her bodice. Lucy began to fight in earnest, her hands flailing, trying to push at his chest. The ale that had emboldened him had sapped her strength. He pinned her arms back, pressing his body against hers. His mouth, impatiently tasting hers, muffled her cries, even as the flavors of mutton and stale ale made her want to retch. The horses in nearby stalls began to stamp, catching wind of her distress.

Weaker, she tried in vain to bat at the hand seeking to hike up her skirts. Wrenching her head to one side, she managed to scream once but was again cut off by Richard striking her across the face.

"Shut up, you whore," he hissed. "You asked for this, with all your simpering and prancing about. I'm just giving you what you want."

Her head spinning from the drink and the blow she had been dealt, Lucy thought distantly that she had heard someone shout. The next moment Richard abruptly released her, and she slumped to the ground. There she lay, quivering in relief and terror, barely taking in the angry voices from the door.

"The lass and I were just talking!" she heard Richard say. "'Tis no business of yours—" The sound of a fist hitting flesh stopped him midsentence.

"She is my business," came the improbable reply. "Now remove yourself before I get you sacked."

She heard Richard swear angrily and then stalk off. Lucy sagged back into the hay, still whirling from drink and fear.

A quiet voice came from the stable doors. "Lucy?"

She looked up, barely stifling a groan. She could see Adam standing there, his figure a shadow. He was half turned away, looking at the dancing lights of the Embrys' mansion and rubbing his knuckles. She felt a hot flush of shame pass through her body, mortified that he would see her this way.

"Are you all right?" he asked, still not looking at her.

Lucy nodded shakily and stood up. "I think so." Her dress was torn a bit, but she hoped in the dark he could not see anything. She wiped her face.

"Come on, then. I'll see you home. I've had enough of this affair anyway." His voice was curt, expressionless.

They started off down the path. She tripped a little, and he grabbed her elbow to steady her. She recoiled, still feeling

Richard's touch on her body. Adam did not move to touch her
again.

Fueled by anger and shame, she recalled the shadowy figures at the front of the house. "Why are you not with your
lady? She will surely be missing you."

Adam frowned. "I bid Judith good night. I've had enough
of dancing and politics. I was on my way home when I saw my
father's silly little serving girl—" He broke off.

What?! Lucy thought. *You saw your silly little serving girl get
manhandled by a brute? Or show her brazen ways?* She wanted to
defend herself, but she didn't know of what exactly she was
standing accused.

The silence hung heavily between them. Lucy bit her lip,
feeling young and foolish. For the second time that evening,
she realized that she did not have her wrap. She shivered. Adam
shrugged out of his cloak and dumped it around her shoulders,
without saying a word. Lucy did not look up to thank him but
hugged it gratefully to her cold body.

As they walked and her head cleared, she grew calmer. The
moon was gleaming through a soft haze, which fell around
them like a blanket. She gazed upward. The stars numbered in
the thousands, tiny pinpricks of light among a mat of darkness.
She wished she were floating among them, keeping her far away
from the pain she was feeling. Although she was still sniffing
a little, her tears had stopped falling.

Adam appeared deep in thought. When he finally spoke, it
was not to say what she was expecting. His voice was quiet,
musing. "Two comets, they say, passed each other in the night
sky. Directly over the city, just two weeks ago."

Lucy remained quiet, trying to envision the spectacle. She was grateful he hadn't said anything more about Richard.

He went on, waving his hand expansively toward the stars, looking like crystals affixed to a deep violet tapestry. "One comet was dull and languid, the other sparkling and furious, moving through the sky like a great flame. Some say it was a message from the Almighty."

"A message?" Lucy asked. "To say what?"

"An omen, perhaps? That his judgment would be upon us? That a scourge is coming?" Adam looked down at her then, searching her face. "You choose."

Lucy scratched her nose. He grinned in response, the tension between them spent. She smiled back. A scourge seemed very far away, not something to worry about, when she was walking beside the magistrate's son in the moonlight, wearing his cloak. Unconsciously, she slowed her pace.

After a moment, he asked her another odd question. "Lucy, do you believe in free will?"

Though again this was not what she was expecting, she pondered the question carefully. "I believe my thoughts are my own, if that's what you mean. I believe I can choose to do good or evil."

"So, you believe we have control over our own actions, over our own fate?" He pulled a branch back from the path.

She stepped through, and he let the branch go. "Yes, perhaps, to a point," she said. "Can I choose to go to market, or to the plays for that matter, whenever the whimsy strikes me? No, I may do such things only when your mother, or Cook, says that I may."

He looked at her then, regarding her intently. She wondered for a second what a looking glass would reveal, since she could feel her hair was completely loose and she had no cap. Her face was probably smudged with dirt, her skirts in disarray. She would never look as poised and graceful as Judith Embry.

Yet she found she did not care as she went on. "I'm not sure I understand what scripture would say, but I suppose men, and women, must make their own destiny. We can, for example, decide who we love, even if the ability to act on that love is determined by others." With a little snort Lucy added, "That's if we understand *politics,* sir, which I'm sure I do not."

Adam looked at her in surprise but stayed silent. They crossed the last field and walked down the street to their home.

When they approached the house, his mood seemed to change. "You're a good lass, Lucy," he said slowly. "Unusual, even." He stopped, seeming to struggle with what he was about to say. Then he was once again a member of the gentry, scolding and arrogant and sure of himself. "Certainly you're too young to touch the spirits in such immoderate measure. I may not be around next time to step in."

Lucy's face flamed. "I didn't ask you to!" she cried, the calm the walk had brought her destroyed. " 'Twas not your concern, it was my evening off. I'm not a child, I'm eighteen! I don't need you to look after me!" Tearing off his cloak, she handed it to him with shaking fingers.

He scowled. "And just what do you think a man like that wanted with a foolish little girl like you, anyway?" Adam asked coldly. "You are a member of my father's household. I would not have the reputation of his servants besmirched."

His words stung her like a slap. The image of Richard's leering face and roving hands on her body burned her. Ducking her head, Lucy ran inside to the solace of her little chamber at the top of the house.

The comfort of sleep did not come quickly. When she did finally drift off, she dreamed that someone was lightly holding her face and moving in to kiss her lips. Somehow, though, Adam's concerned face was replaced by Richard's angry countenance, causing her to awake, her heart pounding in fear, excitement, and something else.

·6·

Lucy found her cloak in the kitchen the next morning. She wondered if Adam had returned for it, or more likely Bessie had recognized it and fetched it back. She didn't know if she was happy or angry as she went out on the stoop to await the raker.

Standing away from two huge basket tubs that held the week's rotting foodstuffs, slops, and bodily excretions, Lucy held a linen cloth scented with rosemary over her face, trying to ward off the unbearable stench. A few months ago, the city government had mandated that all household refuse be carted away, which meant that servants like Lucy had to wrestle with heaping buckets of waste, instead of throwing everything out the window as servants had been doing for many centuries.

As she waited, Lucy gazed into the dirty fog. The Fumifugium. She rolled the word around on her tongue, tasting its full acridity. John Evelyn's word, she heard the master say the other night at supper. The word could only begin to evoke the disgusting cloud of smoke that ever rose from the city's chimneys and became mired in London's ever-present fog. All she knew was that the putrid smoke felt like a murderer, stealing among the Londoners, clouding their lungs, taking their breath, and pilfering lives. Or at least that's what Evelyn had said.

Finally Bessie came out, her face paling as she caught a whiff of the stench. She plopped down heavily on the stoop, without a word of greeting. Lucy could see sweat beading across her forehead, and her face seemed unnaturally pale and waxy, despite two blotches of red on either cheek. She looked ill.

Lucy's mind flashed to something Missus Gray had gossiped about the other day. "Something troublesome is going on, down by Drury Lane. A strange sickness, 'distemper' they're calling it. Bah. Whoever died from distemper?" At the other women's encouraging clucks, Missus Gray added, "I ask you this: Would that explain the bodies being carted out at night? Would it explain the dogs' howling?"

"What say the magistrate, Mary?" Mistress Vane had pressed Cook. "Do you know?"

Cook and Lucy had exchanged glances. They knew what the magistrate thought, but neither spoke. Several houses in Drury Lane, a few miles away from their home, had been quarantined by a fellow magistrate, but according to Master Hargrave, probably not nearly the number that should have been.

Indeed, Lucy had heard him tell the mistress, "The Bills of Mortality have been reporting an unprecedented number of deaths in Drury Lane, but there may be many more. The problem is, families are trying to hide their marks of infection from

the law and may be dumping bodies in other parts of the city."
Here he had looked sternly around the family, his gaze taking
in the servants. "There may well be plague upon us, but it is
our duty not to start a panic."

Without thinking, Lucy felt Bessie's head anxiously for
fever, but it was cool. "I guess you don't have the plague."

"Plague? What? No. I'm all right." Bessie wiped her mouth.
Glancing down the street, she pointed at a man slowly bringing a cart up the street. "Look, here's the raker. I'll be back."

Bessie did not come back outside, though. Lucy had to heave
the filth from the tubs into the cart by herself. She noted with
disgust that the cart was leaking excrement onto the street. "So
much for improved city cleanliness," Lucy commented to no one.

Returning inside, she found Bessie drinking some water
from the kitchen pail. Sweat had drenched the back of her
muslin dress. Without saying anything, Bessie left to attend to
Mistress Hargrave. Sighing, Lucy poured sand across the stone
floor of the kitchen, for Cook had asked her to scour the floor
after breakfast.

Lucy had finished the floor and started on preparing dinner
when Lucas came into the kitchen a short time later, whistling
a catchy tune. He plopped himself at the other end of the
bench, watching as Lucy pared potatoes with a knife. Peering
hopefully into one of the iron bowls cooling on the table, he
spoke.

"Dear Lucy, will you give a poor lad something to eat? Just
a small bite?"

Lucy tossed him a carrot from one of the wood baskets lining the kitchen's ample shelves. "Here, eat this."

Making a face, Lucas nonetheless bit down on the carrot. "I thought you had a heart. I'm beginning to believe you don't care about me at all. I've not had a bite to eat all day."

"As I would wager it is just ten in the morning, I feel none too sorry for you or your clamoring belly. Besides, you should feel lucky Cook is not here to shoo you off, with your tales of woe. Which I don't believe, by the way."

"Hmmm. Don't be so sure. Cook loves me," Lucas said. "By the by, where is dear Cook?"

"She is off visiting her son, Sam, in Leadenhall."

"Ah, yes, the fishmonger. An' you and Bessie did not get to go? What a shame!" Lucas grinned. He knew all about Sam's wandering fingers.

"Yes, we do miss him terribly, but someone must tend to supper."

"Of course. Quite noble and kind of you, to be sure." He looked around. "And Bessie? Off today, too?"

"No, off getting thread from the seamstress. She lives not too far from here. The mistress did need her new bonnet fixed. The winds tore it something terrible when she got caught out in this morning's rain."

"Uh-huh." Lucas leaned over to stir a pot. "And Adam?" he asked, idly.

Hoping the faint blush was not evident on her cheeks at the mention of Adam's name, Lucy shook her head, chopping quickly. "Off to see Miss Embry, perhaps."

Lucas looked at her keenly. "Now why would you assume

that?" He held up his hand. "No matter. He's just as likely at the pub. No, I jest. I'm sure he's off somewhere studying or some such nonsense. He's seemed a bit anxious of late to finish his legal studies."

"How are you getting on with the good Reverend Marcus?" Lucy asked hurriedly, hoping to change the subject.

"Quite well, actually." Lucas chuckled. "I think I may have found my calling after all."

Lucy could not quite tell if he was teasing. There was a little glint to his smile that she had never before seen. A bit of self-mockery, a bit of hesitant pride—he reminded her of Will, trying to find his way in the world. "I'm so glad, Lucas."

Perhaps seeing the admiration on her face, Lucas settled more comfortably on the hard bench. "Have you any more of that cakebread?" he wheedled, licking his lips. "The currants, the spices, mmm."

Shaking her head, Lucy pulled out the last piece of cake-bread from yesterday's supper. Mistress Hargrave had given Cook a copy of *A Boke of Gode Cookery* this past Christmas, but it was Lucy who had begged her to try the recipe. Everyone had heartily enjoyed it. Indeed, she was surprised there was any left.

"I knew it!" Lucas clasped his hands to his chest. "I should marry the girl who produced this cake."

"That would be Cook," she teased. "I'm afraid John will not let her go."

"But 'twas your sweet hands that produced this delight out of thin air. A wondrous feat, to be sure!"

Lucy flicked a towel at him. "Get on with you, and mind you do not spill crumbs on the floor!"

"I'll sweep them up, I promise." Now settled with the cake-bread and a bit of mead, he continued. "So, you asked me about the good Reverend Thomas. He has the most uncanny ability to read a man's soul, and he does not hesitate to berate a man—or woman, for that matter—about the wages of sin. Gentry and digger alike."

"He is like to make some enemies," Lucy said doubtfully. "I should think that people do not like to be confronted with the wages of their sins."

"Quite wise, and so true, Lucy." He licked his plate. "I'm starting to believe in the power of the pulpit, nonetheless, and even more so the purpose of a minister. There are a lot of sinners in this world, and it's the Church who must help them see the error of their ways." He seemed more resolved than she had ever seen him.

She laid a bun in front of him. "I wish I had such a purpose."

"Women's callings are different. You'll find it." Smiling, he took the bread. "Now, tell me, Lucy. How is brother Will these days?"

"He is doing very well indeed with the smithy. In a few more years, he will be a master himself. He could set up his own shop. He should even have the means to marry." Her face clouded slightly. "He's taken up with Bessie, you know, but I cannot make headway about his feelings for her."

"Do you think he wishes to marry? Is he willing to wait, do you think, until he is his own master?"

Lucy smiled. "I don't really know. I haven't truly inquired after his heart in some time now, but Will is always a lad to have several girls after him, with not one a particular favorite. There is a girl back home, Cecily, but 'tis only Mother who favors the match. I find her sweet but a bit dull myself. I'd be happy enough to call her my sister, though, should he choose her."

"Oh, I see," Lucas said, pondering the last drops of mead in his cup.

"I do not think," Lucy continued, enjoying having someone to share her thoughts with, "being truthful, that Will wishes to wed either Cecily or Bessie, at least not now. He plays among the lasses, but I think he still desires a place for himself."

"Well, that be the way of many men, before getting married. Hopefully, he will see his sinning ways before it is too late. A good man will not string a woman along." Seeing Lucy sniff, he added, "Oh, but you are frowning. You're not thinking about Will, are you? My dear Lucy, is there someone you are pining after who has not been faithful to you?"

"Oh, no," she said hastily. "No sweetheart. No one like that."

"Good," Lucas said, his face flushed. "I should not like to see you give your heart away, especially to some fickle lad who doesn't deserve it. Or," he said, leaning closer, "to someone from a family you can never marry into."

Lucy looked up sharply, catching his troubled look.

"It is the way of the world, I'm afraid. Like marries like." He shook his head ruefully. "Of course, that's the good thing about someone like me," he said, his eyes suddenly intent. "I can marry whom I please. Perhaps some charming wench who will conjure up a cakebread whenever I ask." He stood up. Without warning, he kissed her forehead, just below her cap. "Don't change, my sweet. I'm off now, nary a crumb to be found, so we will not face the wrath of Cook."

The door slammed behind him, and Lucy sat on the bench Lucas had just vacated. *The way of the world, indeed,* Lucy thought. She looked around the happy kitchen in sudden distaste. Why did the walls feel like a prison?

·7·

Upon waking the next day, Lucy could see that Bessie had
already slipped out to start her morning work, eager to finish
lacing one of the mistress's fine underskirts. The good mistress
had promised her several of her old petticoats if she made haste
and had these ready for spring. "I shall affix a fine braid of silver fringe that will show when my skirts part, like so," Bessie
had confided to Lucy a few days before. "When I am through,
my underskirts shall be as fine as the Queen Mother's own!"
Bessie had then laughed at Lucy's shocked face. "Oh, Lucy, don't
be such a stick. I saw Mistress Embry with her skirts like so, in
church even!"

"Well, that I cannot protest," Lucy had demurred. "For she
might be doing us all a great service."

"I did not know you had such a fondness for Mistress Embry, Lucy," Bessie had said, giving her a sidelong glance.

Lucy had laughed, a bit wickedly. "Well, 'tis true enough. But I was thinking that perhaps the sight of her skirts would shock the good minister into silence. Surely that would be an act of benevolence itself."

Her teeth chattering now, Lucy forced herself out of bed. She cast about for her heavy stockings before remembering she had left them in the kitchen to dry after yesterday's shower. "I wonder if Bessie would mind if I borrowed her gray worsted stockings," she said to herself. "They are so much heavier and warmer than my own."

Lucy began to rummage through Bessie's clothes chest. To her surprise, she felt something hard wrapped up in a soft summer petticoat. Removing the light muslin wrap, she found a beautiful red lacquered case that Bessie had never shown her. Kneeling on the hard wood floor, Lucy ran her finger along the red trim, enchanted by the workmanship of the meticulously painted curlicues. Only the mistress owned anything so fine.

She shook it slightly. It was heavy, but nothing rattled. Craning her ear toward the hallway, she did not hear anyone in the corridor outside their room. Making a quick decision, she flipped open the lid and stared.

Two beautifully crafted combs and a brush lay neatly within the purple satin that lined the box. A gold mirror was inlaid into the top of the box, allowing a woman to view herself easily as she dressed her hair. Intuitively, Lucy knew this was what Bessie had hoped to hide from her the night of Lady Embry's Easter dance.

Where could Bessie have gotten such a fine piece? Such an item would surely cost dear. Who could have given it to her?

Mistress Hargrave, as kind as she was on occasion, would not have given her so fine a gift. Nor would Sarah. Bessie's family could ill afford it.

A sickening thought occurred to Lucy then. Could she have stolen it? Even as the idea flashed into her mind, she banished it as impossible. Silly for finery as Bessie was, she did not have it in her nature to steal. Thoughtfully, Lucy wrapped the fine lacquered case back in the petticoat, wondering how she could ask Bessie about it.

The day passed without Lucy being able to corner Bessie about the beautiful lacquered case. Slippery, she was, almost as if she did not want to speak to Lucy. Before supper, Lucy stretched to light the tall dining room tapers, one foot on a small embroidered stool, the other balancing carefully behind her.

"Don't move!" a man shouted from behind her.

Startled, Lucy began to turn around. "What—?"

"No, don't look at me! As you were, at the candle."

Surprised into obeying, Lucy turned her gaze back to the hearth.

"Keep that candle up!"

Foolishly, she stared at a cobweb, thinking Mistress Hargrave would probably like that removed. From behind her, she heard the sound of someone rummaging through a bag. "Dash it all, I've not got my sketching pens here," the man said. Then, exasperated, he added, "I would lose the light in a moment anyway. You may as well set the candle down."

Doing as he demanded, Lucy stepped down and looked at

the man. He was lithe and lean, with vigorous black curls falling below his shoulders. He looked exotic, his coloring Italian and perhaps African, his dress brighter than what most men wore, even in the more colorful Cavalier households. This must be Del Gado, she supposed. Cook had told her a famous painter would be dining with the family.

"And who are you, my little beauty?" he murmured, moving just an arm's length away.

Lucy bobbed a quick curtsy. "Lucy, Master Del Gado. I am one of Mistress Hargrave's maids."

"Indeed. A maid." His dark gaze traveled over her slowly. His familiarity made her freeze and then warm inexplicably. "Why is it you and I have never met before?"

"I don't know, sir. I have been with the Hargraves for just under two years."

"They did well to hide you from me, I think. Such a sweet little nymph you are."

Lucy shifted impatiently. Another guest who would be too handy. Her encounter with Richard had made her even more skittish around men. She started to edge away.

Del Gado laughed. "Perhaps you might consider posing for me? I should like so much to paint you. You could even wear this sweet little apron," he said, putting his hand on her shoulder, "although I should not like you to wear much else, I'm afraid."

Lucy's hand flew to her mouth.

"Ah, my little one. I have shocked you. You think I am a rogue, do you not? Oh, do not answer. You will be a great charmer in a few years, I daresay, and I should just like to capture the moment when the innocent lass knows what it means to be a woman. Perhaps I can help that moment along, if you like." He chuckled again.

Unable to move, Lucy just stared at him. Mistress Hargrave stepped into the dining room at that instant, taking in the painter's cheeky grin and Lucy's flushed face. She laid a hand, almost protectively, on Lucy's arm. Her voice tight and clipped, she said, "All right, Lucy, very good. Now, run along to help Cook with supper."

Before the door had shut completely behind her, Lucy heard the mistress say in a low tone. "Now, Enrique, you really must behave. Lucy is a good girl, and I won't have her spoiled by you."

"Not when her mistress needs to be spoiled!" he responded, adding a few words that Lucy did not hear as she fled to the kitchen, her ears burning fiercely.

Supper was an odd meal. The mistress talked breathlessly and gaily with Master Del Gado, her manner unguarded. The painter, fawning over the mistress, responded courteously enough but seemed watchful and a bit tense, content to listen to his patron's nonsense. The master, by contrast, was particularly taciturn, commenting from time to time on some aspect of the fare. Adam seemed more brooding than usual, and Lucas was nowhere to be seen.

Passing a platter of bread, Lucy heard the magistrate quietly ask Adam about Lucas. Seeming to realize her ward's absence for the first time, Mistress Hargrave looked up.

"And where is Lucas?" she asked.

"Lucas and I"—Adam paused—"had a difference of opinion with some men at the pub." He picked up his fork and speared a piece of meat.

Del Gado snickered behind his handkerchief. The magistrate glared at him.

The mistress just looked at Adam expectantly. "And?" she prompted.

Finishing chewing, Adam said, "I fear Lucas is a bit indisposed and is resting upstairs. He'll not be down for supper."

"Oh, dear," Mistress Hargrave said. "Shall I send for the physician?"

"Nonsense," the magistrate replied. "He's no doubt just a little the worse for a day of tippling down. I remember my own days at Cambridge."

Mistress Hargrave pursed her lips, perhaps not liking to remember his carefree student days before they had wed. Lucy wanted to smile but did not dare. "I should so have liked Lucas to see Enrique's first sketches," the mistress pouted. "He has rather good taste, you know."

The master sniffed, ever so slightly. Adam coughed into his kerchief. The mistress looked at them sharply, but both kept their faces on their plates.

"Another time, I can show him," Del Gado said, seeking to ward off a storm. He started to pat the mistress's hand but withdrew his fingers just before making contact. "Do not fear, my dear."

As Lucy refilled mugs of ale, she thought at times Adam seemed to be directing baleful looks at *her,* although she could not fathom why. As if she had been the one to pour spirits down poor Lucas's throat, she thought, miffed by his inexplicable anger.

After she had finished serving supper that night, Lucy passed into the drawing room to ready the room for dessert. Bessie had disappeared again, so Lucy was left alone. Spreading a fine Holland cloth over the sideboard, she saw that Master Del Gado had left his large case in the corner. A small peek couldn't hurt, she thought. The knotted cords seemed simple enough to untangle. She untied them quickly, keeping her ear attuned to the dining room, in case the mistress should require her.

Opening the case, she murmured in delight. The first sketch was of Mistress Hargrave looking stately in a beautiful blue gown. Wrapped around her slim neck was her favorite jewelry— a necklace the magistrate had given her last Christmas. The mistress was indeed captivating.

Lifting a piece of fine velvet, Lucy saw more sketches underneath—still of the mistress, but in these her long hair flowed around her face and bare shoulders. In the next pictures, the mistress's clothes seemed to be dropping off her body, exposing all her womanly parts as she lay supine on the bed in her chamber. She seemed to stare right into Lucy's eyes, a teasing look that rather unsettled the girl. Hardly daring to breathe, Lucy pulled the last piece of velvet up to expose other nude women, each caught in varying states of repose.

Once her initial shock had subsided, Lucy could see that these women, in all their rosy flesh, were beautiful. Though untrained, she could glimpse an ugliness, too. The painter had clearly caught their beauty, but there was a grimness to several that suggested a waning of youth and vitality. As she looked at one more closely, her heart began pounding like a baker working his dough. It was Bessie! Bessie, posing like Venus rising, blond hair flowing about her body. When had Bessie done this?

Hearing Cook call her to help with dessert, Lucy hastily stuffed all the sketches back into the painter's case, hoping that he wouldn't know that she had been snooping through his drawings. She regarded the cords uneasily, quickly tying a few knots in a way that might look similar to his. A moment later, the family entered the drawing room. Nervously, Lucy served the dessert, trying to avoid the avid gaze of Master Del Gado. He sat with his case, fingering the knots carefully.

"Oh, Enrique, we're ever so eager to see your sketches. Are we not, dear?" the mistress asked.

"Yes, of course, my dear," the magistrate answered. Settling into a large cushioned chair, he smiled indulgently at his wife. "By all means, Enrique. Please show us. Although I warn you, my wife can never be more beautiful than how I see her every day."

Lucy felt her throat tighten, hoping the master was not being cuckolded. Del Gado's next words sent a shock of fear through her. "Hmmm. I seem to have tied my knots differently than usual. I have a system, you know."

Lucy stiffened, waiting for him to accuse her. She might get sacked then and there. Even if the master did not believe she had stolen anything, he might not appreciate her going through his guest's belongings. Even if that guest did flirt shamelessly with his wife. She held her head high and still, waiting for him to denounce her. *Mistress and Master Hargrave,* she expected to hear, *you have a spy in your midst . . . and she's standing right there!*

Fortunately, no accusation came; indeed, he just laughed. He pulled out the top sketches, leaving the others hidden from view. No doubt waiting for a more private showing, Lucy thought grimly. She still wondered about the sketches of Bessie.

Master Hargrave was smiling proudly at the sketches of his wife. "Your jewels do you great credit, my dear, but by God, I have a lovely wife." He kissed her hand.

Later, as Lucy returned the clean dishes to the dining room cabinet, Master Del Gado entered the room. He moved toward her rapidly, backing her against the table. Her heart constricted, making her feel caged. Leaning into her, he whispered in her ear. "Do not be afraid, my lovely one. You are afraid I will brand you a thief and have you thrown from the house, are you not?"

She nodded, too afraid to speak.

Del Gado continued. "Rest assured. I shall not do so. You were just curious, were you not? And why not? I am curious myself. That is why I sketch. I am curious about life, about love, about women. I shan't tell anyone that you looked through my things, for indeed I should not like the content of some of those sketches known. Especially, your master might not like it." He took her hands, caressing them gently. "My dear, there are many things that I should like to do to you, and painting you in your burnishing youth is just one of them. However, if you ever look through my belongings again, or speak of what

you saw to anyone"—abruptly his fingers squeezed her hand—
"I will not be so nice. Do you understand?"

Lucy nodded mutely, tasting the tears in her throat. She
wanted to slap him but was afraid, since he was a guest.

Perhaps sensing her thoughts, he kissed her mouth lightly
and stepped away, smiling, the flash of anger gone as quick as
it had come. "Consider my offer. There is much I can provide
you, and I know girls like their trifles. Until, my dear, we meet
again."

Although it was nearly midnight, Lucy still had not gone to
bed. Like most servants, she usually stayed up until the master
and mistress had retired. She moved slowly about the house,
blowing out candles and banking the coals in the hearths,
readying the house for the morning. In the kitchen, she washed
the cup and plate Lucas had used when he finally descended
from his chamber, looking a little worse for wear. Lucy could not
help teasing him about his absence at supper.

"Didn't want to see Del Gado," Lucas had confided. "He's a
cad, and a fraud at that. Posing as one of Van Dyck's students,
while he's probably from the gutters of Seville. Don't know
why our good mistress is so taken with him!" Changing his
tone he had added, "Get me a bite, would you, Lucy dear? I'm
famished."

Knowing that Lucas shared her poor opinion of the painter
comforted her somewhat. Like the still-warm embers, her cheeks
burned painfully whenever she thought about the painter. Lucy
tried not to think of the mistress's own pictures, or of the master,

who might feel chagrined to find he had such a wayward wife. Or perhaps he knew? She put that thought from her mind. It wasn't her place to question the doings of the master and mistress.

Mounting the stairs a short while later, Lucy decided to wake Bessie and ask her outright what in heaven's name had possessed her to pose for Del Gado. The question died on her lips, though, when she found the tiny chamber she shared with Bessie to be completely silent.

Puzzled, Lucy crept back down to the mistress's chamber and put her ear to the door. She heard the master say something in a low voice to the mistress, and the mistress laugh in response. Clearly, Bessie was not in there.

Making a face, she continued down the hall, putting her ear first to Lucas's door and then to Adam's. Surely, Bessie would not be the first comely maidservant to be led astray, but the thought made her sick. She was relieved, though, not to hear any movement behind either door.

Slipping back down the stairs, Lucy quickly looked in every room. She heard Cook and John snoring in their small room behind the kitchen. Peering out the kitchen shutters assured her that Bessie was not out in the courtyard. Bessie had been known to cull morning's first dew from the leaves in the garden, rubbing it on her face, thinking it gave her skin a lustrous sheen. A light snow had begun to fall, but there was no sign of Bessie.

Lucy grew angry. Clearly, Bessie had left the house without permission sometime after the supper dishes had been cleared. "And left me to make her excuses again, I wager," Lucy muttered. "She might have at least warned me."

Four times that night, until the gray morning light finally began to seep through the house, Lucy tiptoed down the stairs and peered out the heavy oak windows. First angry, then alarmed, she became increasingly worried and desperate over Bessie's absence. The magistrate would not take kindly to the disruption of his orderly household.

Finally, with a heavy spirit, Lucy opened Bessie's chest. She stared down in growing dismay. It was completely empty. Everything Bessie owned was gone, including the mysterious box with the combs and brush. She had even taken Lucy's stockings and petticoat. Lucy had thought Bessie was going to mend them, and instead she took them.

Lucy sank back, leaning against the bedpost. She looked up, her gaze falling on the shelves above. Bessie had left her jars and scents, and even more shockingly, her Bible. Lucy picked up the book and ran her finger along its spine. "Oh, Bessie!" She bit into her knuckles. "Don't tell me you forsook God as well as family!"

·8·

By morning, it was impossible to hide the fact that Bessie had left the household. Wringing her hands and sniffling a bit, Lucy told Cook and John first, where they sat having their morning mead.

At the news, Cook set her mug down on the table. "I don't believe it," Cook said. "Maybe the mistress sent her on an errand."

Lucy shook her head. "In the middle of the night?"

"Well, maybe—"

"All her clothes are gone. Some of mine, too." Lucy said flatly. "She's left us."

"Stupid cow," Cook muttered through tight lips. A tear may have glistened in her eye. "She's sure to be discharged now. What will become of her?" Throwing up her hands, she added, "You'd best tell the magistrate and mistress."

Wretchedly, Lucy informed the Hargraves and Lucas about Bessie's disappearance when they met for breakfast. Adam was not around.

"Stupid girl!" Lucas muttered, unconsciously echoing Cook's words. He was clearly unhappy.

The master looked solemn but said little. The mistress was surprisingly calm. "Go check if anything is missing," she commanded Lucy.

Trudging on heavy feet, Lucy went to count the silver in the sideboard. When she pulled open the drawer, she just stared down, her mouth agape. All of the mistress's silver, some of it imported from Spain and Holland, was gone. She felt sick. Tearfully, she informed the master and the mistress. Both seemed pale.

The muscles in the magistrate's face tightened. He seemed to find it hard to speak for a moment. "John, send for the constable."

With a grim set to his face, John took off. He returned not a half hour later, bringing Constable Duncan and their local bellman in tow. Lucy did not know the bellman, Burke, very well, although she had seen him about from time to time, stopping drunkards on the street and banging pickpockets' heads together. He was a stout man in his early forties, his hair already gray. Much older than the constable, he had the air of a man who had spent some time in the army, battering down enemy charges.

After hearing the magistrate's account of Bessie's disappearance, Constable Duncan asked to question Lucy. The mistress slipped out then, to soothe her scattered nerves. Lucy was grateful that the magistrate stayed nearby, seating himself on a low bench by the wall. His presence was watchful but not interfering.

Duncan peppered her with questions until her head was spinning. When had she last seen Bessie? Had Bessie seemed happy? Had she ever spoken of leaving? Of starting a new life? Of ending her current life?

She stayed silent. At the last question, Lucy looked up. "Bessie would never kill herself. Why would she?"

"All right," Duncan said and tried to soothe her. "Let's start from the beginning, shall we? When did you last see Bessie?"

Lucy tried to recall. Surely, she had seen Bessie just before supper, but she had not seen her afterward when it was time to clear the table. She was certainly not around when Lucy was fending off Del Gado.

Her mind drifted again. *Why did you go, Bessie?* she wondered for the hundredth time. *Why would you steal the silver?*

She almost missed the constable's next question. "Did Bessie have a young man in her life?"

Lucy hesitated. She could feel the magistrate's penetrating gaze upon her. She thought about the painter's sketches, which she was not supposed to have seen, and she thought about her brother. Reluctantly, she gave the constable Will's name. She cringed when Duncan and Burke exchanged a knowing glance.

Duncan twirled his quill pen. Lucy found herself looking at the nub, not so carefully sharpened as the magistrate's or Adam's would have been. It looked straggly and out of place, although she could see he had borrowed the magistrate's ink.

A silence loomed as Lucy's head began to spin. Had she missed another question? They seemed to be waiting for her to speak.

Lucy looked hopelessly at the magistrate. She felt like a mouse trapped in one of Cook's baskets. "Will has done nothing wrong."

The magistrate leaned forward in his chair, reaching to pat her hand, which gripped the table. "Don't worry, my dear. The constable is just doing his job, gathering information. We will get this cleared up soon."

Gulping, Lucy gave him Will's address. They all watched the constable scratch something in a little chapbook. He paused, squaring his shoulders with the manner of a man asked to taste something he knew would not sit well on his tongue. "I understand you also have a son, sir. Is he in the house?"

The magistrate glanced at John before he answered the constable's question. "I believe he had a late night with friends, so I do not think it is necessary to get his testimony about a disappearing maid, or a bit of missing silver."

Burke smirked but instantly tried to suppress it under the magistrate's stern gaze.

His manner bland, Duncan said, "Oh, of course. Well, I doubt we need to talk to him, then. I shall go question the neighbors and see if they know anything about this. If you remember anything else, sir, do let us know."

As John ushered them from the house, Lucy saw the magistrate put his head down in his hands. For a moment, he looked older than she had ever known him.

———

When Lucy heard the watchman call the tenth hour of the morning, she was still sweeping snow from the front walk with a bit of birch. She had positioned herself out front, so she could track the progress of the constable and bellman as they talked to each neighbor in turn. Finally, they moved out of view, and Lucy turned to go back inside.

She noticed a small dead bird on the step, wings drawn into its soft downy chest. The little wren bothered her immensely, although she didn't know why. Didn't she see dead birds every day? Game hens, cocks, pheasants hanging upside down, throats garroted, heads chopped off, blood dripping from plucked bodies. Not quite like this bird, though. The stone walk looked almost tomblike, and something about the lay of the bird's tiny corpse on the step made it look almost sacrificial.

Grimacing, Lucy carefully laid the bird to rest under a nearby bush, rather than throwing it in the raker's bucket. No good sign there, she thought, but at least it was no raven. It was common enough knowledge that ravens brought no good to the world. Good thing Cook hadn't seen it. She'd surely be brewing some potion to brush across the step to ward off evil. As the cold edged more into Lucy's bones, she wondered if a wee prayer might not be in order.

At that moment, a dusty cart pulled up in front of the house. She was about to wave the driver around back when she heard a throaty cry from the cart. "Lucy!"

She stared as Adam, dirty and rumpled, toppled out of the cart, helped by a man that Lucy did not know. Adam growled something, and the man jumped back in the cart. Whinnying at the smart crack of the whip, the horses trotted away, kicking up dirt behind them as they passed.

Across the street, a curtain moved, unseen watchers taking in Adam stumbling up the path, slipping a bit in the snow, making his way unsteadily along the stones. What could he have been doing all night? He looked uncommonly disheveled.

Coming to her senses, Lucy sprang to meet him. Drawing his arm around her shoulders, she hastened Adam over the threshold. The smell of drink was heavy upon him, and she nearly gagged. Once inside, away from gossipy tongues, she shook him off, leaving him to lean heavily against the windowpane. Truly, he looked terrible.

"At the tavern, sir?" she asked, raising her eyebrows. *While the rest of us are worrying sick over Bessie,* she thought, *he's off tippling down with his mates.* That was a magistrate's son for you, she supposed—and yet something seemed off.

Adam shrugged, grimacing when he moved his arms. "In a manner of speaking, but not what you think. I was taking care of some unfinished business." He looked at her. "Why am I explaining myself to you? Bring me some warm water and send John to me. I should like to clean myself up a bit."

Without waiting for her answer, he limped carefully up the stairs, gripping the rail. Lucy stared after him a moment, then sent John up to attend him. After heating a basin of water, she carried it up to the second floor, grumbling all the while. The pot sloshed precariously as she knocked at Adam's door.

Entering the room, she found Adam sitting on the edge of his bed, his outer shirt peeled off. Gasping, Lucy saw thin lines of blood soaking through his undershirt. "My God! What happened?"

John shot her a warning look. Adam looked down, seemingly puzzled by the blood on his chest and legs. "Oh, right. I seem to have had a mishap at the market today."

"A mishap, sir?"

"Some damn fool bumped me into the butcher's stall. That's animal blood, Lucy, nothing more. Could you go ahead and wash this shirt out?" he said, handing her the shirt from the bed. "And be a good girl, keep it to yourself."

"But I don't understand, sir, are you all right? You're bleeding. Shall I run for the physician?"

John gingerly dabbed at the blood on Adam's back with a piece of soaked linen. At the word "physician," he looked anxiously at Adam.

"No!" Adam replied, wincing as John dabbed at the deep scratches. "There's no need to tell anyone about this. Do you understand me, Lucy? I must have gotten scratched when I fell. We don't want to disturb anyone. It was just an accident. A minor one at that. Nothing to worry anyone about."

Lucy looked at Adam doubtfully. She looked at John, and he shook his head slightly. There did not seem to be much more she could do. "As you wish, sir."

Later that afternoon, as Lucy tried unsuccessfully to polish the pewter in the drawing room, John touched her shoulder. He looked worried.

"Yes, John? What is it?" she asked.

He grimaced. "It's Master Adam. He seems to have taken a fever."

Lucy shrugged. "Are you sure you haven't mistaken a touch of brawling and drinking for a sickness?"

John knitted his brow, looking doubtful. "Just come see him, would you, lass? Mary is out visiting old Missus Healy, who took sick last week. I could sure use some help."

When they entered Adam's room, her tone changed. Lucy was not prepared for how much more ill he looked than he had in the morning. He looked young, with his tousled chestnut hair, even though he was a good five years older than herself. His face was a deep red with fever, and the cuts on his arms looked angry and raw. When the blanket moved, she saw he had more cuts across his chest. His gaze was wide and unfocused.

Lucy pulled herself up. "Cook must make a bit of a poultice as she did for me—a bit of a bread mold and spiderwebs as I've seen her do with scabby sores. John, you *will* fetch the surgeon. I think he needs to be bled."

After the surgeon tended to him, Adam fell into a deep sleep and did not revive for a full day. Mistress Hargrave walked around wringing her hands, and the magistrate retreated to his study in a black funk. His servant had run off, his silver was missing, and his son was worse the wear for drink. Not a godly household, indeed.

Proper inquiries into Bessie's disappearance yielded no results over the next few days. Lucy knew that Bessie's sister and mother in Lambeth were questioned and their houses searched. After Constable Duncan talked to the Hargraves' neighbors, Bessie's absence was discussed with great glee.

The night Del Gado had joined them for supper was the last anyone remembered seeing her. No one could remember exactly, but several neighbors claimed to have seen her walking down the street that evening. The bootmaker said that when Bessie reached the corner she had turned west toward town, while the soap seller insisted she had turned east toward the forest. No one had seen her past the fork in the road. Depending on who was telling the story, Bessie had either been brandishing a small cutlass or nervously clutching her reticule, and had either been alone or skulking in the shadows with several nefarious sorts.

Everyone agreed, though, that swallowed up she had been, at a time when only the criminal sort walked and God-fearing folk slept easily in their beds.

Easily Bessie had moved from being a simple maid who sought to better her lot in life with the theft of the spoons to being a scofflaw's moll, the likes of Moll Cutpurse robbing gentlemen at knife's point.

"It's lucky she didn't murder you all in your sleep," they hissed at Lucy. "She's a right sneaky one, she is. 'Tis a good thing she took off with just your spoons!"

"She'll be caught sure enough," Janey said with a sniff. Lucy scowled at her, remembering her words at the Embrys' Easter masquerade.

"And she won't look so fine, will she, when she's carted off to Newgate!" chimed in her sister Emma. "Those curls won't be so gorgeous, will they!"

"I'll pull them myself!" Janey shrieked, clearly delighting in Bessie's comeuppance. "Serves her right! Dirty beggar!"

"Imagine! In the magistrate's own household! A little thief!"

"A laughing-stock that magistrate is! Keeping order in his house, I think not!"

"Could not see past the end of his nose, to be sure. The tart must have had him magicked by her pretty ways. Could not even see her for the guttersnipe she was."

"'Twas as bad as being cuckolded!"

Lucy kept her head up, trying to shut out the uglier servant voices that she heard along the street, malevolent as only the most sniping fishwives could be. Echoing what they heard whispered in the withdrawing rooms, they could barely contain their delight at a good family being brought down by scandal.

Thankfully, some voices were kind. Those who liked Bessie and respected the family just shook their heads. "I'll pray for the lass," good Mistress Fields told Lucy, pressing her hand as she passed her on the curb. "Your poor master. He does not deserve this. I should not have taken her for a thief. Let us just pray she's come to no harm."

During these fretful days, Lucy had seen Will only once, and he was so angry and sullen he scarcely spoke a word. Like so many of the neighbors, he believed Bessie had run off with another man.

Returning from market, Lucy stopped to look at a crocus

just popping its head out of the thawed earth. She was glad spring was finally upon them; winter had seemed so long and dark. Pausing at the back gate, she could see Constable Duncan speaking to Janey.

Seeing Lucy, the constable strode across the grass toward her, Janey at his heels. "Lucy, a word if you will," he called.

"What is it?" Lucy asked, running up the back path.

"I'll tell you!" Janey sounded triumphant. "Bessie, the hussy! She's been found. Oh, yes, indeed!"

Duncan grimaced, but stepped back when Cook came racing out of the house, a mass of aprons and pushed-up sleeves. "No, oh, no, you don't, Janey Miller! You wait here, Constable! I'm going to tell her myself!"

"Cook, you're weeping! Why are you weeping?" Lucy asked, increasingly frantic, letting the old servant pull her into the house. An unpleasant tingle ran over her skin.

Cook slammed the door, the pots and pans rattling with the blow. The smell of something burning assaulted Lucy's nose. John was looking helplessly at a steaming mess in the pot, which he had evidently tried to quench with water. He stood up, casting a sorrowful look at Lucy as he passed out of the kitchen.

"The stew, Cook. I think it's burn—"

"Never mind that!" Cook said, scrunching the muslin of her skirts with nervous fingers. She added softly, "Pray, child, sit down, here by the fire."

Lucy sat down on the bench, her fingers clenched in her lap. She felt like a jumbler was tossing things around inside her stomach. She fixed on Cook's red-rimmed eyes. "Is she in jail?

Is she to stand trial?" A vision of Bessie getting egged in the stocks made her sick.

"No, no, child." Cook gulped. "Heaven help us! Bessie, our sweet Bessie! She's dead."

"Dead?" Lucy repeated. A dull rushing sound filled her ears. How could she be dead? Bessie, so full of life and love and laughter, how could she be dead? She swallowed. "What happened?"

"Found in Rosamund's Gate, she was, by a passing tinker. Her body had been hidden under snow and leaves. That's why it took so long, to find her, I mean. The magistrate and Adam just went to identify her."

Cook gripped both Lucy's hands in hers. " 'Twas no accident. Do you understand? Her death was not natural."

"Not natural! But that would mean—did she kill herself? Self-murder?" Unbidden, the minister's warnings about the torments of hell flashed into her head. Tears began to flow again. "Oh, Bessie, why?"

"No, dear. 'Twas unnatural, to be true, but she died at the hands of some rotter."

Lucy could not speak.

Cook nodded. "A knife through her organs, no less."

Numbly, simply, Lucy heard how Bessie's body had been found, stabbed, in a secluded grove. Rosamund's gate. A lover's park, some called it, for along time ago, a man had killed his beloved and then himself, for reasons now long lost. She and Bessie had once talked about the legend. How romantic, Bessie had thought. Romantic that lovers would rather commit suicide to be together in death than be separate in life. Romantic! Ha!

All she could think of was Bessie, freezing and alone in the brush, the March snow melting all about her. She didn't even have her Bible.

Lucy barely noticed Cook holding her, barely heard someone howling. Was it herself? She could not tell.

And oh! That wretched foul-burning stew! Throwing off Cook's arms, she grabbed the boiling pot and heaved it into the muck outside. She then sagged down beside the steaming pile, passing into unheeding oblivion.

·9·

Lucy woke with a start, blinking at the sun streaming through the cracks of her bedchamber shutters. Not sunrise, but rather the full sun of midmorning. Why hadn't anyone awakened her? Why had she been allowed to sleep so late? Bessie should have woken her—

She sat bolt upright. "Oh, Bessie," she moaned. For a moment she could scarcely breathe as her throat clenched with tears. The last day and night had passed in a blur. She'd stumbled downstairs a few times to dump her chamber pot into the great barrel. Cook would press something hot into her hands, but she didn't remember eating much, or doing much of anything. Snatches of conversation, hushed remarks from the neighbors, wafted by her, but nothing made sense. She felt like leeches had been placed all over her body, draining her of blood and spirit.

The emptiness of the bed nearly got her weeping again, but with some labor, Lucy pushed her legs over the edge and stood up. "The day must start," she said to the wooden figures on her shelf, for a moment envying their place in the world.

When she entered the kitchen, Cook took in her neat dress and apron. "That's a good girl," she said. She seemed about to say something else, then stopped. Instead, she gestured to a tray of bread and hot mead. "Could you take that up to Master Adam?"

Lucy found Adam already up, sitting in his chair. A book lay open in his lap, but he was idly poking at the cold ash in his fireplace. When she set the tray on a little table beside his bed, he reached for a bun but did not bite into it. Instead, he crumbled it in his hand.

"Shall I light the fire for you, sir?"

He did not answer, seemingly deep in thought. She shrugged. Fine. As if she cared. "All right then, sir. Good morning."

Just as she reached the door, Adam called out to her. "Lucy, wait."

She paused but kept her tear-stained face slightly away from him, not in a mood to be doing anyone's bidding, certainly no special requests. She just wanted to lie down and hold a sachet to her temple, which had just begun to throb.

"Tell me what you know about Bessie's death."

"Sir?" Lucy asked. "To be sure, I know as much as you." Even those small sentences required a great deal of effort. She dug her nails into her palms to keep from weeping openly.

Adam might have seen that, because he abruptly stopped sounding like a barrister. He jumped from his chair and touched her arm. "Please, Lucy. Sit down for a moment. Here, by the fire." They both glanced at the cold grate. "Well, all right, no fire, but please sit down. I didn't mean to distress you further. Indeed, I am terribly sorry that you lost a friend. I know she was a companion to both you and my sister, and she will be heartfully missed."

Well, that was better at least. Less like a noble. Barely listening, Lucy concentrated instead on a dark knot on the wood floor. It looked like a mushroom, she thought idly. She despised mushrooms.

"I've no news of the outside," Adam said, making an impatient gesture. "This sickness has kept me abed, and I've not seen Father. I need to know what is being said of Bessie's death. Who are they saying did it?"

Lucy made a face. "It's all fantastic nonsense."

"Yes, and?" Adam prompted. "What are they saying?"

She bit her lip. "Well, that Bessie had been in league with the devil." Seeing his brow raise, she gave the slightest of smiles. "Not the real devil, of course, but some devilish man who seduced her. Convinced her to steal the silver spoons. And then he killed her."

"Oh?" Adam prompted.

"He must have taken the spoons, you see. Because the spoons weren't found where she was . . . killed. At Rosamund's Gate."

"How singular. Who was this supposed devilish man?"

At this, Lucy could not help but sneer. "Janey supposes a highwayman."

"Of course. And what say the constable?"

"He thinks maybe it was the gypsies encamped to the south. He knew that Bessie had visited them a few times." How tongues do wag, Lucy thought. An image of Maraid's beautiful and wild face came to her then, asking for silver.

Adam seemed to follow her thinking. "The gypsies do require silver, do they not? Had Bessie particular need for their services?"

Lucy thought about this. Bessie had wanted something from the gypsies but had not confided in her, to be sure. Truly, her manner had been strange for some time—and what about the red lacquered box? If only she could just go somewhere and think. She scratched her arm, waiting for permission to leave the room.

Adam wasn't done. "So Bessie was wearing a green silk dress when she was murdered?" Seeing her flinch, he added, "I'm sorry, Lucy. That was thoughtless of me. When she passed on, I mean. But the dress? What do you make of that?"

The question gave Lucy pause. Certainly, the green taffeta was not a dress to travel in. "Yes," she said slowly. "It was one of her favorite dresses. She wore it to Lady Embry's Easter masquerade. She looked lovely."

Lucy gulped, recalling a vision of Bessie, beautiful in the green taffeta, generously lending Lucy her perfume. Lost in the past, she barely heard Adam comment, "I'm afraid I did not notice her."

The memory was too raw to think of now. Lucy pushed it aside to concentrate on what Adam was asking her, but she kept thinking about the dress. She herself would have worn a more practical work dress, one of her gray muslins, if she were taking a journey. Bessie must have hoped to meet someone, nay, to impress someone. Perhaps those nosy neighbors were right. She sighed.

"What is it?" Adam asked gently. "I can see something has occurred to you. Will you tell me?"

His unexpected kindness loosened her tongue somewhat. "It's just that this was a special dress. Not a dress she would have wanted to walk very far in, especially in such cold weather. She looked so beautiful in it. Not like a servant at all, sir. So she'd have worn it to impress someone." Not some made-up highwayman, either. Someone more like Will, Lucy realized. Someone Bessie cared about.

Adam tapped his fingers on the wall, musing out loud. "Exactly. My thoughts as well. The constable could not be too aware of women's clothes if he didn't know that it was a servant girl's best dress. Of course, it was no doubt the worse for wear when he saw it."

Lucy had only half heard him, as she remembered Will whispering into Bessie's ear. She put a hand over her mouth, the bile rising in her throat.

Adam saw the gesture. "Oh, I am a cad. Forgive me." He paused. "So the dress suggests that she was planning to meet a sweetheart, not have an assignation with a highwayman. Why would he kill her?"

"Perhaps someone else killed her," Lucy said. "Someone else she encountered on the way."

"Perhaps. *Did* she have a lover, do you know?"

Lucy narrowed her eyes, not wanting to speak of her brother's relationship with Bessie. She'd already been forced to mention it to the constable. Adam seemed tense, and his questions did not appear to stem from mere curiosity. She watched him trace a crack in the wall. As she gazed at his bandaged hands and body, she could not suppress the ugly and dark thoughts. What had he been doing to get himself all bloodied? The stories he had told, about running into a butcher's stall, seemed far-fetched. She spoke carefully. "Oh well, you know Bessie. She had an eye for the lads, as they did for her. Now, sir," she said, rising from the chair, "I really must get back to my duties."

Adam scowled at her, his mood changed. "You're not telling me something."

Her heart jumped at how easily he seemed to see through her. "No, sir, there's nothing else," she said.

He jerked his head toward the door, and she scurried out. Rather than going down to the kitchen as she ought, instead she crept to her little chamber, trying to push away dreadful, ill-formed thoughts.

Bessie's death gradually sank in, like a stone slipping into a pond's deepest muck. At night, Lucy slept in fits and starts, lying alone in the chamber she had shared with Bessie, sobbing her way through several handkerchiefs. During the day, she tried to hide her tears in front of the family, but little things could set her weeping afresh. The iron that Bessie had cursed, a bit of ribbon that she might have worn in her hair, an untouched treacle tart that they might have shared when the chores were done—all shredded her deeply. Every movement was an effort, the most simple exchange a chore. She felt she couldn't remember the most routine tasks.

"More ale, did you say, sir?"

"I forgot to light the hearth, sir? I'm sorry, I'll get right to it."

"Pardon me, mistress. I thought you wanted the brocade this evening."

Lucy thought the magistrate might have awkwardly patted her arm once or twice, but she could not be sure. The mistress she saw weeping, sitting at her mirror, just staring at the brush Bessie would use to stroke her hair. Lucy wanted to go to her, but she did not quite dare. Only with Sarah did Lucy cry outright.

Once, in the courtyard, Lucas slung his arm around her shoulders and gave her a quick squeeze. "Our dear merry girl is gone, 'tis true, but as the good Reverend Marcus would say, she lies sweetly in the Lord's own hands." This gave Lucy little comfort, but she nodded at the thought.

Only Adam remained aloof, although she looked up once to see his eyes upon her, as if measuring her in some way. That so unnerved her that she dropped her spinning wool and had to spend quite a long time to get it unknotted.

Lucy hardly dared put into words the ill feelings Adam stirred in her. Something was clearly amiss. The memories of that shared moment in the hallway, and later, when they walked home on Easter night, were images she fought to suppress. Instead, she forced herself to think about the last few weeks of Bessie's life. Bessie had been acting strangely, but what about Adam? Could they have been sweethearts? She thought about how he had questioned her, his bloodstained clothes, his injuries the night of Bessie's disappearance. All pointed to something that pained her deeply.

She tried talking to John about Adam's odd injuries, but a single twitch of the servant's cheek warned her staunchly where his loyalties lay. Cook certainly shared her husband's loyalty to the household, and Lucy could not well speak to any of the family about her sickening worries. In any case, Sarah had been bustled off to her aunt's in Shropshire, an event that sharpened her loss. Nor could she turn to her brother. Will had stopped by the day before, after the family had returned from church, showing a grayness to his features that surprised her. Bessie's death seemed to have hit him harder than she expected. He was a lost soul, distracted by his sorrow, and as such was no use to her.

Lucy contemplated going to Constable Duncan but decided against it. She thought he would listen, but she was afraid to get in trouble. Afraid to be wrong, afraid to be right, afraid to be discharged without a reference. Afraid.

Lucy sat now in the kitchen, looking down at the small cup in her hands. She hardly knew what she was supposed to be doing. Basting the roast, perhaps? Chopping roots? She sighed.

Cook looked at her and scowled. "You're hardly much use to me now. You take the afternoon to yourself. Go to St. Peter's for some solace. The church won't be too full on a Monday. Mind you, not the tavern. Don't you come back until it's time for supper."

"But—" Lucy protested, thinking of all the work yet to be done.

Cook put her arms on Lucy's shoulders and firmly marched her to the door. "Now, not another word," Cook said. "If anyone asks, you are at market, but I think the family is like to give you some space to grieve and pray. The magistrate, he's a good man. I can tell he does not like to see you so distressed. Just take care you get back for supper."

With that final reminder, Lucy found herself out the door and walking down the dirt path to the road. The fog seemed less oppressive, less tyrannical, less determined today, though it still swirled about, questioning her will. She scarcely knew what to do, or where to go. To the church? No, she did not want to be reminded of Bessie, moldering in death. She shook off a little tremor and breathed deeply. See her brother? Unlikely. She wanted to see Will, desperately, but had to wait for his day off so they could talk properly. The market? She didn't want to be around people.

Lucy toyed with the idea of getting a pint. She pictured herself handing over her coin, looking like she had a thousand crowns to her name, the tavern keeper plying her with the best meats and cheeses. Then another image arose, dampening her enthusiasm, as all the men in the pub looked suspiciously like Richard, elbowing their way to sit next to her.

Lucy sighed. So many oafish louts about. People could easily get the wrong idea if they spied her, a young girl, drinking alone in a tavern. Cook would not like it, and, of course, she'd hate to bring shame to the magistrate's household. The fetters on a woman never seemed to break away.

As Lucy wandered, she found herself veering away from town and toward the open fields and glens. Above her, the birds of spring chirped, oblivious of her heavy spirit. As always, her thoughts turned to Bessie. Where had she been going? Who was she meeting? Why had she stolen the silver? Lucy's fists clenched at her sides. "I didn't even know you, did I?"

A fox bounding in front of her caused her to stop short. She looked around, realizing only at that moment that she had wandered right to Rosamund's Gate, where Bessie had met her fate. The field had drawn her like a lodestone. Her stomach churning, she headily imagined the scene.

It had been dark, of course, but perhaps closer to twilight. Certainly, Bessie had not been around to help clear the evening meal. Bessie would have walked down the path that Lucy had just trod. How would she have walked? Gaily, with eager steps? Toward a lover? A highwayman? Had she walked slowly, worried?

Lucy's mind shifted through the possibilities. Did Bessie think she would be caught, the silver in her satchel weighing down her soul? Had she worried that her rendezvous would not happen? Lucy found she preferred to think of Bessie as happy, her customary curls bouncing free beneath her scarf. Would her lover have been waiting already? Would they have eagerly clasped hands? Or would Bessie have stood here alone in the copse, growing more nervous of the forest sounds as each moment passed?

A twig snapped behind Lucy, and she felt the hackles on her neck rise. She leaped behind a large oak tree, not daring to make a sound and too fearful to move. A man clad in blue stepped from behind a tree some yards away, near a small pond, the fog putting him in stark relief against the gray landscape. Adam! What was he doing here?

As Lucy watched, he knelt down, and carefully passed his hands by the flattened grass of the bank, peering this way and that, finally poking his head into a log. From her vantage point, she could see his grim satisfied smile. After pocketing something Lucy could not see, Adam strode off.

For an instant, Lucy stood frozen in her spot behind the tree, then darted over to the pond. Kneeling down in the grass, she looked inside the hollow log. She could see that several stones were stained an odd dark brown. Blood! She snatched her hand away. Bewildered, she sat back on her haunches. This was where Bessie must have been killed.

Even as tears streamed down her face, she found herself deciphering the scene, as it might well have happened. Bessie had arrived first and had waited, perhaps idly throwing stones in the water to pass the time. Maybe her assailant had watched her a while, standing where Lucy herself had been, then silently sneaked up behind her. Bessie would have whirled around, her bright smile wide upon her lips. Too late, she must have realized his intentions as he set upon her. Perhaps they had struggled. Lucy liked to think that Bessie had gotten in a few swipes of her own.

What about her killer, that nameless monster? What had he done? Why did he do it? Was it all about the silver? And, oh! What had Adam found? Although Lucy was trembling, a calm began to pass over her. She knew what she needed to do. She needed to find out what Adam was hiding.

———

Deciding to search Adam's room was easy enough, yet when to do so was another matter. Tuesday passed, Wednesday passed, and the whole time curiosity gnawed at Lucy. What was Adam hiding? He seemed to spend much of his time at his studies, but at night he still went out, though he spoke little of his activities. There could be no good reason for a young serving girl to visit the room of the young master at night, so she knew it could only be in the morning, when she could at least pretend to be cleaning or collecting linens, or some such business. If she were caught poking about his room, though, she'd likely be discharged, as the master would not brook another thief in his household. Lucy knew she had to bide her time.

The day of Bessie's funeral finally arrived, just under a week after her body had been discovered. Dr. Larimer had at last turned her body over to her distraught mother, deciding that he and his students from the physicians' college had learned all they could about Bessie's murder for the upcoming inquest. Graciously, the Hargraves had agreed to pay for the funeral at St. Peter's, truly a fine farewell for a simple serving girl like Bessie. Ten quid, Lucy had heard. "She was a good lass, who served us well," the magistrate had said. "A thief she may have been, but she did not deserve this end."

The funeral drew a large crowd, neighbors and strangers who relished being close to "the true tale of a murder most foul." Booksellers were already shouting their wares. "Murder will out!" came one customary call. Another declared triumphantly,

"Learn how the lovely corpse pointed to her very murderer, even after death."

"What do they mean by that?" Lucy whispered to John, who stood at her elbow.

He looked disgusted. "Some people are saying that when her body was moved, having lost the stiffness of death, her hand pointed to her murderer and her eyes fell open upon him."

"What? How could that be?"

John shifted uncomfortably. "Someone who was there when Bes—the body, I mean, was being examined."

Lucy thought about that for a moment. "You mean, examined in the field? Where she was found? That would mean the constable, or the bellman."

John looked decidedly uncomfortable now. "I think it was after that. When she was being moved to the physician's surgery. When her body was identified."

"But that would mean—" She paused, thinking. "Well, yes, I guess the magistrate was probably there, and—" She looked sharply at John. "W-who do they say the murderer is?"

He put his finger to his lips. "Not now."

The reverend had raised his hand for silence. The crowd stood beneath the bare trees swaying gently in the breeze. Though it was still a bit icy for early April, a few birds twittered above them. The reverend had begun his eulogy, and, as always, Lucy found her mind drifting from his words, fiery and angry as they were.

Lucy struggled with the finality of it all. Soon Bessie's body would be lowered by ropes into the cold, hard ground. Lucy hoped her soul had been welcomed to heaven. Some of the old parishioners swore, though, that ghosts of the wronged and the damned still lingered by the old church, in the hopes of finding salvation.

"We've several crossroads before our home," she whispered to John. Everyone knew that ghosts got confused by crossroads. Still, the thought of Bessie haunting them made her sad.

The servant patted her arm. "Bessie won't be coming to us as a ghost. Never you fear."

The reverend concluded his sermon. "This audacious act is a sure sign of the wages of her sin. But, as Rahab of Jericho was forgiven, so must this young sinner be."

Lucy clenched her fist. Cook patted her cheek. "Don't you listen, my sweet. Bessie was a good girl," she whispered. "She's in heaven now, singing with the angels and tossing those golden curls."

Soon after, Bessie's coffin was slowly lowered into the ground. As the diggers shoveled fresh earth on top, Lucy cast in a nosegay with the few pitiful blossoms that bloomed this time of year. "To my friend. My sister," she murmured. "May you bring your joy and laughter to heaven."

Straightening up, Lucy noticed two poorly dressed, haggard women weeping. One of them was clutching a baby. They must be Bessie's mother and sister, she thought, who had made the long trek from Lambeth. Shyly, Lucy walked over to introduce herself and utter a few words of solace.

"Thank you," the woman whispered. Lucy could barely hear her over the baby's crying. "I'm Rebecca, Bessie's elder sister."

They stood silent for a moment. Then Lucy blurted out, unable to hold her tongue, "Can you tell me? Do you know? Where was Bessie going, you know, that night? Was she coming to see you?"

Rebecca's shoulders slumped. "I wish I knew. She was not coming to see me, or at least I did not know it. Damn the man who killed her!" Her voice broke. "That bastard should swing, and Lord knows if he will ever be brought to justice."

Without even stopping to think how her words would sound, Lucy asked, "Do you think it was a stranger that killed her, then? Not a lover? Someone she knew?"

Rebecca pulled her hand away angrily. "Our Bessie was a good girl. You've no right to say otherwise."

"Oh, oh!" Lucy said, contrite. "I'm sorry to have offended you, missus. I'm just trying to make sense of this."

Only somewhat mollified, Rebecca sniffed. "No sense to be had. She was killed in cold blood, by a monster, and there's little else to say. That I know for certain."

Rebecca stated to walk away. Lucy remembered something else. "Your baby. Daniel? Is he well now? I remember Bessie telling me he took awful sick this winter past."

"Not too sick, God be praised. He's a strong one."

"Oh, but I thought she came to tend him when you took the sickness, too." Lucy floundered a bit under Rebecca's hard stare.

"I think you are misremembering. The babe's not took sick all winter. A miracle, to be sure, when so many others had the sickness."

"Oh." Lucy swallowed. "Oh, well. I'm glad to hear he is in good health."

———

The rest of the family a few steps ahead, Lucy walked soberly home from the funeral. Trudging along, her head down, she spied a scrap of paper in a patch of muddy grass. It was a broadside, no doubt having fallen, unbeknownst, from a book-seller's bag or from the hands of one of the many onlookers who had come to watch the spectacle. Lucy picked it up.

The text was a ballad—"Murder Will Out!" set to the tune of "Three Men in a Tavern"—and the words were striking. The broadside described the story of a young maid who fell in love with a rich lord, who made promises to her that he had no plans to keep. He persuaded her to run off with him, only to rid her of her hard-kept virtue. Then, when he wanted to marry an-other woman, he lured his young mistress to a secluded spot and killed her.

"The cad!" Lucy muttered, but she kept perusing the ballad.

The story did not end with the young woman's death but shortly after her body had been discovered. When they moved her body, her hand fell open, so that one finger ended up point-ing to the young lord, wordlessly naming him as the murderer. Lucy started to crumple the penny piece but instead put it carefully into her pocket.

When Lucy arrived back at the Hargraves' house, she found that Cook had tied a wreath laced with black ribbon on their door. She saw, too, that rushes had been laid in the streets to muffle the sounds of carts and the footsteps of tradesmen and gawking passersby. Cook had prepared a bit of stew for the family, but Lucy found it impossible to swallow. Everyone spoke in hushed tones, and no one spoke directly to her. For this, she was grateful.

As Lucy lit the candles at the hearth that evening, she thought about her conversation with Bessie's sister. It was as she had feared—Bessie had no doubt been keeping company with some gent. She had not been to see her sister as she had said. Where had she been? Why had she lied? Then there was the matter of the dressing case that she had tried to keep out of Lucy's sight. So many times she had covered for Bessie, so many mysterious absences. Was it this same gent who had done away with her?

"I'm going to find out," she said, kicking the stone hearth. "You'll see, Bessie! I'll find justice for you yet!"

The idea of finding justice for Bessie soon felt like a needle threading in and out of Lucy's mind, pricking her unexpectedly, painfully reminding her of her desperate promise. "How can I even begin?" she muttered to herself. "I'm just a chambermaid."

Yet, after Bessie's funeral, the magistrate informed her that he wished for her to assume Bessie's former position as his wife's lady's maid.

For a moment, Lucy was speechless. I've not got Bessie's skill with a needle, she wanted to cry out. I shall ruin the mistress's fine silks!

Hearing his next words, however, she was glad she had held her tongue. "The mistress has taken Bessie's death to heart, Lucy. As we all have. My wife needs a companion more than she needs to have her silks pressed." He regarded her with his steady reassuring eyes. "Will you do that, Lucy? Be her companion?"

Lucy scarcely knew what she mumbled, yet found herself a short while later sitting silently beside her mistress, their sadness wrapped about them like a winding sheet. Listlessly, she unsnarled knots in several skeins of yarn, while Mistress Hargrave plucked impatiently at the happy cherubs she'd been embroidering for the last few weeks.

"Cherubs, bah! I'm starting a new piece," the mistress said, casting aside the wooden embroidery frame. "This one will depict the people of Nineveh being stricken down by God." She shrugged lightly. "Divine providence."

Divine providence indeed, Lucy thought to herself. Bessie deserves real justice, no matter what it may do to this household.

Finally, Lucy found her chance to look for what Adam had been hiding. Taking her leave of the mistress the next morning, she paused in the second-floor corridor, holding a candle to light the darkening passage. Darting a quick glance up and down the hallway, she put her ear by Adam's door. She couldn't hear anything. He must still be downstairs, she thought, having a drink with his father. Now that she had been promoted to the mistress's lady's maid, she had no good reason to enter Adam's room, as she might have done as a chambermaid. Knowing that what she was about to do was pure folly, she opened the door and slipped inside.

Unsure what she was looking for, she headed to Adam's desk. It was neat, like the rest of his room. Beside a stack of four or

five leather books were his pen and ink, pipe, and small pouch
of tobacco. She could see he had been writing something, but
she did not dare move the books to read his words.

With shaking hands, Lucy carefully eased open his desk
drawer. Inside, there were more papers, a bit of vellum, and
some knives for sharpening his pens. Otherwise, the drawer
was empty. She looked around the room. She quickly checked
the wardrobe and his trunk, but neither yielded much beyond
his penchant for finely tailored clothes. Under the bed was his
chamber pot, which she did not linger over, and a pitcher and
basin were on a small table by the window.

Lucy frowned. She was about to leave when she spied the tobacco pouch, which she had earlier discounted. Crossing the
room in three steps, she picked it up. "That's not tobacco," she
muttered, and with trembling fingers she loosened the cords
that kept the pouch closed.

Reaching in, Lucy pulled out two miniature portraits that
could fit easily into the palm of her hand. Each frame held the
image of a single left eye, with only a hint of a woman's eyebrow and cheekbones revealed. One eye was a beautiful light
ocher, and the other was green, the color of moss after rain. Each
eye stared directly at her, in a manner that was both coy and
knowing. Studying the portraits, she knew she did not recognize
either face. Bessie had blue eyes, and for that matter, so did
Judith Embry.

She could tell there was one more small object in the pouch.
As she drew it out, Lucy stared at it in horror. It was a beautiful lacquered comb—a comb she had seen before, hidden in
a box, tucked under Bessie's petticoats, a comb she had never

seen Bessie wear. This must have been what Adam found, she reasoned, at the site of Bessie's murder. Why had he been looking for it? He had definitely been searching for something that day. Had he known something about it? Was there any connection to the miniatures?

Thoughtfully, she put everything back where she had found it, lest she'd be caught in his room. Her little quest had left her with far more questions than answers, and her curiosity was far from satisfied.

"I'd be pleased to go to market today," Lucy called to Cook as she laid out the breakfast dishes the next morning. Last night, as she lay in her bed, staring at the crack in her shutters, she'd begun to realize that she needed to learn more details about Bessie's murder. *Maybe there's some truth to be found in the accounts of her death,* she had thought. *Something someone may have missed.*

Lucy murmured a quick prayer that the rain would hold off till she was home. Though it was just noon, the sky was looking to break open with a quick April shower. It would not do to walk through the market with her hair and dress plastered to her body. Although, truth be told, her mind felt as slushy as the outside world, and right now it was an effort to care about her appearance.

Stepping quickly around the peddlers hawking their wares, Lucy hurried past a carpenter pounding nails into a row of coffins. The solemn nature of the simple wood boxes unnerved her and made her think of Bessie. Wincing from the memory, she moved past another shop with a sign that had only a man's and a woman's hands intertwined. At that shop, Lucy knew, marriages were performed for those too poor or too desperate to get married properly in a church. At last, she stood in front of the apothecary, watching the sign with a unicorn's horn swaying with the hustle of the crowds.

At that moment, a young girl caught her attention. Lucy squinted, trying to figure out why the girl looked familiar. Dressed in a dirty frock, the lass was trying to sell ribbons as soiled as her cloak, looking like all the other ragamuffin children tearing about the streets. Yet there was something about her. "Ribbons for sale!" the girl called this way and that. Tired and wan, she had a thin voice that barely carried over the din. No one paid her any heed as she stumbled, falling into a pile of something steamy.

Lucy dashed over, crouching down beside her. "Are you all right?" Seeing the girl's slight nod, Lucy added, "Do I know you? What is your name?"

Pushing back her dirty cap, the girl looked up. Her eyes were sharp, taking in Lucy's headwrap and servant's clothes. Guarded, she shook her head.

Lucy studied her features. She knew she'd seen her before. Something about the set of her lips. Snapping her fingers, she said to the girl, "You're Cook's niece, aren't you?"

The girl shrugged. "How should I know? Who's Cook?"

"Sorry," Lucy said. "You have an aunt Mary, right? And, I suppose, a cousin Samuel? He's now a fishmonger in Leadenhall, but she's with the magistrate. Our household. You came with your mother to visit us."

The girl was nodding, looking wistful. "Yes, that's right. I remember now. What a grand house that was. That was when my pa died."

"Oh, right." Lucy recalled. "Where's your mother now? Have you a stall nearby, then?"

Something did not seem right. Thin and dirty was not unusual for children living in London's clogged streets among swelling debris and rattling garbage, but the ribbons she was trying to sell looked to be just scraps, a weaver's cast-offs. The girl also looked like she had not eaten for days. Lucy held out the apple she had saved for the long walk home.

The unexpected gift loosened the girl's tongue. "I'm Annie. It's just me and my brother Lawrence now, since my mum died in the last sickness; took a number from the city, it did. Now she's up in blessed heaven with my dear father."

Annie must have been talking about the last cholera outbreak, Lucy thought. She had heard that hundreds had died.

"Have you no family, then?" Lucy asked. "Are you alone?

"Shh!" Annie said, looking around fearfully. "I dunna want to be stolen."

Lucy put a hand to the girl's cheek. She knew only too well that bad sorts did sometimes prey on luckless children, especially those left abandoned on the streets. She lowered her voice. "Why didn't you come see Cook? Tell her your mum had passed?" she pressed.

Annie smoothed a ribbon hanging from the basket, but it still wrinkled unbecomingly. "She was not my mum's sister, you know, but the sister of my poor dad. I've been taking care just fine, excepting that Lawrence took sick, and we had to use the last bit of money for his potions. 'Sides, I did not know where she lived."

The thought of Annie and her brother alone on the streets made Lucy sick, and she said as much. "You must come home with me, to Cook. I'm sure the magistrate will help you. He's a good man, he is."

Hope and suspicion battled on Annie's pale face. "Lawrence, too?" she asked. "He's got a game leg, he does, but he's awful strong. He can haul logs and baskets and help with cooking and the marketing. I can't leave him."

"Yes," Lucy said more firmly than she felt. "We wouldn't leave Lawrence. Listen, now. I've an errand to run. Do you think you could get Lawrence, and your things together, before the clock strikes one? I could meet you, just there. Under the rooster."

Lucy pointed to a set of barrels outside the corner tavern. The Crowing Cock had a picture of a red rooster hanging above its door.

"Yes," said Annie. "We'll be there."

Looking at Annie's pathetic and eager face, Lucy felt a moment's misgiving. *It will be all right,* she thought, squaring her shoulders. *The magistrate is a good man. He will know what to do with these youngsters.*

Turning down Fleet Street, Lucy stopped in front of Master Aubrey's shop. Even from there, the noise of the presses and the men's shouts filled the air. Stepping inside, once again she was assailed by the smells coming from both the machines and the men themselves, sweating at their heavy work. She knew, from her previous visit, that most actual sales were not carried out in the shop; rather, the books went out in the hawkers' leather bags to be sold at stalls around the city or along the streets. St. Paul's Churchyard, London Bridge, Oak upon the Hill, Cheapside, and the Cock and Bull were favorite sites.

The half-formed thought Lucy had concocted that morning now seemed more than a bit foolish. It didn't help when Master Aubrey spotted her and strode over, rubbing his hands on a towel. Red faced and a bit impatient to get back to work, he nevertheless was courteous.

He took in her servant's garb but did not seem to recognize her from her prior visit. "Yes, lass? Do you have a message for me?"

"Er—" Lucy faltered, inwardly berating herself for not thinking through her plan.

Mustering patience, Master Aubrey tried to help her out. "Did your master send you, perchance?" he asked, clearly used to dim-witted servants doing their masters' bidding. "Come on, then, girl, let's have it."

Did she dare? Bessie's merry face danced before her eyes. Yes, she would do it. She tried to speak without guile. "I'm from Magistrate Hargrave's household. I believe you know his son?" She paused, eying the bookmaker from under her lashes, trying to gauge his response.

"Oh, yes, of course. Adam. You've a delivery, then?"

"A delivery? Oh, no. No," Lucy said, momentarily diverted. What *was* Adam's business with the printer? Then she returned her focus to the matter at hand.

"Master Adam would like all the true accounts and broadsides you have about the recent murder of Bessie Campbell."

Master Aubrey raised his eyebrows slightly but otherwise did not seem too surprised. "Zounds! I thought I already gave Adam those penny pieces. Never thought the young man to be so morbid. Hold on, then." He started out of the front room of the shop and then turned back. "I suppose he wants the accounts of the others, too?"

"The others?"

"Oh, yes. There were two other girls, taken in like your poor Bessie." This time, the printer looked right at Lucy, as if seeing her for the first time. A bit of warmth entered his voice. "Your friend, I suppose? Worked together at the house?"

Lucy looked up at the cracked white ceiling, battling with the tears that threatened to destroy her composure. She managed to nod.

"Sorrowful lot that," Master Aubrey sighed. "Mind you, I don't have all of the accounts, but I've got a few. Some I've been saving. I don't know why; I'm not one to paste murders on my walls like some. I've just always thought about these girls. Must be on account of me having a daughter myself." Pausing to add ink to a press, Master Aubrey added, "It will cost a crown for the lot."

"A whole crown?" Lucy gasped. "But they're old!"

"Murder always sells, my dear. Adam would know this. Shall I just send them by your master's house later, then? He can pay my apprentice."

"Oh, no! I mean, he sent the money along." Turning away, Lucy quickly pulled her pocket out of her skirts and looked at her last few coins ruefully. She had intended to buy her mother a present. *This is far more important,* she told herself, handing over the money.

Coin in hand, the printer disappeared into the back of the shop. As she had done when she first visited the shop two months before, Lucy looked around the drying racks, reading the titles, looking at the woodcuts.

"'A Recipe for a Good Wife,'" she read out loud. The piece was accompanied by its rejoinder, "'A Recipe for a Good Husband.'" Looking it over, she blushed at the bawdy advice.

The thought of a husband seemed so distant to her, and yet Lucy knew she would marry in a few years. What her future husband—this nameless, formless figure—would look like was anybody's guess. She had no expectation of his appearance. He was as likely to be fat and bald as he would be young and handsome. *As long as he does not beat me,* she supposed, although in her heart, she wished for love.

So long as he is not in one of the animal trades, she thought, her nose wrinkling. Though it might be a blessing to have meat on the table regularly. Yet the thought of a man climbing into her bed every night smelling of blood and gristle turned her stomach.

Beyond that, she barely dared imagine. Her mother, she knew, would not force her to marry, but she would be expecting that banns be read by the time Lucy was twenty-five, an age when servants commonly scraped together enough money to marry, or when men had finished their apprenticeships. Otherwise, she'd surely be seen as a dried-up spinster, and her options would grow scarce. Lucy knew her mother was especially eager to see her settled before she passed.

As she gazed at the silly woodcut images, several faces of men she knew passed through her mind. Richard, leering at her at the Embrys' Easter masquerade. The painter's eyes, first warm and caressing, then hard and cruel. She shivered, repulsed again. Lucas, his ready grin and red cheeks. Adam, his amused smile in the drawing room, sharing a joke with his father. His hands cupping her face, so close to his own . . . but kissing Judith a few hours later . . .

Lucy came to her senses. *Stupid!* she scolded herself. She forced herself to think of his bloody hands, the blood on his shirt. *Remember why you are doing this!*

Master Aubrey was just returning with a tied packet. Opening the door, he said, "I don't know why Adam wanted these now. We're planning to meet in a few hours anyway, as we've some things to catch up on."

A freezing cold passed through Lucy. She managed to shrug, trying to look casual. "Oh, those gentry," she said. "Who can understand their passing fancies?"

"Indeed," the printer agreed, not paying her any more attention. "Ho there!" she heard him call to his apprentice as she scurried out of the shop. "Mind how you set that type!"

Hurrying down the street, Lucy scolded herself again. "Stupid sow!"

What if Master Aubrey told Adam that she had purchased the woodcuts and folios in his name? She did not know what she could say. *Maybe he will not find out,* she comforted herself. Indeed, why would he?

So upset was she that she had not thought her ridiculous plan through, she almost forgot about Annie and Lawrence.

Luckily, she spotted them, huddled together by the Crowing Cock, clutching a small bag each. Chagrined, she rushed over to them, muttering to herself, "Lucy, you do not have two licks of sense. Two feckless deeds in just one hour!"

Waiting for a cart to pass her in the road, she continued to chastise herself. *What will the magistrate say when he sees these two waifs?* she wondered, putting her worries about Adam and the woodcuts firmly out of her thoughts.

Mustering a smile, she greeted the two children shivering on the corner. Like Annie, Lawrence looked scrawny and under-fed, and he favored his right leg. He barely seemed able to walk but still managed to convey both pride and defiance, which kept her from expressing the concern she felt. Neither looked to be more than ten. "How old are you, anyway?" she asked Annie.

"Almost eleven," Annie chirped, nudging her brother. He duly answered, "Nine."

Lucy supposed there would not be much harm bringing them home for a meal and a bit of a wash. She could inquire among the neighbors if they needed extra help, but she did not think the magistrate would turn them out of the house out-right. Best get a move on. Lucy smiled, trying to look reassur-ing. "All right, children, let's go." Taking their packs in her own strong arms, Lucy started back to Lincoln Fields. The children followed close behind. Neither looked back.

Lucy's fears that the children would not be accepted into the magistrate's household were unfounded.

Cook took one look at them and, with tears in her eyes, opened her arms into a hearty embrace. "Annie and Lawrence!" she managed to choke out. "Whatever has happened?"

Lucy quickly told her what Annie had related about their mother's death, while the children gnawed thick crusts of bread and slurped hot soup.

Cook clucked and tutted as she heard the story. Later, when she thought the children were not listening, she whispered to Lucy, "Their mother was too proud. She should have sent word when she took sick."

"Would not have made a difference," Annie spoke up, a bit of soup dripping from her lips. "It happened right quick. Neither of us could remember your master's name, nor where this house was. Me and Lawrence, we could not well knock on all those fine houses, looking as we do."

Lucy helped them wash for the first time in many months and then made beds for them on pallets of straw in the pantry. It was not long before the children were sleeping peacefully among the onions, near where John and Cook slept. Having heard of their arrival, Master and Mistress Hargrave peered in at them, where they lay close together.

"Poor dears," said the mistress. "That little Lawrence looks unwell. We shall call for the physician in the morning."

"Lucy, indeed, it was providence that you found them," Master Hargrave said. "Mary, the children may stay, provided they help you and Lucy with the scullery tasks. When Lawrence is well in a few months' time, we shall apprentice him out. Make sure you feed him, Mary; he looks too scrawny for being nine years old."

After the master escorted his wife from the kitchen in his customary solemn way, Cook and Lucy exchanged glances. They did not need to say anything, knowing they were fortunate to live in such a good household.

With all the excitement, it was quite late before Lucy finished her chores and retired to her chamber. There, she lit a candle stub and stuck it into a crack in the wall. Finally, she pulled the packet from under her skirts. After undoing the string with her teeth, she spread out the papers, frowning. There seemed to be ten pieces altogether, although four pieces puzzled her on first glance. Another was the ballad "Murder Will Out," which had been sold at Bessie's funeral. She wondered why it had been included; the account was of a murder that had occurred some twenty years before. These she set aside.

The other five were penny pieces, typical of what Master Aubrey and other booksellers peddled in the streets. Jane Hardewick and a woman named Effie Caruthers were the focus of two, and there were a pair about Bessie. The authors, identified either by their initials or more simply as "Anonymous," described the last moments of each wretched girl's life, with the ballads setting the horrific acts to rhyme. None of the murders looked to have been solved.

"Such a shame," Lucy murmured. They all had dreams and hopes and families, and now they were gone. She said a small prayer for their souls before reading through the pages in earnest.

She started with the broadside and ballad describing Effie

Caruthers's death. According to both accounts, Effie had been set upon by a passing woodsman on her way to a rendezvous in a secluded field in south London. The ballad gave little detail of Effie's death, mostly describing the plight of her master, who had lost his favorite servant.

"Good they can banter about her death," Lucy muttered and picked up the accounts of Jane Hardewick's murder.

As with Effie, there was a "true account" and a ballad about Jane. The "true account" she had read long before. She closed her eyes, remembering for a moment poring over the account with Bessie and Cook, unaware of the tragedy that lay ahead.

Lucy shook her head. "That won't do," she admonished herself, and she reread the passage describing what Jane had been last seen wearing. Gray muslin dress, red embroidered sash. Lucy sat upright. That reminded her of Maraid. Uneasily, she recalled the gypsy's words. *The sash comes from a dark place.*

Letting the woodcut drop from her fingers, she picked up the "true account" of Bessie's murder. "'A Murder at Rosamund's Gate,'" she read. "'Being a true account of a most horrible murder at Rosamund's Gate, of a serving girl, who did work at the Magistrate's household in Lincoln Fields. By S.C.'"

Taking a deep breath, Lucy read only the first few lines before swearing. "That rat Janey! This is her swill!"

Nearly every word was a lie, including the same rubbish about Bessie having received a letter from an unidentified lover, who had persuaded the "heartless trollop" to meet him at Rosamund's Gate with the magistrate's silver. Much of the piece focused on how Bessie had brought ruin on the magistrate's household. Even worse, it contained several passages suggesting that her lover had been someone much closer—someone known to, or even part of, the magistrate's own family.

Chilled, Lucy compared the woodcut account to the ballad, which was much shorter but also mentioned the lover's note. "All lies," she repeated to herself.

Tossing the woodcuts aside, Lucy looked back at the discarded pile, the four pieces she could not quite decipher. They had no pictures, and the text was much smaller and harder to read. Although the words were in English, their meaning escaped her, especially in her current tired state. The papers looked like legal documents and could have been in a strange language for all the sense she could make of them.

The last of the pieces looked like a petition to the king, and try as she might, she could make no headway. It seemed unrelated to the deaths of the three girls. Perhaps Master Aubrey had included it by mistake. Lucy was too tired to ponder it anymore. Blowing out the candle, she laid down her head and quickly fell into a dreamless, but troubled, sleep.

·II·

In the morning, Lucy found Lawrence cleaning out the hearth. His face blackened by soot, he still grinned at her. "Morning, ma'am," he said.

"Just Lucy, Lawrence," she corrected him gently. "Did you get enough to eat?" she asked, although the telltale signs of porridge and jam were well in evidence on his collar and cuff.

"Yes, ma'am. I mean, Miss Lucy," he said, returning to work.

Lucy moved into the kitchen, where she found Annie sitting close and trusting beside Cook, her small hands busily scrubbing vegetables for the midday meal.

"I guess you can get back to giving yourself airs now, as a lady's maid," Cook said, her voice gruff but kind. "I guess my Annie here can do your work just fine, though she be a bit peaked."

"Fair enough," Lucy said, sliding onto the hard kitchen

bench. Using the long wooden ladle, she spooned a few bites of porridge into her bowl. Her stomach grumbled happily as the food slid, warm and delicious, down her throat. After swallowing, she added, "I just wish I could sew half as fine as Bessie, or it will be back to the slops for me."

"Never!" Cook declared. "The master is pleased he could move you up, I think. Have a smart one, like you, to tend the mistress. Now, Annie," she said, turning to her young ward, "let's leave Lucy to finish her breakfast in peace. I shall show you around the house myself; goodness knows I knew the ins and outs of chamber pots and hearths in my day. Lucy can give you the particulars later."

The kitchen unexpectedly empty, Lucy sat down, resting her head on her elbow. Trying to read through the penny pieces the night before had given her a headache, and she had not slept well. She was nearly dozing off when a low voice from behind her caused her to start, her heart beating painfully.

"I believe you have something of mine?" Adam asked, appearing in the kitchen doorway. "Let's have it."

"Oh!" Lucy blushed.

Unlike Lucas, who often came sniffing around for a bit of pudding or a piece of treacle tart, Adam, like his father, was not a common sight in the Hargrave kitchen. His dark hair was pushed back from his face, and he looked like he had been out getting some exercise. For a moment, she wondered what he did when he was not studying. Fencing, perhaps, or even sparring? Of course, the gentry didn't dirty themselves as the boys back home would; they would use special gloves and padding. Will and his lot would have a good laugh.

Adam repeated his question in a tone that brooked little humor.

"I don't know what you mean," she stammered, trying not to recoil.

"Come, Lucy. You know exactly what I mean. Did you think Aubrey would not tell me about your request? Did you want me to seem a fool before my friend?" Adam tapped his foot. "Make haste, if you will. It would not be seemly for me to enter a chambermaid's bedroom, but by God, I'll go right up there and search your things to find what is mine. Your honor be damned."

"Lady's maid," Lucy muttered without thinking.

He folded his arms, his frown deepening. "What?"

"I'm a lady's maid. Your mother is a lady, is she not? And I'm her servant, am I not? Then I'm a lady's maid, sir, and not a chambermaid."

"Of all the damndest—"

Pushing past him, Lucy added, "I shall retrieve what you request shortly. You may meet me in the drawing room."

His raised brow made her think she might have gone too far. "Sir," she added hastily.

Racing to the drawing room, she quickly unwrapped the scarves that crossed her bodice, pulling the papers out. Making a snap decision, she kept "A Murder at Rosamund's Gate" hidden. Adam walked in a few moments later, just as she was refastening her dress.

He looked at the small pile of papers on the table and then back at her. "You were *wearing* all of that under your skirts?" he asked, incredulous.

Lucy smirked. "Under my bodice, actually." Suppressing an inner groan, she bit her lip. Why on earth had she mentioned her bodice? She talked quickly then, to cover her embarrassment. Putting her hand on the papers, she said, "I paid for these, you know. A crown. My money," she emphasized, in case he didn't get it.

"The price of using my name, I'm afraid." Adam held up a hand to quell her protest. "Now, I am interested, however, in knowing what my mother's charming little *lady's maid* wanted with these nasty, sordid pieces." He eased one of the flimsy sheets from under her hands.

Despite the great show he was putting on, Lucy had the feeling he knew exactly what they all were.

"Yes, I see. Bessie's murder, of course." He looked at the others. "Hmm . . . and Jane Hardewick's, and even little Effie Caruthers's. Tut tut. Dreadful business all, to be sure. What is going on in that silly little head of yours?"

Lucy shook her head.

"Oh, come now; it's easy to see what you're thinking. A connection between them. Tell me your reasoning." His voice was lazy but commanding. "Really, I insist."

Although she remained standing, Lucy leaned against the table. "Well," she began, "I found it hard to piece it together, truth be told. I thought Dr. Larimer had said that the two girls, Jane and Effie, had both been killed the same way. Yet this one"—she picked up a pamphlet and in a halting manner read, " 'The True Account of a Most Treacherous Murder,' says Effie was killed by a passing woodcutter. This makes no sense at all." Lucy laid the sheet down on the table. "It seems odd that Effie had left the house with her satchel of clothes, planning to run off with someone, then she just happens to have the ill fortune to be set upon—what? Why are you laughing? 'Tis not a humorous event!"

"No indeed," Adam said, the mocking grin disappearing for an instant. "Her murder is no laughing matter. I think you know she was not hacked to pieces by, what did you call him? A passing woodcutter?"

"But," Lucy reasoned, "why would the picture here show it like this? It makes no sense."

"For that confusion, you may blame Master Aubrey. He will simply select woodcuts that he had used for other texts, a common practice among printers. See, he'll use that woodcut whenever the crime seems to suit. However, there may be some truth here, even if the author may have made up other details to better sell the story."

"Did Master Aubrey write this story, then? About Bessie?"

"Not likely. He probably just bought this from a Grub Street hack, put it in his press, and sold it as new. None would be the wiser, and it's even less likely that anyone would care."

Lucy picked up another ballad. " 'Murder Will Out!' " she read. "This is the one some crier was selling at Bessie's funeral. 'Twas quite disturbing for her family, you know. And it had nothing to do with Bessie. This murder happened twenty years ago!"

Adam looked pained. "Yes, well, this one was not from Aubrey's shop. See here, a different bookseller and printer are listed below the woodcut. He probably just traded it for one of his own," he explained. "Booksellers often trade their wares. As for why this particular one was sold at Bessie's funeral, would you care to speculate?" His gaze was hard.

Sidestepping the question, she sought to change the topic with a question of her own. "How do you know so much about this, sir? About what booksellers do?"

Adam shuffled through the papers but would not be baited. "I know something about the booksellers' trade, I suppose." He rapped the table with his knuckles. "Come, Lucy," he continued. "Show me why my father sets store by a *lady's maid's* intellect." Again he stressed "lady's maid" in a slightly mocking way. "Look beyond the woodcut image. Look beyond the barbarous words. Those are just meant to tantalize, to seduce. Does anything strike you as true? What can we learn here about these murders?"

Lucy thought for a moment. "Well, all the girls were similar. Each was young, alone, unmarried, a servant. Pretty."

Adam sniffed, unimpressed. "That could describe a goodly portion of all the lasses in England, at least of a certain class, including you. Go on, what else?"

Lucy tried again, attempting to hide her irritation. "Well, each had received a letter—"

"Yes, that is the more interesting question." Adam tapped his fingers on the table. "What does the presence of these letters tell us? How foolish these girls were? 'Dear Jane, meet me at midnight. Do not tell anyone, for I plan to kill you when I see you.' Does this make any sense?"

"Well, no, not when you put it that way."

"Thus, there are at least two questions here. Did such letters indeed exist? If so, were they used to lure these girls to their eventual fate? That is, did the alleged lover intend to kill them, or were they killed by a third party?"

Now Lucy was getting annoyed. "You seem to have already worked this out, sir. Perhaps you would care to explain? I have not your experience with such things."

"I should say not. Master Aubrey—a good man, indeed. Certainly not a liar in our everyday world. He wouldn't cheat the baker, or fib to a clergyman, or spread stories about a friend. However, he might see fit to find ways to sell a few more papers with more, shall we say, embellished true stories."

"Everyone loves a good murder," Lucy said, frowning. "Master Aubrey told me so."

"Yes, exactly," Adam said. "A good murder sells penny pieces, and crimes of passion make good reading. Not to mention good profits."

"How can we know the truth?" Her voice caught a little. Tears were close, but she blinked them away.

"There's the rub. Let's see what else you have."

She showed him the more official-looking folios. The petition he merely glanced at and put in his pocket.

"What was the petition for? It said to get someone out of jail? Is it the killer?"

"No, that's nothing. Something our good printer friend may have included for my, er, amusement. No bearing on this case." Adam tapped the other papers. "What about these? What do you make of them?"

"Testimonies, I think. Are they? Am I right? I couldn't make out head or tail."

"I had not seen these," he said, skimming them with skillful eyes. "These are different types of court records and are not publicly circulated or sold. Generally they pass only between judges and magistrates, so that they can be kept informed of changes in the law or updated about recent events. They are supposed to stay with the court. I do not know how Aubrey got hold of them."

"What do they say?" she persisted. "Please tell me."

"This one is a deposition, where two witnesses recorded their testimony before the Effie Caruthers trial. And this one is the sworn statement of Robert Preswell, who swears he was nowhere near Jane Hardewick when she was murdered, although neighbors suggest otherwise. He does admit to fathering her baby, which may be enough to condemn him." He snorted. "In themselves, I'm not sure they add more to what we already know. And, really, Lucy, what do you hope to accomplish here? It's all rather unseemly stuff for a lass such as you."

"I have to know the truth," she cried. "Can you not see that?"

"The truth can be painful, have you thought about that?" he countered. "I'm afraid—"

She never knew what he was going to say, for she heard Cook calling for her. "The mistress must want me," Lucy said.

"Indeed. And Lucy," he said, as she started out the door. He held a coin. "A half-crown for your troubles, for bringing me my package and for so closely, ahem, guarding it on your person. But not a word, if you will. It's best not to talk about Bessie's death. We shan't want to upset anyone. Don't you agree?"

After he walked out, she had the feeling he had been about to say something else but then changed his mind. She did think, though, he was warning her. She looked at the last penny piece that had stayed hidden under her skirts. Like the others, it insisted "Murder will out" and described how Bessie's arm did willingly and truly move on her own and did, with the will of God, then point to her killer. Lucy read the passage again: " 'After her body was found, a crowd gathered to see her. Then, her eyes did open of their own accord and her finger did point to a certain young gentleman studying law at the Inns of Court who most certainly did live in the same household as the comely wench—"

"I thought you were hiding one more from me."

Lucy whirled around. Adam had doubled back, moving so stealthily she had not heard him.

"Give it to me."

She shook her head dumbly. " 'Tis nothing, sir."

"Oh, my dear Lucy. As if I am not well aware that there was one that accused me so directly. And I can see by your rapid pulse that you believe every word of it. Or, at least, the part that has to do with me."

"No, sir, I don't. It's full of lies." Her protest was weak, and they both knew it.

"It is quite true, I'm afraid." Adam laughed at her shocked expression. "I was indeed there, and her arm did drop and look to point at me. I was as surprised as anyone, although perhaps more surprised that the silly tale has gotten about." He frowned.

"Tell me, Lucy. Why would I want to kill Bessie, a girl I scarce had a single conversation with? I wish someone could tell me." He stood close to Lucy, his eyes fixed on her face. "Do *you*, Lucy, really think I could have killed her?"

The image of Adam stumbling up the front walk, covered with blood and feverish, the morning after Bessie's disappearance flooded Lucy's mind. She blanched at the memory and stepped back from him.

For a moment, he looked hurt and puzzled, then his familiar mocking gaze returned. "I guess I have my answer. The scullery maid thinks I'm a murderer. I should just like to know my motive." He reached over and picked a tendril of hair from her shoulder. She stood, frozen, as he rolled the lock between his fingers. A final tug and he let it go. "Best have a care, then. Living with a murderer under your roof may not be so good for your health." She heard his scornful laugh all the way down the hallway, and she sat down hard on her bench.

Lucy was still mulling over what she had pieced together from the penny pieces as she walked home from market the next day. She remembered what Avery had said about the witches taking the clothes off a dead woman's body. She reread the passage about Jane having last been seen with a red sash.

Could the gypsies have had something to do with Jane Hardewick's death? she wondered. Not that she'd ever dare ask Maraid such a thing. She couldn't anyway, because she'd heard the gypsies had cleared out and were off to who knew where. Besides, according to Avery, Jane had already been dead when the witches removed her clothes, so they may not have been the ones who killed her.

None of it made any sense. Lost in thought, it took Lucy a moment before she realized that an older man she did not know had fallen in step beside her. Uneasy, she began to walk more quickly, not nearly as carefree as she had been before Bessie's death. She looked about; a few other people were walking back from market, but none that she knew.

"Hey there, young lady," the man called. She began to walk faster. The man tried again. "Lass, please wait. Thee dost work in the house of Adam Hargrave, dost thee not?"

Hearing the peculiar form of address and the mention of Adam, Lucy stopped and turned warily around. Breathing heavily, she regarded the man. He was dressed in sober woolen clothes, a nondescript gray. His beard was neatly shaved in a good somber fashion, shading a careworn face. She thought he was likely about forty years old, but his gaunt frame aged his body even more. He looked and sounded for all the world like a Quaker. His next words seemed to confirm her guess.

He held up both hands. "I have no wish to harm thee. I am a Friend. 'Tis Lucy, is it not?" Seeing her surprise that he knew her name, the man smiled, looking years younger. "Adam Hargrave said thee art a good and loyal lass, and that thee could be trusted, should I ever need to send him a message."

Flattered by the unexpected compliment, Lucy held out her hand for a note. "What is the message, sir?"

He shook his head. " 'Tis not a message I dare write down. Pray tell Adam that we are set for tonight. When the moon is high. By Jamison's paddock. Will thee remember that?"

Lucy repeated the words dutifully. "I'll remember to tell him, sir."

"And Lucy?"

Something about the man's grave and humble stance commanded her respect. "Yes, sir?"

"This message is for Adam only, dost thee understand?"

She gave a quick bob before walking thoughtfully home.

Later, Lucy lay in bed, huddled in her brown muslin dress, having foolishly made up her mind to follow Adam that night. When she had delivered the message to Adam that afternoon, he had simply nodded and then bent back over his thick law volume. Clearly, he was not interested in continuing any conversation with her.

She cracked open her shutters, peering down at the cobblestone street below. The rising moon was bright. Her heart beat quickly as she thought about leaving the safety of the house. For Bessie's sake, she would do it. Her dreams of late had been restless. In them, Bessie kept coming to her, dressed in her green taffeta. Rather than the beautiful girl Lucy remembered, this specter had long jagged scars down her body and entrails spilling from her gown. Each time, the specter would stretch out her arms, searching, pleading. *Lucy! Help me, please!*

The last time Lucy had awoken, breathing heavily and sweating, a sheet wrapped around her neck like a shroud. To Lucy, the message of the dreams was clear. No matter her own fear, no matter who the murderer turned out to be, truth must out— and she had to play a role in its discovery. If Bessie's murderer turned out to be Adam . . . Lucy shook her head. She didn't know what to think. What could he be doing, so secretly, this late at night?

"He simply can't be a Quaker," she said out loud. The magistrate would throw his son into jail if he took up with that wretched sect. "It's easier to believe him a murderer than a Quaker." She laughed, without mirth, to herself. Yet, of course, it wasn't easy at all to think Adam had killed Bessie. Because he was the magistrate's son. Because he had once been kind. For other reasons, too, that she knew would be too heartbreaking to face.

Though Lucy could barely keep her eyes open, her patience was finally rewarded when she saw a furtive shadow slip from the house. Hurriedly, she laced up her shoes and tiptoed down the stairs. Hearing the reassuring sound of Cook's and John's snores from the kitchen, she pushed open the back door. As she stepped out, she made a small prayer that no one would awaken in her absence.

Lucy raced lightly down the street, thankfully bathed in moonlight, hoping that Adam was still heading in the direction she had glimpsed from the window. She was not sure where Jamison's paddock was and was relieved when she caught sight of Adam's tall, wiry form walking swiftly down the road. Lucy caught her breath. He was moving toward the fields where the tinker had found Bessie's body. What was he doing?

Adam moved toward a farmer's paddock, where Lucy saw that several people were already waiting. Puzzled, she stepped behind a tree to watch. No one greeted Adam when he approached, although a few glanced at him silently. All were dressed simply in Quaker garb. Lucy recognized the tall, thin man who had approached her earlier. Soon, eight people had gathered. One of the women held a sleeping child in her arms. Nervously, Lucy realized that this was indeed one of the secret conventicles banned by the king and the Church. For a long time no one spoke, although Lucy thought she heard a woman weeping. A moment later, someone spoke quietly. Adam kept his head bowed, as if in prayer.

Finally, another man spoke. Lucy had to strain to hear him. "The king has seen fit to cast another dozen of our brethren into jail. Mistress White is alone with three young babes. How can we help her?"

The woman shifted the sleeping baby in her arms and spoke quietly. "I can spare some victuals."

Another man declared, "Myself and Garret here shall visit our brethren in Newgate and seek to sustain their spirits."

One by one, each Quaker promised ways to help their imprisoned brethren. None looked very wealthy, so Lucy thought they could scarce afford it.

Throughout it all, Adam had remained silent. Finally, he spoke. "I shall draft a petition to the king and deliver it to Whitehall."

The tall man nodded gravely. The group began to disperse, everyone sidling off in different directions, the meeting apparently over. The baby still slept sweetly in his mother's arms. Adam said something else to the Quaker who had spoken to her, and she saw him nod.

Lucy pressed herself against the tree, hoping Adam would pass her by without noticing. As she shifted her weight, though, a twig cracked beneath her foot. Adam stiffened and stared into the copse where she stood hidden in the shadows. Lucy was glad that clouds were passing before the moon, offering some cover.

"Who's there?" Adam called. "Show yourself!"

A long moment passed. Lucy longed to peek out from behind the tree trunk, but she was afraid he would see her. The chill of the night began to seep into her bones, and she desperately longed to move her legs and arms and to get some life back in them. Warily, she slid from her hiding spot, trying to avoid the great pools of light that spilled through the branches. Looking around, she heaved a great sigh. Adam had left. She started down the path.

The next instant, a man's hand clamped tightly over her mouth, and an arm about her waist immobilized her. In her panic, she began to thrash about, remembering how Richard had attacked her.

Adam's voice came angrily into her ear. "Lucy. It's me! Stop it!"

She stopped squirming, and he let her go, standing a few feet from her. His clothes were rumpled as if he had not sat comfortably in a while, but his stance was watchful. He looked like he could knock her down without a second thought.

"What are you doing here?" he demanded. "Spying? Certainly a foolhardy thing, to spy on a man who you believe to be a killer. I guess this is my chance, then. We're alone. No one around." Lucy gaped at him, at a loss for words. Adam went on, ignoring her distress. "Unfortunately, the opportunity will have to pass. I seem to have no knife, or rope, or even a bit of cloth. I suppose I could smother you with your cloak, but that seems a lot of trouble. Plus, I prefer to keep you alive."

Adam ran his fingers through his dark hair. "Oh, come on, Lucy! Where is the intelligence my father alleges you to have? Or is it you are blessed with too keen an imagination? Please understand, I've no wish to kill you! Not now or ever!" In a different tone, he asked, "Now, will you please tell me what you are doing here, in the middle of the night? I trusted you enough to think the message could be relayed to you, but clearly I underestimated your distrust of me." He shook his head. "What did you think you were going to find out? That we were meeting tonight to murder someone? There must be so many easier ways to go about it! Yet I did manage to lure you here, it would seem. So perhaps my plan was not so far-fetched."

Although Lucy bristled at his mocking tone, she thought about how he had silently prayed with the Quakers. Something about the obvious trust they placed in him confused her.

He continued to wait for her answer, almost daring her to ask the question on the tip of her tongue. Still, she couldn't very well probe him about his bloodied hands here in this desolate spot. Why else would she have come, if not to spy on him?

A sudden flash of inspiration came to her instead. "My conscience!" she declared, trying to keep the note of triumph out of her voice. "I knew that man was a Quaker. I knew you would be meeting with them, and my conscience told me to follow you." She thought that was a safe enough answer. Everyone knew that Quakers were led in all their decisions by their conscience and did not feel the need to obey earthly authority or rules.

"Hmm," he grunted, a disbelieving look on his face. "If that were true—"

Lucy sought to shift the conversation. "You're a Quaker, then?"

A long moment passed. Lucy thought he wasn't going to respond. When he did, it was in his old measured way. "No," he admitted. "I'm not. But I do have some sympathy for their cause." Then, unexpectedly, Adam began to talk, and kept talking as they walked home. He had long questioned the Church of England's policies and doctrines on certain matters, and he certainly did not approve of King Charles's hardening response to the nonconformists. He had, he admitted, written a tract or two pleading their cause. "Father would not much like that if he knew, Lucy," he said, a warning evident in his voice. "Of course, I'm not too likely to use his name, am I?" he muttered more to himself than to her.

She nodded, uncertain what to say.

Adam glanced at her. "I must say, there is something else that interests me about these Quakers."

"Oh?" she asked, pulling her thin cloak more tightly around her. For a moment, she was reminded of their walk from the Embrys', although she thought it unlikely he would share his cloak again with her. "What is that?"

"They move in and out of the jails. They pick up information. That kind of information can be useful."

"What kind of information?" Lucy asked.

Instead of answering her, Adam stopped and looked down at her, a questioning look on his face. "So, how can I account for this sea change?"

She stopped, too. "Sir?"

He moved slightly toward her. "You're no longer looking at me so fearfully. Have you finally displaced the misbegotten fancy that I'm a murderer?"

For the first time in a long time, she smiled in his presence. "I'm not sure."

She was unexpectedly gratified when he gave her a rare answering grin. "Well, so long as I know what you're thinking."

·12·

I'm here to talk to Master Adam about the murder of Bessie Campbell."

Lucy gasped. Constable Duncan was speaking to John just outside the kitchen. Had it only been eleven days since she had informed them of Bessie's death? Casting aside the fine frock she had been mending, Lucy rushed into the hallway, Cook at her heels. Seeing the constable there, standing smartly by the door, reminded Lucy of the first time they had met—when he had come bearing news of the hapless Jane Hardewick. With a shiver, Lucy remembered how Bessie had flirted with the young constable. Now Bessie was gone.

"You have news?" she asked before she could help herself.

The constable glanced at her, his face stern. "Perhaps," he replied. "Something new has come to light."

John returned. "This way, sir, the magistrate is within."

A moment later, Adam appeared, his face drawn and pale. As he passed, he raised his eyebrows at her, looking cool and arrogant. When the door closed behind him, Cook and Lucy unashamedly put their ears to a long crack in the wood. John settled onto a nearby bench, playing with his unlit pipe.

Then they heard Duncan speak. "I'm going to cut through the chaff. Can you explain, *sir,* why you arrived home, after having been out all evening, with torn clothes and bloody limbs, on the same morning that your servant went missing? This same servant who was later found murdered, having been run through and through with a knife. Can you explain this?"

They gasped. Lucy held up her hand for quiet so she could hear. How had the constable known? She looked at John, and he gave a slight shake of his head. No, the constable's knowledge did not come from either of them. Dr. Larimer's assistant, the surgeon who had tended Adam, she realized, might have come forward. Or perhaps one of her nosy neighbors had seen more than she knew.

Lucy's mind was clear, but her stomach was churning. Somehow, now that Constable Duncan was there, questioning Adam, she could hardly bear it. He couldn't have anything to do with Lucy's death, he just couldn't. Yet she had to have the answer that had been plaguing her for weeks.

"Pub fight." Adam's tone was terse, angry. "At the Muddy Duck. Plenty of oglers, I might add. A few might be coaxed to speak, if a few bits more found their way into some pockets."

"Indeed," Duncan said. "We did hear about that. Not too common for the magistrate's son to be involved in an everyday brawl." Though his tone was even, a note of disdain had crept into the constable's voice. "Here's the thing," he continued. "We've heard tell that you, Adam Hargrave, threatened to kill the girl in question—"

"What!" Adam exclaimed. "That, my dear sir, is a blatant lie."

"Do you deny, sir, that your brawl was over your serving wench, Bessie Campbell?"

Adam said something, but his voice was muffled. Cook and Lucy signaled the same confused question. *What in the world—?*

They scarcely had a chance to ponder, hearing Duncan speak again. "Can you explain, sir, your absence later that evening? Do not suppose, sir, that we do not have witnesses. I should like to hear your own accounting."

Again the heavy oak door kept Lucy and Cook from hearing Adam's response. Frustrated, Lucy could only press her ear more closely to the crack between the door and the frame. Here the constable evidently was reading something. "He did arrive home, at a most unseemly hour, blood all over his clothes, a crazed look on his face, like a man having spent the night satisfying unnatural cravings—"

"Unnatural cravings?" the magistrate shouted. "What nonsense is this?"

"—thereby being helped in by his servant," the constable continued, "another hoyden by the name of Lucy Campion and—"

"Enough!" roared the magistrate, causing his listeners to jump. Lucy felt, rather than saw, Cook give her a sidelong glance.

Into his next statement, Master Hargrave put the full weight of his magisterial authority. "I'll not let some prying neighbor with too much time on her hands impugn my son in such a way. Wild look in his eyes, indeed! Blood on his shirt! By God, I shall go to your superior this instant! His name, man!"

Adam said something then. They heard the magistrate sink heavily into a chair.

"Why in heaven's name . . . ?" they heard him say, his voice strangled. "Whose blood was it?"

Lucy pressed her ear so hard against the door that she began to hear ringing. Her fist was pressed just as tightly to her mouth. She was dimly afraid that she would burst the door open by accident, but she little cared about making a disturbance.

"My own blood, I swear," Adam shouted, "and that of a dumb beast!"

Oh, he's going to try telling them he ran into the butcher's stall again, Lucy thought faintly. *They won't believe it.* She could scarcely believe that she had accepted that nonsense as truth.

There was silence again. For a moment, all Lucy could hear was John's slight raspiness as he breathed in and out. Then the constable said something. His words were inaudible, but the meaning was clear.

Adam seemed to be speaking to his father, not the constable. His voice sounded more pleading than confident. Certainly, he had dropped the self-mocking tone. Luckily, his voice was elevated, so they could discern almost everything. "Just hear me out, sir," Adam said. "This will sound absurd, I know." He paused. Lucy could imagine him running his hand through his hair. He seemed to be searching for words. Then he spoke again. "I was at a ring in Southwark the night Bessie, God rest her poor soul, disappeared."

"A ring!" Master Hargrave exclaimed. "What were you doing, at such a low sport as that?"

Lucy strained to hear Adam's next words. Whatever she had expected, it was not that Adam had spent time at a cock and dog fight. She wrinkled her nose in disgust and disappointment. Still, she wanted to hear his explanation.

" 'Tis no sport!" Adam answered. "Putting a pea in a poor dog's ears to make him mad! I believe such sport is wrong, and against God's own law!"

Casting her mind back to that awful night, Lucy considered Adam's words. Grudgingly, she realized that some of the cuts and blood could have been the result of a man's being mad enough to step into the midst of such bloodlust. The fever that had followed would fit, for it was well known that those animals could sicken a man, and even kill him, even if he had not lost blood. But what about the odd slashes across Adam's chest and arms? No animal had made those!

As if hearing her thoughts through the door, Duncan spoke again. "We have it on good conviction that those marks on your body were not from a beast."

Adam murmured something that Lucy did not catch.

They all jumped as Master Hargrave roared, "Who dares whip my son?"

Lucy's hand flew to her mouth.

"I think," Adam said wryly, "there are many who would

whip a man who busts up their sport. One in particular would be glad to have everyone know he had whipped me, if he had not perhaps preferred that I swing from the hangman's noose."

The constable said something. Adam raised his voice. "I should give you his name and address if I had it, but alas I do not. Perhaps if you asked around, down in Southwark, you might get proof of my innocence, but I think it will be unlikely, angry as they all were that I had ruined their sport. Now, sir, either arrest me or leave, I pray you. I've things to attend to here. Good day."

Lucy and Cook tried to jump away as Adam threw open the door pretending they had not just been huddled with their ears pressed to the wood. Seeing them, he stopped short and glared. Lucy opened her mouth to speak but could make no words come out. Adam looked at her, his glance so contemptuous that a deep hurt arose within her chest.

She realized then that Adam thought she had informed the constable about his injuries. Then a deeper realization surfaced. *Who will believe Adam's story?* Even she had thought Adam had been lying. *He will likely be arrested,* she thought, feeling her stomach twist. *If that be the case, he is as good as tried and hanged.*

Just before dinner, the magistrate called Lucy to his private study. The constable had left three hours before without arresting Adam, but she knew that a bellman had just delivered a note to the magistrate. He was holding it in his hand when she tapped on the open door.

"Sit down, my dear," the magistrate said, gesturing to his

own large comfortable chair. Lucy sat, perching uneasily. She did not come into this room very often, since the master did not like his stacks of paper to be disturbed, and she certainly never sat in the magistrate's own chair.

"I'll be with you in a moment," he said. "I just need to finish this letter."

As Lucy waited, her gaze drifted to the portrait of the family above the fireplace. The magistrate was seated at the center, in his robes, taking the viewer's gaze head-on. The mistress, looking lovely in a midnight blue gown, sat beside him, smiling warmly down at baby Sarah in her lap. Adam, dressed to imitate the magistrate, stood solemnly at his knee. Although he was looking up at his father, there was a slight smile on his lips.

For the first time, Lucy noticed that in the portrait, Adam's right hand was positioned as if he were pointing. Following the direction of his index finger, she looked to the bottom right-hand corner of the painting, where, in the dark shadows, the family dog was tussling with what might have been the household cat. She smiled herself when she saw it.

The magistrate, about to speak, followed her gaze. "Oh, yes, indeed, I always assumed that Adam was smiling at me, his honored father! What a laugh I had one day, working on a court brief, when I looked up and saw this little joke painted in the portrait! It makes you see it all in a different light, doesn't it! The honorable Master Hargrave has been supplanted in honor by a scuffling cat and dog!"

Lucy nodded but looked questioningly at the magistrate. His smile faded, and he seemed to have difficulty finding the words. "Constable Duncan, the king's man who was here earlier—a good man, actually, I inquired around. Well, he be-lieves he has identified Bessie's murderer."

"Oh, no! I don't believe Adam did it, sir!" Lucy cried. "Not for one moment! They've made a dreadful mistake—"

Master Hargrave held up his hand. "Thank you for that. Your loyalty is commendable. No, I'm afraid it is not Adam."

Lucy exhaled, still feeling uneasy. The magistrate stared at the letter in his hands again. "I'm quite pained to tell you this. They intend to arrest your brother, William, for Bessie's mur-der." He crumpled the letter in his hand. "The constable was good enough to send this note. He wanted you to learn this news from me, not out on the street. Will is to be kept in Newgate until the spring assizes in a few weeks."

A great buzzing filled Lucy's ears; she could not stop seeing the sickening image of Will swinging from Tyburn tree. The bile rose in her throat. She had to swallow several times before she could focus. "Will?" she repeated. "How can that be? He had nothing to do with this!"

"He was courting Bessie, and depending on which story they plan to tell, either she threatened to break off their en-gagement, or he did not wish to be trapped in wedlock to her. Either way, witnesses state that he threatened to kill her."

"No!"

"Adam told me so himself. Indeed, it was that same mis-begotten pub brawl that got your brother into trouble."

Will and Adam—together at a pub? Lucy shook her head.

"Such words will not stand up in every court," the magis-trate continued, "but they could well damn him in some of my fellow judges' opinion."

"I don't believe it!" she said. "It can't be true."

The magistrate unexpectedly looked sad. "There is the truth, my dear, and there is the law. But your brother's guilt shall not be assumed, by me or any of my peers of the Bench, until he stands to defend himself in a few weeks' time."

·13·

Lucy moved quickly through the market stalls and the sellers, not wanting to be intercepted by an acquaintance. She was headed to Newgate for the first time, instead of staying to shop for cheese and lamb for supper. A market basket slung casually over one arm, Lucy darted effortlessly between the peddlers and fishwives, glad for once that her small size allowed her to move so nimbly. Two weeks had passed since Will was arrested, and Lucy hoped he was faring well enough in jail. Everyone said Newgate was a fearful, terrible place.

Lucy stopped when Newgate loomed darkly before her, casting a monstrous shadow. Nervously, she walked toward the entrance, where two bored guards stood stiffly. The sight of soldiers always made her a bit nervous, reminding her of that terrible day so long ago when Cromwell's armies had waged war against the king's men on her father's fields.

She remembered how she and William had huddled in the hay for hours, until the air grew silent and cold. Finally, they had ventured forth to find their parents. Lucy remembered little enough of her father, who died a few years later, but she would never forget the sight of him kneeling on the ground, crying as only a broken man could and crumbling fistfuls of dirt as his fields smoked all around him. He had lost everything, but she did not truly understand until she was much older. Her mother, she still remembered, was holding the hand of a young red-coated soldier with a great scarlet wound across his chest. The boy was dead, but still her mother had held his hand. "So young," she had repeated over and over. "His poor mother shall never know his death." It was Will who had protected her, that day and through those next anguished weeks, as their family numbly retrieved their farm from the rotting corpses.

Now Lucy lifted her chin, mustering her courage. Just as Will had not failed her so long ago, she could not fail him now. Booksellers milled about the dusty courtyard, their pockets and sacks bulging with chapbooks and penny pieces, spreading the news of recent executions. As she drew closer, a horrible stench assailed her nose.

One of the guards took notice of her. He had a shock of red hair and freckles that stood out against his pale skin. "Whatcher want, little girl?" he asked, leering down at her. Lucy was glad that she had worn her oldest, loosest smock, so that she would seem too young for their lechery. The other glanced at her but then turned his attention back to the courtyard, not caring for such small sport.

Lucy straightened her shoulders but tried to sound like a young witless girl. At least it was easy enough to sound afraid. "If you please, sir, I should like to see one of your prisoners." She decided she would not give Will's name unless absolutely necessary, since he was there on capital charges and they might not let her in to see him.

"Oh, yeah? Whatcha have there?" The guard pawed at the basket.

Instinctively, she clutched the basket closer, remaining childishly silent.

"Who you coming to see?" The guard tried again.

Reluctantly, she told them, and this time they both guffawed. "Oh, yeah? Nothing's going to save that gent, for sure. He'll be swinging within the month!"

A chill seeped under Lucy's skin, as if she had been out walking in a freezing rain.

"You may as well just go home, little girl."

Lucy shook her head defiantly, trying to hold fast to her nerve. She would not go home without seeing Will. A thought struck her. "Perhaps you fine sirs could do with a spot of wine?" she wheedled.

For the first time, the men looked interested. The one who had done all the talking held out his hand. She quickly handed him the flask. "Now let me in," Lucy demanded.

He took a long swallow and, wiping his mouth with the back of his hand, tossed the flask over her head to the other man. The second guard wordlessly unlocked the gate and then muttered something to a guard standing inside. More kindly now, with a few swigs of spirits inside him, the red-haired man pointed into the dark passageway. Lucy shivered but moved forward.

"All right, lass, you've paid the toll," he said, smirking. "Just follow Matthews here, and give him a shout when you're ready to come out. And miss—" Lucy turned to face him—"mind you take care in there. We won't come in to look for you."

The guards' laughter followed her as she stepped into the cold, dark passageway. Lucy stopped, adjusting to the darkness. Pitiful cries and moans echoed about her, and a distant dull clanging of metal made her toes curl. A great stench assaulted her nose, and she stopped for a moment with her hand to her mouth, completely overcome.

Prisoners, chained and shackled, rotted away on dirty straw pallets, their hair matted and tangled and their beards long and wild. In varying states of undress, they sat in pools of their own vomit, excrement, and blood. Some lay beside their wooden trenchers, as if they had given up the very will to eat, not even bothering to swat the flies that buzzed about their faces or to shoo away the rats that defiantly claimed morsels of moldy food. A few prayed in corners, beseeching God to deliver them from their terrible suffering.

As the prisoners saw Lucy, they reached their hands out piteously to her, some begging her for food, others merely mouthing their pain, not even realizing that their lips no longer made sounds. When one of them grabbed her arm as she passed, Matthews raised his baton and swiftly brought it down on the prisoner's head. Lucy winced as the prisoner fell back to the floor, blood gushing from his brow.

Even as Lucy turned her head from the horror of human

misery, another sight caused bile to rise in her throat. She vomited right there in the corridor. Two corpses, beheaded and dismembered, lay strewn about the floor of a small room that led from the corridor. The stench of human flesh and something else violated her nose. She dimly wondered what the sickly, spicy smell could be, and she began to sway.

Dimly, she recollected John telling her once how the hangman would boil the heads of men who had been drawn and quartered in a mixture of bay-salt and cumin seed, to keep them from putrefying before their relatives could claim their bodies for burial. *Why had he told her that?* she wondered dully. *Why had she wanted to know?* Gagging, she stumbled down the corridor. She held her posy to her nose and breathed deeply, hoping to ward off the evil humors.

"In here." Matthews gestured gruffly. "Don't be too long now."

As she stepped fearfully into a small, dank room, two men exclaimed her name, one astonished, the other angry. "Lucy!"

"I'll let yer out in half an hour," the guard grunted. "Best be ready, or I'll lock ye up, too!"

Not sure if he meant it, Lucy nodded, trying to hide a gulp, her attention fixed on Will. He sat on a dirty straw pallet, his back against the stone wall. His bloodshot eyes contrasted weirdly with his pale face, and frankly, he was filthy. Lucy was relieved to see, though, that otherwise he looked well enough. Adam, his hair and clothes immaculate, sat on a low stool beside him.

In two steps, Lucy crossed the cell and knelt by Will. "Brother, how do you fare?"

For a second, Will just clasped her hand and tilted his head back, eyes closed. No one spoke. Then he opened his eyes and stared at her. "Lucy, what possessed you to come? How did you get in here?"

Adam stood stiffly in the corner, his arms crossed, his face a mask.

Lucy tossed her head. "I needed to see you! Oh, Will, I don't understand! How could they have—?" Seeing his ashen face, she realized that weeping would not help. Instead, she held out her basket. "I brought you some victuals. I had to give the guards the flask of wine, for I feared they would not let me in if I did nothing to smooth the way."

Lucy regarded her brother. He reminded her of a lame horse she had once seen at a neighboring farm, broken in spirit and health, knowing he was defeated, before being felled by a farmer's merciful knife. Sighing, she turned her attention to Adam. "What are you doing here?"

"He thinks he can help me, help me plead my case," Will said, taking an indifferent bite. "I think it's a bit of a lost cause myself."

"No! Will! You mustn't say that!" Lucy cried, aghast.

"I agree, Will," Adam said. "These charges do not make a whit of sense, and I'm determined to get to the root of it."

Without thinking, Lucy laid her hand on Adam's sleeve. "You must! Will must be proved innocent!"

Looking down at her, Adam shifted uncomfortably. Lucy pulled her hand back hastily.

"I don't think there's much anyone can do," Will said. "I

shall commend myself to God. He knows my spirit. He knows my conscience and my innocence. That is all that matters." Dispirited, he sank back down on his pallet, returning his gaze to the ceiling.

Lucy felt uneasy. "No, Will! You must defend yourself at a trial, else you will be hanged for sure!"

"He's not going to be executed!" Adam glared at Lucy. "I will be back tomorrow. Come, Lucy. It's time for you to go."

After quickly embracing her brother, Lucy allowed herself to be led out of Will's cell, Adam gripping her arm firmly. Her head down, he hurried her past the sickness and atrocities and out of the jail without a word. Once they were outside Newgate and in the bright sunshine, Lucy shook off his hand. "What are we going to do?" she asked.

Adam frowned. "What possessed you to come to Newgate? 'Tis no place for a woman, especially one as young as you, and unaccompanied to boot! You're lucky you got out alive."

Lucy scowled back. "I think that it is my right to visit my own brother! Anyway, 'tis no matter to you!" Resentfully, she recalled herself. "Sir."

For a while, neither spoke as they crossed the field back to the path that would take them to Lincoln Fields. The first few flowers of spring were starting to poke up in the grass. Any other day, Lucy would have enjoyed the soft freshness all about her, the sunlit promise in the air. Today, though, her heart was tight and cold, and there was little she saw but the well-trod ground beneath her. Try as she might, she could not shut out the terrible images that had just assaulted her senses, nor what

Will was facing now. Thinking about what Adam had said to her brother, she asked, "Do you really think you can help my poor Will?"

Without responding, Adam appeared to be judging the large patch of mud and dung heaps that covered the trek. A number of carriages must have passed by recently, their wheels spinning the mud, creating deep harrows, and leaving swill from the horses. With a quick measured leap, he crossed to a bit of dried grass. Lucy jerked her skirts up and followed him.

"Right. Well." Adam ran a hand through his hair. "Here's the thing, Lucy. The testimony against your brother is rather compelling."

"What do you mean? How can that be true?" Lucy demanded.

Adam brushed a few leaves off a mossy tree trunk that lay close to the trek. "Here, let us sit a moment," he said. "Let me see if I can explain it to you. Indeed, it will help me make sense of these facts, as they were, to see what truth we can find."

He didn't speak right away. Lucy, anxiously tapping her foot on the ground, had to will herself not to speak.

"Here's what I understand," he began, slowly working out what he knew of Will's movements. "Will had been visiting with Bessie earlier that day—"

"He was?" Lucy exclaimed. "I never saw him!"

Adam regarded her steadily, with the slightest lift to his eyebrows. She flushed, realizing what he meant. "Oh." Then curiosity got the best of her. "Where were they?"

"Well, as a matter of fact, in a secluded field by the house. It seems a neighbor may have seen them there. Will was not

altogether clear on this point, but as near as I can make out—"
He hesitated.

"It was where she was killed, wasn't it?"

"Yes, I think so." He sighed. "But, as I was saying, he was
with Bessie from about noon to two. They seem to have had
a bit of a row, though, from what Will has told me. Afterward."

"A row? What were they arguing about?"

Adam shrugged. "I'm not sure. At that point, I believe, he
went to the Muddy Duck for a spot of ale, which is where Lucas and I found him."

"He didn't tell you what they had argued about?"

"Not in so many details, though I think I got the gist.
Bessie seems to have been with another man. Del Gado. The
painter."

Images of the pictures Lucy had glimpsed in Del Gado's
satchel rose in her mind. It was too bad Will had learned what
Bessie had done, Lucy thought. Will, for all his teasing roguish ways, was not a man to be second to another. He talked
of girls like Cecily who kept their virtue, but she knew he would
lie with a pretty girl if he could. He was no doubt very angry
with Bessie for being with another man. Lucy exhaled. She
turned her attention back to Adam's account.

"Unfortunately, as I learned later, some witnesses—a tinker
and a potter's wife—saw them yelling and Bessie rushing back
to the house sobbing." He paused. "At any rate, we had barely
ordered pints when I saw an acquaintance. I went over for a bit
of a chat." He hesitated again.

"Well?" Lucy demanded. "Then what?"

He continued. "In the meantime, Will and Lucas had a bit

of a chat, too. For about three-quarters of an hour, I would imagine. My acquaintance and I finished our conversation, and I returned to the table. At that point, we were joined, unbidden, by another. A bit of a lout. You may remember him—Richard, that oafish stableboy that we, ahem, met on Easter night."

"Richard!" Lucy croaked. Recollecting the livery man who had pawed at her in the stable turned her mouth dry as hay. "What did he want?"

"Richard and his men had a few drinks in them. Indeed, they were itching for a fight. 'Twas William, I believe, who took the first swing, though Lucas, too, soon entered the fray."

"Lucas? Why?"

"Richard had claimed to have seen Del Gado's pictures of Bessie, describing them in great detail. Lucas holds both you girls in high regard, and Richard's words did taunt him to strike a blow."

His answer puzzled her. "What do you mean? What do I have to do with this? I had never even met Master Del Gado before he visited the house. The night Bessie disappeared. I certainly never posed for him."

Adam looked away, grimacing as if he had tasted a bit of wormroot. "Well, Richard implied that you were both lasses of easy virtue, and that since you were serving in my house, I had found a way to, that is to say, we had—" He stopped.

"We had what?" Then she took in his discomfort. Realization flooded over her, and she flushed. "Oh! But you would never—!"

"I would never?" Adam asked. She thought he smiled.

Lucy flushed even more. "I mean, I would never—!" She stamped her foot. "Oh, you know what I mean! But why did he say that? About you and"—she swallowed—"me?"

"I think you know that, while I share the scruples of my father, other men like Richard do not, and would not think twice of having relations with, er, a comely young lass living in their household," Adam said, anger rising in his voice, "her virtue be damned. They assume that all men are like themselves, coarsely fulfilling their needs as they choose, no matter the cost to those who would suffer for those needs."

"I know that, Adam. You are a good man. As is your father. I thank you for that," Lucy's voice was small.

He frowned. "Lucy, I hope you are not thanking me for not dishonoring you and destroying your virtue. Such is the world we live in, to be sure, but I hope you cannot believe I would view you or any other servant as chattel for my needs." He swatted a fly buzzing by his face. "Let us move off this distasteful subject. Suffice it to say, Lucas grew angry and punched Richard. I saw no need to keep restraining Will. We all three quickly got into it. After a bit, I recalled myself, and"—he snorted—"my position as a magistrate's son."

Lucy rubbed her jaw, trying to take in everything he was saying.

He continued. "I then convinced Will and Lucas that it was time to leave. Here, we parted company. Lucas and I went home, Lucas, I fear, the worse for wear. Will left, too, and that was the last we saw of him that day. He told me, at the time, he was going to the theater to visit a lady love of his. Hoping, I'm afraid, to forget poor Bessie."

The orange seller! Lucy thought in a flash.

"However, this was not true. He has since told me that he was, indeed, still furious with Bessie. He felt he was cuckolded by her, and he was truly enraged that she had let her virtue be compromised in such a way. He was looking to finish the fight with Richard, blaming me for having ended the fight too soon."

"No!" Lucy said.

"I'm afraid so," he said grimly. "As it turns out, they did exchange a few more wallops at the pub. Not right away, though. Later. For Richard had come after me, having known my intention to interrupt the cock and dog baiting in Southwark."

"That was after supper, then, that you went down to the ring," Lucy recalled. "So Richard left the pub and sought you out? What, to continue the fight with you?"

"Something like that," Adam said. "Someone at the Muddy Duck must have overheard the conversation I had with my acquaintance, so Richard knew where to find me. I admit that I was quite surprised when he appeared in the baiting ring just as I was trying to stop that sorry spectacle."

He grinned without mirth. "I stood with several Quakers, but I quickly found myself sadly outmatched. He and his men focused their attack on me, which is how I got those stripes from Richard. He was glad to strike me down, I can tell you that. Thankfully, other Friends came about. They disavowed my fists, for they are a peaceful folk who refuse to raise a hand against their fellow man. One, Jacob, plied me with spirits to soften the pain and sheltered me in his own abode. In the morning, he helped me home, bringing me in his cart, as I could scarcely stand. The rest you know." He paused. "I shan't be in a hurry to enter a ring like that again, I tell you. Now you know the extent of my wretched heroism."

Lucy shivered. She remembered seeing Adam's bloody torso after he had stumbled out of that cart. Privately, she thought he was rather brave to have tried to stop the despicable cruelty. She squirmed now to think of the low opinion she'd been holding of him recently. How wrong she'd been! For a moment, she wanted to cry.

Unaware of her internal turmoil, Adam went on. "Will says now he went back to the Muddy Duck and got bloody hammered on ale while waiting for Richard to return. The problem is, he cannot remember most of the details because of the drink. He remembers exchanging a few wallops with Richard, and then he went off, finally sleeping off his drinks in a ditch."

"Well, then!" Lucy pronounced in triumph. "There's surely folks at the pub who can say they saw Will then? The tavern keeper? Barmaids would no doubt remember him; he's a fine fellow. What? Why are you shaking your head? Where are you going?"

Adam had stood up and was walking along the path again. "No, Lucy. I'm afraid there are no witnesses who can help. There are plenty, to be sure, who saw him take drinks and brawl with Richard, but the field where Bessie was killed was close, not one mile off. Richard claims—with great malicious speech—that William rushed off 'with a murderous look in his eye,'" Adam spat. "The lying blackheart even says that William swore to have Bessie's blood ere the night was over! Later, his mob of curs alleged they saw him running away from Rosamund's Gate with blood all over his hands."

"No!" Lucy stopped, feeling faint. She peered up at Adam. "That's not possible!"

"Yes," Adam replied grimly, "which is why it will be so hard for William to refute these claims. If I had my way, such words of hearsay would not be permitted as evidence, but indeed they may damn his portrait of innocence."

"That's a monstrous lie!" Lucy cried. "Bloody bastard! I would wring Richard's disgusting neck, but that would mean I'd have to be near him! Can you not talk to your father and ask him to speak to the justice who will preside over Will's—"

"No! Lucy! He cannot! We cannot subvert the justice system—"

"You said it yourself!" Lucy said, sobbing. "It's all hearsay and lies! How can you let this happen? What goes on in all those books of law anyway, that there are no means to help my brother in this most dreadful hour?"

His face was anguished. "Lucy, I—"

She turned away. "I've got to find a way to help my brother. Since you cannot, I will find someone else who can."

·14·

Lucas?" Lucy called, knocking softly on the vestry door. Still unsettled by her conversation with Adam the day before, she thought to seek out Lucas. Walking in, she felt the air change, growing cooler. The slight chill of the church always surprised her, so pleasant in the summer, so frigid in the winter. She stepped quietly through the nave, where several candles were already lit. Finding a penny in her pocket, Lucy put it in the offering box, lighting a candle for Bessie and for her own father, dead near five years now.

Lucy remembered when she first starting attending St. Peter's with the Hargraves. The small stained glass window above the altar—hidden for the years Cromwell had controlled England—had just been replaced. The smooth wooden pews and the choir loft had retained their peaceful quality, a striking vestige of the church's Catholic past. The rood screen served as a dim reminder of long-ago religious controversies.

Not seeing Lucas, she sat down in a pew, looking reverently at the newly restored images of Jesus. If she looked hard enough, she could still make out an image of the Virgin Mary smiling over a nursing baby. Unlike the other images on the altar, it was not surrounded by lit candles. Pictures of Mary and St. Peter recalled the beliefs of the bloody papists, and most people knew not to speak of them much. It was rather remarkable that such an image had survived, and yet Lucy was rather glad that it had.

Lucy didn't know how long she'd been praying when she noticed an odd thumping sound from beyond the central part of the church, toward one of the apses at the south side. Wondering if it might be Lucas, Lucy moved toward the sound, noticing in passing that someone had just lit a small taper by the portrait she had been admiring earlier. An object on the floor, near the bench, caught her attention. She picked it up. It looked like a necklace made of smooth wooden beads on a sturdy cord. It was then that the thumping sound started again, and what sounded like someone groaning.

From the other direction, where she stood with the odd necklace, she heard footsteps. Lucy stepped back into the shadows. Lucas appeared and stopped abruptly when he saw the candle. Frowning, he snuffed it out with a quick pinch of his fingers and then passed into a curtain on the other side of the apse. There was a muffled shout—was it Lucas?—and she heard someone respond in low angry tones. The odd thumping stopped. She began to creep away.

"Lucy?" Lucas called, suddenly back in view. "What are you doing here?"

Lucy held out the necklace. "I found this." She jerked her head. "Over yonder. I thought someone must have lost it. Um, is everything all right? I thought I heard a noise."

He gave her a sharp look but took the cord of beads from her. "Do you know what this is?"

Lucy shook her head. "No, but it looks so worn and smooth, I would suppose that its owner must be missing it. She will want it back. It's pretty."

Lucas laughed. "If that be true, I can assure you *I* will not be approached by its owner."

At Lucy's puzzled look, he laughed again, adding, "It's a rosary. Used by the Catholics to pray."

Lucy stared at him. "That would mean that a Catholic was here, praying in this Anglican church?"

Lucas took her arm and began to steer her back toward the vestry. He had pocketed the rosary. "There are papists everywhere, I'm afraid. They come here, I think, because we are an old church. You probably don't know this, but the catacombs below are full of marble saints, albeit without their heads. Knocked off last century when Henry the Eighth stopped being Defender of the Faith." Lucas chuckled. "But I do not think you came here to talk about the bloody Catholics, or our ongoing war against them."

"No," she said. "Not right now."

"This way," he said, leading her through a small door at the north end of St. Peter's. Lucy had never ventured through this part before, the offices and living quarters of the men who ran

the church. As soon as she was sure no one was about, she
turned to him, finding his eyes fixed eagerly on her.

"Please, Lucas!" Lucy said. "I need you to help William."

"Help him?" Lucas asked, turning slightly away. "How?"

"I thought perhaps we could go talk to the constable! Adam
said there was no use trying to talk to the presiding justice. I
thought, though, if we could talk to Constable Duncan and—
why are you shaking your head? You know Will did not murder Bessie."

"Alas, I do not know that, dear Lucy."

The starkness of his words made Lucy's mouth fall open.
"But you, you could not think that?"

"Heartsick I am to say it," Lucas said, taking Lucy's hand.
"Sad as I've been over Bessie's death, it pains me deeply that
your brother has been accused of this terrible crime."

"But—" Lucy interrupted, tears threatening to spill.

"By God's grace, Lucy! I do not know that he did not do it,
and I could not swear to it in court as a man who will be taking the cloth soon! At best, I could say that I believe his heart
is not that of a murderer, yet I know that he was very angry at
her that day."

Seeing her stricken face, Lucas tried to explain. "Well, you
see, dear Lucy, when Adam and I saw him, he was quite bothered by Bessie."

"Surely not angry enough to *kill* her!"

"I should think not! As God is my witness, he was angry
with her. She had all but cuckolded William, he who wanted
to marry her!"

"Marry? Truly, he said that?" Will had been genuinely distraught by Bessie's death, but with all his lady loves, it was hard to believe that he would have actually wed her.

"Yes, indeed. He told me so. In a few years' time, of course. He wanted to be his own man, with his own trade. Indeed, Richard, that boorish cur from the Embrys', was egging us on, saying that he had seen—" He stopped short, deferring to her sensibilities.

"Del Gado's sketches of Bessie," she supplied. "Yes, I know."

"Well, nothing inflames a man so much as to know that his lady love is stepping out on him."

"That was before she knew William! I know it to be true!"

"That may be so. I just know that he was angry. That, and the babe, of course." He tapped his pen on the paper, as if willing a sermon to appear on the blank white pages. "I believe poor Will felt trapped. He may have wanted to marry her, but not just yet. And who's to say the babe was his? I can tell you, Lucy, with my hand on this Bible, that he was enraged enough to murder her."

Lucas's words were not making sense. "Babe? Trapped?" Lucy asked, confused. "What babe?"

Lucas looked sorrowfully at Lucy. "I just assumed you knew. I won't drag this out, then. Bessie was with child when she died. The child, of course, being Will's. Or so Bessie told him. As I said, he wasn't sure."

Lucy stumbled out of the room, tears blurring her vision, dimly hearing Lucas calling her name. With child? Oh, no! Poor Bessie! She clutched grimly at the stone walls. Waves of nausea threatened to overcome her as she trembled weakly. She remembered Bessie's illness, her tiredness, her bouts of moodiness. She remembered seeing Bessie letting out the seams of her work dresses. Too many sweet cakes, Bessie had laughed it away, and Lucy had believed her.

"Oh, Bessie." She sighed. "Why couldn't you have told me? I, who loved you like a sister!" Shaking, she began to weep.

A hand on her shoulder made her look up, expecting to see Lucas. Instead, Reverend Marcus was staring down at her. Lucas hovered in the doorway, his anguished face reflecting the torture and pain she felt.

"Grieving young Bessie, are you?" the reverend asked her.

For a moment, Lucy was surprised that the reverend knew who she was, but she realized, of course, that he'd seen her all these many Sundays past, standing by the Hargraves in their pew. She nodded, a little afraid. Even though he did not sound as fierce as he did when he took the pulpit, Lucy still felt afraid of him. Those eyes! They were too probing, too knowing. Lucas seemed to stiffen, and to Lucy, he looked afraid of what the reverend was going to say.

"I came back here to check on Lucas's sermon. He is to take the pulpit in my stead this Sunday morning, and I am afraid he is ill prepared, having not committed his sermon to paper and to practice."

Lucas, looking like a chastened schoolboy, shuffled his feet.

The reverend continued, his tone mocking. "Something about subduing the lust of the flesh, I should think. Avoiding the temptations of young she-devils. Young Bessie's tale will serve as a suitable parable, I should think."

A red-hot anger coursed through Lucy at the reverend's words. Seeing Lucas's misery was the only thing that kept her from screaming at the man. She wanted to rip and shred and tear at the reverend—just as his words had shredded her—no matter that he was a man of the cloth. Using Bessie as a parable, indeed! She clenched her fists tightly, her fingernails cutting into her skin.

"You'd best be getting back to your chores now," the reverend said, his eyes boring deep into her. It was clear he wanted her to leave. "Idle hands are the devil's tools."

Lucy began to feel her way blindly out of the church. Just as she reached the door, the reverend called to her. "Lucy!"

Reluctantly, she turned around. The reverend stood at the altar, much as she had seen him every Sunday, dark, captivating, and forbidding, the weight of the Almighty behind him. Even without his clerical garb, he was frightening in his godly authority. "I shall ask Lucas to add one more thing to his sermon. It comes from the Book of Exodus."

"Yes?" Lucy asked, desperate to leave the church.

"'He that smiteth a man, so that he die, shall surely be put to death!'" He began to laugh.

With that, Lucy fled St. Peter's, feeling his eyes boring into her every step of the way.

At dawn, Lucy awoke, a fantastic thought bouncing about in her head. Perhaps if she could find out more about the other girls, Effie and Jane, she could discover something new about Bessie's death. Although she could almost hear Adam questioning her logic, Lucy believed in her heart that they were connected.

"Adam thinks so, too," she whispered. The contents of his tobacco bag suggested this to be true. The murders had to be connected. Unless there truly were three monsters running about, as Dr. Larimer would believe. Lucy laughed uncomfortably to herself.

Still in her shift, she rummaged through her trunk and found the crumpled penny piece that related the sad but true tale of Effie's murder. She smoothed it out and found what she was looking for. Queen's Row in Southwark.

It seemed less risky to go to a stranger's house in a distant part of London rather than to Jane Hardewick's old employers, the Eltons, who might recognize her from church. "Since I'm planning to be a servant for hire, I can't have them carrying tales back to the magistrate," she said to herself. "I just need to find out how to find Queen's Row."

Before she could lose her nerve, Lucy tiptoed to the master's private study. To her surprise, she saw a light from under the door. The magistrate must still be awake. Trying to avoid a pang of conscience, she filled a tray with some rolls, a bit of Cook's jam, and a draft to keep the chill away. "Here you are, sir," she said, placing the tray on his desk. As she suspected, he had not lit his hearth, and she bent quickly to take care of it.

"Oh, Lucy, I was just thinking how I'd like a bite to eat. These briefs can be quite dry and cumbersome. You must have read my mind."

Madame Maraid's knowing face, poised over her crystal, passed into Lucy's thoughts. If he had been almost anyone else, she would have done the same silly impression of the fortune-teller. Instead, she suppressed a smile and concentrated on getting the information she needed from the magistrate. "Indeed, sir, 'twas no trouble. I'm sorry you've been up all night, sir." Lucy fidgeted a moment, looking at the map on the wall behind him. The details were hard to make out from across the room.

"Yes, Lucy?" the master inquired politely, shifting the papers on his desk. He followed her gaze. "Ah, you are looking at the map of London."

"Oh, well, sir, the map, sir," she stumbled. "Well, I've never really looked at a map up close, sir. I've never put it all together."

The magistrate put down the quill he had been rolling in his fingers and shook his head. "We must rectify this situation immediately. Come here, Lucy, let me show you how it all fits together." He beckoned to her, and she shyly stood beside him.

"I don't want to be a bother, sir. I can see you have work to do."

"Pah!" he exclaimed. "I should rather talk about this map anytime." He pointed to the middle of the map. "First, let me show you the Thames, one of the most important rivers in Europe. And here, you see"——he moved his hand toward the middle left——"is the original Old London, Londontown as the Romans called it." As he talked, he grew more excited. "Have you ever seen the Roman wall? No? You must stop by, the next time you are at market. I would show you myself, had I the time. But I shall show you how to find the original fortresses."

Quickly he pointed to the different parts of London, showing her the Tower of London, Whitehall, Lincoln's Inn,

St. Giles, and the main thoroughfares, Fleet Street, Newmarket, and Burrough High Street. "Here on the other side of the Thames, to the south"—he pointed at the bottom of the map—"is Winchester Palace, St. Mary Overy, Shakespeare's Globe, and the Rose."

"Where," Lucy broke in, "would one find Lambeth Palace?" After he showed her, she ventured, "And how would one get there? Take London Bridge, I suppose?"

"Aye," he agreed. Then he looked at her, his face grave. "How is your brother William holding up?"

Tears blurred her eyes. "He didn't do it, sir! I know he didn't."

He nodded. His eyes were kind, but Lucy could tell he didn't believe her.

As she walked to Southwark, Lucy worked out her story, munching on a bit of bread and cheese from a sack, thinking through her plan. Although a godly respectable household would be unlikely to take in a stranger with no references—indeed, even in the city, people looked askance at strangers outside the local community—she had thought of a way to get around that natural distrust.

Lucy had decided she would tell them her mum had died. Even thinking this terrible thought made her cross her heart and look for forgiveness toward the heavens. The fog that swirled about her was an ever-present witness to her feckless acts.

Before long she had crossed the Thames into south London. After pausing a moment to admire Lambeth Palace, she finally found her way to Walworth. She was terribly thirsty but had not seen any public wells along the way. She fingered the coins in her pocket. She hated to use them so frivolously, but she thought she might find a place to stop in for a pint and cool off.

There were a few shops and taverns, and she soon found the Elephant and Castle. A little nervous about being in a public house by herself, she scooted into a table in a dimly lit corner.

A tavern girl, little older than herself but far more worn in spirit, approached her with a friendly smile. "What will it be, miss?"

Lucy ordered a pint of ale and pulled out her bite of bread and cheese. Looking around the dimly lit pub, she saw there were only a handful of people in the room. There were a few women, Lucy was grateful to see, for she did not think her mother would approve if she could see her right now. A snatch of conversation from a group of young men in the corner caught her attention. Although they were not in scholars' robes, she guessed they were students from Cambridge or Oxford.

"This was most certainly a stop in *Canterbury Tales*," one man said, gesturing to the room. "Chaucer's pilgrims were definitely here."

Lucy looked around the room, noting the careworn timbers and uneven stone floor. She'd heard of *Canterbury Tales,* from listening to Sarah's tutor. Indeed, these young men reminded her of him—young, passionate, conversant in literature and philosophy. Now they seemed to be debating whether Chaucer had been influenced by Aquinas, another scholar she had learned about from her brief time in Sarah's classroom.

Lucy envied them. She'd seen a picture of Oxford once, and the image of its graceful spires had filled her with a great longing. Not just to see the university, though of course the notion drew her, but to be a part of it. To live and dream, to study and share her thoughts, to ponder the words of great men. Lucy scarcely dared to think of it. To be a man, to be a scholar—she could only imagine the freedom and the headiness of reading and writing without being encumbered by scullery duties.

The clamoring of nearby church bells brought Lucy up with a start. "Make haste, Lucy!" she scolded herself. "You've got work to do!"

Finding Effie's house required a little ingenuity and even more luck. Lucy did not want to make it obvious that she was seeking Effie's house specifically, so she found herself making conversation with different shopkeepers and sweeps to find their house. She didn't want to raise anyone's suspicions by her questions, or worse, become an object of gossip. She varied what she asked, taking different approaches that she thought would give her more information. To some, she pretended to be Effie's cousin ("Oh, you poor thing!" the older women would cluck). To younger men sweeping stoops or working leather, she batted her lashes a bit, saying she was really hoping to find work in the neighborhood.

As she slowly gathered information, she finally stood before the house on Queen's Row that the young tanner had pointed out to her. "They doubtless need help in that house," he had said. Though the white house he indicated was one of the biggest on the street, the magistrate's home was far more fine. "I know they've had a hard time keeping a serving lass since their one girl got herself killed."

"Killed!" Lucy feigned surprise. "In the house?"

"Oh, no! Not in the house! In some park, she was!" Suitably impressed with himself, the boy added, "But don't you worry, miss. I'll be glad to keep watch, neighborly like, you understand. You won't likely be running into the same fate poor Effie ran into, not when Roger is around!"

"Who killed her?" Lucy asked, as casually as she could. "The girl, I mean. Effie, did you say?"

Roger looked mysterious. "No one knows for sure. My money's on the master. He's a mean sort, he is."

Lucy's face blanched, but she kept walking, resolute. Roger, taking a moment to catch up, said, "Wait a minute. Maybe you'd best work somewhere else."

"I'll be fine," Lucy said curtly, wanting to shake him off.

Roger even wanted to come to the house with her. That she could not let him do, of course. "Don't you worry, Roger dear," Lucy said, repeating firmly. "I'll be fine."

At his dismayed look, she added, "If I get the job at the house, maybe we can go walking where no one's like to kill me." Giving what she hoped was a sufficiently flirtatious giggle, Lucy walked away without looking back.

Going around back to the kitchen, she knocked firmly on the stout oak door. Just as she'd hoped, an elderly servant opened it. She looked cross and sweaty. "What do you want? We've no deliveries expected today."

Bobbing a quick curtsy, Lucy took a deep breath. "If you please, ma'am. I am looking for work."

The woman, who looked to be in her sixties, stared at her, mistrust evident in her wrinkled face. She sniffed. "Who was so bold as to send you to us in this manner? I was not aware the master had gotten around to hiring a new lass."

Something flashed over the woman's face. Something Lucy caught but could not quite grasp. Fear? No, it looked more like guilt, and it was gone in an instant.

Lucy gave her brightest smile. This was not going as she had hoped at all. "I know, Missus—?"

She waited for the servant to supply her name. When she didn't, Lucy went on, her words more hurried. "Well, it's like this. My mum did die, just a few weeks back, and my dad did run off when I was just a babe. She used to do some odd jobs, laundry, sewing, and the like, but now I'm out on my own. I just thought I could work here a few days, not for pay but for a bit of food. Then I could get a reference and maybe set myself up proper. I'm a hard worker, I am."

Toward the end of her little speech, Lucy let her voice shake. The servant crossed her arms, filling the whole doorway. "The master, he ain't running no charity here. You'd best be off to the poorhouse, then, or I'll be calling for the constable. This ain't the place for you. You'd best run off."

"Missus Jones?" a man called from within the kitchen.

The servant stiffened, glaring at Lucy. "Now you've done it," she whispered.

A heavyset man in his thirties appeared behind Missus Jones. "What have we here?" he asked.

"A girl, sir. Looking to work here. Without no friends or family to vouch for her, either."

"Is that right?" he asked. His eyes were small and greedy,

and his face was fleshy and round. The overall effect was that he looked like a pig her family had once owned.

Lucy nodded. "Just for a little while, in exchange for food and a good reference, so I can get set up proper. I had heard you might be needing a maid."

The man laughed in a way that made Lucy nervous. "Yes, that's true. I think you'll do just fine. Come on in. I'm Anders, Samuel Anders."

"And does the young lady," the servant nearly spit out, "have a name?"

This Lucy had already prepared. "Sarah Johnson," she said quickly. "My mum and me, we used to live by Walworth. I've lots of neighbors who can vouch for me there."

The man laughed. She was starting to wonder what she had gotten herself into. "Jones here, she can show you around. Do some scullery tasks for her; the good Lord knows we haven't had the grates and pots cleaned in some time. Then, in about two hours' time, come see me, and we'll decide about your reference."

Lucy spent the next two hours scrubbing and cursing herself. Jones seemed to take a great pleasure in bringing her the most disgusting things to clean. What maid in her right mind would go do another full day's work for free?

After a while, Jones left Lucy to her efforts. By comparison, the pots at the magistrate's house were a pleasure to clean and polish. This house, too, was somber and chilly, and compared ill to the magistrate's warm and cheerful household.

Finally, Jones came back in with a pot of tea and some hard

rolls. "I reckon you've worked hard enough," she said gruffly. "Come sit with me."

Lucy sat down, holding her cup of tea gratefully in her cold fingers, well aware of Jones's scrutiny.

"I'm wondering why you came to this house. Surely, other homes are closer?"

Taking a bite of the roll, Lucy just shrugged. "I did hear tell that a maid who had worked here left sudden-like. So I thought—"

"Left sudden-like!" Jones exclaimed. "You cannot tell me that is what they"—she gestured angrily at the other homes on the street visible through the window—"are saying."

"Yes, all right. I did hear that your maid—Effie, was it?— had been killed. In a field some miles off . . . ?"

Unexpectedly, Jones seemed to choke up. "The girl was dirt stupid, that's true enough. To run off with a lover? I do not believe it to be true. More like run off from him!" she hissed.

"Him?" Lucy asked. "Who? I don't understand. "

"The master, of course. I knew it was only a matter of time before she fled. Taking up with all sorts, she was. I thought for a time she'd even become one of those dratted Quakers, but she was hardly the godly sort, if you catch my drift. Still, she did not deserve what happened here, or in that there field. The master, he did on more than one occasion—"

She broke off, hearing a door shutting in the hallway. Lucy looked at her in sudden fear. "He'll be waiting for you. If you want a good reference, best do what he asks. Better yet, take yourself out of here, fast as you can. Make your bed, as it were."

Afraid, all Lucy wanted to do was to bolt out of the kitchen and run all the way back to the magistrate's household. Yet if she wanted answers, this was the best chance. "I think I'd like the reference," she said.

Jones's face was set back in her hard mask. "Suit yourself. Don't say I didn't warn you."

She went into Anders's drawing room, noting with distaste how dirty it all was. The dust was thick, the grate had not been cleaned, and the chairs looked in sad array. Clearly, little effort had been made to keep the house tidy.

Anders cleared his throat, sounding a bit like a bullfrog Lucy would hear at the lake. "Jones tells me you've been cleaning pots all morning and have met Jones's particular standards. I can assure you, she is most discerning."

Lucy somehow doubted that, but who would turn down free labor?

"However, I must see you clean before I can lend my good name to a recommendation. I see you still have your apron on, and a clean rag. Let me see you clean that grate. On your hands and knees, my lass." He laughed jovially.

She looked at the grate and back at Anders. He was perspiring. Lucy remembered the stable, and what had nearly happened there. Shakily, she knew no one would heed her screams. Missus Jones was not like to help. It was bad enough for a young woman without a friend in the world, but for an old woman that could be the end. Jones probably overlooked her master's transgressions. Perhaps that was why she looked guilty when she mentioned Effie. Poor Effie! Had she been trying to escape the master's household when death caught up with her anyway?

Anxious to get away herself, Lucy began to cast about for an excuse to leave the room. "Let me get a bin," she suggested, trying to stall. "This grate looks like it has not been cleaned in some time."

"Never mind the bin," Anders said, his voice growing gruff and his body flushed. "Lift your skirts." He lunged toward her, his movements bovine and lumbering. Lucy nimbly jumped aside, but he still stood between her and the door.

"Help!" she screamed. "Oh, help!"

"There's no one to help you, my dear. Do let me take this moment"—he grabbed her with great meaty hands—"to thank you for first servicing my house and then servicing me. It's been so long since my Effie left. I've been craving female company."

Hoping to divert him, she screamed, "Was it you? You who killed Effie? That's what they all think, you know!"

Momentarily startled, he stopped. "What?" he roared. "I did not kill Effie! 'Twas those damn Quakers, I have no doubt! Why would I kill the best lay I'm likely to get—"

His face, already a mottled purple, started to twitch. Dropping her arms, he began to claw at his throat, gasping for air, flopping about on the floor. "Did—not—kill—Effie." He groaned softly, spittle dropping from his lips.

Hesitantly, Lucy looked at him. "Uh, Missus Jones?" she called.

The door opened. The servant must have been listening at the door. She came in and calmly regarded Anders, who was still twitching, but less violently than before. They both watched him in silence. Then he stopped.

"Is he dead?" Lucy whispered.

"Let us hope so." Jones bent over the body. "He's not breathing, and I can't hear his heart. Good thing, bloody bastard." She straightened up and glared at Lucy. "Look, girl. He was a bad one, he was. I heard you asking him about Effie, and I don't know why. I will tell you, though, that there's no way that he, bullying coward that he was, told you a lie on his deathbed. He didn't kill her."

Lucy gulped. "Do you know who did it, then?"

"One of those blasted Quakers. She was mad about one of them, stupid git. Didn't know, did she, they're all touched in the head. Found out too late, didn't she." Jones shook her finger at Lucy. "Best you count yourself lucky and hightail it back to where you came, and pretend you never set foot in this misbegotten house. I've some things to take care of here."

Lucy got her meaning full and clear. Jones wanted Lucy to go so she could pick through Anders's belongings for anything of worth, a common enough practice, to be sure. Indeed, Jones had already pulled out a sack and started to fill it with things she could easily peddle. Likely as not, she'd tell no one of Anders's death until she had near robbed him blind. She could clear out, a richer woman than she'd ever been, with none the wiser about her criminal misdeed.

Lucy fled, saying a small prayer for Effie, who had not been protected as she should have been. As she passed the Thames, she longed to jump in and wash away the vile aura that enclosed her.

·15·

May Day came and passed. The grimness in the city kept people out of the streets, a heavy fog further quelling the Londoners' spirits. No blooming bouquets, no dancing, and nary a maypole in sight, only withered dried flowers keeping death at bay. Every time Lucy went to market, she heard gossip about the spreading distemper. Spotted fever, some called it.

"It's them godforsaken lot in St. Giles," one neighbor sniffed, a burly woman known to everyone as Goodwife Cruff. "We know they have the sickness. I heard tell of near three dozen secret burials, just last week."

"The mayor should just board the whole lot of them, and let them rot," another fishwife added. "We've no need of their sickness here."

The master insisted that the household keep to its schedule

the best they could, so he and his wife sometimes still dined with friends and neighbors. Lucy was helping the mistress for supper at the Drakes'.

"Nothing too fancy," the mistress said to Lucy. "We are a household in mourning, even though Bessie was but a servant, she was one of us for five years now. It would be unseemly to dress too fine."

Lucy nodded, absently smoothing her mistress's hair into a knot pinned securely onto her head. She was still preoccupied with what she had learned, or rather what she hadn't learned, from being at Effie's house. What had the Quakers to do with this? Would it be worth asking Adam about it? Surely, he would laugh at such wild accusations. Besides, weren't there hundreds of Quakers all over London, holding their secret conventicles, preaching in the streets, filling the jails? The whole day had been for naught, having brought her no closer to understanding what had happened to Bessie. Her thoughts were jumbled, flashing back to Anders's dead body. *I've got to get a hold on myself,* she sighed.

"The black combs tonight, I think, dear. The red roses do something wondrous to my hair." The mistress reached into the small box on the dressing table that held her most precious earbobs, combs, and jewelry. "You know, I find that I miss Bessie quite dearly. Does that surprise you?"

"Oh, no, mistress," Lucy said, trying to smile. It still hurt her deeply to talk about Bessie. "I know Bessie was quite fond of you. I know she felt well treated and protected here."

"Protected," Mistress Hargrave repeated, pulling idly at a

loose thread on her skirt. "Yes, that's a funny thing to say. How protected could she have been? I should have done more. I would have helped her find a place for the babe."

Their gazes met in the mirror. The mistress spoke again. "Yes, I knew she was with child. What I don't know is—" She broke off. A second later she gripped Lucy's hand. "Do you know? The child?"

Lucy shifted uncomfortably. It hurt too much for her to bear thinking about. The mistress continued. She was trembling, Lucy could see. "The father? Who sired the babe? Tongues have begun to wag, you know."

Lucy gulped, for the mistress's words were an unwitting dagger to her gut. "I know not the truth, mistress. Bessie never unburdened her soul to me."

Mistress Hargrave went on, unaware of the pain she was causing. "I am the mistress of the household. It is I who is supposed to look after the good virtue and morality of my servants. In this, I have failed most abjectly. I lie awake at night. Could it have been a member of this household? Adam? Lucas?" she faltered, fidgeting with a small linen. "My . . . husband?"

"No, mistress!" Lucy averred. "That cannot be true. Even the most heinous gossip knows how devoted he is to you." Tears threatening to spill, Lucy added, "The babe was begot by William, my brother, I would suppose. Everyone knows they were coupling." *Or perhaps the painter,* Lucy added to herself but did not dare say.

The mistress looked contrite. "Ah, Lucy! You must think me heartless. I'm very sorry. How could I have forgotten?" The mistress rubbed a curing oil onto the fine wrinkles on her cheeks. "Do you think that is indeed what everyone believes? That it was your William, and not my son and not"—she paused—"my husband?"

"Indeed, mistress." Lucy could barely keep the bitterness out of her voice. "'Twas Will's passion for Bessie that seems to be setting the noose around his neck."

As she took the combs from her mistress's outstretched hands, Lucy's eyes widened. The combs were black with gold and red filigree roses, obviously made by a craftsman of uncommon skill. "Oh, these combs are beautiful," Lucy said breathlessly. "Where did you get them?"

"Oh, I can't quite recall," Mistress Hargrave replied. "The magistrate must have gotten them for me, during his travels. I believe they are Spanish or perhaps Flemish."

As Lucy carefully slid the combs into her mistress's hair, she knew she recognized them. The mistress had been wearing them in the painter's sketches. The combs were in the same style as the lacquered hairbrush set that Bessie had kept so hidden beneath her linens. *How odd,* she thought. A little notion began to nip at her mind. "Mistress Hargrave, how is your portrait coming along?"

If she wondered about the flow of Lucy's thoughts, the mistress didn't let on. She spoke without a hint of guile. "I don't rightly know. Bessie used to run such errands for me. Perhaps I shall send him a note by and by." The mistress grew more decided. "Yes, I'll write him a quick note that you could run over to him, inquiring about the status of my portrait and whether I need sit for him again."

"Yes, ma'am," Lucy said, her mouth tight. She busied herself with fixing the mistress's collar.

"No need to let anyone know of this little visit." The mistress put a stray hair back in place. "I should not like the magistrate to think me vain."

Early the next morning, Lucy slipped out of the house and made her way to Putney-on-the-Green, where Del Gado lived. The houses there were decent, mostly white with wood beams, a style that had become pervasive when Henry VIII had been king. These structures were not balanced so precariously against each other as was common in some of the more run-down parts around the city. Everyone knew that King Charles admired Del Gado, having specially commissioned him to paint his favorites at court. Most notably, the seductive and infamous Nell Gwyn, rumored to be the king's own mistress, had been lovingly rendered on canvas. However, the painter lived in a rather scandalous way, if the stories about him were indeed true.

When Lucy got to the house, she carefully compared the number to the address on the note. Yes, number five. She moved to the rear of the house, thinking to hand the note to a footman. The mistress had not asked her to wait for a reply, but she would not mind a bit of refreshment and a chat. Maybe she could get some answers.

When her first tentative knock went unnoticed, Lucy rapped on the wooden door with more force. A moment later, a young woman answered the door, and Lucy found herself gaping at her. Usually she could place a person in an instant, servant or nobleman, tradesman or convict. Everyone she knew dressed according to their station in life, and even when their fortunes rose or fell, it was not too hard to discern the place they fit in society.

This woman, however, defied expectation. She did not have the look of a lady, for her dress was cut shockingly low and her long dark hair fell loose about her shoulders. She wore no cap. Only the apron over her skirts suggested her to be a servant. What kind of servant was she, though, to be in such disarray and brazenly regarding Lucy's small, neat form? "What?" the woman asked, disinterested.

Lucy held out the note with a shaking hand. "This for Master Del Gado," she said. "Could you please give it to him?"

"You can bring it to him yourself," she said, a flounce to her skirts. "I'm no servant. 'Sides, he likes to see lasses when they come to the door. Though 'tis not likely he'd be interested in drawing the likes of you." She smirked.

Lucy hesitated at the door. She had no doubt that Del Gado had painted this girl many times, and more besides.

"Who is it, Marie?" Del Gado's lazy, elegant voice drifted from a partly closed door.

"Just a servant with a note for you, Enrique," Marie said. To Lucy, she said, "This way, girl."

Her manner haughty, Marie pushed open the door. She led Lucy into what should have been a drawing room, but this room was barely furnished and had none of the pleasing elegance of the Hargraves' home. A fire was crackling in the hearth, to be sure, but the room was dusty and the chairs looked grimy from the smoke. A few pieces of pewter lined the shelves. Cobwebs hung from the ceiling, and a mouse hole could be seen in the corner. A few sparse candles made long shadows that danced oddly when the air moved. The whole room emitted a depressed, neglected feel.

Looking about the room, Lucy was shocked by the portrait of a nude woman occupying a place of honor above the great fireplace. She appeared to be stepping from her bath, long tresses of auburn hair partially hiding her body from view. No innocent was she, Lucy thought, for her gaze was at once knowing and intimate and mysterious. A slight cough forced her to turn away.

Del Gado was regarding her carefully, smoke arising lazily from his pipe. Marie stood behind him where he sat in his chair, her arms wrapped around his neck. Her easy clutch made it clear she was not merely Del Gado's servant.

"Ah, my little curious kitten from the Hargraves'," Del Gado said, tapping his pipe into a small tray. "What has brought you here to my den?"

Lucy handed him the note, which he quickly perused. "So, your mistress wants me to resume the portrait," he mused out loud. "Alas, I've grown a bit weary of painting your dear mistress. She is a mite too wan for my tastes. I find it too hard to awaken *that* tiger!"

Marie's arms tightened around him. With difficulty, Del Gado extricated himself from her embrace and swatted her plump bottom. "Leave us a moment, love."

Flouncing out of the room, Marie flashed Lucy a warning. Catching the look, the painter smiled fondly. He stood up. "Yes, Marie is a tiger, too, but she has become predictable. I am weary of her. I need a new muse. Someone younger, fresher . . ." He took a step closer to Lucy and breathed deeply. "Sweeter."

Transfixed by his voice, Lucy stood stock-still.

"Perhaps you, my dear, should like to pose for me? I have many things to offer a girl such as you," Del Gado suggested.

"I do not want to pose for you," she whispered.

As if she had not spoken, he continued. "No, I can see, no mere trifles for you, no combs or dressing boxes or gilded mirrors or perfumes. A girl like you wants something different; I can sense it." He reached for a curly wisp that had escaped from her cap. "Perhaps you would like a small picture for your lover so he can delight in your loveliness. A token that you can bestow upon him." Lucy flushed, and he laughed, dropping his hand. "No, I can tell you want something from me but do not wish to say. That intrigues me, my love, yes, that intrigues me. Just know that when I think of it, you'll not refuse. I desire to know you, little one; I sense something in you, but no matter. I do not know yet where to place you, how to capture you." Del Gado's eyes drifted over her body knowingly. "You are still a girl, but the woman in there . . ." He sighed. He moved to open the door.

Knowing, even as she spoke, the pure folly she was venturing upon, Lucy seized her chance to find out what he knew. She pretended to reconsider. "I do not think my mother should like it if I posed"—she paused—"as you would have me."

"Ah, mothers. She would never know, my sweet. I can already see you, my little Psyche, a nymph in a simple white robe, perhaps just slipping off one shoulder here, revealing—"

Lucy interrupted before he could touch her. "You say you would give me something in return? Perhaps you could just do my eye. As you did for Jane Hardewick." Lucy held her breath.

A frown creased Del Gado's brow. He stepped back. "You knew Jane?"

"We worked together before I came to the Hargraves," she lied, figuring he would never know. "We were friends."

"And she showed you the eye?" he asked. The excitement that he had just displayed was fast fading. Lucy nodded, hoping he would not press for details.

"Yes, lovely girl. Made Marie jealous, which isn't too hard to do these days." He licked his lips. "I had to use a special ocher to get the brown of her eye right."

A dark shadow crossed his face. For a moment, he looked— what? Angry? Desperate? Disappointed? "Shame about the girl, though. Waste of lovely young flesh." Del Gado looked at Lucy sharply. She merely nodded. Then he stepped back, the earlier vulnerability she had glimpsed now disappeared. "Tell your mistress I shan't need her for any more sittings; the portrait the magistrate commissioned is finished. I'll have it sent over shortly. And Lucy," he added. "Remember. There's much I can offer you—more than you can imagine."

·16·

After supper had been cleared that night, Lucy brought a mug of mulled wine to Adam, taking care to leave the door wide open. A few thick law books lay about his room, various passages marked by any number of odd objects, including a feather, a rock, and a shard of wood. A sheaf of printed pamphlets was strewn across his writing desk. Placing the steaming mug on his desk, she waited nervously for him to look up.

After one last notation, his quill stopped scratching on the paper. "Thank you, Lucy." When she did not move, he added, "Yes, Lucy? Is there something else?"

He knows what I'm going to ask, she thought. She nodded at the papers on his desk. "Is that William's case?"

Adam grimaced slightly. "Yes. I'm afraid I haven't much new to tell you. I'm trying to work out the questions he must put to his accusers."

"You cannot ask the questions for him? I'm afraid he will not remember what to ask."

"No, I wish I could. You see, the law of this realm is set up so that a man may face his accuser and be able to question him. That is all well and good, but I have seen many a time when an accused man grows flustered, or is tongue-tied, or simply forgets to pose the right questions to his accusers. I've often thought that barristers should be the ones to pose the questions in court, so long as the accused agrees." He rubbed his forehead. "All I can do is try to keep him focused, so he'll ask the right questions," Adam said. "It's rather tricky, you see. He must plead a certain way, so we must think through what words he should say. We must, in essence, work out his defense. It shan't be 'learn the neck verse' either. Worst piece of advice a fellow can get!"

"How so?" she asked.

He explained. "One of the prison clergy taught it to him. The neck verse is the Fifty-first Psalm. It's a common enough strategy. If the accused can memorize it and speak it to the magistrate and jury during his trial, sometimes that means the prisoner can be passed off as clergy."

"Clergy are not harmed?"

"Sometimes they are spared. A fool's strategy, I can tell you that!" Adam slammed down his book. "The whole case is based on hearsay! There is no definitive evidence that Will did it."

"Because he didn't," Lucy said.

Adam glanced at her. "Of course. Unfortunately, Will had a motive and means—two things the law is most concerned with. Bessie was with child, probably his, and the jurors are likely to believe he did not wish to be hindered with wife and child when he's widely let it be known that he wishes to be his own master."

"Still, he had no need to kill her," Lucy said. "He could just have denied her, as men usually do in situations like these."

If Adam heard the bitterness in her voice, he did not let on. "Well, she was murdered in a fit of rage. It might be argued that Will killed her because he could see no other option. The courts might well have made him marry her, if she claimed he was the father to her babe."

Lucy looked up at the ceiling, despairing of his logic.

"Or," he continued, "the jurors could be convinced that Bessie was blackmailing him. And there were, of course, the stolen items. The constable might also say that Will had convinced her to make the theft and then killed her to maintain her silence." He raised his hand to stem her protest. "We know that was not the character of either Will or Bessie. The jurors, however, do not know that. So we must create doubt in the minds of the jury. That is our only hope here." Adam began to pace around the room, his steps on the wood floor softened by the leather slippers he wore.

Lucy watched him quietly. *Does he regret his offer to help?* Her lip curled. *He must think the case is impossible. What hope is there for William?*

Adam's next words confirmed her fear. "We could say that he had been drinking, which is of course true," he mused. "When he discovered her infidelity, and about the baby . . ."

"No!" she cried. "I won't allow it! It's not true!"

He went on as if he hadn't heard her. "'Tis unlikely to get

him out of jail, but it should do well enough to keep him from swinging at Newgate, to be sure. That will have to do."

Lucy wanted to slap him. This was her dear brother he was speaking of, not some common oaf out of the gutter. A life in jail was as bad as swinging. She marshaled her anger and tried to stay calm. Her tone was icy, reasonable. "What about the painter, Master Del Gado?"

"What about Del Gado, Lucy?" he asked, stacking the papers into a pile.

"He certainly knew Bessie. Indeed, he knew her intimately."

Adam shrugged and picked up the wine. "He had no motive."

"Yes, but he also knew Jane Hardewick!" she cried. "Quite well! What do you make of that?!"

Adam set the mug down heavily. "What do you mean? How could you possibly know that?"

"Sir, I was at Master Del Gado's today, and I—"

The force of his glare stopped her midsentence.

"Why were you at Del Gado's? For God's sake, Lucy! Are you completely addled?"

Lucy flinched. "I'll have you know that your mother, Mistress Hargrave, sent me and—"

"Of course she did." Adam picked up his mug again and set it down without taking a sip. "No thought about sending a girl like you into a scoundrel's den like that."

Lucy shuddered as he unconsciously echoed Del Gado's own words.

"By God, Lucy, it isn't right. Anyone can see you're a decent respectable innocent girl! Mother shouldn't have sent you there;

John should have gone to check on her precious portrait, which I *imagine* is the excuse she gave you! I've a good mind to say something to her!"

"Oh, no, sir!" Lucy cried. "Please don't! Mistress Hargrave did not want me to tell anyone she had sent me. I mean, I wasn't to tell the master. I mean . . ." She trailed off.

"All right, Lucy. I won't say anything. But sometimes my mother—" He muttered, "I mean, look at you! A girl like you! A man like him! Your brother would never allow it!"

Thinking of her brother made her remember why she had come to his room in the first place. "Oh, yes, sir! Do you think that Master Del Gado may have had something, er, to do with Bessie's death? I mean, he did paint her, and I know he gave her the box with the dressing brush and combs . . ."

"Combs?"

"Well, the combs like the ones your mother wears." Her voice faltered; she was unsure how to put her thoughts into words. "When I was dressing your mother's hair, I saw her combs. They were just like Bessie's, painted, I'm sure, by the same hand. I asked her about them, and she said they were a gift from your father. Forgive me, sir, I think they may have been from Master Del Gado." Lucy twisted her hands uncomfortably.

"Never mind about *that,*" Adam responded tersely. "I daresay everyone knows about mother's, er, *sessions* with the painter. Everyone excepting Father, that is, but that is neither here nor there. I'm afraid I'm not following you."

"It got me thinking. I knew Bessie and Mistress Hargrave had both posed for Master Del Gado, and I think he gave them the combs—"

"Yes, yes," Adam interrupted. "I understand *that*. What does this have to do with Jane Hardewick?"

Suddenly, Lucy felt trapped, like a hen before the butcher's knife.

He went on. "So somehow you assumed that Jane Hardewick had posed for Del Gado, too? You thought, what, that you would just ask him? Tell me, Lucy." Adam's voice grew hard. "Exactly how did this leap in logic come about? I'm quite eager to know."

Lucy glanced at his writing desk. The tobacco pouch was nowhere to be seen. Following her quick look, his eyebrows raised. "I see. In your infinite devotion to this household, you thought to make sure that all nooks and crannies, including the pouch containing the miniatures of two eyes, each from a different nameless woman, were thoroughly cleaned. Clearly, I underestimated how much a chambermaid—ahem, *lady's maid*—will snoop."

Lucy's hand tightened into a fist, but she willed herself not to cry. She felt something dear had slipped away. He no longer trusted her, she could see. A different thought arose, and she heard herself speak. "Why did you have a portrait of Jane Hardewick's eye, *sir?*"

Adam crossed his arms, his own face taut. "I found it where the poor woman was murdered. I assume it depicts her eye. I have no doubt you saw that I also found Bessie's comb. This object I also found where she was killed."

"But why—?"

"Why did I go searching these morbid scenes? Simple enough. I believe that when a crime has occurred there is often evidence that is overlooked. Our constables and our bellmen, good men though they may be, are given these positions because they've proved themselves capable of banging together the heads of drunken men. They know how to keep men from tearing each other apart in pub brawls. They know how to stop a bread riot." He shook his head. "For God's sake, they know how to keep watch, tell time, and shout a report at the hour. But what do they know of evidence? What do they really know of the law? Read enough legal testimony and it's obvious how many things are overlooked."

Lucy was not to be deterred. "And the other eye portrait? I know it was not of Bessie. 'Twas not the shape of her face. Whose eye was it?"

"Alas, I do not know. I found that miniature, too."

Awfully convenient, she thought, but did not dare say. Reading her doubt, he added, "I did find them. The first, I found on the street in front of our home, believe it or not. I still do not know to whom it belongs."

"On the street? In front of our home?" she repeated. "That would mean"—she broke off, a sickening thought coming to her.

"That this monster may have passed you in the street? That you may have seen him?" He ran his hand through his hair. "That he may have seen you? Believe me. I've thought all these things." He turned away then, not seeing her shiver. He went on. "So I too have been suspicious of Del Gado, knowing that this form of expression is peculiar to his hand. Even before that swaggard Richard showed us those sketches of Bessie, I knew enough of that dastardly painter to know that he usually ends up bedding his models. Forgive me the coarseness." He sighed in frustration.

"Yet, I'm sorry, Lucy, but I don't think the painter had any reason to kill Bessie. Unfortunately, he lacks motive."

"But he——" She paused, grasping for the right word. "He seduced her! You said so yourself."

A muscle twitched in Adam's face. For a moment he seemed amused, which renewed her earlier anger. How could she ever have thought he was kind or compassionate? Her cheeks turned a delicate shade of pink, but she continued breathlessly, her words tumbling out as she tried to make him understand.

"Don't you see? Perhaps it was he who got her with child! She had nowhere to go, nowhere to turn to, maybe she threatened to expose him for the"—again she paused, trying to find the worst words she knew—"for the dung beetle cad that he is!"

She imagined the scene. It all fit perfectly, yet Adam was shaking his head.

"I know, Lucy, I know Bessie was a good girl and he took that from her, but the jury won't see that. Perhaps if there were ever women on the jury! If you will forgive me for speaking so bluntly of your friend, the jurors will just see her as a fulsome wench, ripe for the plucking. Surely, they will see her transgression as her own folly. Indeed, we know him to be a philandering cad. The plight of a serving girl who has been taken in by the gentry is of little consequence."

Adam's words shocked her. "That's not fair!"

"No, Lucy, it isn't. After all," he said, pacing around the room, studiously avoiding her stare, "what is a serving girl to anyone in the privileged ranks? Indeed, it was foolish for her to have believed he would marry her; society would never condone such a match." He held up his hand at Lucy's hiss. "There's no denying Del Gado's of noble blood, though I daresay there's nothing noble about him. The reputation and standing of his family make him still notable in society, even though he's no doubt run through his inheritance and seems to laugh off his title. Indeed, for him, such an attachment would be a laugh, as he is unlikely to settle down with one girl when so many throw themselves before him for the taking."

Tossing some kindling on the fire, he continued. "Indeed, I am sorry to say that a rake like him might well see his reputation bolstered by his philandering. His art will only become more fascinating and sought after by foolish women with indulgent husbands." He stirred the fire with a poker. "And Bessie, little twit she could be, how would she not know this! She could not have expected marriage! There was nothing she could do to him, nothing with which she could entice or threaten him. Nothing that would induce him either to marriage or to murder."

"She was not a little twit!" Lucy said hotly.

Ignoring her, Adam said, "He is a man whose passions run deep, yet he is a man so self-interested that he will only pursue a woman until he has grown tired of her. As I suspect he did with our Bessie, and with my mother, another good-hearted but silly soul. It's good that you are so little likely to tempt a man like him, or you, no doubt, would be his next prey."

Stung by that last remark, and by what he said about Bessie, Lucy drew herself up in barely contained fury. "Bessie and me, maybe we're just simple girls. Bessie was just a bit dumb, getting herself mixed up with a member of the gentry who would cast her off. Perhaps that's what men of your kind do to a poor lass who has naught to offer but love." Her voice became shrill. "We've got feelings! And Del Gado *said* he wanted to paint me, he said so! So I guess he sees something in me, even if I am not tempting to some!" Stifling a sob, she added, "If there is nothing else, sir, I am off to bed."

Adam looked taken aback. "Lucy, I want to help, but I can only do what I can."

Her fury blazed again, true and full. "I do believe, sir," Lucy began hotly, "that you say you love the law and have studied all these wonderful books"—she waved her arm around the study—"and yet I do not think you can get beyond those words to see that the heart and soul, nay, the very life, of a good man are at stake." She wiped away a tear. "William may not be the best man, but he is a good man, and honest and true, and he deserves that the law regard him as such. And Bessie, whatever you think of her, was a good and true lass, too, who deserves the same justice as the very highest of high. Our lot in life may be to serve the likes of you, but we deserve more, sir. We deserve more!"

Her voice having broken at the last, she fled, not daring to see the effect of her words. Running up the steps to her little room at the top of her house, she moaned, her face in her hands.

"What did I just say?" She groaned. She did not think Adam would have her discharged, but would he refuse to help William now? She cursed her heedless tongue and spent a restless night hearing her words repeated in her mind, until the sun bid her to her Sunday morning chores.

As the family was leaving the church the next morning, Lucy edged up to Adam, her cheeks flushed. The words she had said—nay, shouted—yesterday still echoed in her ears, but she had to know how her brother was doing. "I was wondering, sir, how is my brother? I forgot to ask when we," Lucy stammered, "when we spoke yesterday."

"As well as can be expected, Lucy," he said, his tone cool. Clearly, he did not want to continue their conversation.

"I am seeing him today—"

"Lucy! Alone? That's hardly wise!"

"Oh, no," she said hastily. "Lucas is going to accompany me."

"I see. Well, take care. You can let him know that I shall, of course, come with him on Tuesday morning."

And then be done with him, and by extension be done with her as well, Adam's tone seemed to imply. Their growing friendship had been checked; no doubt, the right and proper thing to do. An unexpected wave of sadness washed over her as she watched him leave the churchyard.

Within a few moments, Lucy found herself alone, waiting for Lucas, as the other parishioners climbed into waiting carts or passed down the dusty paths toward town or their homes. Walking among the peaceful stones and crosses, Lucy read the names and epitaphs on the graves. MARY WORTHINGTON, BE-LOVED WIFE. ELIZABETH MOORE, DEAREST MOTHER.

Lucy wondered idly about their lives. She wondered if that

would be her one day, someone's wife and mother, buried after a life of love and happiness. Such a life would probably not be surrounded by books. Her husband was not too likely to read much, just the Bible or some dreary sermons. She would miss the magistrate's household, she thought, and though it was like to be a long way off, she already resented her future husband for taking her away from the security and happiness she found living with the magistrate.

She heard someone calling her name, interrupting her reverie. "Who's there?" she asked, peering among the white alabaster angels that gracefully protected the bones of long-dead parishioners.

Avery popped his head from behind one of the graves. Fingers on his lips, he waved her over.

"What's wrong, Avery?" she asked. "Did you lose your kitten again? I'm sorry, I've no time to help you to find her today."

He shook his head. "Kitty is here." He patted his pocket. Sure enough, there was a movement, and a little white head popped out. Lucy petted it. "I'm to tell you, someone wants to talk to you."

Lucy studied him. His gray hair was matted about his face, but his eyes seemed clear. "I'm waiting for Lucas right now, Avery. Who wants to speak with me?"

"I don't know her," he said. "It's about your brother. Me and Kitty, we're so sorry, miss, that he's in Newgate."

"My brother? What news?"

"Will was with me," said a woman, flouncing toward them, "the night that the cheap vixen was killed."

The orange seller! From the theater! Lucy grew excited. "He

was with you? When? What is your name, by the way? I'm sorry my brother never told me—"

The woman sniffed. Up close, Lucy could see she was not as young as she had appeared when she was bantering with customers at the Globe. She could see lines around the woman's mouth and a single gray strand in her brown hair. Avery faded away, leaving them alone.

"Name's Maggie Potts." She licked her lips. "That's right, I was with Will all day, all night. Your brother, he's a swell lad. I shouldn't like to see him swing, especially for a daft git such as her that got herself killed."

Lucy frowned. "When? He was with Bessie—I'm sorry, but it's true—and then at the Muddy Duck, which is where he was, sousing himself silly, until Richard came back to the pub, and they seem to have had a bit of a brawl. Many people saw it, I heard tell—"

Maggie put her hands on her hips. "Well, it was after that. No matter. I've got some girls who can swear to the same."

"So he was with you?" Lucy pressed. "That night?"

The woman smirked. "Sure. For a few sovereigns, I can say whatever."

"A few sovereigns?" Lucy echoed, startled.

"Pay me five and I'll even testify in court. I can be real convincing." She swung her bodice a bit. "I can get them jurors to like me, no problem. They're just men, right? I should have been a player myself, not just selling stupid oranges all day."

Lucy hesitated.

"Look," Maggie said, pulling out a flimsy pamphlet. "Do you want Will to end up like this poor sod?"

With shaking fingers, Lucy pulled open the crumpled bit of paper. " 'Order Regained, or The Last Dying Speech of Robert Preswell, convicted of murdering Jane Hardewick of Lincoln Fields, before he was hanged at the Tyburn Tree.' "

Lucy skimmed the document, feeling a bit faint. Apparently, several neighbors had heard Preswell confess to fathering Jane Hardewick's child, while another neighbor testified that he had borrowed a knife just that morning and "had an evil glint in his eye when he did ask for it." While even in his last dying speech Robert denied murdering her, everyone agreed that justice had been achieved, and order restored.

"Hanged Friday last, he was," Maggie said, looking at Lucy. Her eyes seemed to gleam.

Lucy could only shake her head helplessly. "I don't understand. If you were with Will, you must come forward! 'Tis the honorable thing to do. Please! If you care two bits for my brother."

"I've given you my terms. Five sovereigns." Maggie looked around. "I'll be serving at the Anchor tomorrow night. Don't tell anyone."

Before Lucy could speak again, Maggie melted away as Lucas appeared.

"Ah, Lucy," he said, holding out his arm. "Shall we take a turn here in the churchyard?" He looked ruefully at the stones that lay cracked and fallen all about them. "Morbid though it may be, there are some interesting words among them to be read."

Lucas grinned in the old way, pausing before a modest gravestone.

"Here's my favorite," he said.

Lucy read the inscription aloud. " 'Here lies dearest mother, who was verily poisoned by her serving maid who she had beaten for many a year, who then herself fell into the hearth and died.' " She looked at Lucas. "*This* is your favorite?"

"Divine atonement, do you suppose?" he asked. "Who says the good Lord does not have a sense of humor."

"Or at least he who makes the stones," she added with a slight smile.

"I do believe that sinners get what they deserve. I also believe that sometimes the good Lord in his wisdom uses man to enact his justice on this our earthly plane."

Lucas's bald words drew Lucy up short and reminded her of why she had come. "The hour is growing late, sir, and I fear we shall not have time to get to Newgate and back without the mistress missing me very much."

As they walked down the cobblestone streets, she related what Adam had told her about Will's defense.

Lucas nodded. "The neck verse," he said, "was probably not a very good idea. Upon reflection." He changed the subject. "Lucy, who were you talking to, back at the church? Before I walked up? Avery I know, of course, poor soul, his mind addled by the war. Who was the woman? She looked familiar, but I can't quite place her."

"Oh, that's Maggie Potts. She's, er, a friend of Will's."

"Indeed?"

"She says she was with Will the night of Bessie's death and would swear to it in court."

Lucas gave a low whistle. "That would save Will, to be sure."

He glanced at Lucy. "Tell me, Lucy. Why, then, do you not look more overjoyed? When Miss Potts's testimony could set him free? Or," and he looked at her shrewdly, "is there a fee to be had for this helpful testimony?"

Lucy hung her head. "I'm to meet her at the Anchor with five sovereigns. She tends the tavern there when she's not working the plays."

"Pray, do not resort to desperate measures, Lucy," he said, putting his arm around her slumped shoulders. "God, and I, will help you through this terrible time."

Lucy began to weep in earnest then, and she scarcely knew for what she was crying. Bessie's death, the strain of Will's trial, and even Adam's disdain . . . all of it overwhelmed her. Lucas let her weep, and she was grateful that he asked her no questions.

·17·

Lucy and John walked to the Old Bailey Tuesday morning, the morning of Will's trial, with heavy hearts. A light drizzle chilled Lucy, yet she felt too numb to care. Neither said anything, but John kept his hand at Lucy's elbow to help her along the muddy path. Adam, she knew, had gone early to be with William and to accompany him on the short walk from Newgate to the Old Bailey. Sunday's visit with Lucas to see Will had left her more afraid than before. Will seemed so dispirited, a grayness in his very soul.

As they approached the great medieval fortress, the bells of St. Sepulchre began to toll. A small group of dirty children, laughing and chasing each other through the square, began to shriek and clap their hands.

"'Oranges and lemons!' say the bells of St. Clement's," one little boy called, running away from the group.

As they sang, Lucy found herself humming along, a distant chant from her childhood; yet she soon found their words and game to be far bleaker than what she remembered.

" 'You owe me five farthings!' say the bells of St. Martin's," the rest of the children called, lining up on the other side of the square.

" 'I do not know,' say the great bells of Bow," the boy chanted back.

Then the children started racing toward the boy, their arms chopping through the air. "Here comes a candle to light you to bed. Here comes a chopper to chop off your head! Chip chop chip chop! The last man's *dead*!!!"

Lucy turned away, slightly sickened. It was like the stories they all had heard. The bellman would bring his candle to the accursed prisoner's cell and lead him to his execution. Not to have his head chopped off, of course, yet surely to be hanged.

Once at the Old Bailey, John found them a seat on a crowded bench. He'd been to sessions before and seemed to know what was going on. The sessions were full; Will's was one of ten trials before this particular magistrate. Among ordinary cutpurses and forgers, Will's trial stood out. No monstrous mothers here; no women accused of killing their babes. His was the trial the muttering crowd had pushed into the courtroom to see.

Soon the jury filed in and seated themselves in two long rows of six on either side of the judge. Lucy recognized a few tradesmen and merchants, as well as two or three nobles, clearly bored by their civic duty. As regular members of the jury, they could supplement their wages or, in the case of the nobles, cover their losses. Most judges preferred their own jurors so they would not have to explain court procedures over and over again.

"And these are supposed to be William's peers," John whispered in disgust to Lucy. "The king of England could be such a peer."

Lucy nodded, twisting her hands in her lap. Will turned around then, looking both fearful and a little defiant. Lucy felt her heart leap when she saw him. His face was pale and brooding, yet he seemed to brighten when he saw her, giving her a little cheer. He raised a hand in greeting. She managed a tremulous smile, even as her stomach churned as if she had drunk too much ale.

The judge was already seated at his bench, shuffling through the papers, waiting for his clerk to finish sharpening his pen. Lucy squinted, trying to imagine him without his long white sheep's wool wig. An image of him leaning back, relaxing over a goblet of Rhenish wine, came to mind.

"Oh, I know him!" Lucy whispered to John. "He's come to the house; he's a friend of the master's!"

"The master probably had a hand in that, I suppose," John said in equally low tones. "Will is likely to get a fair trial."

Lucy felt a little better already. From what she knew of the judge, he was a quiet man, but he always spoke courteously to her when he came to the house and had always been friendly and kind. Now he nodded to his clerk, who called the first case.

The first two cases were dispatched quickly, a maid who had stolen her ailing mistress's best bonnet and her purse containing five shillings, and a youngish man who had stolen a pail and a brush from the local stabler. Both were consigned to spend two hours in the stocks outside the courthouse. Lucy had little sympathy for the maid, given that she'd taken advantage of her mistress in such a low way. Her flouncing about made Lucy wonder why she did not look more distraught at her punishment. Sitting in the stocks for three minutes would surely be unbearable.

"I wonder what else she stole," John muttered at her side. "She's hiding something, to be sure, that one is."

That's it. Lucy nodded, fascinated. *The maid thinks she's put something over on the court, to take her punishment so easily.* Yet as she was being led away by the bellman, the judge stopped her. "I suggest, miss, that you take a more honorable foray into your livelihood. Although I have no proof at this time, 'twould not be hard to send around the bellman, say, every day, to check with your mistress to see if anything else has gone missing. Do you understand?"

The girl nodded, more sullen now. Lucy smiled. She was glad that the young chit had not tricked the magistrate. He seemed a good man.

The other theft was quite strange. Why take a bowl and brush? she wondered. The magistrate asked the same question, not bellowing but speaking quietly to the boy, as if they were not sitting among a roomful of strangers. Lucy had to strain to hear the boy's words.

"For my horse," the boy whispered.

The magistrate looked puzzled. "You own a horse?" he

asked. The boy seemed barely able to own his own shirt and shoes, let alone pay for the upkeep of a horse.

The boy grinned, a long, lazy grin. "Yes, of course. He's right here now. He follows me everywhere I go."

The crowd burst out laughing, and the boy, puzzled, grinned wider. Clearly, the poor boy's wits were addled. He, too, was sent off with a warning and would have to sit in the nasty stocks.

Next, four women were called, and they rose at once. "Sibil Heaman, Margery Rively, Mary Jessey, and Susan Williams," the magistrate intoned, "you stand accused of taking an unlawful conventicle at the house of Sibil Heaman of Limehouse parish, under color of exercising religion other than the king's own. This is in defiance of the Conventicle Act of 1664. How do you plead?"

"Innocent before the Lord," the women cried as one, their gray-woolen-clad arms flapping.

"Quakers, are you?" He sighed. "Guilty as charged. Six shillings each or another night in Newgate."

"We obey no authority but the Lord! He shall smite the evil and bring solace to the righteous—"

"Yes, yes," the judge said, wiping his brow. "Our recorder has faithfully described your trials and tribulations for your next chapbook. Constable, if you will?"

Next to be tried were two more pickpockets, one nervous and scared, the other grinning impudently. The judge regarded them sternly. Looking closely, Lucy recognized the younger one. Sid! He was the one she had tricked so long ago at the market.

"Sid Petry and Geoff Hicks, you have been accused of pick-pocketing on at least five separate recent occasions. How do you plead?"

Sid quailed. "Guilty, Your Highness."

There was a tittering in the crowd, as the older boy shoved him. "I meant, not guilty, most noble sire."

The room laughed again; for a moment, the judge's lips twitched. "Indeed, 'sir' is fine. I shall enter a plea of not guilty on your behalf. What about you, young man?" He directed his gaze at Geoff, who kept his cheeky smirk.

"I can think of no reason I am here," Geoff stated blandly. "Those witnesses are all liars, and them jurors will just agree with them. They're all liars, too."

A group of men and women began to scream at him. The judge raised his hand.

"Guilty or not guilty?" the judge demanded.

Geoff shrugged. "There ain't no justice for me here."

"In that case, if you do not wish to plead or to be tried by this court, then the court will adjudge a verdict of *peine forte et dure.*"

The judge beckoned the constable, who stepped forward. Like him, many of the jurors looked impassive, but several looked openly stricken. Others whispered to their neighbors. "What does that mean? What shall happen?"

Geoff looked around, sensing something amiss. "What? What does that pen, pen . . ."

"*Peine forte et dure.* It means, my insolent boy, that you shall be taken back to prison and live out the final days of your life in that dirty vile place. You shall be stripped to the waist and hoisted above the ground, so that your arms can be tied to two corners of the dungeon, and your legs in the same fashion. You shall then have iron placed on your body, adding to your weight. For three days, you shall thus hang, with just a bit of barley to eat, and maybe just a spot of water, and then no food or water at all, hanging until you are dead. That, or an hour in the stocks."

The crowd murmured again, enjoying its own shock. Lucy balled her fists in her lap. "Oh, he wouldn't! He couldn't! Why can't the stupid boy just admit it?" she muttered to herself.

Sid began to sob. "Geoff, Geoff . . . that would hurt so much!" he cried. This plaintive wail made a few laugh and others look nervous.

The judge slowly lifted the gavel in the air, looking meaningfully at the boy. He finally seemed to catch on. "Guilty, then, I guess! The stocks ain't so bad, compared to all that!"

"Just so," the judge agreed. "One hour in the stocks. Constable?"

Geoff and Sid were led away to take their turn in the stocks outside. Lucy was glad that was all. He shouldn't be pickpocketing, but no one deserved that *peine* punishment. Well, except the vile cur who killed Bessie, of course. That thought brought her back to the matter at hand.

Sure enough, William's name was called next. Thankfully, the judge ordered a short meal break, reminding the jurors that dinner was available in chambers. William was given a piece of bread and a drink of water from the pail in the corner. He grimaced, yet took a sip from the ladle anyway.

While a few people went off to use the necessity, or down a

quick pint at the pub around the corner, most left someone holding their spot on the bench. Everyone had come to see Will's trial. A murder trial was far too sensational to be missed, especially when the accused was so young and handsome.

Since John was there to guard her seat, Lucy pushed her way to the front, where Will sat, dejected. She pressed a bit of gingerbread into his hand. "Eat. Please, dear."

Neither Will nor Adam acknowledged her presence. She had apparently interrupted Adam's final instructions. "So remember, Will, I cannot ask questions of the witnesses myself—God in heaven, how I wish I could!—but do not let a witness retire until we have finished. When I nod, all right?"

Will just stared ahead, inclining his head slightly to show that he heard.

Adam continued. "It's important! 'Tis very difficult to call a witness again. The judge will not like it, so we must be careful to get all the evidence necessary on the record. We must lay a careful foundation. Do you understand me?" He shook Will's shoulder. "Will?"

Will nodded, but Lucy doubted he really understood very much at all. He was on trial for his life and had entered a mad daze. A bell rang somewhere, sending the spectators eagerly back to their seats. The show was about to start. Lucy kissed Will's cheek, rough with the day's stubble despite that morning's required wash and a shave.

Her kiss seemed to revive him, help him focus. "Mother?" he asked. "Did she—?"

Helplessly, Lucy could only shake her head. She had received a note just that morning, written by one of her mother's neighbors, saying that their mother would not be attending Will's trial. She was simply too overwrought by the notion that her son could stand trial for murder. *Dear Will, Trust in the will of God. His Light shall prevail. Your Loving Mother, Theresa Campion.* That was all the note said. Furious, Lucy had ripped the letter to shreds.

"Be strong, brother," she whispered. She didn't know if he heard, but at least his face seemed less pale.

The next hour was one of the worst in Lucy's life. The little bit of joviality and humor that had appeared in the first half of the assizes had dissipated. The murder of a young woman, even if she was just a servant, was a serious and grim matter indeed. Even the jurors who had looked so bored before sat up, listening intently, when the case was called.

Lucy craned her head all around. The orange seller, Maggie Potts, was nowhere to be seen, which, truth be told, didn't surprise her all that much. Evidently, when she had not heard from Lucy, she had decided not to present herself to the court.

A pang of guilt and regret nagged at Lucy. Should she have bought her testimony? Principles don't mean all that much when one's brother stands facing Old Jack's noose.

Constable Duncan stood up to serve as prosecutor, since he was the king's man called when Bessie's body was first found. Pulling out a piece of paper, he read slowly. "On March 31 in the Year of our Lord 1665, Elizabeth Ann Campbell, known as

Bessie to her friends, late servant at the good Magistrate Hargrave's household, him of the King's Bench, was done found murdered—"

Here a wail broke out. For the first time, Lucy saw Bessie's mother and sister huddled at the bench. They had not been there earlier. Who had cried out, Lucy did not know.

"—found murdered," Duncan continued impassively, "stabbed five times in the abdomen and chest."

Quickly presenting the case, Duncan explained how William and Bessie had become biblically familiar, "as was fine and proper since they were courting." However, after Bessie had been with another man and found herself with child—surprisingly, Del Gado was not named—William discarded her. Because she would not cease seeking him out, he had sent her a letter, asking her to meet him in the field, where he "did plan to seduce and murder her, so as to silence her and the babe once and for all, in manner most foul."

As he spoke, Lucy watched the judge and jury consult the penny chapbooks describing Bessie's death and nod as the details of the story were confirmed. The jurors occasionally glanced at William, judging him, gauging his reaction, deciding the merit and value of his life. Her brother stared stonily before him.

The judge then called the physician to the stand, explaining, "Though not common practice, the learned members of the court, my fellow judges, have recently decreed that the physician who tended to a deceased, particularly one so obviously the victim of foul mischief, should be called to give true and honest testimony about what he found."

The physician, Larimer, took the stand and made quick work of describing the state of Bessie's body: that she had been stabbed by a man, until she was indeed dead, with some wounds to her hands as if she had tried to stop the blows. "The first strike seems to have been to her abdomen, forceful, but not the death blow. If I were to guess, he started coolly with some precision, then grew in anger or passion. He must have been stirred by bloodlust. Some men's blood does boil that way." Upon a more complete examination, he then found her with child. "A vile beast, that man was," he finished, staring at Will.

The crowd murmured in agreement. Lucy saw several jurors nod their heads as well. This was not good.

Will sat motionless. Adam nudged him, gently at first, and then harder when he failed to move. "Oh, right." William gulped. "Do you know, for sure, that it had to have been a man who inflicted those wounds upon"—here he stumbled over Bessie's name—"the girl?"

The physician stroked his beard. "To my mind, 'twas too violent an act to have been wrought by a mere girl. To betray her own sex in such a way! However, I have seen enough criminal travesties in my time to say that such a thing, though thoroughly unnatural and unbefitting the gentler sex, could have transpired. Yes, it might well have been a woman. Although I think that unlikely."

The jury nodded again. Other witnesses were called, including several tavern customers who detailed how William had been angry that day, and how they had seen the couple arguing early that afternoon. They saw him shake her until "her head did near shake off." Even more damning were the witnesses who had been at the pub later in the day. They all claimed that Will said he was out for Bessie's blood.

Throughout all the testimony, a great angry red flush colored Will's face and neck. Adam appeared to be taking notes. Once or twice, Lucy saw Adam press Will's arm, warning him to be careful with the words he spoke, so as not to incriminate himself before the judge and jury. Dutifully, with each witness, William posed the questions that Adam whispered to him, showing holes in each person's testimony.

When a woman stood up and claimed that Bessie's finger had appeared to point to Will, Adam tersely had Will read the original pamphlet, where that same woman claimed the finger had pointed to the magistrate's son. Lucy could not believe that such an unnatural story could be used as evidence, yet it was duly entered into the court record, with the notation that the woman had switched her story.

Finally, Richard Cuthbert's name was called. The onlookers craned their necks and began to whisper, knowing that he was the key witness. He was the one who heard Will say that he would kill Bessie with his own hands. He was the one they were waiting for, to condemn Will to his death.

Richard sat down, sullen and cocky. The constable asked him to explain what had happened the night of the murder. "Me and him got into a bit of a fight," he said, nodding shortly at William.

"What were you and the accused fighting about?"

Richard grinned, smacking his lips. "I told him that I'd seen some pictures of the git he'd been keeping company with."

"Is that when he struck you?" the constable asked.

Richard scowled. "No, it was what I said about the other one," he muttered, losing his bravado.

"The other one?" Duncan asked. The conversation was clearly not going as he expected.

"Yeah. I made another comment about the other girl I'd seen him with. Quite a fine one. Didn't know she was his sister."

Lucy felt her face flush as a few people turned to look at her. She recognized some of her neighbors, their faces lit up by this tidbit. Gossipy old hags.

The judge leaned toward Richard, with a warning in his own voice. "Do you mean to say, young man, that you said something lewd about the defendant's sister? Lucy? A lass that I know for myself to be a decent good girl? And that's when the defendant hit you? In defense of his sister's good name?"

"Yeah," Richard muttered again. Seeing the disappointment on her neighbors' faces, Lucy couldn't help feeling smug about being in the judge's favor.

"So," Duncan continued, trying to bring the questioning back on track, "that's when you got into the fight. What did he say to you afterward?"

"Nothing."

The constable gestured impatiently. He pulled out a flimsy piece of paper. "Do you recall stating to me that the defendant had said, " 'I'm going to kill her, Bessie. Yeah, I'm going to murder that lying whore'?"

"No, I don't remember saying that."

William looked at Adam in surprise. Adam only lifted one eyebrow, his eyes steady on the liveryman.

The judge looked at Richard accusingly. "Do not mock this

court of law, young man. Did you hear the defendant say that or not?"

"No. I didn't hear him say it."

The constable wiped his sweaty brow with his cap. "Richard Cuthbert," he said sternly. "Did you or did you not see the defendant covered in blood later that evening?"

"Yes, I did," Richard agreed.

The crowd looked eager. Now they were getting somewhere interesting. The constable smiled. "And where was that?"

Richard was silent.

"Where did you see the defendant?" the judge asked him. "Young man, I will hold *you* in contempt of court if you do not answer the question."

Sullenly, Richard replied, "I saw him in my stable."

"Your what? Your stable? What could you mean?" Duncan shouted. With a quick look at the judge, who was frowning, he said, "Beg pardon, Your Honor. That's not what the witness told me!"

Opening the paper again, Duncan read loudly, "'And then, that night, not a few hours later, I did see William, the blackguard, had fulfilled his promise, with blood all about his body, blood I knew had come from his unfaithful mistress, who to my mind he must have killed in the field near mine, that field they do oft call Rosamund's Gate, where lovers do die.' Do you deny seeing this?"

"I did not see this," came Richard's low reply.

"What, pray heaven," Adam said, rising to his feet, "was William doing in your stable?"

The magistrate ignored Adam's breach and looked expectantly at the man squirming in the witness chair.

Richard hesitated. "He was tied up."

The crowd gasped. Adam continued. "And how did he come to be tied up in your stable?"

"I wanted to teach him a lesson. My men," Richard said, looking somewhat sheepish, "tied him up. He came to me, drunk and swinging, ranting about that wench Bessie. I knocked him out and tied him up and then left." He smirked then at Adam. "I had other things to attend to. A few hours after sunrise, we untied him and threw him in a ditch."

The crowd began to buzz, and the judge held up his hand. He looked at Richard sternly. "Are you saying that the defendant was tied up from the time he came to you until the next morning? When he was found, with bloody hands, in a ditch?"

"I guess he didn't recollect what happened after I knocked him out," Richard muttered, both defiant and a little ashamed. "I was just funning with him. I untied his hands before we left him. Didn't want him to rot there. I sure as hell didn't expect him to swing for the girl's murder. I've no wish to have a dead man swinging in my thoughts all the time. Burt and Joe, they'll tell you it's true."

The constable, seeing the case slip away from him, spoke directly to the judge. "The defendant could still have killed her and crawled back—"

"Kill her in broad morning light? Then go back to that very same ditch, to be found by that tinker on his way to the market?" Adam asked, the disbelief clear in his tone.

The magistrate cocked his head. "Indeed, sounds far-fetched, but I must consider it—. What was that?" He turned to Richard, who was now looking more shamefaced.

"Saw that tinker," Richard muttered.

"How's that?" Adam and the magistrate asked simultaneously.

"After me and my mates unbound him, we saw that tinker on the road. I've done business with him before. I'm in livery for the Embrys. Sometimes they need something hammered out for the carriages and whatnot. So not more than ten minutes could have passed since we left him, when the tinker found him."

The magistrate sighed. Lucy and John, and the rest of the courtroom, leaned forward.

The magistrate fingered his mallet. "As much as I hate to see the murder of a young lass go unresolved, I should hate far more to see an innocent man be wrongly accused and hanged."

Lucy held her breath. The magistrate then said the words she could scarcely have dreamed he would utter. "The court thereby declares the defendant, William Campion, acquitted of all charges and set free."

The crowd roared in approval. Londoners were a good-natured group; they were equally glad to see a man justly acquitted as to be sent to the gallows. The magistrate banged on his desk.

"Master Campion, it is in your right to have the court charge Richard Cuthbert with giving false testimony and assaulting you. If you choose to press charges, Richard will pass not less than three nights in jail, spending two hours each day in the stocks."

Richard grimaced. William hesitated, then swiveled to

look at Lucy. She shook her head. No need to renew Richard's rancor against them.

William seemed to understand. Reaching for Lucy's hand, he said firmly, "No, Your Honor. I should just like to put all this behind me."

On the way out, Lucy held Will's arm tight, sobbing with relief, the crowd around them still cheering.

A young lad darted up and pumped Will's arm. "I never thought you did it!"

Will managed a weak smile. Adam and John flanked them both, pushing their way through the crowd. Within moments, the crowd that had gathered outside the Newgate prison door had sought other grisly entertainment.

As they passed, Lucy heard a bookseller selling chapbooks reading off another man's last dying speech. A hanged man would have his "true confession" read before he was hanged; whether it was true or not mattered little. "He was very willing to die!" the bookseller cried out, trying to be heard over the growing crowd. He was a small man, with greasy hair and ill-fitting clothes. He looked tired but was working hard to earn a few pennies. "He did not live well, but his soul shall find redemption in death."

"Aw, give us the good stuff!" one man called. The crowd murmured in agreement. Penitence was fine and good, and showed that justice prevailed, but everyone wanted to hear the more sensational details. They wanted to know they were right when watching the man die.

Adam had his hand on her back then and almost seemed to be pushing her. The ground outside the prison was rocky and rough, and she almost tripped. She looked up at him indignantly, about to say something, when she realized what he was trying to keep her from seeing.

A gallows had been erected at Tyburn, and there a man was swinging, still alive. His body was rigid, his face was blackened, and his head hung at a queer angle. He bobbed about. "Cut him down!" the crowd began to cheer, while others called with equal fervor, "Rack him back up!"

The executioner obliged both calls, cutting the condemned man down and putting another noose around his neck.

Lucy didn't even know she was fainting until the ground rushed up to her. She felt strong arms swoop her up and carry her. When she opened her eyes, great tree branches waved gently above, and long grasses tickled her cheek. She could hear little of the hubbub and fuss of the town, and the executioner's scaffold was nowhere in sight. Adam and William were talking in low tones. John was chewing on a stalk of grass, listening.

Seeing that she had woken up, William mustered a grin, a semblance of his cocky self. Yet he still looked wan and pale. "All right now, sister? John and Adam carried you near a quarter of a mile to get you away from that ungodly scene."

"That man!" She gulped as the horrible image of the man's bulging eyes and blackened tongue came to her. "It could have been—"

"Aye, lass." John cut her off. "But your brother, he's fine. Thanks to Master Adam here."

Adam shrugged but still looked ashen from the trial. It

seemed to have taken a lot out of him. "Let us say no more of it," he said, stretching out his long legs. "Let us just breathe in this good clean air."

And not think of the rotting stench of Newgate or the stifling tension of the courtroom. Lucy still could not fathom what had nearly happened. "Richard? What about him?" she asked. "What could have possessed him to recant? He actually seemed . . . penitent?"

Adam looked at the palms of his hands. "I think he may have had, how shall I say this, a little Friendly persuasion?"

"Whatever do you mean?" Lucy asked.

"A week ago, I heard tell that Richard had been thrown in jail for a bout of public drunkenness. It was not too hard to grease a few hands to get the jailers to put him in a cell with three Friends."

John guffawed. "The Quakers worked him over!"

Adam sighed. "Something like that. Except, of course, with words, not fists. I've no doubt that enough talk about conscience and hell will make even a hardened criminal confront his ways. Richard, for all his faults"—here he looked significantly at Lucy—"is not an evil man. Let us just thank God that he found his conscience before it was too late for Will."

No one needed to say anything, but the enormity of what had almost happened was still overwhelming. In the distance, she heard the church bells toll two o'clock. For a moment, Lucy watched a bird making languid circles above them. Was it a hawk? No matter; at this distance, it was beautiful and free and as far removed from earthly desires and hatreds as Lucy could ever wish to be. She did not realize that tears were slipping down her cheeks until she felt a handkerchief pressed into her hand. Gratefully, she looked at Adam, but he was frowning, watching a distant figure stumble toward them.

"What's this?" John asked.

Lucy squinted. It was a woman, running, clutching her skirts. Something was clearly amiss. The woman puffed heavily toward them where they stood on the hill, her gray hair falling messily from her cap. Judging from her dress, she was probably a merchant's wife. The hill proved overmuch for her, and with a hand to her chest, she staggered a bit before falling to her knees.

Instantly, their small group was on their feet, racing toward her.

Adam, a half step behind, called to the woman, his voice imperious. "Woman! What is wrong?"

"Can we help?" Lucy asked at the same time.

The woman tried to catch her breath. "It's happened," she said, panting heavily. The others waited impatiently. She seemed unable to speak, her eyes deeply distressed.

"What? What's happened?" Will asked, shifting his feet.

The woman threw up her hands. Her next words chilled Lucy to her very bones. "The plague," she said helplessly. "It's reached the west side."

·18·

Lucy's brief moment of happiness was cut short, a terrible sense of dread muddling her senses. Everyone knew that the last time the plague hit the city, thousands had died. There had also been Flanders and Paris.

"John," Adam said, "you must escort Lucy home. I must go to the courts to see Father home safely. Will, you can come—"

"Will," Lucy interrupted, "must go home, to mother and Dorrie." She turned to her brother. "Promise me. I've got the protection of the magistrate and John, but they need you."

"Mother, who did not even come to the trial," Will said, kicking a clump of dirt.

Lucy embraced him, pecking his cheek. "Please," she whispered, helping him swing his pack over his narrow shoulders. "You must give her the chance to make amends for the wrong she has done you."

She watched her brother for a moment as he briskly walked off. No one would ever have known that he had been almost condemned to hang a few hours before or, seeing his jaunty step, that the world might be coming to an end. *Will I ever see him again?* She said a little prayer for him.

Turning back to Adam and John, she found Adam's gaze on her. He looked away. "Well, I'll be off," he said. "I'll see you back at the house. Take care."

Indeed, their hurried journey home, no more than two miles, was strange. Just as the magistrate had foretold, all of London began to panic as the threat of plague, long hanging over their heads, finally became reality. Everywhere, people were running, crying, despairing—everyone trying to figure out what to do, where to go. Doomsayers and prophets wandered the streets, predicting God's wrath.

"London, you are Nineveh before the great flood!" one man shouted, his hair matted with sweat. "Sinners all! Heed me as you would Jonah, lest the Almighty smite you down!"

Catching Lucy's eye as they stumbled by, another woman tugged at her sleeve. "You're going to hell, you know," she said, almost pleasantly. "Unless you turn your ways."

Church bells began to toll, some deep, others bright, but all strangely mournful, their cacophony heightening everyone's unease. The fog seemed uncertain, too, at times cloaking the city's misery, at other times lifting like a curtain to reveal life in all its sordid frenzy.

Finally, John and Lucy reached the Hargraves' house, where

a flustered Cook greeted them at the door. A short while later, Adam returned from the Inns of Court with the magistrate.

Within moments of their arrival, Master Hargrave convened the household in the drawing room. His grave voice bespoke the seriousness of the situation. "We will pack what we can into the carriage, mostly provisions and clothing. Adam and John, you must get another horse and a cart. In the morning, we will journey together to our family estate in Warwickshire." To his wife he added, "Thankfully, Sarah is still with her aunt in Shropshire."

Cook and Lucy started to prepare for the long journey with heavy hearts, cooking, packing clothing and victuals, and tying dried herbs into bundles. The mistress disappeared to her room to put a few things together. Master Hargrave set aside his copy of Gadbury's *Alogical Predictions* and his almanacs and began to shutter the house so that it would not be broken into while the family was away.

All of them were grim in their tasks, trying not to think of the despair and terror that lay beyond the safety of their home. Lucy hoped they were safe, anyway. She had heard that in Amsterdam, looters began to break into homes as the plague spread. She hoped Will was with her mother and Dorrie. Perhaps they would be safe out on the farm. At least he would not die with a noose around his neck.

Lucy also tried not to think of the other things she had heard; people murdering one another in the streets for a bit of moldy bread or rotting horseflesh, as their limbs dropped off. The dancing was the worst; the rhythmic contortions that she had heard tell would happen to a body when the grim reaper came to call. Lucy shuddered as she tied the dried meat into a sack.

Against her will, Lucy could not resist peering out the drawing room window at the fantastic sights. People were screaming at one another, loading up carts, trying desperately to decide what they needed to do to survive. Everyone was boarding up windows, nailing doors shut, hoping that looters would not break in.

Wagons and carts kept passing by, women, children, and servants clinging crazily to the sides, as the menfolk sought to rush their families out of the city. Some people cried; others held on tightly with pinched pale faces. One child pulled a wet thumb from her mouth and gave Lucy a little wave, even as bread and blankets fell out the back of her family's cart.

At one point, Lucy even saw Janey sneak out a side window of her master's house, with two other servants close behind, their arms laden with packages and clothing. Lucy narrowed her eyes, thinking they probably had the candlesticks hidden under their cloaks.

Their neighbor, Mistress White, stopped by for a moment. Her family had opted to stay. "'Tis all in God's hands anyway," she said.

Lucy felt a great lump in her throat. "That's probably true," she muttered to Cook. "Still, I'm glad we're leaving."

By early evening, they had seen most of their neighbors shut up their homes and flee, some heading to the docks, hoping to find passage on a boat or barge. For the umpteenth time, Lucy checked her pocket for her certificate of health, which the master, with great foresight, had sought to procure several weeks ago. The certificates would allow them to pass safely through the streets and get sufficient lodging and victuals as they passed through the towns to the magistrate's country estate. "I have it on good authority that the Crown will bar all passage from London without these passes," he had told them all. "You must keep them on your person at all times."

Lucas stopped by once, too, to check in on them. "I do not think you should wait long," he said. "I am greatly worried. Can you not go now? I'm afraid death will be upon you and it will be too late."

"Adam and John have gone for a second cart and horse," Lucy explained. "The master thinks the morning will be soon enough, and if we have sufficient provisions, we shall not have to stop often along our journey." She changed the subject. "Will you be coming with us, Lucas? To the family's seat in Warwickshire?"

Lucas shook his head. "Reverend Marcus is convinced this scourge is a test of our mettle. It is God's will that we remain and tender solace to the afflicted. We shall be keeping the church open, as a refuge for those in need. I daresay, too, there shall be many sinners seeking absolution." His eyes gleamed. "Lucy, I believe I shall be needed here, to help those who've been touched by the wages of sin. It is my duty—my calling!—to stay and minister to them."

"Oh." There seemed little else to say. After bidding her to keep safe, Lucas took his leave of her, and she could not help but feel alone.

"Miss? Lucy?" A small voice came from behind her. Lucy turned around. Annie was standing there, her face puckered in a frown. "The mistress is in a state," she said. "Lucy, she needs you."

"I'll go and see to her."

She found her mistress tearing through her skirts and petticoats, throwing them into a heap upon her bed. "Oh, Lucy, you're here. I need you to press these dresses before you pack them for the journey."

Lucy suppressed a groan. Such pressing would take hours, precious time that could be better spent on more important tasks. Truly, what was the woman thinking? Smiling through gritted teeth, Lucy began to lay the dresses out for pressing.

"Lucy," the mistress called. "I think you forgot to pack my new hat."

"Ah, mistress," Lucy said carefully. "I fear there will be no room for your hat."

"Nonsense," the mistress replied. "Isn't the master going to get us a second cart and horse? That should be able to hold all three of my trunks, I think—quite nicely, I might add."

It wasn't for her to tell the mistress what she could and could not bring, and she imagined that the magistrate would talk some sense into her.

As she packed the trunk, the mistress prattled on, her speech increasingly rushed. "My, it's hot. Lucy, don't you find it very hot in here?" The mistress fanned herself. "I haven't even begun to dress for the ball."

"The ball, missus?" Lucy asked, confused.

"Yes, of course. Please send for Bessie. Where is that silly girl? I've not seen her all day! Where could she be?"

A growing fear spread over Lucy. Something was very wrong. She forced herself to remain calm. "Oh, Bessie, missus, it's her day off today."

"Bah!" the mistress said, sitting down at her dressing table. "Come do my hair, Lucy. I want it pinned up."

As Mistress Hargave pulled up her hair, Lucy noticed a large black welt on her long slender neck. Her mouth gaped. The black mark!

Her insides churning, she looked closely at her mistress, noticing for the first time how flushed she looked, how her eyes glittered with fever. Lucy's eyes returned to the black mark. Everyone knew that meant the Black Death had seized upon a new victim. Then, without saying a word, the mistress vomited into her urn, wiping her mouth daintily afterward. She smiled at Lucy as if nothing unusual had occurred.

"Oh, missus," Lucy said as calmly as she could. "There's plenty of time before you need to prepare for the ball. You look a bit peaked. Perhaps you'd care for a bit of rest before then? I'll get a nice fire going."

She patted the coverlet, hoping to entice her mistress back into bed. The mistress smiled. Like a child, she obediently lay down in the bed and pulled the covers up to her chin. "Yes, perhaps I am a bit tired," she murmured. "Pray return in an hour, if you please, Lucy. I don't know why Bessie is not back yet; it's rather late even if it *is* her day off."

"Yes, missus," Lucy replied, tucking the blanket around the mistress. She smoothed the hair back from her flushed face. "I'll be back soon."

After she backed out of the room, she raced down to the

kitchen. Cook was showing Lawrence how to salt pork and pack it into the barrels as she chopped vegetables for their supper that evening.

For a moment, Lucy could not move her mouth. Finally, she managed to croak, "She's got it. The mistress, she does. "

"Got what, girl?" Cook asked, dropping some old mutton into the pot.

"The Black Death!"

In a flash, Cook had flown up to the mistress's room, returning not five minutes later, panting heavily.

"Lawrence!" she called to the little boy, who was now peeling potatoes, oblivious to the despair about him. "You must run to the physician's house. Drag 'im away from his supper, if you must. Say the mistress is very ill."

"Should I tell him Annie is sick, too?" the boy asked, hooking his hands in his pants. Cook and Lucy exchanged a worried glance.

Not wanting to alarm the boy, Lucy asked him casually, "What do you mean, Lawrence? Annie is sick?"

"Yup," the boy said, unconcerned. "She's been lying down there this last hour." He pointed to the shelf behind the kitchen. "Dizzy-like, she said."

The two women quickly conferred.

"No," Cook decided. "No, don't tell the physician about Annie. Lucy, you go check on her. Lawrence, just tell the physician that the mistress is sick. Don't mention your sister. And, lad, run!"

The boy took off then, banging the door behind him. Cook went to tell the master, who was still nailing down windows.

He ran immediately to be at his wife's side to await the physician. Lucy sat by the little girl's pallet, stroking her head. Annie
had no black marks that Lucy could see, but she was shivering
violently. Lucy went to her own room and brought blankets
down to wrap around Annie's scrawny frame. She was holding
a cup of tea to the little girl's head when the physician came.

He glanced at the child, but his attention was on Mistress
Hargrave. "Now, Lucy," the physician said. "Tell me, does your
mistress have any black spots on her neck, or under her arms,
or in her"—he coughed—"private areas?"

"Yes," Lucy replied. "She does. She also has fever and has
been vomiting; I scarce know what to do."

Without any more questions, the doctor hastened to the
mistress's chambers, where he remained for about a quarter
of an hour. When he was done, he found them in the kitchen.
Hearing Annie moan on her pallet in the pantry, he bent over
her as well with a frown.

Straightening up, he turned back to them, his voice weary.
"Well, there is little enough you can do, I'm afraid. As I told
your master upstairs, you must keep her warm and comfortable. Dry. If she gets to flailing about, as some do, then tie her
arms and feet to the bedposts with strips of cloth. Keep her
linens clean."

Cook and Lucy nodded their heads. Dr. Larimer regarded
them intently. "Heed my words. Three days it is, from when
the symptoms first appear, to the end. If you can survive it,
then you should be fine. You must take care of yourself, too;
eat, drink, think happy thoughts. Have you any posies to hang
about?"

"Posies? Why, yes, sir," Lucy said. "We kept the blossoms from last summer's garden."

"Well, keep them below her nose. Add some lavender if you have it. Also, rub some of this on her chest." He handed Lucy a small pot. She sniffed it, making a face. "It will help her breathe. All right, Lucy? Can I depend on you to keep your head about you? The life of your mistress may well be in your hands. And that of the little girl there, too."

"Yes sir," Lucy stammered. "I understand."

"I've told the magistrate that I shan't report this as plague, but he knows what to do."

Shortly after the physician left, the magistrate seated himself rather uncomfortably on the low bench by the fire.

"Have some soup, sir," Lucy urged him, somewhat unnerved by the presence of the master in the kitchen. She cut a large slice from a new loaf and handed him the plate. "And some bread."

He nodded. "How's Annie?" he asked, somewhat absently.

"Feverish, chills. No black marks like—" She broke off. "Sir, I'm sorry!"

As if he had not heard the last comment, he simply said, "Right. Well, that's good." Then he looked at Cook and Lucy. "Well, Mary. Lucy. We're in a spot of trouble here, I'm afraid. Your mistress does indeed have the plague, and maybe little Annie, too. As a justice of the peace, I am obliged to think of the public good."

Master Hargrave crumbled a bit of bread in his fingers, looking distantly at the crumbs. "Believe me, I want nothing but to load us all into the carts and pack us all off to my family

home in Warwickshire as we planned. Escape this damnable
mess. However, I very much believe we'd not be escaping the
plague, but we'd be bringing it along with us."

Leaning over, he began to poke the fire with a stick. Cook
and Lucy looked at each other.

"No, indeed," he continued. "I believe we must do what is
right. That means we must quarantine ourselves. No one must
enter this household, and I'm heartfelt sorry to say, no one must
leave, until the sickness has passed."

They gasped. *What if the sickness does not pass?* Lucy thought
miserably.

"We must have courage, and have faith in the good Lord,"
the magistrate continued, noting their pale faces. "Above all,
we must do our part to contain the sickness. That means that
we must all be very brave and resolute."

He looked at Cook, his face anguished and drawn. "Mary,
I'm sorry, but we cannot let John come back in the house, if
but to save him." Blinking back tears, he swallowed. "My own
son, I cannot look upon." Straightening his shoulders, he took
a deep breath. "When they return tonight, we must send them
out of the city to fetch Sarah and to take her to the family seat
and keep her safe. Mary and Lucy, I'm so sorry. You both deserve better than this, but with perseverance and courage, I
believe we will survive."

Cook looked as stricken as Lucy felt. A bitter and heavy silence fell over the room. From beyond the door, Lucy heard
Annie moan softly. For a long moment, Lucy and Cook looked
at each other, complete understanding between them. They
loved this household—there would be no sneaking out windows

as Janey and other servants were doing, no doubt all over London. The magistrate deserved their loyalty and courage, even though Lucy wanted to run crying to her mother. Even the mistress, with all her vanity and silliness, was a good woman and deserved better.

"Right, sir," Cook said briskly. "You can count on Lucy and me; we will take care of the mistress as if she were our own kin."

Unexpectedly, the magistrate blinked and swallowed, looking quite overcome. For a moment, the three were quiet. Lucy wished she could embrace him, offer him some comfort in this terrible time. Annie's soft moans called Lucy back to her bedside, and the magistrate returned to his wife's chamber, to sit vigil by her side.

It was nearing seven o'clock when Lucy finally heard John and Adam rap at the kitchen door.

"It's us!" John called. "We've got some chickens that need to be put up and wood. I do not want to leave them on the stoop."

Lucy went to the crack in the door. "Nay, Master Adam, John. I cannot let you in."

"Lucy, what nonsense are you speaking? Hurry, we have our hands full and still much to do," Adam said.

Lucy shook her head fiercely at them, as though they could see her through the door. "No, I cannot! The mistress, she has come down with the plague. I dare not let you in. Cook and me, we will take care of her, but we are afraid that you and John could get the sickness. It would be best"—she paused, a catch in her voice—"if you go on to the Warwickshire estate without us."

There was a short silence on the other side of the door. "My mother? She has the sickness?" Adam asked, his voice husky. "The . . . plague?"

"Yes," Lucy replied, trying not to cry. "Your father has bid us to be quarantined. You are to paint a cross on the door, so the neighbors will know to stay away. "

On the other side of the door, she heard a muffled oath and some muttered discussion. "Wait, Lucy," Adam called out. "Do not be rash. I will fetch the surgeon. He can confirm—"

"No, sir," Lucy interrupted. "We've already had the surgeon. He told me and Cook some things to brew, but there's little else we can do for the mistress or little Annie, except prayer. And posies."

The sound of a fist hitting the heavy oak door made her jump. "Lucy, let me in!" Adam demanded. "John must stay away. He can get Sarah from my aunt's and take her to Warwickshire. But Lucy, that is my mother in there. I should be with her."

From beyond the door, she could hear John protesting. "And I should be with my sweet Mary, and little Annie and Lawrence."

"No!" Cook said sharply, coming to stand behind Lucy at the door. Her hands were on her hips, and her face was stern.

"John, dear. Master Adam, sir," Cook said, speaking as she might to small children. "It must be as the magistrate said. Lucy and I will tend the mistress and the others. Rest assured, sir, we will nurse them as we would our own family. If you were in here, you'd just take ill and be in our way."

Lucy could almost laugh, if it were not so serious. Again a muffled discussion ensued beyond the door.

Then Adam called back. "We do not like it, but we accept my father's wishes. We will bring you provisions, enough to make it through the next few days."

A few days. Lucy shivered. The doctor had said the sickness would run its course in a few days. A sudden moment of terror overcame her. Would they survive? Would they be trapped? She wanted to scream for them to open the door, to not let the reaper come for them, but she remained silent.

Fiercely, she pushed the thoughts away. Knowing the men were just outside the door was making her weak. "You must go!" she cried. "Please!"

"Master Adam, sir," Cook called back. "Do not forget. You must then nail our door shut and not return for three days."

Again, silence. Whoever returned might find a grisly sight indeed in three days, if the plague did run its regular course. Lucy bit her lip. Someone coughed.

"Right, then," Adam said. "We will stable the new horse and return with nails."

Then John spoke. "God bless and preserve us all."

Not much later, Lucy heard the grim sound of boards being nailed across the front door. Pounding, pounding, pounding . . .

Lucy's heart raced. She felt like they were being sealed in a tomb. John was the coffin maker, and they were the dead. The dead must be kept from the living.

———

Deep in the night, Lucy stole softly into the mistress's chambers, to check on her as she slept. She and Cook had taken turns tending Annie, the mistress, and now Lawrence, who had just fallen ill. The master had not left his wife's side, holding her hand, gazing at her dimly lit form. With her curling hair spread across her face and bodice, and the lines of complaint gone from her mouth, she looked beautiful. Del Gado's portraits popped into Lucy's mind, but she pushed the image away.

"Sir," she whispered. "Perhaps you should try to get some sleep."

Master Hargrave lifted his anguished face to Lucy's. "Lucy, I have to stay with her. God knows I've been away from her for so much of our life together; I must be with her now." More to himself he added, "I know she sometimes found enjoyment with others, but I never blamed her. If anything, I blamed myself for being away from her side so much. She's the only woman I ever loved."

As if hearing him, from deep within her deathly stupor, the mistress smiled ever so slightly, and a small sigh escaped her lips.

Lucy nodded and stoked the fire in the hearth a bit. As she replaced the warm potatoes at her mistress's feet, the magistrate looked up, recalling her presence in the room.

"Oh, Lucy. Adam told me that William was declared innocent, was he not? You must be much relieved."

She nodded. The events of the day, of the trial, were so far off. With the mistress being so ill, she barely had time to think about her brother.

"Your friend was the one who presided over his case," Lucy said, smoothing the cover around the mistress's still form.

The magistrate smiled slightly, looking old and tired. "Yes, Ernest, he's a good man. I knew he'd give your brother a fair trial. Adam insisted that he be the one to hear the case, you know. I don't really have much say over these matters, but we justices usually work out the demands of the docket, and change things around when necessary."

Lucy gazed into the fire, tiredly holding a mug of cooling mead, trying to stay warm and awake.

"The evidence was very circumstantial, I know, but heavily against William's favor. Something must have decided Ernest's mind. Do you know?"

" 'Twas amazing, sir. Richard, the bast—, excuse me, sir, the man who had accused William, lied about him and, in fact, ended up recanting at the last moment."

A glow came to her voice as she spoke. "Adam, well, he ended up asking the questions for Will. Richard came to admit that he had tied Will up, so it was impossible that my brother could have done the foul mischief upon Bessie."

Lucy did not mention the Quakers' involvement in "working Richard over," as John had put it. She thought Adam might not like it if she told his father about his friendship with the Quakers.

"So Adam got Richard tied up in knots instead." The magistrate chuckled. Then he cleared his throat, his face growing serious. "For what it's worth, Lucy, none of us ever believed that your brother had any part in that dastardly business. But the law must run its course. I'm just sorry that he had to spend so much time in that bloody prison."

Both fell silent. Lucy drifted a bit, trying to recall the bliss of the afternoon, those moments when she, John, Adam, and Will had walked home, before this new terror had gripped their hearts. The joy of Will's release seemed to have swept away her earlier animosity toward Adam, and indeed, he seemed to have thawed a bit toward her.

A movement from the bed caused the magistrate and Lucy to stir. The mistress was awake, gazing at the magistrate. "What is going on, dear?" she asked, her voice raspy. "What are you doing in here?"

The magistrate pulled his chair close to her side and held her hand. "My dear," he said, raising her hand to his lips, "you are ill, very ill."

The mistress's lips trembled. "What do you mean?"

In short, measured words he told her, his voice despairing. Lucy slipped from the room so that they could be alone.

·19·

I believe she will die today," the magistrate said as he walked heavily into the kitchen the next morning. "It is God's will. She keeps calling for Adam and Sarah. At times, she is a madwoman—I scarcely know her."

He gazed at her portrait and shook his head sadly.

"What is today?" he muttered, setting his diary on the table. "May 10, 1665. A day that shall never pass from my thoughts."

He wiped his brow. Seeing his flushed face, Lucy ushered him off to his own chamber, promising to take care of the mistress. Cook, too, did not look well. Despite her inward despair, Lucy led Cook to her pallet behind the kitchen, where she tucked several blankets around Cook, Annie, and Lawrence. Although Cook protested, they both knew that Lucy alone had to bear the burden of the household.

As she prepared a bit of stock, Lucy heard a sharp rap at the kitchen door. It was Adam.

"How is my mother?" he demanded through the heavy door.

"I'm afraid, sir, that—" She stopped, unable to tell him what the master had said. "Your father was with her all night. And now"—she paused unhappily—"Cook, Lawrence, and your father have taken ill, too. Your father may just be exhausted and need to be refreshed in spirit and body."

She heard Adam's sharp intake of breath. "Lucy, let me in."

"What? No, Adam! I cannot!" she protested. The magistrate had been very stern with her, saying that no one could be admitted until the sickness had passed.

"Lucy, this is not right, that you should take care of my parents alone, sacrificing yourself."

"But Adam, you are still not sick; you could survive this. You should go to your family's estate as your father wished. I can take care of everyone."

"No, Lucy, you cannot. I will not allow this." His voice was hard.

"Adam, there is no use in all of us dying!" She did not know when she had started referring to him so personally, but he did not seem to mind.

Lucy jumped back as he pounded the door in anger and frustration. Then he spoke. "Lucy?"

"Yes, Adam?"

"Are you sick, too? Do you have the sickness?"

How curious his voice sounds, Lucy thought tiredly. *He sounds so concerned for me.* "Adam, I don't really know. I think I'm still fine, though."

"Lucy," she heard him say, and then the terrible, wonderful sound of nails being ripped from the door. "There is no law against someone choosing to enter a quarantined house. 'Tis only against the law for someone to leave. Let me in. Now."

With a sigh, Lucy unbarred the door. Adam looked haggard and unshaved, his clothes rumpled. His eyes had heavy rings about them. Had she seen him on the street, she'd not have known him for the elegant Adam Hargrave. She wondered where he had slept. Of course, she had not glanced in a looking glass for some time, so she assumed her appearance was no less disheveled. He barely looked at her.

She bid him to sit by the fire. "What news have you of the city, sir?" she asked.

"It's not good. Thousands have fled, and they are no doubt spreading the plague themselves. The mayor of the city has ordered thousands of dogs and cats killed, so as to stop the plague."

"Oh, poor Avery," Lucy murmured. At Adam's surprised look, she tried to explain. "I fear he shall lose his kitten in all this madness."

"Cats?" he exclaimed. "Lucy, are you truly so concerned about cats? I tell you that thousands are dying, and you concern yourself with some poor besotted fool's cat?"

"It's all he has left!" she said, her voice trembling. "He lost everything in the war, his fingers, his sweetheart, his mind! The cat *is* his family! Can't you understand that?"

"I'm afraid I'm more concerned with people, especially my own family and members of my household."

He sighed, then continued as if the tense exchange between

them had not occurred. "Bodies are being taken away by the wagonful. I'm beginning to think we'd do as well to wait this out here. At least Sarah is safe with our aunt in Shropshire, and hopefully John will get to her soon."

A shadow passed across his face. "I should like to go see my mother now."

"Yes," Lucy said, knowing it would be useless to have it otherwise. "Perhaps you can feed her some broth. She must eat."

Adam rushed up the stairs. She heard him knock and then utter a muffled exclamation.

A moment later, he shouted to her from the top of the stairs. "Lucy! Come here! I need you! Now!"

Frightened, Lucy flew up the stairs, fearing the worst. *The mistress must be dead,* she thought.

She burst in, and in a glance understood—and shared—Adam's panic. The magistrate lay slumped on the floor beside his wife's bed, his body at an unnatural angle. Though he had been fine but a half hour before, now his skin had taken on a sickly gray pallor. At least he was breathing, although his short, shallow bursts did not seem right.

Quickly, Adam turned his father onto his back, loosening his clothes and chafing his wrists. "He's cold." He looked around. "Bring me that blanket."

As she laid the blanket across the master's chest, she peered closer. "Dear God, Adam!" she said, frantic. "He's not breathing! He can't die! We can't let him!"

Thinking furiously, Lucy suddenly remembered Will telling her once how a man had beaten life back into another man. Without stopping to think, she took a deep breath and sealed her mouth right against the magistrate's and blew. Squeezing her eyes shut, she thumped on the magistrate's heart.

Adam jerked her back. "What in heaven's name do you think you're doing?"

Ignoring him, she breathed into the magistrate's mouth again, holding his nose, so that her breath would not escape. She hit his chest again. This time she saw his chest rise, and so did Adam.

"Good God, Lucy! What did you do?"

The magistrate's eyes flickered and opened. He opened his mouth, his breaths short and raspy. Lucy laid a hand on his arm, half comforting, half restraining. "Shh, sir. Shh. You're all right. Please just rest."

"Help me get him into the bed," Adam ordered.

Together, they struggled to lift him onto the bed. Within moments, the master had dropped off to sleep, his breathing regular and even, and his color no longer ghastly pale. He seemed all right.

Adam, however, still seemed stunned. "Lucy, I don't know what to say. I've never seen anything like what you've just done. Where on earth did you learn to do that?"

She could only shake her head. He stepped closer to her. "Thank you," he said.

Unsteady, Lucy backed away from the bed, trying to hide her shaking hands. "I'd best check on the little ones and Cook now, sir, if you can sit with your father and mother. I'll be back soon. You should get some rest."

———

The rest of the day and evening passed in a blur. Lucy slept in patches, checking on the little ones who nestled with Cook. Occasionally, she looked in at the Hargraves, where Adam half slept in a chair in their room. The mistress was increasingly incoherent, thrashing violently, but the master seemed to just be sleeping mostly. His face still looked healthy beneath his fast-growing beard. She saw no sign of the deathly pallor from the previous evening. She wondered at this and asked Adam, when she came to the chambers with hot tea and soup.

"It's odd, I agree. For what it's worth, I do not believe he has the sickness that my mother has. He has none of my mother's black spots; I think it was something else that stopped his breathing and his heart." Changing the subject, he asked, "How are the others?"

Lucy wrung her hands desperately. "I do not know, sir, indeed I don't." Sometimes Cook and Annie looked better, but little Lawrence—oh, poor unhealthy Lawrence. The image of his feverish little face and body hurt Lucy desperately.

Half in a daze, Lucy drifted from person to person, changing poultices, emptying pots, replacing covers, bathing foreheads, changing soiled linens, wiping off vomit, and placing warming potatoes in their beds. Gratefully, she saw that Adam was taking care of his father's necessities and was keeping careful watch over his mother. He also helped by keeping the kitchen fire going and trying to feed his parents the stew Lucy had made. Mostly they did not speak, caught in a common nightmare for which there were no words. Sometimes he helped her hold someone who thrashed about, caught in the mindless throes of fever, but even then their words were terse. "Hold her head!" "Do not let him bite his tongue." "Watch it!"

Dimly, Lucy worried what she would do if Adam took ill, but he still looked fine, if haggard. Early Saturday morning, though, when she came to check on the mistress, she found Adam had finally fallen asleep. To be sure, he was slumped awkwardly in his chair, his head on his mother's bed. Gently, she moved him into a more comfortable position, covering him with a soft blanket so he would not catch a chill. She could not resist touching his cheek, feeling the stubble that had arisen in the three days since he had seen a razor. Seeing him stir a bit at her touch, she stole away. A few minutes later, as she sat beside Annie, waves of dizziness came over her.

"I can't get sick!" she whispered frantically to herself. As the nausea filled her, she laid her head down and, for the first time, finally slept.

Jerking awake, Lucy did not know what time it was or how long she had been asleep. She thought it might be Sunday's dawn, but with the shutters nailed down, it was hard to know. Church bells still tolled steadily, but for the dead, and there was no bellman calling the hour. Mindlessly, she checked the fire and saw that Adam must have banked it in the few hours she had slept.

Annie and Cook both looked better. Their fevers had broken, and they were sleeping heavily, their bodies exhausted from the battle against death.

As she smoothed Lawrence's matted hair from his head, she

hummed a tuneless little song. Poor little urchin. She could tell he was about to die, and he'd never had a chance to truly live. She was holding the boy's hand when Adam came down, his face stricken as he peered in at her, a mute plea in his eyes as he passed.

From the next room, she heard Adam sink down on the kitchen bench. Wordlessly, she left the pantry, knowing in that instant that his mother had passed. She sat beside him and put her arms around his neck, as if it were the most natural thing in the world. Instinctively, he nestled his face in her shoulder. Wrapping his arms around her waist, he wept.

She didn't know how long their tears flowed, or how long he held her tightly. Gradually, the room began to take on light. Lucy was starting to feel strange in his arms, dreamy and wonderful, especially when she felt Adam brush his lips against her forehead.

Lucy heard herself murmur something, but with the queerness of it all, she didn't know what she had said.

The next instant, he had grasped her by the shoulders and looked closely at her. "Lucy!" he exclaimed. "You're sick! You must go to bed!"

"No," she protested weakly. "I can't, they need me."

"No, child." Cook's voice came from the kitchen wall. Though it lacked Cook's normal blustery raucousness, Lucy was very glad to hear her speak at last. Lucy and Adam hurried into the pantry to look at her.

"I believe I'm starting to be fine now." Cook began to raise herself from the bed but fell back into the covers.

Adam hurried over to pull another blanket over her and

Annie, who was still slumbering peacefully. "No one is getting up right now," he said firmly. "I'm going to get Lucy to bed and—oh, my sweet, I'm so sorry."

Lucy was staring dumbly down at little Lawrence. His cherubic face still had a bit of a rosy flush, but he had taken on the fixed features of death. Little Lawrence had died! The room began to swirl, and she gave in to the light-headedness.

When she awoke, it was dark again and she was confused by her surroundings. She heard Adam's voice as though from a distance. "Please eat, Lucy. Please take some soup."

She opened her mouth obediently and swallowed, hot liquid coursing in a welcome way down her throat. She felt it all the way into her stomach. She blinked at Adam. "Where am I?" she asked.

Adam smiled, a quick harried grin. "You're in my chamber. My father insisted that you rest here, considering how you took care of everyone." Reading her thoughts correctly he added, "Now, no more questions until you've taken some more soup." He raised the spoon to her mouth. Again she swallowed obediently, but then everything came back to her with a start.

"Your mother, I'm so sorry! Oh, and little Lawrence! What about your father, and—?"

"Everyone else is fine," Adam broke in. "Don't worry. You're the only one who's sick now."

She felt weak. "Am I going to die?" She gulped.

"Oh, I expect so." Unexpectedly, he grinned. "But not today.

You did give me, us, a scare, though. You don't have the plague. You're just worn out from taking care of us."

Lucy looked about his room. One of the windows had been opened, and with the blankets on top of her, she felt comfortable and warm. "Oh, Adam, you shouldn't be here like this, tending to me and all. It isn't right! I'm the servant, not you!"

"Hmm . . . perhaps. I was hoping, though, that you might repeat some of the things you said to me when you were still stricken by the madness of fever."

What! Lucy thought wildly to herself. *What did I say to him?* He must have read her question, because he just grinned and brushed the hair back from her forehead. Surprised and confused by the gesture, she turned her head on the pillow so that he could not see her face.

Three days later, the household huddled together at the kitchen table, poring over the weekly Bill of Mortality. With the deaths of the mistress and dear little Lawrence, they found themselves drawing together, like soldiers after a siege. Dr. Larimer had stopped by once, his last visit on his way out of London, and had brought them the latest news. Thank goodness, he had lifted their house from quarantine since there was no sickness among them any longer.

Despair seeped over Lucy as she ran her fingers down the number of deaths that had occurred last week. "Dear God," she whispered, "7,165 deaths from plague in one week alone!"

Three hundred and nine poor souls had died from fever, fifty-one from griping in the guts, and another nine from stopping of the stomach. One was "planet struck." One poor man in St. Giles Cripplegate had burned himself to death in his very own bed, having left a candle alight nearly. Another unfortunate had gotten himself killed by a fall from the belfry at Alhallows-the-Great. All the tolling the church bells were doing these days, it was no small wonder.

The magistrate looked sober. "We have survived the plague by the grace of God. Now, we must leave. Good Dr. Larimer has assured me that other diseases and miseries will soon follow, and these we might not be equipped to withstand. We shall ready the carriages and leave in the morning."

Adam was silent but looked steadily at his father. Some understanding passed between them. His father sighed and nodded, as if accepting a decision in court. The magistrate looked sad, though, leaving Lucy to wonder over their wordless exchange.

As they loaded the carts the next morning, the magistrate gravely informed them they would surely see some grisly and terrible sights while still in London. "I can only imagine the devastation and misery that lie before us, but we are fortunate to have excellent horses and a sturdy carriage to get us on our way. I would advise you, Lucy dear, and Mary, to avert your eyes, for there are some sights no women should have to see. Indeed, no humans should have to see such things."

Lucy remembered the carnage she had witnessed in the

battle as a child and shivered. "We are strong," she said stoutly, and Cook squeezed her hand.

"I know you are, my dear," the master said kindly, and a little sadly. "You are becoming an old soul."

After the carts were loaded, Lucy came in to make a last check of the house. She stood in the kitchen for a moment, remembering how Adam had clung to her in the moments after his mother's death, remembering what it felt like to have his arms around her. As if she had conjured him, she heard Adam enter the room and stand behind her. She did not turn around.

His voice close to her ear, he whispered, "Are you still wondering what you said to me that night?"

Lucy nodded, the tempo of her heart harmonizing with the quickness of her breath. He turned her around gently to face him, and she looked up hesitantly. His eyes laughed into her own. He leaned down, his breath soft against her cheek. "You told me to kiss you again. So I will. "

Even as a deep flush heated her cheeks, he pressed his lips to hers, softly at first but with a growing urgency. Lost in amazement and confusion, for a moment she could only think, *but he's the magistrate's son! I am just a servant! This cannot be!*

She put a hand to his chest to push him away just as he set his hands on her shoulders to gently hold her apart from him.

"Perhaps I should not have done that, but I damn well wanted to." Then, as if nothing out of the ordinary had happened, he added, "We'll resume this conversation when this is all over. Right now, I've some business to take care of that can't be put off."

"What? In London?" she gasped, still reeling.

"Yes. I may join the family later, if I can." He gave a short laugh.

Lucy stared at him. Was he daft? He might not survive London, given the death and certain misery surrounding its inhabitants.

"Father is calling. You must go. For now, Lucy, take care, and Godspeed."

WARWICKSHIRE

March 1666

·20·

Taking a break from packing, Lucy wandered out to her favorite stone bench at the Hargraves' home in Warwickshire. It had been a long ten months since those terrible days in May, when the family had fled the city. Tomorrow, they would finally be journeying home, having had word that the plague had let up in London. To what they'd be returning, no one dared to guess.

The household had grown smaller—just herself, the master, Cook, John, and little Annie, who had become like her own true sister. Lucas, of course, had first stayed in London to minister to the sick and sinful, then spent some time in Oxford, where he had begun his theological studies. Adam had never come to the family home at all. He had chosen to remain in the city, for reasons only he and his father seemed to know.

She flushed now to think of his kiss and, even worse, her

own foolishness. She forced herself to think instead of Sarah, who had stayed through the winter but then returned to her aunt in Shropshire. The magistrate had let his daughter leave, of course, but was puzzled by her request. Only yesterday, they had found out what Sarah had intended.

Lucy pulled Sarah's letter from her pocket and smoothed it out. As was common, letters got passed around the family members and the household. No one noticed that several had ended up in her hands.

> *Dearest family,*
>
> *I am most thankful to hear that you are well and in good spirits. Although I still miss dear Mother every day, I find that I am refreshed in my spirit, having become a handmaiden of the Lord. Ever since I found the light and joined the Friends (should you pass this letter to Lucas, our godly fellow, pray do not let him call me a Quaker! Although I will answer to Quaker), I have found my calling. It was God's will, Father, that you sent me to Shropshire. I am preparing now to journey to Jamaica and Barbados with my dear aunt! Perhaps, after that, we will journey to Boston, and trumpet the Lord's word there. I shall not come to London for a while, so that, Father, you will not feel you must send me to Newgate, under that terrible Conventicle Act. I hope, though, that we are together in spirit.*
>
> *Yours in Christ,*
> *Sarah*

Lucy had seen the magistrate's face when he first read this letter. Although he crumpled it in his hand, he had smiled wryly. "Well, that gypsy told Sarah she was going to travel, eh, Lucy? And that I wouldn't like it? Maybe there's something to all that chicanery after all."

Beneath Sarah's letter, Lucy had also hidden three letters from Adam. They were not addressed to her, of course, but rather to the whole family.

"Why would he write to me?" she softly berated herself. She stared down at the letters, trying to decide if she wanted to read them again. The papers were practically falling apart, she'd held them so often.

She sighed. Thinking about Adam felt disrespectful to the magistrate. He'd hardly appreciate his son cavorting with one of his servants, Lucy thought—although, over the last few months, Master Hargrave had seemed to welcome her as a daughter. When he had first thanked her for saving his life, in his grave and somber way, Lucy had felt embarrassed for them both, but a great tenderness had surfaced between them.

When the magistrate discovered her reading the same penny chapbooks they'd brought from London, he'd handed her a leather-bound copy of Shakespeare's comedies.

"No more of that twaddle," he had said, and after she was done, she found Jonson, Marlowe, and the like left for her.

The magistrate seemed to seek her out, too, asking her opinion on different matters and listening closely to her responses. Once he read her a passage from a bit of legislation that he was putting forth to Parliament, and she could only shake her head. "I don't know those words, sir," she had told him.

"What?" The magistrate had chuckled. "Oh, right, of course. I forget sometimes. Well, let's rectify that."

"Sir?"

"Let's start from the beginning."

Every evening, sometimes for an hour or more, the magistrate had taught her about the law. It began as a means for him to pass time, but Lucy sensed he really wanted to share his thoughts.

"It was after William's trial, actually," the magistrate explained, "that I apprehended how imperative it is that we have new standards of evidence. Your brother, I'm sure you realize, came very close to being judged guilty, and would have been, had that hearsay evidence held. While judges should be allowed a measure of latitude, it should not be a different standard of justice at every circuit court. The people must understand their rights."

The magistrate tapped his pen against the sheepskin on his desk. "That is why I run these ideas by you, Lucy. They should be comprehensible even for a young girl, although I think few young girls would show the inclination you have demonstrated toward understanding the law."

"I'm sure you will make that change," she had replied, without thinking how forward it might sound.

Unexpectedly, the magistrate had taken her hand in his for an instant. "Thank you, my dear. I am a lucky man to have such a good and loyal companion beside me."

For Lucy, the opportunity to learn had changed something in her. Her thoughts were bigger than they had ever been before. She was starting to make more sense of the magistrate's ideas and words. Cook said she was starting to "talk like gentry."

The biggest change came, though, when Lucy began to write. At night, with only a nub of candle, she had begun to write her own ideas. Sometimes she would kept the Bible open beside her, since it seemed that people liked to draw on scripture, but other times she just wrote from a place deep in her soul.

The first piece she wrote was about Lawrence. She called it "On a Young Boy Dying," and it detailed her young friend's short life. This she kept to herself, tucked in a little chest. She cherished her scraps of paper, imagining what her pieces would look like, all neatly printed out on one of Master Aubrey's presses, but she knew she would not dare. *Master Aubrey!* she thought with a pang. She hoped he had survived the plague.

Fingering Adam's letters now, Lucy wished they had been addressed to her. Unable to help herself, she opened the first one again. It had come within a few months of the family's settling in Warwickshire, in August 1665.

Dear Father,

I am glad to hear that you are in better spirits since those terrible days when we lost my mother. My heart is with the family and household. I have found London to be very strange these last few weeks; as you know, the Mayor ordered all of the stray cats and dogs to be rounded up and executed, the fear being that they were the conveyers of the plague. On this point, I am not convinced, as the evidence of the sickness seems to travel among other vermin, like the ever increasing rats. One near bit me the other day, but I did beat it

off with a staff. If you please, tell our Lucy that she need not worry;
I have helped her dear friend Avery to find safety and shelter for
himself and his cat. I did also meet with Will, who told me that
both Lucy's mother and sister are safe and out of danger's way. Fa-
ther, you did ask me in the last letter if I had seen Lord Embry yet,
but I can only say that I heard that he and the family, including his
daughter Judith, had safely escaped the sickness and have not yet
returned. I have not had the pleasure of renewing our acquaintance
or of discussing with her father the particulars of the shipping in-
dustry. My love to you and Sarah and the household.

With warmest regards,
Your son, Adam

The second one was from early January.

Dear Father,

Thank you for your letter. It is indeed good to know that all
members of the household are in raised spirits. London seems to be
ridding itself of the lunacy that beset it since last summer, and
thanks be to God, the rats are lessening, perhaps being driven off by
the cold. The tolling of the bells has mercifully stopped at last; one
could surely be driven mad by their monotonous call. Shops are open-
ing. Indeed, many MPs and JPs are starting to return; we've heard
tell that the Inns of Court shall be reopened before long. It has been
rumored that the king will be returning to London soon; we can but
hope that he will see it fit to do so, as I think it would do the hearts
of the people good to see their great sovereign among them.

I did see Lord Embry and his daughter Judith at a Twelfth
Night gathering; since near everyone is in mourning it was quite a

small affair. I recall with some regret and happiness Easter night past; this had not near the gaiety that comes when hearts and minds are joyfully engaged. I am glad to hear that our Lucy is reading so well; perhaps she can help Cook puzzle out some new recipes from this book I have enclosed. Please tell Lucy that I have seen her brother in London and he sends his best regards.

St. Peter's has been cleared of all the sick and dying who had sought shelter there in the darkest days of the sickness. I assume Lucas will be returning from Oxford soon, to put his new learning to use in the pulpit.

Will you and the household be returning soon to London? There is an issue we must discuss, sir, post haste. My heart is with you and Sarah and the household.

Yours truly, Adam

His third letter had just come a few days days ago, on the twenty-fifth of March, and was terser than the other two.

Father,

When shall we expect your return? I fear that London very much needs you here. I have been bidden to tell you that with the great death toll that has been brought to Parliament and the courts, you must return to the bench post haste. I myself have sped through my exams at the Inns of Court and will be entering the circuit. I will be leaving at the end of the month to take up the county assizes in Kent. I hope to see you ere I go, as I would very much like to apprise you of an arrangement I am making with Lord Embry.

Yours, Adam

Lucy looked at the three letters again, admiring Adam's small, neat script, reading her own name in his hand. Every time she was grateful to know that her family had survived the plague. It was hard to be so long away from Mother, Will, and little Dorrie, and she was grateful that Adam had thought to include the news in his letter.

She could not help but reread the passage that referred to Judith Embry. *I did see Lord Embry and his daughter Judith at a Twelfth Night gathering; since near everyone is in mourning it was quite a small affair. I recall with some regret and happiness Easter Night past; this had not near the gaiety that comes when hearts and minds are joyfully engaged.* He must have been remembering how he had kissed Judith that night, Lucy thought with an odd pang. She tried not to think of the last thing he wrote, but the words slunk into her mind anyway. *I hope to see you ere I go, as I would very much like to apprise you of an arrangement I am making with Lord Embry.*

Lucy shook her skirts. *That's how the gentry speak of marriage,* she supposed.

This last letter from Adam was what finally roused the magistrate to action. With great regret and even greater apprehension, the family began to pack their belongings to prepare for the weary journey back to London. The life they had forged for themselves, while not exactly happy, had created a bond built on a sense of shared grief and companionship—a bond that no one was sure would continue when they returned to the harsh reality that London was sure to be.

Only Lucy was glad of the tiresome preparations, working feverishly, trying to quiet her mind with busy hands. She was so tired each evening that she would just drop off to sleep, although her dreams were restless. What would they be coming back to?

On the first of April, the Hargraves' carriages stopped before the Red Rooster Inn, five miles from London's limits.

"All Fools' Day," the magistrate had commented as they jumped off the cart. "It may be fitting, although I suspect we will find little to laugh at when we get to the city. Let us stop here for a quick dinner and a bit of news."

John stayed outside to look after the horses and carts while, with some trepidation, the others went inside the tavern. As they ate their leek and meat pies, people traveling from London warned in hushed tones of the grim landscape ahead.

"At least all the corpses are gone, carted off to Houndsditch, I hear," one woman said.

"And the king's men have stopped the looting," added another.

"The plague was an omen," a third woman said, noisily slurping her soup. "Sixteen sixty-six. The Year of our Lord. Bah!"

"The year of the devil, to be sure!" A man banged his fist on the table. "London is paying for her sins."

Lucy and Cook looked at each other, and Annie snuggled closer.

"Stuff and nonsense," Master Hargrave declared, chewing a bit of lamb.

The magistrate's words steadied her when at last the spires

of St. Paul's and St. Giles came into view. Makeshift camps were everywhere, people in tattered rags cooking over open fires.

"Banned they were for suspicion of sickness," John muttered, "and, poor souls, they have not found a place back inside the city."

As their carts passed carefully through the bedraggled groups of huddled families, a familiar face caught her eye. "Maraid!" she whispered.

As if she had heard, the old gypsy looked straight at her. For a moment, they stared at each other, Maraid as proud and fearless as she'd ever been. Lucy smiled slightly and gave a little wave, glad she had survived the sickness. Unexpectedly, Maraid crooked her finger, invoking the age-old calling of the blessing. The cart jerked and moved on, and within moments, the gypsies were out of sight.

As their horses trotted closer to the city walls and they began to breathe in the familiar smoky haze that engulfed the city, Lucy tried to prepare herself for what they would find.

Right away, though, Lucy could see London little resembled the bustling, noisy town she remembered. The streets were thick with rushes, laid down in mourning, quieting the wheels of their carriage. As it was twilight, few people were in the streets. House after house was shuttered and closed from the street; black crepe draped from many windows. Most doors were marked with a great cross signifying the plague had come to the inhabitants inside, with a grim number below indicating how many in the house had been claimed by the reaper.

Annie gripped her hand tightly, and Lucy gave her an answering squeeze.

As they turned down their own street, Lucy could feel her companions grow tenser, expectant. Their own house was still mostly shuttered and dark, but the wood across the door had been pried off, great holes showing where the nails had been. Adam must have removed them, for the master had sent word that they would be arriving.

For a moment, they could only stare. The last days they had spent in the house, the sickness, the anguish, the death of the mistress and Lawrence, weighed heavily on her heart. Lucy longed to touch the master's hand, wishing to soften his despair. Instead, she put her arm around little Annie and hugged her close.

Cook brushed a tear from her face. "Right, then," she said, bustling past them. "We'd best get everything inside before dark. I'll get a good fire going. Lucy, come help get supper on."

Supper that night was a sad affair. The master sat alone at the table for a while, eating little. When Lucy came to bring him some ale, she found him in the drawing room gazing at the portrait of his wife. She coughed into her hand. "Here's some ale to warm you, sir."

"Ah yes. Lucy. Thank you, dear." They heard a step in the hall and a muffled greeting. "Ah, here must be Adam."

Adam swung open the door then and quickly embraced his father. He nodded stiffly at the others, immediately turning back to him. Lucy quietly poured out a second flagon of ale for Adam. When their fingers touched, he glanced away.

As she walked out of the room, she heard the magistrate

say, "Now, Adam, tell me about this business with the Embrys."

Lucy put her hand to her stomach, feeling queasy. Would banns announcing Adam and Judith's betrothal be read, now that the family had returned? She stumbled up to her old small chamber, which stifled her with memories. Gratefully, she saw that someone had made her bed with fresh sheets, and there was even a flower by her old mirror. She held the flower to her nose and sniffed deeply.

When had Cook done this? she wondered. Or had Adam? She dismissed the thought as soon as it came to her. *Don't be daft,* she scolded herself. The magistrate's son was not likely to be making the beds of his servants. More likely, he had hired a local lass to take care of it. Still, it was kind, she thought as she gratefully snuggled in the clean sheets, exhausted after the long journey. No chance of weevils or bedbugs biting her legs, which she had feared. In her last waking thought, she blessed the small kindness.

Over the long summer of 1666, Lucy saw little of Adam or the magistrate, as they were both involved with restoring the Inns of Court to some semblance of order. On the few occasions she did see Adam, he seemed intent on ignoring her. The one or two times she directly addressed him, he answered her curtly, so, out of embarrassment and anger, she soon stopped trying. Only once did she see an expression of regret on his face, which further fueled her sense of shame.

Cook mentioned once that Master Adam spent a great deal

of time at Lord Embry's when he was not in session. "Everyone expects him and Lady Judith to be betrothed within a fortnight or two. Most likely before Master Adam sets out on the circuit."

Lucy just nodded, trying to ignore Cook's knowing and sympathetic gaze.

Gingerly stepping through the streets, Lucy skirted the piles of debris that still littered the walkways. Haggard men with yellow eyes, faces drawn from the miseries they had suffered, drove carts led by bony horses. As the August sun beat down, she hoped the city government would start sending the raker around again. The new mayor's efforts to clean up the city were slow, but at least the streets were less foul than when she had first braved them upon their return.

At the market, Lucy walked listlessly among the stalls. At the butcher's stand, she inspected the sad, stringy meat arrayed before her on a bed of straw. Everyone, whether peddling or buying, looked gaunt and beaten by the tragedy of the previous year.

The normal happy din of the marketplace had been replaced by a sense of feverish desperation that made Lucy's stomach churn. *You must buy my wares,* Lucy seemed to hear. *My kids are sick, and my husband, he died. The rent is due, and the master won't keep me long if I can't empty out my basket.* And from those without coin, eying the straggly baskets of others, *Feed me! Clothe me! Why should you have what I need? Give me! Give me!*

Looking away from the misery surrounding her, Lucy

noticed a flash of blue. A woman, her back to Lucy, was wearing a blue cloak that looked exactly the same as one Bessie
had once loved. As the butcher handed Lucy a cut of meat tied
in string, she idly watched the girl walk through the stalls.
Her hood slipped, revealing an abundance of tousled blond
curls.

Lucy stopped short, her mouth open. "Bessie!" she whispered.

Knowing she was being foolish, Lucy began to move after
the girl, who weaved easily through the market stalls. Intent
on her, Lucy did not see a man pushing a cart of half-rotting
vegetables. She tripped, falling against a few women gossiping
together. They glared at her. Lucy stumbled about, picking up
the packages she had knocked over.

"Watch where you're going, then!" one of the women called,
only slightly mollified.

Lucy peered through the crowd. She did not see the woman.
She shook her head, wondering what had possessed her. "I
must be mad."

That night, Lucy dreamed of Bessie again. As before, Bessie
was disfigured and still, lying on the cold ground. Her golden
curls were a dirty mop around her head. She was wearing her
green dress. In the dream, Lucy felt herself move closer and
closer to the body that looked frozen to the earth. Lucy sniffed.
The cloying scent of lavender assaulted her nose.

Against her will, she moved closer and closer to Bessie's still
form. She gawked at Bessie's face, pale and lovely, her rosebud

lips tinged in blue. She looked like one of the tiny alabaster statues that the mistress had once kept on her dresser.

Then her eyes opened and stared straight into Lucy's own.

She stretched a gaunt arm toward Lucy, the tattered remains of her precious green dress fluttering. Her mouth began to move as Lucy watched, horrified.

What do you want? Lucy asked in her dream. *Bessie! Tell me!*

Bessie lifted her face imploringly to the heavens. A single tear rolled down her face. Then she was gone.

Lucy woke up then, confused and weeping. "Oh, dear Bessie! I haven't forgotten you!"

The image of a woodcut she'd once seen came into her mind. The ghost of a midwife, who had been murdered by her husband, haunted her old servant to tell her how her husband had murdered several villagers besides herself and buried them under the tiles of the house. Was it true, then? The souls of the wronged did not remain still.

Lucy buried her head in the blanket, but it was a long while before she fell back asleep.

Still troubled the next morning, Lucy moved slowly about her morning chores, stopping to refill mugs of hot cider for Master Hargrave and Adam. Looking keenly into her face, the master asked if she were well.

"Yes." Lucy hesitated.

The magistrate lifted his eyebrows. Adam set his cup down on the table, waiting. Keeping her head down, Lucy murmured, "It's just that I dreamed of Bessie last night."

"Ahh," the magistrate said, taking another sip. "There are many ghosts here now, I fear."

He sounded sad. Lucy wondered how well he had been sleeping these many nights since they had returned home.

Lucy took a deep breath. "It's more than that, sir. In my dream, I felt her soul is still lost. I'm troubled, I am."

The magistrate nodded understandingly. "Because we never brought her justice, you mean."

She nodded again, not trusting herself to speak.

"Well, my dear Lucy," the magistrate said, his voice gentle, "no one has come forward with news. Indeed, it is as like as not that her murderer is long gone or dead from the plague. It may be that our Bessie will not get justice in our temporal courts on earth, but indeed, she shall find justice in the next."

His words offered some comfort, but Bessie's forlorn face still weighed heavily in Lucy's thoughts.

The first day of September, the household set off to St. Peter's to hear Lucas—newly returned from Oxford—deliver his first sermon.

The magistrate had mentioned that Lucas would be sharing the Reverend Marcus's pulpit duties, a necessity with so many people seeking solace from the madness around them.

Thankfully, the church still possessed its sense of timeless strength and grace, a virtue so necessary in this tumultuous time. Every week, Lucy recognized more faces as the parishioners slowly returned to London, although there were many people she did not know. Nearly all looked haggard and grim, as if they had been at war. The practice of families staying in carefully kept rows had been abandoned. Lucy remembered how when they first had returned, they had discovered another family sitting in the magistrate's family pew.

Without a word, Master Hargrave had simply moved to another pew and, after letting Adam slide in, had sat down. The magistrate had then patted the seat beside him. "Here, Lucy," he had said. "With us."

Although surprised, Lucy had slid in beside the master, and next to her came Annie, Cook, and John. Cook had shrugged, and John had grinned a bit, but both took the change in stride. No more standing for hours at the end of the pew.

Today, Lucy waved to Avery, who gave her a slow answering grin in return. She had been so glad to find that Avery had survived the plague. He had found new clothes and no longer looked the dull-witted ex-soldier as when she had first met him. Indeed, as she had since learned, the church had hired him to maintain the graveyard in exchange for his keep in a little lean-to out back.

With a pang, Lucy could not help noticing that Judith Embry, still resplendent in her finery, was also there. Her face was drawn as she sat stiffly beside her parents, her eyes flitting to Adam. She could not see if Adam was also watching Judith.

Cook clutched Lucy's arm. "Look there!" she whispered. She pointed at a woman with great blond curls across the aisle, several pews up. "She looks like our Bessie, don't you think?"

"Yes. I saw her once at the market. I wonder who she is."

To her greater surprise, Lucy saw Del Gado enter the church and sit down beside the woman, saying something in her ear.

Marie, his old companion, was nowhere to be seen, but certainly she might have been among the thousands who had not survived the plague.

The reverend stepped out to signify the beginning of the service. Beside her, Annie gave an excited squeal. "Look, Lucy," she whispered. "It's Lucas."

Watching Lucas, she thought he seemed different. He had not the reverend's fire, but his words were earnest, sincere—compelling. He looked to have taken to his new calling. Perhaps, like herself, he had lost a bit of the tenderness of youth, having witnessed so much death and misery over the past year.

After the service was over, the family waited outside to congratulate Lucas on his sermon. As she waited, Lucy noticed Constable Duncan and a soldier approach Del Gado, the woman who so resembled Bessie still clinging to his arm. Lucy could see that the constable, while still handsome, looked far older than his years. The last year had not been easy on him; that was plain enough.

Lucy nudged Cook, who got the hint. They sidled closer, trying to hear the constable's conversation with the painter. Lucy noticed that Adam also seemed to have moved closer as he conversed lightly with an old acquaintance.

"No, I hadn't seen Marie since before the babe was born," Lucy heard Del Gado telling Constable Duncan. "She most certainly had left before then. No doubt to be with the baby's father, as the babe most assuredly was not mine."

Constable Duncan coughed politely. "Miss, if you would excuse us? I'd like a private word with Master Del Gado."

Nodding, the woman stepped away, nervously rubbing her hands on her skirts. The three men moved down the path, out of earshot.

Lucy and Cook looked at each other. Cook nodded toward the woman, a question in her eyes. Adam, having sauntered over, caught their wordless exchange. "What?" he demanded. "Tell me."

"It's her cloak," Lucy whispered behind her sleeve. "Bessie's."

He glanced at the woman's cloak. "How can you possibly know that?" Adam asked. "There must be a hundred cloaks like that—"

Cook added, "Look at the burned patch. There, above the hem."

As Adam peered closer, Lucy recalled that day with a start. Bessie had come in from the cold, her eyes intensified by the blue of her cloak, her cheeks rosy. It was not long after Bessie had met Will, Lucy remembered. Even when they realized her cloak had caught a spark, Bessie had just laughed when John stamped it out.

"How did she get it? The cloak, I mean?" Cook wondered out loud. "It disappeared from the house along with her other clothes."

The suspicion that had been gnawing at Lucy would be held in no longer. "Del Gado?" she murmured, thinking about her suspicions from so long ago.

They all watched as Del Gado took his leave of the constables, without a backward glimpse at the woman he had accompanied to St. Peter's.

"I wonder what brought him to this parish," Lucy murmured, watching the woman disappear back into the church. "Perhaps he's moved out of Putney-on-the-Green."

Adam nodded. "We must find out."

"I'll go and see him," Lucy said.

Adam turned on her fiercely. "You'll do no such thing!"

Cook cocked her head, her expression inscrutable. "I must head back, lest dinner not be ready for the magistrate. Lucy, don't do anything foolish."

Lucy shrugged. "Fine. You talk to Del Gado, then," she said to Adam. "I'll talk to her. Find out about that cloak."

·21·

Lucy moved back into the empty church. The woman was sitting alone in a pew, her head bent in prayer. Casually, Lucy sank into a pew a few rows back, thinking about how she could best approach her. Only a few people remained in the church, and she did not want to draw attention to their conversation.

"Lucy?" Lucas asked, standing beside her. "Are you all right? I saw you come in here."

She smiled and patted the place beside her. "Oh, I'm fine, Lucas."

"I was so glad to know that you had survived the Black Death," Lucas continued, sliding into the pew. "You're looking well. Tired, though." He also inquired after her brother, adding, " 'Twas a miracle that he was acquitted of the crime."

Lucy smiled, feeling comforted by Lucas's presence. "Yes,

'twas helpful that Richard discovered his conscience, and in such a timely way!"

"Yes, indeed," Lucas said. "I have not seen you since I stopped by that fateful day. I've long thought about you, though, hoping you were well. I was quite distressed when I learned that Mistress Hargrave had succumbed to the dreadful illness. I also heard that you did not spare yourself in taking care of the family. How do you fare now, Lucy?"

"I am well." She glanced over at the woman, who was still praying, her mouth moving. "Your sermon was wonderful."

"Do you really think so, Lucy?" Lucas asked, seizing her hand in both of his. "I've missed our little chats. You're so different from other girls. Not like a—" He stopped.

"A servant." She could not keep the bitterness from her tone.

"Lucy, what's wrong? You know I never treated you like that, right? That may be how Adam and the magistrate view you, but I never did, did I? When I lived at the house? We were friends then, weren't we? I sometimes wished—" His hands tightened.

The young woman got up, bowing respectfully before the altar. Lucy started to stand up, but Lucas pulled her back down. "I've thought about you a lot, you know, Lucy," he said.

Lucy watched the woman pause to light a candle on her way out, missing whatever Lucas said next.

"Lucy?"

"Oh, sorry, I was just woolgathering." She paused. "Lucas, do you know that woman there?"

He glanced at the young woman. "Oh, yes, that's Maud Little. She stayed here at the church during the sickness. She lost her parents and brother to the plague, she did. I'm surprised she came here today, I must say. She usually attends a different parish."

"I saw her talking to Del Gado outside."

She thought back to what she had overheard the constable say to Del Gado, thinking about the sinewy woman he had lived with at Putney-on-the-Green. "What happened to Marie, do you know?"

"Well, it looks obvious, doesn't it? Del Gado, no doubt, tired of poor Marie when she became pregnant with his child. It seems likely, knowing the man to be an utter cad, that he then kicked her out when a more comely wench came along."

"Do you think that the painter may have"—she lowered her voice—"done away with Marie? I think she is missing. I heard Constable Duncan asking Master Del Gado about it."

Lucas put a finger to her lips. "It's best not to speak of such things in the house of the Lord." Unexpectedly, he asked, "Lucy, have you given much thought to your own future?"

Her future. That was something she thought little enough about. "No, I haven't." She sighed.

"Well, you might come along and join the Embry staff, I suppose, but Miss Judith may not take too kindly to a servant as comely as yourself."

"Mistress Embry?" Lucy asked, a pit in her stomach. She felt like she had been eating too many of Cook's sweetmeats.

"Oh, and I thought servants knew everything," he teased, not noticing her hands tighten in her lap. "Yes, I expect to be given the nod soon to read the banns for her and Adam. For some reason, though, Adam hasn't finalized the agreement."

Lucy's smile felt frozen on her face. It was one thing to assume this would come to pass, and another to actually know it to be true. She felt sick and wanted to leave the church.

Lucas went on, oblivious to her discomfort. "So, you may stay on with the magistrate, of course, but I've heard that he's looking to return to the country estate. That would be hard, to be so far from your brother and London life, I suspect?"

She sought to change the subject. "Come, let us take a turn outside. There is something I should like your opinion on." As they started to walk, she quickly she told him about the dream. "It's true. It has occurred to me that Bessie's soul may be lost. Her murderer has still not been brought to justice."

Lucas took her arm. "I do believe her soul is with God, so please do not fret on that account. But," he said, seeming to echo the magistrate's words, "I also believe God's vengeance will be served, even if not on this earthly plane."

They walked through the graves, stopping at Bessie's headstone. ELIZABETH ANN CAMPBELL, BELOVED DAUGHTER AND SISTER, 1644–1665.

"Dear friend," Lucy added softly, feeling a tremor in her heart.

"Let us say a small prayer," Lucas suggested. As they bent their heads, Lucas quickly said a few words. "Amen," he finished, taking her arm again. He led her carefully among the gravestones, far more plentiful than before the plague. "Just remember, Lucy," he said. "'Tis as the magistrate said to me after the death of my mother. Hard though it may be, we must honor and respect the dead, but we must live. That is what the good Lord wants from us."

His words comforted her. She touched his arm, liking that he seemed to brighten. "You must come to the house to dine, Lucas. I'm sure the magistrate would like to see you."

Lucas took a deep breath. "Lucy, you know, I care about you and—" His face grew red. "Well, you know I make a good living here, and, well, you know, a minister's wife has some position in society. Perhaps—" His voice dropped off, his eyes saying more than his words.

Ducking her head to avoid seeing his hopeful expression, Lucy quickly shrugged into her cloak. "I'm sorry, Lucas, I must be getting home."

"Of course," Lucas said. He seemed stunned, and she was sure he was still staring at her as she hurried from the church.

Lucy came out of St. Peter's just in time to catch Maud Little ambling down the main path. The hood of her cloak had fallen back, revealing her gold hair.

"Miss?" Lucy called, not even sure what she was going to say.

The woman turned around. "Yes?"

There the resemblance to Bessie stopped. Her eyes were brown, not blue, and rather than sparkling with merriment, they were set deep in her gray, pockmarked face. Indeed, she exuded death more than life. Like so many of the survivors drifting through London's streets, she bore scars that were vivid reminders of the havoc the plague had wreaked upon the city's woeful inhabitants.

"I noticed you," Lucy stammered. "I mean, I noticed your cloak earlier. It's lovely."

Maud looked down, as if surprised to see what she was wearing. She smoothed the folds. "Oh, yes," she said vaguely, then waited.

Lucy started speaking quickly. "I mean, I was wondering where you had got it; the cloth is so fine. I should like to get one for my sister. Holland cloth, I've heard it called."

Maud frowned. "Well, I don't really know, now do I?"

Her dark, liquid eyes seemed confused, haunted even, like so many who had lost so much during the plague. What had those eyes witnessed? For a moment, Lucy felt she was drowning and tore her gaze away. "The painter, did he give it to you? The cloak?"

"The painter?" She seemed confused. "Master Del Gado? Is that who you mean?"

Lucy nodded, holding her breath.

"No, I just met Enrique. Someone told me that he might like to paint me, give me a few crowns if I posed for him. But no, this I got when I was at St. Peter's during the sickness."

"You got the cloak at the church?" Lucy's mind began to spin. "Are you sure?"

"Yes." The woman smiled distantly. "My little brother found it, way in the back room, you know, where the reverend works. He'd gone exploring, you see—he was but ten—before he got the sickness."

The woman was looking fearful and perhaps a little ashamed. "Why, does the reverend want the cloak back? I never told him I took it. Maybe I shouldn't have taken it?" she stammered. "I'm sure he wanted me to have it."

"Of course," Lucy said, her thoughts whirling. Something was not quite right.

Adam was sitting by the fire when she came home, her mind still aflutter. She busied herself with tasks, setting the table before dinner. She hoped to avoid him, but he followed her into the kitchen. "Did you talk to that woman?" he asked. "Who was wearing Bessie's cloak?"

Lucy nodded, pulling dishes noisily onto the table. "Yes, her name is Maud Little, and she said the most surprising thing—"

Adam wasn't listening. "Well, I went to see Del Gado. Do you know what I learned?"

Lucy polished the inside of a cup with her skirt, caught off guard by his anger.

He spoke deliberately, as if he had been tossing the words over in his mind for hours. "I learned two things. For one thing, he seemed genuinely perplexed, and a little frightened, that so many of his models had ended up dead. I think I actually believed him. I also learned that you promised to pose for him," he spat. "To think I worried about you with a scoundrel like him."

"Your own mother posed for him!" Lucy snapped back. "Besides, I suppose it makes no difference to you that it has been nigh on a year since he asked me to pose for him. I never said I would!"

"You didn't say you wouldn't," Adam countered angrily.

"Just don't think Father will keep you here if you are ruined. He's got an image to maintain, you know."

"As do you, I suppose," Lucy said, her hands on her hips. Words she had held back for so long finally tumbled forth. "Your Mistress Embry will help preserve your reputation."

Adam looked like he had been struck. "What are you talking about?"

"Well, I'm sorry, *sir*," she said. "I must wish you all good luck on your impending nuptials."

"Lucy, those banns have not been read and you know it."

"Sir, you do not need to explain yourself to me." Lucy took a deep breath. "I can tell you now, I will not be coming to work for the new Mistress Hargrave."

Unexpectedly, he seemed somewhat amused. "Well, now, I should not expect you to do so."

His reaction was not quite what she had expected. "As I might be getting married myself, you know."

Adam lifted a brow. "Indeed. Anyone I know?"

How she wanted to erase that smirk from his face. "Well, Lucas has asked me." She thought back on the conversation from earlier that afternoon. "I think."

That did wipe away his smile, but she could not tell what he was thinking. "Well, I should think that a woman would know if an offer of marriage had been made. What did you tell him?"

"I haven't decided," she said, sailing out the door. For a moment, she felt triumphant; then, in the next, unbearably sad.

·22·

Dawn had not yet broken when Lucy slipped out of the household. She knew it was folly, but she had to go back to St. Peter's. On her way out, she had whispered to Cook where she was going, lest the household be unduly alarmed by her disappearance.

"I do not like it, Lucy," Cook said, trying to focus on Lucy's face. "What can you possibly learn by sneaking around in the church? At least wait till light, and tell Lucas. Have him look out for you. What if the reverend catches you, poking about his things?"

"He shan't catch me," Lucy said. "I must find out what else may be there. Please, I have to go!"

She walked briskly, hoping she would not encounter anyone she knew. The branches above were still thick and green. Although it was early September, the leaves had not yet taken on the hues of fall. Once she thought she heard someone behind her, but when she spun around, no one was there.

She almost felt relieved when she saw St. Peter's looming before her. Without dousing her light, she slipped in through the rear church chamber and into the vestry, where she knew Reverend Marcus, and sometimes Lucas, resided. There was a closed door to the west of the rectory, where she imagined they slept.

Looking about, Lucy tried to imagine how the deeply recessed main room might have looked. She knew that during the plague, thirty or forty people might have set up pallets in here, tending their sick and dying family members. She thought about how a ten-year-old might have scampered about, before he got too sick to move, perhaps hiding in an untended corner, trying to flee the sickness.

There—in a shadowy corner, she spied a few trunks, which she immediately hastened toward. Kneeling down to unlatch them, she had to wipe away heavy cobwebs and layers of thick dust. None of them had been opened for months, and the smell of camphor and cedar wafted toward her nostrils. The first contained bedding, and the second a number of old, fairly filthy clothes.

In the third, she spied a bit of bright cloth hidden under some moldy blankets. Bessie's reticule! What could it mean? She opened the small bag with shaking fingers.

There, on the top, were Bessie's fan and her pocket and a small lace kerchief that she had painstakingly embroidered when she was but fourteen. Underneath, something glinted in the lantern's soft glow. Lucy pushed back the cloth. The Hargraves' missing silver!

She stepped back, frowning. She thought about what she knew of the reverend. Could he have—

She heard steps echo in the passageway. A voice came from behind her. "I'm sorry you found that, Lucy." Lucas moved toward her from the shadows. "I saw your lantern and I wondered who was here."

"Lucas?" Lucy asked, her voice faltering. "Did you know Bessie's things were here?"

He slapped the wall. "I would have made a life with you, Lucy! I would have lifted you from being a servant. Something our Adam would not do."

As he spoke, he edged nearer to her. His hand shot out and pulled her cap off. The face she had so long trusted seemed suddenly to slip away, as though a vizard had fallen to the floor. His features looked cold and hard and something less definable. Lucy stood completely still, frozen to the ground.

Lucas began to loosen her long hair, entangling his fingers in her tresses. "Oh, Lucy, I knew Adam wanted you. Sometimes I thought it was endearing, the way he resisted his feelings for a servant. So honorable, our Adam. Any other man would have just taken you, as I'm sure you know. But don't fool yourself, my dear. Our Adam knows the lay of the land; he'll marry his precious heiress and have everything he ever wanted. He'd keep you on the side, too, if he weren't so conflicted about your honor!"

Lucy stepped back into the shadows, feeling the wall behind her, trying to move away.

"You should have seen him that day in the pub! When that lout Richard talked about you! Adam, our errant knight, leaped to defend your honor. I don't know who was more surprised, though, us or him." Lucas chuckled at the memory. "Oh, 'How can I have feelings for a serving girl?' he would say to me. 'She's so sweet and good,' he would say. 'Do you know, Lucas,' he said once, 'she taught herself to read? Do you know what kind of mind she must have? A man could go a long way ere he met a woman like her! But a servant, no less!'"

Lucy listened, dumbfounded, barely noticing that his hand had caught hold of her sleeve. "Then, you see, when that oaf Richard spoke of your attributes, thinking that Adam, as the master's son, had already tasted your wares, they all laughed at Adam championing your virtue as if you were a fine lady. Only I knew William to be your brother, so I kept my thoughts silent!" He licked his lips, his gaze darting about. "There's something I must show you, Lucy. I need you to understand."

"Understand what, Lucas?" she asked, her voice faltering.

"Understand why he was driven to kill those hoydens, I suppose?" asked a voice from behind them.

They spun around. Reverend Marcus!

The reverend continued. "I'd long wondered, Lucas, since I had of course seen you with a few of those girls before their . . . unfortunate demises."

Lucy's mouth gaped open, her fingers still holding Bessie's pocket. She heard a lot of noise in the church, muffled shouts and then the church bells tolling. In the far reaches of her mind, she dully wondered what was going on, given the earliness of the hour.

Lucas laughed scornfully. "Those whores, you mean. A few

of them with child, all of them with no morals, spreading their pernicious lies, polluting our congregation. I did it for you, sir—"

"Liar!" the reverend shouted, his face dark with fire. "Whores of Babylon they may have been, but I did not ask you to take the hand of God as your own!"

"Yet it was you who gave me the authority of the Church," Lucas said, picking up a long pole, used to light tapers, that had been resting against the stone wall. He glanced at Lucy, still cowering by the trunks in the corner. "Well, I can thank the magistrate for this position as well. I did not want the Church, and yet I came to realize that this was the hand of divine providence at work. This I learned from you! God has sanctioned my actions. He has seen fit to give me power to act in his name."

No, Lucas, no! Lucy thought, but she could not speak, terror having frozen her body and tongue.

"You have taken lives, Lucas, which did not belong to you but to God." The reverend wagged his finger. "He will not thank you for the evil you have unleashed into this God-fearing community."

"And how will this God-fearing community respond, when they learn that a bloody papist has been devoutly leading them in prayer every week?" Lucas narrowed his eyes. "Oh, yes, I've kept your secret, Reverend Marcus, but before I go, I will leave out your monkish trappings—the hair shirts, the rosaries—for all to see."

For a moment the reverend was struck dumb. Anger, guilt,

and shame warred on his features. Then he regained his voice.
"You will suffer!" he shouted. "Indeed, you will suffer the most
horrific torments, on earth and in hell!"

"I think not!" Lucas laughed, brandishing the pole. "For it
is you who will suffer, for seeking to stop the hand of God! Just
as Evangeline, the filthy wench, dared turn against me! I did
know then, as I know now, that I had been given this power
from God. Still, I taught her then, as I shall teach you now!"

Lucy screamed as Lucas lunged forward, striking at the
reverend in a frenzy. Unable to protect himself from the sudden onslaught, the reverend quickly fell to the ground with a
sickening thud, blood seeping onto the cold stone floor.

Barely pausing, Lucas pulled a small knife from his belt
and with one smooth practiced motion swung the blade into
the reverend's chest. His body contorted grotesquely for a moment and then, one last groan escaping him, lay still.

A sudden silence filled the chamber. Nauseous, Lucy could
not move, could no longer scream. Even Lucas seemed struck
by what he had done, sweat beading on his forehead. He worked
his mouth, as if trying to find words to explain what had just
unfolded.

Then the sound of steps racing down the hallway galvanized
him. He clamped one arm tightly around her chest, and held
the knife against her throat with the other hand. Adam appeared in the doorway, panting heavily. "Lucy!" he cried. "I
heard you screaming!" Stopping short, he looked around the
room. Instantly, he took in the scene, from the blood pooling
through the reverend's robes to Lucy shaking under the blade of
Lucas's knife. He paled but stepped forward. "Let her go, Lucas."

Lucas snarled. "Come to rescue your lady love, I see. How charming! Then come get her, why don't you!"

He slammed Lucy down the steps into the catacombs. Desperately, she tried to catch herself, but she only succeeded in halting her descent slightly. In tremendous pain, she saw Lucas trip Adam as he lunged down the steps after her. Adam shouting her name was the last thing she heard. She struggled to get up, but the ache caused her to slump heavily to the floor.

When she regained consciousness, Adam was lying near her, a length away. Lucy could see that both his feet and hands were tied. She began to scream for help, but only a rusty, dry wheezing sound came out.

Lucas smirked. "Don't bother, Lucy," he said, idly scratching the dirt floor with his knife. "No one will hear you. Not with all the excitement up there, anyway."

Lucy could hear the sound of bells and men shouting. The noise sounded very far away, but the church was so solid that everything was muffled and eerie. "What is happening?" she asked, scrambling to keep calm. "Outside, I mean."

"Well," Lucas said, still scrabbling in the dirt, "it seems that London is in flames."

He offered this startling pronouncement as blandly as if he were purchasing a loaf of bread. She heard Adam exhale sharply.

"What?" Lucy gasped. "What do you mean?"

"Oh, yes, it's been going on some hours now. Started on Pudding Lane, I've heard tell. Just a mile off. They've come here, asking for buckets, ladders, squirts, and such supplies we clergymen are supposed to keep, but there is little enough man can do against almighty providence, of this I have no doubt."

Lucas drew himself up, as if he were standing at his pulpit. "Ring the bells, go on, I told them, if only to warn the people of London that their time is nigh, and that judgment day is upon them!"

Hairs raised on Lucy's neck, and she glanced nervously at Adam.

"I see you staring at me," Lucas continued. "I can see in your eyes that you think I am a madman. Perhaps I am, I do not know."

He got up and started pacing the floor, the stone columns of the catacombs causing his steps to echo menacingly, as if the ghosts of a thousand lost souls had come to sit in on his hapless victims' plight. He threw up his hands. "I couldn't tell you when it all started."

"You said 'Evangeline,'" Lucy whispered, her throat scratchy and hoarse. She was trying not to look at the reverend's body, lying on the hard stone floor. Lucas must have pushed the body down the steps after she fell.

"Evangeline?" Adam asked slowly. A look of dawning comprehension crossed his face. "Good God! Evangeline!"

"Adam, why you don't tell our dear Lucy about Evangeline," Lucas said. "She looks confused. You seem to know all about her." Sniffing, he added, "I barely remember that little tart."

Lucy looked at Adam, who still seemed dumbstruck. "My God. I could never put it together. It just seemed too fantastic, too improbable . . . but Jane Hardewick, Effie . . . it all makes sense now." A growing sense of horror showed on Adam's face. "I remember Evangeline. That is, I remember you speaking of her."

"Indeed?" Lucas asked. "I hardly recall."

"It was just once. The summer that Father and I had visited, four years now, just before I went to Cambridge. Father had wanted to speak to your mother, since he knew she wanted you to become his ward. You had spoken of a girl, a young miss, the daughter of the tavern keeper. She worked in the local inn," Adam said, a distant look on his face as he remembered the scene. "You had convinced me to stop in for a pint. I remember you pointed her out to me. You said her name was Evangeline, a heavenly name, you said. I thought her a comely lass, but one rather free with her smiles. I recall you said she had promised to go walking with you. Did that ever happen, I wonder?" He stared at Lucas, who shrugged. "For it was not too long later that we received a letter from your mother, who mentioned that a local lass had been found killed in the field. A young man hanged for it, I believe."

"Yes, George Pickering. I did not know him well." Lucas smirked, chilling Lucy. "Although, you know, I recall seeing them together once."

He paused, rubbing a spot of blood into the dusty ground with his boot. "We had gone walking. Me and Evangeline. We held hands, and when we got into the trees, she let me kiss her. But then she asked me for a bit of coin, which I didn't understand. She said she liked me well enough, but she was trying to get a dowry together, because her father, the tavern keeper, kept drinking away her chances." He looked at Lucy. "There was a lad she had her eye on. George. His family had some money and would not like him marrying the likes of her. So she wanted money from me. I was bemused, bewildered. How could such words come out of her mouth? I stumbled away, gagging. And she laughed as my world tumbled all around me."

Lucas came closer to Lucy. "Later, I could hardly think. I would flush, then freeze, then flush again, just thinking of it. I barely slept that night. To think of her selling herself so she could lie in his arms. I who loved her! The whore! My fury grew. The next evening I resolved to follow her. I knew she would slip away, after the evening meal had been served at the inn, to meet that scurrilous George. And she did!" He took a deep breath. "She darted out of the tavern, the vixen that she was. I watched her through the trees, watched them. He took her willingly enough, but then afterward, I heard her say something about him wedding her. Then he laughed, the cad, saying she had confused 'bedding' with 'wedding.' I could almost take solace in the despair upon her face. Then he punched her, leaving her weeping. When I was sure he was gone, I raced to her, wanting to comfort her. Still wanting her, despite the vile disgusting thing she had just done. She was glad to see me."

Lucy watched him helplessly, unable to speak, tears slipping down her cheeks.

Lucas paused again, caught up now in recalling his deeply hidden pain. In the candlelight, his face glistened with sweat. "She was glad to see me, that is, until I told her I would still marry her, though I was but fifteen. She called me an 'untried calf, baaing for my mother.' Though my fury rose with her words, I hid the hate that started to swell inside me. She begged me to go and talk to George. She held out this necklace to me, wrapped in a handkerchief that she had embroidered for him, and begged me to take it to George, so that he would think fondly of her. At that, my forbearance snapped."

"And you killed her," Adam said.

Lucas shrugged. "I did not want to, but something rose up within me. I wanted to smash her lovely lips and make her wish she had not scorned me. My hands around her neck, I looked deep into her eyes. She could not talk and could only make strange rasping sounds. I relished her fear." He smiled. "Then her eyes closed, and she was gone. I shook her, but her eyes did not open. 'Twas at that moment the enormity of what I had done came to me, and I did not feel fear but power! I looked at the small package that was still in her fist, and I pried it loose. The necklace I kept as a tiny remembrance of her, but the handkerchief I stuffed back in."

Lucas laughed then. The sound was was so pleasant, so ordinary, it turned Lucy's stomach. They could have been chatting in Cook's kitchen over a piece of pie. " 'Twas only later I learned that the handkerchief had George Pickering's embroidered initials on it. G. P."

"I left her there, lying in her bed of sin and greed. George, as it turned out, had already told his mates about bedding her, and even that he had struck her before he left. When she did not return, the constable was not too long in finding her, and he put everything together. 'Twas not so surprising that George was tried and hanged for the harlot's death."

Adam spoke softly, still groggy from the blow he had

received. "My father had known of the case, but we never pieced it together. Then you came to London." He waited.

"Ah, London." Lucas sighed. "This amoral, sinful city. So many Evangelines."

"Effie? And Jane Hardewick? And"—Lucy swallowed— "Bessie?"

Lucas smiled. "They were all the same. Effie was next."

Lucy could hear a great clanging in the distance, bells tolling far away, carriages rushing all about, people shouting. Hurriedly, she spoke again, hoping to keep Lucas talking. "I don't understand."

From his corner, Adam said, "They're all the same, because for Lucas, it was the same story over and over again. Wasn't it, Lucas?"

Ignoring Adam, Lucas spoke, his eyes shining a bit with the memory. "Effie I came to know later. I came across her in a park in another part of London, on her day off. Like Evangeline, she was beautiful, and she let me buy her supper in a nearby tavern. Over our ales, she told me how she despaired of her master's advances. I thought to save her, but then she told me about some lad she hoped would marry her. And he a Quaker at that!" Lucas made a rude sign. "I thought I could turn Effie from her path to iniquity before it was too late, but she was dead set on this Quacker. She even showed me a portrait of her eye that Del Gado had made for her, which she intended to give to him. I pressed her on the terms of her payment to the painter, and as I suspected, she had given herself to him. This I could not abide."

Lucas paused, looking at the bloodstain on his fingers. His

gaze was distant, unfocused. "I could not get Effie out of my mind. A few days later, I sent her a letter from her professed lover, the Quacker, hoping to talk some sense into her. As luck would have it, the poor uneducated girl had to go to a local merchant to have it read. It was I that met her in her lover's stead, and when she refused me, I killed her."

"Monster!" Lucy whispered.

"You have to understand," Lucas pleaded. "I was trying to help her. At the time I did not understand what I came to understand later. I was acting as the hand of the Lord."

"And you took the eye portrait?" Adam asked, as if probing a witness in court.

Lucas willingly responded. "Yes. You know, I was so taken with that eye that I kept it in my pocket. I'm not sure why. I liked remembering Effie before her eyes closed." He shrugged again. "Jane was much the same, in love with some Robert fellow, except that I prepared more for her. It was easy to see that she would not give herself over to me, and by now I had begun to truly understand my role."

"Your role?" Lucy whispered.

"As God's instrument. I told you that! Don't you remember? I found my calling. For I even hastened the inevitable by sending Jane to the painter, convincing her that Robert would want her likeness, knowing full well the painter would finish her debauchery. That's why it didn't bother me that Robert was hanged. He had spoiled her. I kept that eye portrait, too." Lucas paused. "Where those miniatures are now, I do not know. A pity."

Lucy glanced at Adam, who shook his head slightly. Lucas,

however, intercepted the look. "Ah, you've seen them. Take them from me, did you? No matter."

"Effie's I found by chance, practically at our front gate," Adam admitted. "You must have dropped it. I always wondered about it, thinking at the time it was just a pretty piece. The other, that of Jane Hardewick, I found where you killed her. It was not till later that I learned Del Gado had painted them both, so at the time I saw no connection between them."

"I see." Lucas digested this information and then continued. "Now I've grown tired of recounting all the acts I did as the Lord's soldier. I'm afraid, Adam, Lucy, it's time to give you over to His great embrace." He pulled out his knife.

Desperately, Lucy seized on a way to stall him. "But Bessie? Why Bessie? You cared about her! We were all friends! You did not know those other girls so well, but Bessie, you knew her!"

Lucas bared his teeth in the semblance of a smile. " 'Twas the monster inside me. You said it yourself. The rest, Will, the painter, was easy enough to set in motion."

He bent close down by Lucy's ear and whispered, "This time I controlled it all, and this time I was more powerful, more purposeful. I could hardly sleep some nights for how much I enjoyed the prospect of what I was going to do."

"Bessie! Tell me about Bessie!" Lucy cried.

Lucas carefully traced the line of Lucy's jaw. She had to will herself not to shudder. "It was the painter's fault, you know. He dirtied so many girls, but, of course, they were all so willing to be sullied. No virtue, no honor." Straightening up, Lucas ran his fingers along the stone wall and gazed for a moment at the likeness of St. Peter etched into the stone. "Bessie, like so many of them, fell under his spell. I told her not to pose for him! I warned her. What happened was her own fault."

"No!" Lucy began indignantly, but a movement from Adam stopped her.

Lucas continued. "Yes, it was. The family was taking supper that night, you know, the night we got into the fight at the pub, and I was resting. She came to my room and actually asked me my advice about her baby."

"She did?" Lucy asked, shocked.

"Oh, yes, she did. She was eager for my forgiveness and my help. It was all so easy. I told her that I would set everything right with Will. I told her that I had planned to meet him that evening for a drink, and that I would persuade Will to go to the park to meet with her. She was so desperate, you see, wanting to believe that her precious Will still loved her, despite what she had done with the painter!"

Snorting, Lucas continued. " 'Twas not so hard later to find her and let her know that Will wanted to see her. 'Tonight,' I told her, 'Will wants to take you to Knightsbridge.' She seemed surprised, so I said, 'Yes, Bessie, he wants to marry you. There is one there who will sell you a license.' For indeed, there are those who presume to marry sinners without posting banns. Not condoned by the Church, of course, but when she asked, I convinced her it was all right, God would understand and forgive. Imagine!"

His hand clenched. "As if the good Lord would forgive such fornication in his name!" For a moment his eyes glazed over. "No matter. I told Bessie to pack nearly everything she had, but to leave some things out, lest Lucy suspect too soon and raise a hue and cry. I had the foresight to write a note, in case she needed to be convinced. 'My dear Will has written me a letter!' she said!" Lucas grinned. "Can you believe it?" He could have been commenting on the antics of a fishwife henpecking her husband at the tavern. "Why *do* these girls always have to bring the letter along? I have to admit, I wondered if she would. That's why I didn't sign Will's name."

Ignoring Lucy's stare, he continued. "She worried, you see, about stealing the silver at first, but I assured her that Will would be making money soon enough. Then she thought the whole thing a lark, I can tell you that. She had some thought she would pay the magistrate back once her Will set up his own shop." He scowled, momentarily diverted. "I thought she'd be branded a thief! Instead, they threw the harlot a fine funeral, far better than she deserved."

Lucy felt a deep wave of sadness flood over her. Poor, sweet-hearted Bessie! "And then?" she croaked, a tear slipping down her cheek.

"The rest was easy enough," Lucas boasted. He reminded Lucy of one of her mother's old cocks, strutting about the stone catacombs as if he were king of the hens. His leer disgusted her, yet she could not tear herself away.

"She was quite easy to dispatch. They always are, you see. They expect to see their lovers, of course, but I am their trusted confidante. They allow me to comfort them. They allow me to come"—he licked his lips—"close. You can imagine how angry I was when I realized she had not actually packed everything as I told her to do. And she wore that silly dress! I had to sneak into the room you two shared and pack her satchel, hoping my memory would serve me right. I hid it out back, and then 'twas easy enough to take it to St. Peter's later."

"That's why my petticoat and stockings were missing," Lucy said slowly. "I could never understand why she took them."

"Yes, well, she didn't," Lucas replied. "My only regret, of course, is that her death hurt you. I did not want to hurt you, Lucy, you must believe that! Since Will was your brother, too, I felt slight remorse over what I had to do. Then I remembered their Philistine ways and I knew I was the trumpet and instrument of the Lord, completing what needed to be done. I was ever so surprised and, to be truthful, somewhat glad, when Adam came under suspicion first. Adam!"

Lucas laughed, the sound echoing oddly throughout the lifeless catacombs. "Even better! Your precious Will would not be injured, and Adam could be punished for the impure thoughts he harbored toward you! For sure, I thought the blood from the ring would prove him guilty, but, of course, that was not to occur. So I renewed my efforts against Will, knowing that it was God's command that he be smited by the mighty hand of earthly justice."

"You're mad!" Lucy cried. "A lunatic!" She spat on the ground. "Monster!"

Lucas turned back. She could see no trace of her old friend on his harsh countenance. "Such ugly words from such pretty lips. Not to despair, my dear, your body will soon match the ugliness of those words you just hurled upon me, when I am through with you."

He advanced toward her, and she flinched. Behind him,

Adam was trying to tell her something. He wanted her to keep Lucas talking, until they could figure a way out. She tried a different tack, trying to sound admiring. "What about Richard? Did you pay him to say those lies?"

The crazed look that so chilled her vanished for a moment. Lucas laughed as if she were a favorite pupil who had pleased him. He reached a hand down to smooth her hair. She accepted the caress, trying not to flinch.

"Richard, that idiot," he said pleasantly. "A weak mind, to be sure. I only had to buy him a few pints and I, shall we say, persuaded him to remember the story a slightly different way. Then those wretched Quakers got to him." He sniffed. "Convinced him to see the light or some such nonsense. Worked over his conscience, I've heard. What a crock! When he recanted his story, I was quite annoyed, I must say." He shrugged. "I had taken other precautions, but, it seems, not enough to convince the jury."

Seeing the strange light return to Lucas's face, Lucy sought desperately to keep him talking. "Other precautions?" she asked.

"The orange seller, of course."

Lucy thought back. "Maggie didn't show up to testify at Will's trial. She had said she would, that she could prove Will had been with her. I didn't believe her, though—but I told you I might pay for her testimony." She stared at him in horror.

"Exactly. When you told me that, I knew I had to make quick riddance of her as well."

Lucy stared at him. "You killed her, too?"

Lucas laughed fondly. "Well, yes. What had been done to her was never discovered, as far as I know. I strangled her quickly that night, near her home, and dumped her body. St. Giles, you know. So much deadly sickness there, I don't think the carters thought too much about another body lying in a ditch. She looked, no doubt, to be just another unfortunate soul caught up in the early days of the great sickness. An early victim of the plague, as it turned out."

The faint din from above was growing louder, and now they could hear a weak battering sound. Lucas sighed. "It sounds like the church has some visitors. Sinners, no doubt, in need of comforting for their wicked ways. I'll tend to them, and then to you, never fear."

·23·

Lucas ran lightly up the stairs of the catacombs. They heard something heavy being dragged in front of the door leading to the chamber. Lucy and Adam looked at each other.

"Why did you come here?" she asked.

He wiped off the blood trickling down his cheek. "Cook came to me. She was worried and told me of your wretched plan. She told me what you had learned about the cloak, what you had tried to tell me last night. I wish to God I had listened to you. She was worried about the reverend, but as I ran to the church, I began to piece together things that had been bothering me about Lucas. I was terribly afraid I was too late, and when I heard you screaming—"

He broke off. Lucy crawled over to him. As he struggled to sit up, Lucy reached around him and managed to tug apart the ropes binding his hands. He flexed his fingers and then began to untie the bonds at his ankles. When they were free, he touched her hand where it lay in her lap. "Lucy, listen to me. I've been a fool."

Lucy sat back on her knees, pulling away from him slightly. She rubbed her hands together. The catacombs were making her body numb.

"Lucy, I would tell myself I couldn't understand you. Your willfulness—yes, your willfulness—your principled ways, your dedication to justice, and your peculiar understanding of Hobbes, which I've heard tell about." He twisted his lips at the last. "The truth is, I just couldn't reconcile your notions in a servant. Simply, I couldn't place you. I've let convention and tradition blind me."

She made a noise, and he raised his hand. "Do you remember that day long ago in the market? When we saw the pickpocket take that poor woman's worldly possessions? While I rued the lack of a bellman, I just dismissed that woman's plight as a cautionary tale. But I saw you—yes, I saw what you did. You got that woman's pocket back, through means"—he smiled at the memory—"of which I no longer approve."

Remembering the roguish Sid, Lucy blushed.

"I saw you give that pocket back to the woman. Both scrupulous and unscrupulous at once. It made me wonder about my own singular pursuit of the law, and my faith in the purity of our system of jurisprudence." He smiled slightly. "That's even why I went to the site of Jane Hardewick's death, and of Bessie's later. Because I overheard you saying that if you were a man, you would never let their murderers go free, and that someone must champion the powerless. Your words made me realize how weak I'd been, how I'd hidden behind the law."

Despite their circumstances, his words warmed Lucy. "You never hid behind the law."

"I just could never place you," he continued. "You were clearly a favorite of my father's, and for good reason, as I came to learn. And when you stood before me wearing that Easter gown, I could only think, 'These are the eyes I want to wake up to.' I pushed you away, because I thought that was right." He raised his hand to her cheek.

As Adam spoke, Lucy found herself lost in his gaze, so close to her. Somewhere, she heard his words, but she recalled herself with a start. "We have to find a way out! Before Lucas returns!"

"In a moment," he said. She looked up in indignation, only to find her face grasped gently in his hands. He kissed her then, a kiss that grew in ferocity and intensity when she began to kiss him back.

Moments passed. Only when she pitched forward into his lap and they toppled sideways did she attempt to disentangle herself and smooth her skirts.

Panting slightly, she looked around. The single candle that Lucas had left looked to be near its end. "We must get out of here."

Perversely, despite their danger, she could not help voicing the question that had plagued her for so many months. "What about Judith?" she asked, deliberately not using the title held by her nemesis.

"Help me to my feet," Adam said.

She put her body under his shoulders and helped him stand.

He wavered for a moment but then smiled down at her. Leaning down, he kissed her nose. "Let's try to find a way out of here, and then I'll tell you all about it."

They began to walk, cautiously, not quite steady on their feet. Lucy's head was beginning to pound. Holding the dying candle aloft, Lucy spied a few more candle stubs in a corner, which she quickly ignited and stuck in cracks in the stone walls. The catacombs opened before them, with great vaults and scattered skeletons, relics of long-dead Catholic saints and great patrons who had donated to the church.

Stricken, Lucy saw that many of the statues did not have heads, their hands raised in supplication to a God they could not see or feel. With a shock, she remembered what Lucas had told her about how the heads had come to be removed. Those that did have heads were balanced precariously—one quick movement could set a heavy marble block tumbling down.

Looking around, Lucy remembered something else Sarah's tutor had once told them. "I heard tell of secret passageways that had been created for the papist priests. Perhaps we can find them."

"Yes, I was thinking the same thing."

Taking her hand, Adam began to feel along the wall. The catacombs stretched out ahead, great ominous shadows shrouding what lay before them and soon, what lay behind them. Lucy began to feel dizzy. Finding another way out seemed near impossible.

"You asked me about Judith," Adam said conversationally, as though they were strolling along the river. Lucy noticed that he was still scanning the walls carefully, a slight furrow to his brow. "Well, my father had become aware of certain, shall we say, questionable transactions concerning Lord Embry's shipping line to the West Indies and the Americas. He asked me to see what I could find out, since his hands were tied as a magistrate, and given Lord Embry's status in the House of Lords and the King's court."

"By courting Judith?" she asked, doubt creeping into her voice.

"By *pretending* to court Judith," he clarified, "but yes. Not particularly gentlemanly of me, I must say. At first, I had no real objections, desiring only to help my father. I just thought I would be one of her string of admirers, which would give me a chance to speak with the family in a more informal way, and see if I could learn anything of interest to report to my father. That changed."

"When Judith picked you."

He shrugged. "Yes, I suppose."

Lucy tried to pull her hand out from the crook of his arm. When he held fast, she exhaled softly. "Did you learn anything?"

"Other than that Judith is a shallow, rather vain creature with hardly an original thought in that perfectly coiffed head of hers? Yes, indeed. I learned about her father's shipping patterns, and I was able to inform my father about several illicit operations that were transacted. Illegally gained goods; unlawful transactions in Portsmouth, Greenwich; that sort of thing. But Lucy, I—"

He broke off and pointed, putting the fingers of his other hand over her lips. She nodded, following his gaze. A glimmer of light was coming from the ceiling. There must have been a grate in the floor in one of the transepts off the main altar. They could see it was partially covered by rush matting. Perhaps a way out, if they could just reach it. Lucy began to feel hopeful again.

Then, from behind them, they heard the sound of a big stone being moved by the entrance to the catacombs. Lucy clutched at Adam. He pulled her back in the shadows behind one of the great tombs, keeping her hidden.

They heard Lucas call down, his voice echoing oddly through the catacombs. "I'm coming for you, my children!" They heard him step onto the stairwell, his every step sending echoes through the chamber. Lucy scarcely dared to breathe.

They could see Lucas then, carrying a great lantern. "I know you are hiding, my little church mice, but I can find you now! It's only a matter of time."

Lucy's heart beat so loudly she was afraid it would carry a deadly echo to Lucas. They were both so groggy that she did not know if they would be able to fight him. *He will kill Adam,* she thought, the despair seeping over her.

Suddenly, Lucy heard the most beautiful sound she had ever heard. It was Avery, calling her name in the church. He must have heard her scream earlier, when the reverend was killed.

She was about to shout his name in return when Adam gave her a fierce look. "Shh!" he whispered.

Motioning, Adam clasped his hands together, indicating that Lucy should step into his intertwined fingers. Soundlessly, he raised her up, so that her hand could push up through the grate. She tried to push the rush matting away, but it was old and heavy. Several seconds passed before she could wriggle her fingers through. Tears flowed down her face; she desperately hoped Avery might see her hand.

"Avery," she whispered. "Avery!"

Yet her soft words did not carry. Feeling Adam start to tremble under her weight, with renewed strength Lucy managed to get all of her fingers into the grate and pushed as hard up as she could. The grate, freed of the matting, moved up easily.

Unable to bear its weight, though, Lucy had to let it go, so that it banged and reverberated about the chamber and in the transept above. Desperately, Lucy screamed, "Avery! We're here! Under the grate! Help us!"

At the same time, Lucas swiveled and bore toward them in the catacombs, his boots echoing madly on the stone floor. Above them, a lantern shone down in their faces, and they saw the grate miraculously lift. Avery's gentle face peered anxiously down.

"Avery!" Lucy screamed again, clawing at the air, trying to get a grip, desperately keeping herself from toppling to the floor. "Help us!"

The next instant, Lucy felt herself lifted through the grate by Avery's massive arms. Adam helplessly put up his own arms, as if to follow, but he was a few feet too far from the opening in the ceiling. Avery bent down to catch Adam, his claw hand stretching as far as it could. Lucy lay across the man's barrel legs so that he would not fall through, but they were still too far. Lucas was rapidly closing the distance between him and Adam.

"Adam!" Lucy pointed. "The pedestal!"

Instantly comprehending, Adam pushed over the marble statue of a saint and stepped onto the plinth it had occupied, which allowed him to reach Avery's outstretched hands. For an instant, Adam dangled precariously as Lucas pounded forward, the knife in his hand held high. Feverishly, Avery and Lucy helped pull Adam through the narrow hole just as Lucas bore down.

Unable to stop, Lucas plowed straight into a massive statue standing tall in the shadows. The impact brought him to his knees and caused the statue to wobble dangerously. He gazed up in horrified supplication as the angel's head lolled grotesquely on its shoulder. The next instant, the great stone head plopped down on Lucas with a sickening crunch.

Stunned, Lucy could not understand what she was seeing as she lay on the floor above. The head of the angel rested atop the prone body of Lucas, its cherubic face mischievously looking upward. "Here is the Lord's blessing upon you," the kind, gentle eyes seemed to say, even as Lucas's blood began to pool from the angel's curling marble hair.

"I don't understand," Lucy heard herself saying, allowing Adam to pull her gently away. She buried her face in his chest.

"It's over, dear. It's over."

When Lucy and Adam opened the church door, they stared out in stark disbelief. In their own excitement, they had forgotten the fire that was gripping London. *The city is burning. London is in flames.*

They could see the golden hue in the distance. Everywhere bells were clanging and people were racing about. They all coughed in the smoke that darkened the sky.

"We must get a constable," Lucy said, her mind still caught in the drama that had just unfolded. "Tell him what happened."

Someone called to Adam. "You there! You must help us! Join the water line or help move the livestock! All able men to help the city!"

"No!" Lucy said, seizing his arm. "You can't! You're injured."

"Lucy, I'd be hardly a man if I turned my back on the city. You must go to my father and tell him what happened. Keep each other safe. I've hidden behind rank and privilege long enough. I shall see you at our home. You must see to Father and, if the fire looks to spread, leave London! Then, by God's grace, I shall see you at the family seat in Warwickshire."

For two days, Lucy waited for Adam to return. Exhausted, she had sobbed the whole story out to the magistrate, who after an initial moment of shock listened with his customary calm. He seemed to see all but say little.

Pressing a cup of hot mead into her hands, he patted her awkwardly on her shoulder. "We'll have our boy back soon," he said.

To pass the time, Lucy composed a whole piece about Lucas. "The Murderer at Rosamund's Gate, Revealed." If there were a bookseller about, maybe Master Aubrey, perhaps he'd buy it.

"If anyone is left after the fire," she said to herself. Inside, her resolution grew.

Finally, they got word that the wind had turned, moving the fire back on its already spent ashes, so that it came to burn itself out, snuffed as quietly as a candle put out at midnight. Adam came back, tired, red-eyed, but full of a new vigor. He embraced her before turning to his father, then went to his bed to sleep.

When Adam awoke, he asked Lucy to walk with him. The sun was just rising. The smell of smoke was still everywhere, but none of the homes near them had been touched. He told her a little about what he had seen—the screaming women and children, the dogs barking, the water lines, and the men sweating, desperately trying to bring water from the fireboats. The fire was a beast, seeking to destroy homes, churches, and markets in a single monstrous breath. That so few were killed outright was truly a marvel.

Adam paused. "But the damnedest thing," he said, "was the pigeons."

"The pigeons?"

"Yes, they did not want to leave their nests—they were often in the roofs and eaves of people's homes. They would not fly away but would stay in their little holes until their wings caught fire and they would just flop to the ground, dead." Adam drew in a great breath. "It's a new day," he said.

Lucy agreed. She pointed to the mansion at the end of their street. Out front, a servant was sweeping the steps with a brush broom. Lucy waved, then squinted. "That's Ruthie—and I see she is wearing her mistress's clothes. I did hear that nearly all the household had lost their lives in the plague. 'Tis likely to be her home now. Can she do that, I wonder?"

Adam shrugged. "Not legally, but if the master had no family, and since the courts are barely back up and running, she may well call it her home. It's happening all over London."

Everywhere they walked, they saw evidence of a changing society. Overnight, it seemed, servants had become landowners, tavern keepers, merchants, tradesmen. Low and high had switched.

"There's talk, too, of a new London," Adam said. "Some fellow, Christopher Wren, has already been commissioned by the king to sketch out a new plan. Supposedly, our city will come to rival the great cities of Europe."

"A new city where servants can marry as they please?" she asked, giving Adam a sidelong glance.

He laughed and pulled her closer. "That, to be sure."

"Or perhaps a new city where a woman might choose not to marry and set up her own shop? Her own trade?" Her smile was mischievous, but her tone was serious. "Where a woman can speak?"

He kissed the top of her head. "Perhaps it's that as well. 'Tis a new age dawning, I foresee."

Lucy smiled and glanced across the street, her attention caught by a woman staring at them in disbelief. It was Judith Embry, and she was lacking her regular well-coiffed appearance. Indeed, she even looked slightly bedraggled, as if she did not know what to do with the new changes in fortune so many were facing. As Lucy returned her gaze, Judith dropped her wicker basket into a great slop puddle at the side of the road, oblivious to the ruin caused to what goods lay inside.

Refraining from smirking, Lucy simply nodded at Judith. Adam, who was looking the other direction, did not notice Judith at all. As the gap between them narrowed, though, Lucy could not resist winking, and she grinned when she heard Judith's outraged gasp. A cart carrying recently slaughtered pigs passed between them on the narrow path, and Lucy and Adam, now arm in arm, moved on.

Soon after, all their possessions carted away, the house felt empty and a little desolate. The household was taking up residence in a new home, one with far fewer memories. Lucy had not told them yet, but she was not sure how long she would stay with them. Something great was pushing inside her, and she wanted to find out what it was. Lucy felt a powerful stillness as she made a last pass through the great hall. She could almost see Bessie, Lawrence, and the mistress moving through the shadows, finding their own ways toward light.

Lucy pulled the great door shut behind her, latching it tight. Slipping the key into her pocket, she rested her forehead against the heavy oak. Silently, she traced a crack with her fingers, marveling for the first time at the vast rings woven by nature into the old wood. *How had she never seen them before?* she wondered. *How long the tree must have lived before the woodsman felled it with his ax?* A single tear slipped down her cheek. Nineteen months before, a knock at this very door had brought death and sadness. Now, the door was shut and a new world awaited.

She did not know what lay ahead, but the street looked wide and open. She could see Adam and the magistrate in quiet conversation by the carriages. They looked toward her expectantly, and she wondered if they could sense her resolution. She waved and walked toward life.

HISTORIC NOTE

Although the main characters are fictional, I tried to render *A Murder at Rosamund's Gate* as historically accurate as possible. The persecution of the Quakers, the treatment of servants and women, the trial and imprisonment of criminals, the plague, and the Fire of London were all important aspects of Restoration London.

At times, I took minor liberties for the purposes of creativity and readability, using far more modern phrasing and spelling than people would have used in seventeenth-century England. For example, a ballad describing a criminal's activity might actually say "As the Prancer drew the Quire Cove at the Cropping of the Rotan through the Rum pads of the Rume vile, and was flog'd by the Nubbing-Cove." According to J. Coleman's *History of Cant and Slang Dictionaries* (Oxford, 2004), this statement would translate to: "That is, The Rogue was drag'd at a Carts-arse, through the chief streets of London and was soundly whipt by the Hangman."

Similarly, the constabulary and magisterial duties were not as clear-cut as I conveyed them; indeed, there was no real police force in London for another fifty years. I sometimes assigned policing roles to English soldiers as well (the emerging "Redcoats"), on the premise they would take a role in maintaining an orderly society. Along the same lines, the gentry was not a solidified group, and "master" and "mister" seem to have been used interchangeably at this time, referring to men who owned their own livelihoods and homes.

I did retain, however, the Julian calendar for all dates and events, since England had not yet adopted the Gregorian calendar used by most of Europe (indeed, Great Britain did not reform its calendar until 1752, at which point the government retroactively adjusted all dates). The Julian calendar differed from the Gregorian calendar by having ten fewer days and starting on March 26, not January 1. I kept the original dating system to be internally consistent with contemporary accounts (such as the famous diaries by Samuel Pepys), and because certain religious markers had to occur on the correct day of the week (for example, Easter has to land on a Sunday). If I used the revised Gregorian calendar, those dates would be off. Thus, my book begins in March during Lent, which technically occurred at the end of 1664, according to the Julian calendar year. Easter (March 26) started the new year of 1665. So as not to confuse the reader, I just said the story opens in 1665.

Lastly, I took license with two other aspects regarding Restoration culture. It's unlikely that someone would have thrown a masquerade ball after Lent, especially for Easter (such activities usually occurred around Twelfth Night or Shrovetuesday); however, I thought that the Embrys would be the sort to indulge themselves, following the lead of King Charles II. Also, the miniature eye portraits were not popularized until the late eighteenth century, although they were created for the same intriguing purposes described in my story.